AFTER CHRISTMAS

BY
JANICE LYNN

HER MISTLETOE WISH

BY
LUCY CLARK

MILLS
BOON
&

Janice Lynn has a Masters in Nursing from Vanderbilt University, and works as a nurse practitioner in a family practice. She lives in the southern United States with her husband, their four children, their Jack Russell— appropriately named Trouble—and a lot of unnamed dust bunnies that have moved in since she started her writing career. To find out more about Janice and her writing visit www.janicelynn.com

Lucy Clark is actually a husband-and-wife writing team. They enjoy taking holidays with their children, during which they discuss and develop new ideas for their books using the fantastic Australian scenery. They use their daily walks to talk over characterisation and fine details of the wonderful stories they produce, and are avid movie buffs. They live on the edge of a popular wine district in South Australia with their two children, and enjoy spending family time together at weekends.

AFTER THE CHRISTMAS PARTY...

BY
JANICE LYNN

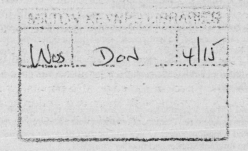

MILLS
& BOON

First published in Great Britain 2013
by Mills & Boon, an imprint of Harlequin (UK) Limited.
Harlequin (UK) Limited, Eton House, 18-24 Paradise Road,
Richmond, Surrey TW9 1SR

© Janice Lynn 2013

ISBN: 978 0 263 89927 6

Harlequin (UK) policy is to use papers that are natural, renewable and recyclable products and made from wood grown in sustainable forests. The logging and manufacturing process conform to the legal environmental regulations of the country of origin.

Printed and bound in Spain
by Blackprint CPI, Barcelona

Dear Reader

I am so blessed in that I come from a family where Christmas is always a special time and always has been. My family didn't necessarily get a lot material-wise, but the love and memories we have are worth more than anything a shiny package could ever hold. Sadly, I've run across people who have had a tragedy around the holidays, or who haven't been so blessed, and I think how terrible the holidays must be when there are reminders everywhere one looks.

Nurse Trinity Warren is just such a person. She's good-hearted, but grew up in a household where Christmas not only wasn't celebrated, but also became an embarrassment for her because her home life was so different from that of her peers. And getting dumped by her ex in a very public way at her hospital Christmas party sure didn't do anything to pump up her Christmas joy.

His name might not be St Nicholas, but Dr Riley Williams loves Christmas just about as much as the jolly red-suited man. Not used to being ignored by the opposite sex, Riley finds his interest piqued by Trinity's seeming indifference to him and her professed dislike of the most wonderful time of year. Showing her the magic of the season is the challenge his bored heart has been searching for, but can he really fall in love with someone whose life motto is bah-humbug?

I hope you enjoy reading Trinity and Riley's story as much as I enjoyed writing it. Drop me an e-mail at Janice@janicelynn.net to share your thoughts about their romance, Christmas, or just to say hello.

Merry Christmas!

Janice

Dedication

To my parents, James and Brenda Green, for making
all my Christmases so full of good times, good food,
and lots of love. Love you both very much!

**These books are also available in eBook format
from www.millsandboon.co.uk**

*Janice won The National Readers' Choice Award
for her first book*
THE DOCTOR'S PREGNANCY BOMBSHELL

CHAPTER ONE

IF THE PRETTY little blonde were a chameleon, Dr. Riley Williams was positive she'd have blended into the hotel ballroom wall long ago.

Who was she? Obviously not someone's date as only a fool would have left her alone. She had to be a hospital employee he just hadn't had the pleasure of meeting.

She sipped on a glass of what appeared to be rum punch and nervously surveyed the room as if she'd rather be anywhere than at the Pensacola Memorial Hospital Christmas party.

He took a sip of his soda and continued to listen to Dr. Sanders discuss an upcoming heart program the hospital was sponsoring while Riley's attention was really on the blonde.

Never had he seen a less likely wallflower. Although she did seem as delicate as one of the orchids his mother loved to grow. Fragile even.

Every bit as beautiful.

Looking almost hopeful, she smiled at a group of women that passed by but they never paused in their hee-hawing to say hello. If anything, she seemed to wilt further. A pity because he'd liked that brief glimpse of a smile.

The need to see that smile again hit hard. Surprisingly hard. He liked women. A lot. Always had. He imagined he always would but he didn't envision himself ever settling down. The long hours and demands of his career would keep him from ever tying a woman to him. A family deserved time and attention.

A plump pink lower lip disappeared between white teeth. Every muscle in Riley's stomach contracted and he'd swear the air in the room had thinned.

Never had he had such an instant, strong reaction to a woman.

He placed his half-full glass on a passing waiter's tray. "Excuse me, gentlemen, but I just spotted what I want for Christmas."

Several of his colleagues followed his line of vision and grinned.

"Trinity Warren. She just started last week," a cardiologist who was one of his partners informed him. "On the cardiac unit. I'm surprised you haven't already noticed her."

With the way his insides were stirring, so was he. Then again, he hadn't been around the hospital much this week. He'd taken a few days off work to spend some time helping his mother with odds and ends of Christmas decorations and shopping. For too long since his father's heart attack sadness had filled her at the holidays. Seeing her renewed joy in the festivities did Riley's heart good.

"Trinity Warren..." He let the blonde's name roll off his tongue, wondering at the way his pulse pounded at his throat. "She works on our unit?"

He didn't usually become involved with women he worked with. Too messy.

"She's been in orientation with Karen this past week. Quirky sense of humor, great smile, patients like her, seems to really know her stuff."

Yeah, well, he'd really like to know her stuff too. Up close and personal. Plus, that glimpse of her smile had been great. He could only imagine what her full-blown one would be like. His imagination was working overtime at the moment.

He studied her, watching as she cast her big brown eyes downward to stare into her glass before taking another sip. Her tongue darted out to lick punch from her full lips. He swallowed. Oh, hell. Without even trying, she was sending his blood pressure through the roof.

How much he wanted to see her pretty mouth curved into a smile stunned him, to see her eyes dancing with pleasure. Want was the wrong word. He needed to see her smile, her pleasure.

"You want me to introduce you?"

He glanced at his best friend and one of the several partners in their cardiology group. "Have you ever known me to need you to introduce me to a beautiful woman?"

"Figured you needed all the help you could get," Trey teased.

"Besides, I'm onto you," Riley continued, hesitating just a little longer, feeling his friend's interest in the woman too. "You're just looking for an excuse to talk to her yourself."

Trey grinned. "If I'd spotted her first tonight, I wouldn't have needed an excuse to talk to her. I'd be over there now, rather than talking to your ugly mug."

"But now?"

"Now I've seen the determined look on your face."

Trey shrugged. "She doesn't stand a chance and neither does any other man in this room. Go for it."

Relieved his friend didn't have a vested interest, Riley didn't deny his claim. Besides, Trey was right. Trinity Warren didn't stand a chance when he turned on the charm. Before long she'd be smiling and enjoying her evening—with him.

Nurse Trinity Warren was smart enough to know that facing her fears was the best way to move on, to put her ho-ho-ho hang-ups to rest. But, seriously, had she really had to come to this Christmas party?

Leaning against the hotel ballroom wall, she took a sip of her third cup of fruit punch. Was she nuts or what? By coming here, she was sticking her neck under the proverbial guillotine. Two years ago she'd vowed to never attend another Christmas party, to ban Christmas for ever. Bah, humbug! That had been her motto.

Only she'd relocated two weeks ago and her new nursing director had said she needed to attend. So here she was, pretending she was having a good time and that she wasn't contemplating a dash to the ladies' room to toss the liquid-only contents of her fluttery stomach.

She smiled at a group of women who worked in the billing department as they paused near where she held the wall up. She didn't personally know them. She knew very few people outside the cardiac care unit. But she had seen the trio around. Waving their hands with animation and talking a mile a minute, they didn't notice her.

"He is so hot," one of the women said, fanning her face with a bejeweled hand decked out with rakish long manicured fingernails and a sparkly ring so big it had to be fake.

"He's yummy in his scrubs, but in those dress slacks and fitted button-down open just right at his collar…" a heavy-chested blonde gave an exaggerated sigh "…he's outright lickable."

Trinity followed their line of sight to see who had their tongues wagging. Oh, my. Um, yeah, they were right.

He was hot.

And lickable.

And a lot of other things that had her looking away really fast so her retinas didn't start smoking.

Startled at her tongue-slurping reaction, she glanced back toward the object of their admiration. Her gaze collided with his. Wow. Something about him made her burn. Probably because he looked as if he'd walked straight out of every woman's fantasy. The mischievous gleam present in his blue eyes said he was well aware of his many manly charms and that she threatened to spontaneously combust any moment just from his visual perusal. He knew he was that hot.

She gulped back another sip of punch, hoping it would cool the burn. It didn't.

Which didn't make sense because she'd banned men right along with Christmas two years ago. Especially a man like the one grinning at her. A man like that one would incinerate the already shattered bits of her heart.

"Oh! Shh! He's coming this way," one of the women squealed, slapping the other's arm and sloshing a little of her Cosmopolitan onto the ballroom floor. All three of the women struck we-weren't-just-talking-about-you poses and one gave a fake laugh as if whatever they were discussing was of the utmost interest and batted her lashes flirtatiously.

Really? Trinity wanted to roll her eyes. She glanced Mr. Lickable's way again to see if he'd caught onto the women fan-girling him.

Yet again her gaze collided with electric blue and this time didn't let go, couldn't let go, as if there was some magnetic force at play that held her eyes in place.

She forgot how to inhale. Literally and figuratively. She couldn't breathe.

Wow. He really was a beautiful man. Dark brown hair that had just a touch of golden curl and looked invitingly soft. Tanned skin that hinted he spent a lot of his time outdoors and, living next to the Gulf of Mexico, he probably did. He had a face and body gorgeous enough to give any movie-star hunk a complex.

Then there were those eyes.

So intensely blue that they had to be contact lenses, because no one's eyes could really be that blue. Or that full of mischief. No doubt he'd been one of those kids who'd stayed on Santa's naughty list.

Yes, the women were right. He was hot, so hot her mouth felt like the Sahara but the rest of her rivaled a rainforest and was probably putting damp spots on her dress. Great. Managing to shift her eyes, she took another sip of her punch, draining the clear plastic cup. Oops. Now what was she going to do with her nervous hands?

"Do you want something else to drink?" Mr. Hotness himself asked, walking past the we-weren't-just-talking-about-you women and planting himself right in front of Trinity.

She glanced to either side, expecting to see some

parched Delilah close by. He couldn't be talking to Plain Jane her, right? And if he was, *why*?

The trio was staring at her in dropped-jaw surprise. She was surprised herself. She wasn't chopped liver, but she didn't kid herself that she was the model type this guy most likely dated either.

The last swig of punch had done nothing to help her dry mouth, which was problematic. Her tongue stuck to her palate, refusing to budge. She was positive anything she attempted to say could and would be held against her.

"I'll be happy to get you more punch," he added, causing a wave of eyebrow rises from their spectators. "Or anything else you might want." One corner of his mouth lifted in a sexy grin. "I'm a man who aims to please."

If the heavy-chested blonde had fallen into a fit of vapors right then and there, Trinity wouldn't have been surprised. She was about to need resuscitation herself.

He was flirting.

With her.

Eyes narrowing suspiciously, brain reeling, she peeled her dry tongue free of the roof of her mouth. "Then perhaps you should aim elsewhere."

Because, really, what would be the point of encouraging him? She wasn't interested in a relationship, or anything else.

Rather than take the hint and move on, his devilish grin widened, digging dimples into his cheeks. "You don't like to be pleased?"

Darn it. He was quick tongued and she'd set herself up for that one. No matter how she answered, he'd twist her words. The mischievous gleam in his eyes assured that.

She shoved her empty cup toward him. "Punch."

Fantastic. She sounded as if she had a mouthful of peanut butter and the IQ of a rock, but at least letting him get her punch would give her a reprieve.

Taking her cup, he laughed. "Then punch it is, but don't think I'm letting you off the hook. We'll discuss what gives you pleasure when I get back." His eyes sparkled. "I could make a few suggestions even."

Heat washed over her body, melting her from the inside out at the thought of just what those suggestions might be.

Not that it mattered. She so wasn't having that conversation with him.

"I wouldn't hold my breath if I were you," she mumbled.

She didn't meet his gaze and earn another laugh from him and an "Is she crazy?" from one of their billing-department eavesdroppers.

They probably thought she was, but the reality was that she didn't want to attract a man like him. Chase had been as high octane as she went and look where that had gotten her. Burnt. Burnt. Burnt.

"Who needs to hold their breath when you've already stolen mine?" he quipped with another flash of his perfectly straight pearly whites, sending her up in a puff of smoke. Then, in a decent imitation of a famous movie line, he added, "I'll be back."

The women sighed then giggled as if he'd said something super-romantic then brilliantly funny. Trinity just stared. Her gaze zeroed in on his retreating figure.

"You go, girl," the heavy-chested woman told her,

stepping closer and giving a thumbs up. "I'm pea green with envy. You're tonight's lucky girl."

She winced that the women had obviously overheard his pleasure comment. Great. She didn't want gossip. Lord knew, she'd dealt with enough of that during her lifetime already. Especially at work. And, seriously, although he was the hottest man she'd ever set eyes on, she didn't want a man in her life. Not ever again. Maybe she should leave before he returned. If her director got upset that she'd left too early, she could always claim she hadn't felt well. With her nervous stomach, she'd be telling the truth.

Glancing around, she easily spotted him in line to refill her punch and chatting with a few people whose faces she recognized but didn't recall which hospital department they hailed from.

Who was he and why had he sought her out?

What did it matter?

She was not getting involved. Especially not with someone who worked at the hospital or had anything to do with the hospital. Been there, done that, had the gaping hole in her chest to prove it.

A sick feeling took hold in her stomach, like she might really lose its contents. Time to go. Fast.

Eyes locked on the exit, she made a beeline for the ballroom door, intent on making her escape. Just after she stepped into the long hallway that would lead her to the hotel's over-decorated foyer, a hand grabbed her elbow. She jumped.

"You okay?"

Him. Great. No doubt there would be scorch marks where his fingers burned into her skin. She grimaced and started to say she was heading to the ladies' room, but why lie?

She turned, faced him, felt her breath hitch again at just how lickable he really was, then inhaled deeply because she was strong. "Look, I appreciate the offer of more punch and boring conversation, but I've had enough and I'm headed home."

His forehead creased. "You're leaving? Because of me?"

"No." Heat infused her face. Hadn't she just asked herself why she should lie? "Look, I'm not a party girl. You should go talk to someone else."

Understatement of the year.

"I don't want to talk to someone else. I want to talk with you. Besides, you're problem is that you've been partying with all the wrong people." His wink told her exactly who she should be partying with.

Determined not to be swayed by his outrageous charm and the way him saying he wanted to talk to her warmed her insides, she arched a brow. "I suppose you're my right person?"

A full-blown smile slashed across his handsome face. "I've been called a lot of things in my life, but I'm not sure Mr. Right is one of them."

She started to correct him, to let him know that she hadn't been implying that he was calling himself Mr. Right, but before she could, he reached out and ran a tingle-inducing fingertip across her cheek. Hello, lightning bolt!

"There's always a first so, sure, I am the right person for you to be partying with tonight. I'm Riley, by the way." His smile cut dimples into his cheeks again and he stared straight into her eyes. "I don't want you to go."

Not offering him her name, she closed her eyes. It was all she could do not to lean towards him, be seduced by the appeal in his voice. Was he like the Pied Piper of women or what, because she just wanted to follow him wherever he led.

"Stay. Dance with me," he whispered near her ear in an enchanting tone that made her want to dance to his tune in more ways than one.

Mesmerized, she stepped towards him, her body almost pressing to his.

He inhaled. "You smell amazing. Good enough to eat."

Um, no. She was not going to let her mind go where his words threatened to take her. Not going to happen. Only her mind went exactly where it wasn't supposed to go. *Bad mind.*

Keeping her eyes squeezed shut, she parted her lips to say no, that she was leaving and couldn't be tempted by visions of sugar plums and whatever else he dangled in front of her. Apparently, he took her movement and open mouth as an invitation. Without hesitation his lips covered hers.

Shocked at the unexpected kiss, Trinity's eyelids flew apart, startled to find his intent blue eyes open, watching her, as his lips gently brushed over her mouth. Tasting. Tempting. Teasing. Rocking her world to the very core. Wow.

Shockwaves rippled to the tips of her toes and she questioned if time was standing still because the hotel seemed to fade away to just the two of them, just his eyes searching hers, his lips branding hers.

When he pulled away, reality immediately sank in. Hospital Christmas party. Surrounded by new coworkers. The most gorgeous man ever had just kissed her. Hello, had she lost her mind?

"Why did you do that?" She took a step back, wiping her lips as if trying to clear away his kiss. Sandpaper couldn't have erased his kiss. Riley. Riley's kiss. He'd permanently branded her lips, her entire body. The man started fires.

He pointed up to the doorway she'd stepped beneath.

"Had to." He shrugged nonchalantly, as if the kiss had been no big deal. To him it probably hadn't been. His knees weren't the ones shaking. "Tradition."

She glanced up, eyed the large clump of mistletoe tied with a red ribbon that hung over the doorway. Her gaze dropped back to him suspiciously. "You're a traditional kind of guy and just couldn't resist?"

"Absolutely, just ask my mom. She'll tell you I'm the apple of her eye." He grinned. "Now that we know I'm a traditional kind of guy, that you smell and taste like the sweetest candy, and the pressure of our first kiss is out of the way, let's go party. I guarantee a good time. Plus, you can tell me all about you while I hold you in my arms on the dance floor, Trinity." His eyes sparkled with devilment.

Feeling oddly out of sorts that he knew her name despite the fact she'd purposely not told him, that he was piling on the charm, she felt what little resistance she had to him ebbing away. "Do you always get what you want?"

One side of his mouth curved upward. "Not always, but it is Christmastime and I've been a very good boy."

She doubted that. Besides which there was nothing boyish about his broad shoulders and testosterone-laden aura.

"I'm hopeful there will be something sweet under my Christmas tree this year. An angel." He raised his brows. "You have plans? We could start a new holiday tradition."

She should go. She knew that. Her tattered heart was no match for this man's charisma. But the thought of going back to her lonely apartment just didn't appeal. Not even with Casper there, waiting for her. Her cat might love her but, whether Trinity wanted to admit it or not, she craved the temptation Riley waved in front of her.

An escape, albeit temporary, from the deeply embedded loneliness that had taken hold of her soul from the moment Chase Langworthy had dumped her publicly at their hospital Christmas party two years ago and plunged her into depression and Scrooge-dom.

Darn him for doing that. Darn her for letting him.

She took the punch glass Riley still held and downed half the contents as if she were chugging a shot of whiskey. Ha, she never drank alcohol, but she needed something to give her the push to do what she suddenly wanted to. She'd pretend the punch was liquid courage. She'd pretend that she was the kind of girl used to men like him flirting and wanting to dance with her. She'd pretend she was the life of the party.

"Okay, Riley..." She drawled his name out. She would do this, would have fun. "I'll dance with you, but I should warn you that I dance much better than I kiss so you might struggle to keep up."

She had no clue how she managed the confident words, the brilliant smile, or where they had even come from. The only time she ever danced confidently was around her living room with only Casper around to yawn at her antics. Still, head high, she headed back into the ballroom.

Riley's pleased laughter behind her warmed parts of her insides that hadn't felt sunshine in a long, long time.

CHAPTER TWO

WHAT A PLEASANT enigma, Riley thought of the woman he held loosely in his arms. She really did dance like an angel. But she was crazy if she thought she danced better than she kissed.

No one danced better than this woman's lips had felt against his. A meeting of their lips that hadn't been an angelic kiss but one that lit hot fires all along his nerve endings. He still burned. Of course, that might be because her curvy little body swayed next to his and every cell in him had an apparent surge of testosterone.

What other excuse could there be for that brief brushing of his mouth against hers to have set him on fire the way it had?

If he didn't quit thinking about how much he'd wanted to deepen that kiss, about how he wanted to take her somewhere private and kiss her again and again and on places other than her juicy mouth, she was going to know exactly what he was thinking. He was intuitive enough to recognize she wasn't the kind of girl who went for one-night stands.

And he wasn't the kind of man who sweet-talked a woman into doing something she'd regret.

Exactly what he did want wasn't entirely clear, but he sure wanted something.

Her.

He brushed his cheek across the top of her head, the light touch sending shockwaves of awareness through him. Yes, he wanted to know her in every sense. He'd always been the kind of person who'd known what he wanted and had gone after whatever that might be. He wanted Trinity with an intensity that made his head spin.

"How long have you been a nurse?"

Tilting her head back, she blinked her big brown eyes at him. Most of the women he knew would have had make-up accenting their large almond shape, would have made the most of the naturally thick lashes rimming her lids to lure some unsuspecting man into her snare. Not Trinity. As best he could tell, Trinity had nothing on her face except the light sprinkling of freckles across her nose and a little mascara coating those already long lashes. Her hair was clipped back with loose springs, framing her heart-shaped face. She looked as if she could be sweet sixteen.

"Trinity?"

Her beautiful face had become pinched, as if she were troubled by his question. "Long enough that I know about men like you."

Her instant defensiveness confused him. "Men like me?"

"You shouldn't get ideas about me." Her face flushed a pretty shade of pink, but she held his gaze. "I'm just here to dance, nothing more."

Riley liked the spunk shining on her upward-tilted face and had to fight the urge to kiss her mouth again.

"You shouldn't get ideas about me," he warned. "I'm simply making conversation with the beautiful woman I'm dancing with. Nothing more."

Her gaze narrowed. He grinned. After a moment she sighed in resignation. "Fine. You win." A sly smile slid onto her mouth. "This round."

He looked forward to future rounds. "And?"

"I've been a nurse for four years," she admitted, as if giving away some top secret. That would likely make her around twenty-six.

"Where did you nurse prior to coming to work for Pensacola?"

She tensed in his arms and stopped moving. "You don't have to play Twenty Questions or even make conversation at all. For the record, I'm a girl who appreciates silence in a man."

Riley chuckled. Oh, yeah, he liked this woman. "Shut up and dance, eh?"

She nodded.

"Problem is, I want to know more about you." Lots more. "Where did you nurse prior to coming to Pensacola?"

She sighed. "How about I save us a lot of time and send you a copy of my résumé?"

He stared at her stubborn expression.

"Oh, all right," she relented, and pushed his chest, motioning for him to start dancing again. "I went to school at University of Tennessee in Memphis and went straight to work at one of the hospitals there. I worked in the cardiac unit until I took the job here in Pensacola."

"Now, was that really so painful?"

"Excruciating." But a smile played on her lips. He

really liked her smile. And the sparkle of gold in her brown eyes.

"Now, be quiet and dance."

He laughed at her order. Talking with her was like a breath of fresh air. Stimulating. Fun.

"I have a friend who went to medical school in Memphis. He says it's a great place. What brought you to Pensacola? Family?"

With a look of what he hoped was feigned annoyance that he hadn't taken her order of silence seriously, she shook her head.

"Friends?" he persisted, despite her glare.

"Nope," she answered after a moment's hesitation.

The music picked up tempo. When she went to pull back he tightened his hold. "Boyfriend?"

"Ha. Exact opposite."

No hesitation there. He frowned. "You have someone in Memphis?"

"Not any more."

There was enough sadness—or was it regret?—in her voice that he felt a little guilty at just how much relief flowed through him at her denial.

"I'm glad there's not someone waiting for you in Memphis. Or anywhere else, for that matter." Because he hadn't liked the thought that she might belong to someone else. "Very glad."

For the first time since they'd started dancing she mis-stepped and caught his toe. "Sorry. I didn't mean to hurt you."

"You didn't," he assured her, thinking that as petite as she was she could stand on his toes and not hurt him. She was like a pixie. A curvy pixie. He couldn't recall ever having the urges that rushed through him when he looked at Trinity. There was something about her. Something intriguing that had him hooked. Was it just that she wasn't the type of yes-girl he was used to? "Recent break-up?"

She gave an ironic laugh and shook her head. "Forever ago. If you insist on talking, let's talk about something else. Anything else."

As much as he'd like to know more so he could understand what made her tick, Riley didn't push. Instead, he loosened his hold and caught her unawares by spinning her out and back to him. "Fine, we'll save the talking for later and dance now," he told her as he caught her.

Looking more than a little relieved, she smiled, then caught him unawares by dipping backwards in his arms and laughed as if she'd been set free. "Deal."

Trinity felt light-headed. Giddy almost. Despite her boisterous claim about her dancing skills, she stepped on Riley's toes more than once. He didn't seem to mind, just kept smiling at her and making silly little comments that made her laugh.

For once she relaxed enough to just enjoy the music, to let loose and move to the beat even if she looked ridiculous. Something about the way Riley looked at her, the way every bit of his attention was focused solely on her, boosted her confidence and let free her love of music.

Riley. He smelled so good. Spicy. Musky. Heavenly.

Her gaze dropped to his lips.

Somewhere in her brain she registered that something was wrong with her thought processes, that she wasn't thinking clearly. Still, she licked her lips, won-

dering if the flavor of him lingered there from his impromptu kiss. *She wanted to taste him again.*

"You're killing me, princess."

"Princess?" Had anyone ever called her princess?
And had she really just giggled?

A kiss under the mistletoe and a few fancy steps
to one of their coworker's karaoke singing "Rocking
Around the Christmas Tree" and she'd morphed into
someone she didn't even recognize. Who knew that pretending to be the life of the party could be so much fun?

"Well, you have me royally torn up so, yeah, princess." He grinned, his gaze going to her just-moistened
lips. "Don't tease me, Trinity."

He'd said her name. She liked him saying her name.
Her cloudy mind registered that she hadn't officially
introduced herself. "I'm Trinity, by the way." Which
seemed a really dumb thing to say as he'd called her
by her name repeatedly. She grimaced at her lapse and
wondered what was wrong with her brain.

He smiled indulgently at her. "Trinity Warren. I
know."

"How?"

"I asked about you before I came over."

She blinked, wondering if she'd misheard. "You did?
Why?"

His hand pressed against her lower back. "I wanted
to know more. I've never dated a woman who works at
the hospital. Too messy."

"Dated a woman who works…" Was he saying he
wanted to date her? Or just letting her know that he
didn't date women at the hospital so she wouldn't take
any of tonight the wrong way?

"Messy?" she prompted, then added, "Not that I'd date you."

He grinned at her comment. "I am going to prove you wrong but, yes, messy. If things don't work out, there's a mess to deal with when the two people involved work at the same place."

"Ha. Tell me something I don't know." She was an expert on that particular mess. Chase had worked as the IT manager for the hospital where she'd worked in Memphis. She knew all about dealing with messes. Especially when he'd made their break-up so public.

"You'll have to explain that comment," Riley commented close to her ear.

"Not likely." Because she had no intention of ever telling anyone in Pensacola of her humiliation. She'd come to forget things, not to rehash them.

His hold at her waist tightened a fraction. "You're a really private person, aren't you?"

None of her personal business had been private in Memphis. Chase had dumped her for another woman in front of the whole Christmas party. He'd been drunk and had... She grimaced, not letting the memories take hold. "Generally, I prefer to blend in than be center stage. If that means I'm a really private person, you're right."

He pulled back enough to stare into her face. "Funny, because when I look at you I can't picture you anywhere but center stage."

His kind words sounded so sincere that her knees threatened to buckle. She wanted to throw her arms around his neck and...actually, her arms *were* around his neck. She leaned closer, breathed in his musky scent.

He pulled back, stared into her eyes. "You're a leading lady, Trinity. You could never blend into the background."

Heat infused her face and she started to point out that earlier tonight she'd blended in quite well until he'd made an entrance into her life. Now lots of people were looking at her and trying to figure out why he was dancing with her. Didn't they know? Tonight she was the life of the party. Tomorrow she'd go back to the real world.

"You're smooth with the lines, Casanova."

His hand moved across her lower back, holding her close. "No Casanova and no lines. Honest. I'm just telling you the truth. You're a beautiful woman."

"I think you're a player."

"You think wrong."

The woman's comment about her being tonight's lucky pick ran through her mind. "You're telling me you're as pure as snow?" She gave him a skeptical look. "I'm not buying it."

"Not sure how pure snow is these days but no one would label me as pure anyway other than my mother, who thinks I hung the moon, of course." He winked.

Trinity rolled her eyes. "Okay, snowflake."

Her nickname obviously caught him off guard and he stared at her a moment then shook his head, laughter shining in his eyes. "I enjoy spending time with the opposite sex and I'm no saint, but you can call me 'Snowflake' if you want to. But for the record, I don't say things I don't mean."

"No red-blooded man ever does."

"Suspicious little thing, aren't you?" He grinned. "Fortunately, I'm an open book and you don't have a quiz in the morning. So how about for the rest of the night you don't analyze this and just enjoy yourself?"

"With you?"

He tightened his hold at her waist. "That was the idea. I'd be very disappointed if you left me to enjoy yourself with someone else."

Despite her uncertainty, the giddy feeling was still inside her so she just shrugged as if she couldn't care less one way or the other. "So long as you don't suggest we sing karaoke."

That naughty look twinkled as brightly as the colored lights adorning the Christmas tree in the corner of the ballroom. "Too bad, because my number is coming up two songs from now and I plan on you joining me."

"You plan wrong."

He reached into his dress pants pocket and pulled out a slip of paper. "Due to the time constraints, the Christmas committee had interested parties draw numbers earlier this evening." He waggled his brows. "This interested party got a winning number."

"I'd ask if you ever don't win, but having to get up in front of all these people and sing doesn't sound like a prize." Grimacing, she glanced at the duo currently belting out a number. "Not a good one, at any rate."

He laughed and touched his finger to her nose. "You're funny, Trinity. I like that."

"Not really." She wasn't funny. She hadn't been since…since Chase had broken her heart and she'd withdrawn into her shell, trying to protect her tender inside.

Why had she done that? Why had she let him steal so much from her? Why was she still letting him steal so much of her life? For goodness' sake, she had moved to a beach town because she'd assumed the locals wouldn't put so much emphasis on a holiday associated with snow. Pathetic.

"Fine, I'll sing with you, but just to warn you, I'm an even better singer than I am dancer and we both know how I excel at that." She stepped on his toes, hard, to prove her point.

"My ears can hardly wait." He grinned down at her. "Like I said, fun girl."

CHAPTER THREE

TRINITY'S HEAD HURT. Not just a little. Her mouth felt as if something had crawled inside and died. Her stomach warned she might just upchuck.

She rarely ever got full-blown, miserable sick, but this morning she just felt bleh. Thank goodness she wasn't scheduled to go into work today, just to take call. Maybe she'd get lucky and her phone wouldn't ring.

Digging deeper beneath her covers, she groaned and snuggled up next to the warm body beside her.

Warm body? Hello. There wasn't supposed to be a warm body in her bed!

"Good morning, sleeping beauty," an unexpected voice broke into her haze.

An unexpected and very male voice.

A voice she immediately recognized, even though she'd only met him the night before. Why was he rambling on about sleeping beauty being a princess and her looking like one? Right. Because, like all fairy princesses, her hair and make-up remained perfect while she slept. *Not.*

She twisted to look at him. "Riley."

"You were expecting someone else?" A lazy brow rose beneath sleep-tousled hair and he looked way too sexy for first thing in the morning. Apparently fairy princes really did remain perfect while sleeping.

She was in bed. Her bed. Between the covers. With Riley. Her heart pounded against her ribcage. Not good. She scooted away from his warmth until she reached a cold spot on the sheet. Too bad half her butt was now hanging off the edge of the bed.

"I wasn't expecting anyone." Her words came out half-croak, half-cry.

Pulling the covers tighter around her, she tried to register the fact that she was in bed with Dr. Riley Williams. Even more confusing, she tried to remember how she'd gotten there. How he'd gotten there.

"What are you doing here? You shouldn't be here."

He shouldn't. She barely knew him. She didn't do one-nighters. Not ever. She didn't do anything. Not before or after Chase.

At her accusing tone, Riley's grin slipped. "You asked me to stay."

That threw her. "I did?"

"You did." His confident tone and coolly assessing blue gaze brooked no denial.

She'd asked him to stay. They were in her bed. Although her black dress was gone, as were her hose, she still wore her panties. But no bra.

In bed with a sexy cardiologist with nothing on but her granny panties. Awesome.

She closed her eyes, took a deep breath and asked the twenty-million dollar question that kept echoing through her throbbing head.

"What did we do?" She sounded accusatory again, but she wasn't able to control the rising panic within her.

What had she done? She'd finally broken away from

the chains that had bound her to Memphis, had moved to Pensacola to make a fresh start, and she'd ended up in bed with the first man she'd stood under mistletoe with? How could she?

Christmas.

It was the blasted holiday that wreaked havoc in her life. Always had. Always would. She really should go to some remote location every December and not come home until well after New Year. If only.

Riley had the nerve to look offended. "You don't remember last night? Our coming here? What we did after we got here?"

"If I remembered, would I be asking?" Really, she'd thought him smarter than that. Or maybe she was just cranky because a thousand things were running through her mind and not one of them good. "Did we have sex?" she demanded, while her throat still worked because, seriously, the tissue threatened to swell shut any moment.

From where Riley lay next to her, he stared, not saying anything at first, just watching, making her wish she could pull the covers over her head, making her wish her stomach didn't churn.

"I can assure you—" confidence and perhaps annoyance oozed from his words "—that had we had sex, you'd not only remember, you'd have woken up with a smile on your face and not that look of horror."

Face aflame, relief flooded her, as did curiosity because sex up to that point in her life hadn't been that memorable. There had just been Chase but, still, she had been practically engaged to the man. Sadly, she had never woken up with a smile on her face. Quite the opposite. So maybe Riley thought she'd remember if they'd had sex, but maybe she wouldn't have remembered. Maybe she just hadn't been impressed and had blocked the experience from her mind.

"You're saying we didn't, um, you know?"

Cool amusement at her lack of ability to say the actual words shone in his eyes. "We didn't have sexual intercourse last night, if that's what you are attempting to ask."

No sexual intercourse. His tone mocked her question but, come on, they were in bed and she was only in her skivvies. Which meant that they had done something, right? The way he was looking at her said they'd done something. But what?

Letting her gaze run over his face, his lips, the strong line of his jaw, his throat, his bare shoulders, his chest, his... She gulped. Had she touched him? Kissed him? Run her fingers over those broad shoulders? Those washboard abs? Had she seen him naked? Face afire, she glanced back up, met his gaze, and winced. He so knew what she was thinking and he liked it.

An inferno burned her cheeks.

"Riley, I..." She pulled the covers even tighter around her, holding on in case the material got a sudden urge to slip below her neck and put her chest and abs on display for his inspection. No washboard anywhere in sight at her midsection. More like a laundry basket. Taking a deep breath, she tried to pull her thoughts together and away from their bodies. "I don't do this."

"This?" His face was unreadable, his eyes dark. She didn't like the look and found herself wishing things were different. That she was different. That she could have woken up in bed with him and not freaked out but reveled in a night full of passion. That she really had woken up with a smile. That she could have been good enough that he could have woken up with a smile. That instead of lashing out at him with accusatory questions she could have teased him awake with kisses and had a morning full of passion.

A morning she'd remember always.

A morning he'd always remember.

A morning that would leave them both exhausted and smiling.

But that wasn't her. She was a woman who disliked Christmas, disliked men, was terrible at sex, and although she'd come to Pensacola to forget her past, she could only handle confronting one hang-up at a time. She seriously had her work cut out for her even with that.

"What is it that you don't do?" Riley prompted when she failed to elaborate.

Everything. She sighed, took a deep breath and went for broke.

"Wake up in bed with a man and not remember how I got here and what we did while here." She grimaced. She sounded horrible. Waking up next to him was horrible. He probably thought she was horrible—in bed and out of it. "I don't do that. Ever."

"I just told you, we didn't do anything, not really. We ended up here because I drove you home from the Christmas party and you invited me in. And, although there's another bedroom, there is no bed."

Which meant he must have at least considered sleeping elsewhere.

"I wasn't doing the floor," he said matter-of-factly, "and I'm too tall to comfortably sleep on your girly sofa."

She did have a girly sofa. A plush Victorian piece

that she loved because it had been the first piece of furniture she'd ever bought for herself, but it really wasn't that comfy. Not that comfort mattered so much, because she never had company or spent much time there.

Trying to recall the previous night's events, she closed her eyes, thought back. The Christmas party. She'd danced with Riley, sung one silly reindeer song with him, celebrated that he'd won one of the door prizes when random names had been drawn from a stocking, then they'd left. He'd driven her home. They'd walked into her house and then he'd kissed her. No mistletoe required. Just a simple good-night kiss that had somehow morphed into something more, something hotter, something that hadn't been simple at all.

Wow, if his kiss had been that amazing she might have really woken up with a smile had they had sex. Then again, had they had sex he'd know how lame her lovemaking actually was.

Her panties weren't the only thing she was wearing.

She reached up, touched the door prize he'd won and given to her. "You won this."

He shrugged, causing the covers to slip a little lower at his waist. "I gave it to you."

He'd taken the pearl necklace out of the velvet box and fastened it around her neck. There had been something mesmerizing about him putting the necklace on her. Something erotic and gentle and totally captivating.

Kind of like his abs.

No wonder she'd asked him to stay. He'd been the perfect date.

Only they hadn't been on a date.

"You can have it back if you want it," she offered, in case he regretted having given her the piece. Maybe he'd expected bodily payment for the beads. Ha, had they been out of a gumball machine he might have gotten his money's worth, but that's about it if Chase's claims about her skills could be believed.

Riley's brows formed a V. "Why would I want them back? Don't you like the necklace?"

"It's lovely."

"Not nearly as lovely as you are."

He was smooth with the lines. Too smooth perhaps. She swallowed.

"You told me I was beautiful last night."

Actually, he'd repeated the compliment several times.

"You were." His eyes bored into hers. She didn't have to be looking directly at him to feel his stare. He stirred beneath the covers, but he didn't reach for her. Somehow she knew he wanted to.

"You are," he continued. "Very beautiful."

Last night, in her haze, he'd made her feel beautiful. Like the most beautiful woman in the world. This morning she felt like a woman who'd gone to bed without washing her face or brushing her teeth. She was rank and knew it.

"Why would you say that?"

"Because it's true."

The sincerity in his voice told her that he was either the world's greatest liar or he believed what he said. Maybe he really did have fantastic blue contact lenses and they were blurred with sleep, leaving him blinded to the truth.

Making sure to keep the covers pulled over her almost bare body, she rolled over to face him directly. She could feel his body heat, could feel the magnetic pull of him. She wanted to touch. Really really wanted to touch. His sheer physical perfection robbed her of thought. Or maybe it was his bare chest that made her brain waves frazzle. He was the one who was beautiful. Eye-poppingly, mouth-wateringly, finger-itchingly, body-twitchingly beautiful.

It occurred to her that the happy trail leading beneath the covers didn't appear to have anything material impeding its path. At least she was wearing underwear.

No sexual intercourse, he'd said. That left a lot of possibilities. Oh, my.

"What happened to your clothes?" she choked out, more and more flustered that he was naked in her bed.

Although she recalled the removal of her clothes, she didn't recall how he'd gone from fully dressed to whatever he still wore beneath her covers.

He was wearing something. *Wasn't he? Just because she couldn't see any outlines, it didn't mean boxers or cotton briefs weren't there, right?*

His eyes glittered. "You don't recall ripping them off me with your teeth, princess?"

She'd taken them off him? With her teeth? Her jaw dropped then clamped shut in case her teeth got any fresh ideas.

"Okay, it was bad of me to tease you." His grin turned devilish. "You didn't use your teeth."

She'd... She closed her eyes and tried to recall the events of the night before. "We had sex, didn't we?"

"I already told you that we didn't have sex." He sounded annoyed that she'd asked again, that she hadn't taken him at his word.

Unable to resist a moment longer, she reached out beneath the covers to touch his chest. His bare chest. To see if the feel of his skin was familiar, to see if touching him would cause a rush of memories.

"Then why are we naked in my bed?"

"I wasn't planning to spend the night anywhere so I hadn't packed any pajamas…not that I normally wear anything to bed. But I'm not naked. I'm wearing boxers and would be happy to show you if you'd like proof." He covered her hand with his, brushed his thumb across her skin. "Besides, you looked as if you needed me to stay. My guess is that you don't drink often."

Still reeling from his offer to show her his underwear and just how tempted she was to take him up on that offer, she focused on the other part of what he'd said. "I don't drink at all and I didn't drink anything last night except fruit punch."

"That was rum punch you were drinking, Trinity. It had alcohol in it."

"The punch was…but…" Hadn't she felt funny? Hadn't she noticed that the more she'd drunk the less nervous she'd been? *Dear Lord*. "I was punch drunk."

Looking as if he wanted to laugh, he just grinned. "You were a bit inebriated but no worries, you were a cute drunk."

A cute drunk. As if such a creature existed. No one was a cute drunk. At least no one Trinity had ever had the misfortune of seeing drunk. Her mother had certainly never been cute. Chase had not been cute.

"I didn't know there was alcohol in the punch."

"It's okay, princess." His thumb paused and he gave her a sympathetic smile. "I figured out that you weren't at a hundred percent. That's why nothing happened."

She tried again to remember the events of the night

before, but only bits and pieces came back to her. "You wanted something to happen?"

He gave her a look that questioned if she had really asked that. "Of course I wanted something to happen."

"Why?"

He laughed but the sound came out a little stilted. "That's a question with a very obvious answer."

"Because you're a guy?"

"Despite what the female population may believe, not every guy wants sex to the point of doing so with any willing woman."

Which meant she'd been willing but he hadn't been. Urgh. What was she thinking? Of course she'd been willing. The man was hot and got under her skin to probe places she'd rather keep locked away. She'd been under the influence to where her fears wouldn't have come into play to remind her of yet another reason why she should keep her legs closed.

"I'm confused. You wanted something to happen, but even though I was willing, nothing happened?" Even as she said the words, the reality that they were almost naked, lying in her bed, hit her. That he could have taken advantage of her and he hadn't. She liked that. A lot. Possibly because most of the men in her life had taken advantage at every opportunity presented. Not sexually, necessarily, but in any other way they could.

Riley made a sound that she wasn't sure was a low laugh or a growl. "Yes, princess, I wanted something to happen. A lot of somethings. Had you been sober, this morning would have been very different."

She didn't doubt that the morning would have been different. Had they had sex, he probably would have snuck out at some point during the night. Or perhaps he wouldn't have bothered to sneak, he'd have just gone, and left her to her non-sexual self. She knew her strengths and weaknesses and if she hadn't, Chase had done a really bang-up job of pointing them out to her and anyone else who had cared to listen. Sexual prowess wasn't in her bag of tricks.

"I'm sorry."

"I don't want you to be sorry," he surprised her by saying. "What I want is to see you smile."

She bared her teeth in a semblance of a smile because, really, he deserved a smile. He was unlike any man she'd ever known and that made her want to know more…and terrified her, too.

"Not exactly what I had in mind, but it's a start." He smiled so warmly at her that the nausea within her actually eased. "Now, the most pressing question is whether you have any food in this joint so I can cook us something or would you like to go out for breakfast? I'm starved."

In reality they did neither. Not long after she'd draped the comforter around her shoulders and rushed into her bathroom to clean up her mess of a face, he tapped on the door.

She cracked the door open to peer at him. He was fully dressed in his clothes from the night before.

"I've got to head to the hospital. I'm on call today, and they've had several chest pains come into the emergency room. Apparently the cath lab is a madhouse. Dr. Stanley is going to be tied up there for some time and there are two more chest pains on their way by ambulance."

Trying not to look too disappointed that whatever

their morning had been going to bring had been interrupted, she nodded. "I understand."

Apparently she didn't do such a good job at hiding her doubts.

He tilted her chin toward him so he could fully see her face. "For whatever it's worth, I don't want to go."

His fingers on her face were so warm, so tender that she sucked in her breath. "What is it you want?"

"To spend the day with you. Maybe help you drag out your Christmas decorations because your apartment is sadly lacking in Christmas spirit. Or, for that matter, we could decorate my tree. It's been delivered, but I haven't had a chance to trim and decorate it."

He had a live Christmas tree? Who did that in these days of commercialized Christmas? Not that she'd be doing either of his suggestions. She'd had her fill of Christmas spirit the night before and preferred to stick her head in the ground until the season passed. Just look what happened when she tried to get into the spirit of things. She'd ended up drunk and waking in bed with a man she barely knew. No, thank you.

"Honestly, what we did wouldn't matter so much just as long as I got to spend some time with you."

From somewhere in her bedroom her cellphone started buzzing.

"If that's who I think it is, you'll probably get your wish. I'm on call today, too, and if you've been called in, I'm likely to be as well," she mused, pulling her robe tight around her while she dashed toward where her phone had ended up the night before.

"The hospital?" he asked the moment she disconnected the call.

She nodded.

"Maybe the chest pains will end up gastro related rather than cardiac and we won't have to stay long. We could grab lunch," he suggested.

"Maybe," she replied, dropping the phone back into the small black evening bag she'd carried the night before.

"Trinity?"

She glanced towards him.

"I like you."

She wasn't sure what to say.

"I'd like to see you again."

Was he a glutton for punishment or what?

"Despite whatever impression I gave you last night, I'm really quite boring," she said, wondering if she should also warn him about how much baggage she carried. The airport's claim area had nothing on her.

"I don't believe you."

"You should," she warned. "I've known me a lot longer than you have."

He laughed then glanced at his watch. "I could never be bored around you, funny girl. Unfortunately, I have to get moving and your car is still at the hotel where the Christmas party was held. You'll have to ride with me to the hospital so get hopping. We have lives to save."

"Sure thing, snowflake."

CHAPTER FOUR

Although Riley hadn't been on the schedule, he still spent most of the day at the hospital.

Fortunately, so did Trinity.

He'd been able to easily maneuver her into the cardiac lab with him. Right or wrong, he wanted her near him. The panic he'd seen in her eyes that morning worried him. Plus, she was going to need a ride to pick up her car at the end of her shift. He was way too smart to miss out on the opportunity to play white knight and give her a lift.

Doug Ryker, a fifty-three-year-old, had woken up with chest pain that had increased as the sun had come up. When he'd started clutching his chest, his wife had called 911. An ambulance had brought him to the emergency room. His cardiac enzymes had been elevated and, at the minimum, he'd needed an arteriogram.

That's where Riley came in.

He'd met the gentleman's family very briefly while the patient was being prepped. Now Riley was scrubbed and ready to proceed. Trinity was his nurse.

He stole a look at her. If she noticed, she ignored him and focused on their patient.

Too bad there wasn't a sprig of mistletoe around because he'd love to pull down her mask and kiss those plump lips of hers. Did she remember their kiss beneath the mistletoe or had she blocked it from her mind along with the rest of the night? Just how much did she remember about their evening together?

'Twas the season for good tidings and cheer. Riley couldn't think of anything that would cheer him more this Christmas than getting to know the lovely woman he'd spent the night holding and had developed a fascination for that he couldn't quite explain, much less understand. Maybe it really was the season?

He loved Christmas, everything about it. The sounds, the smells, the spirit of giving, all of it. If someone popped a bow on top of Trinity's head and set her beneath his tree to unwrap, he'd be a very happy man.

He glanced over at the angel monitoring Mr. Ryker's vital signs.

She caught him looking. Instant hot pink tinged what he could see of her upper cheeks peeking out from behind her surgical face mask. He winked and her color deepened.

Something warm and fuzzy, like the smell of cookies baking, filled him. Something that just made him feel…happy.

Odd that the feeling felt strange, because he couldn't think of anyone he'd label as happier than him. He was totally happy go lucky. Yet he couldn't deny that the feeling felt alien.

And addictive because already he knew he'd want more when the feeling waned.

Maybe everything would go well with Mr. Ryker's arteriogram and the man wouldn't need anything beyond a few stents. Then, Lord willing, Riley would ask Trinity to go to a late lunch.

"Vitals are good," she said, probably more just to say something rather than to actually inform him.

After she'd prepped Mr. Ryker's groin, Riley numbed the area with an anesthetic and made a penciltip-sized incision. Carefully, he threaded the cardiac catheter through the femoral artery and up into Mr. Ryker's heart.

Mr. Ryker's elevated enzymes had already conveyed that there was cardiac tissue not getting proper perfusion. Riley had hoped he'd find a single small blockage that could be fixed easily with a stent to restore blood flow. He found much more than that. Unfortunately.

Mr. Ryker's mammary artery had a large area of calcification and stenosis. Plus, there were other areas of calcification scattered throughout the arteries. Riley carefully positioned the catheter tip and placed a stent, then another, corrected the blockages that he could via an artificial material holding the artery open. Unfortunately, the stents weren't nearly enough to restore blood flow to the tissue. He withdrew the catheter.

"He's going to need a coronary artery bypass graft," he told another nurse, while Trinity applied pressure to where the catheter had been withdrawn. "Find an available vascular surgeon stat and let's get Mr. Ryker into the operating room."

So much for taking Trinity out to eat any time soon. They'd be here for several hours yet.

Trinity wasn't sure how she'd gone from being in the catheter lab to the operating room as that wasn't usual protocol. At least, it hadn't been standard at the hospital where she'd worked in Memphis, but there she was. In the operating room. With Riley.

She was working as his assistant and blowing CO_2 into Mr. Ryker's open chest. That helped keep blood from interfering with Riley being able to readily see where he was making the anastomosis in the mammary artery to loop the vessel into the right coronary artery. While keeping the CO_2 blowing at just the correct angle, she watched him carefully cut away a pedicule and reroute the artery. Painstakingly, he sutured the arteries together, making sure not to damage the vessels.

Another nurse dabbed at his forehead. Trinity found herself wishing she was the one touching him. Silly really. They were at the hospital. Working to save a man's life. Touching the cardiac surgeon while he performed a procedure should be the absolute last thing on her mind.

She'd touched him the night before.

On the lips under the mistletoe and again on the dance floor and again this morning when she'd reached out to touch his magnificent chest. Who knew where else she'd touched him during the night? After all, she'd woken up spooned against that long, lean body of his.

She swallowed back the knot forming in her throat and refocused her attention on the CO_2.

After what seemed like hours she snuck a peek. His blue eyes, which were normally so full of mischief, were focused intently on the job at hand, on how he meticulously placed sutures, making sure the vessel remained patent, that every movement of his hands were precise.

He'd been full of fun and teasing the night before, and even this morning. Now he was as serious as serious could be. Which one was the real him? The mischievous player who'd stolen a kiss from her under the mistletoe or the brilliant, intense heart surgeon attempting to save his patient's life?

"How late do you have to stay?" Riley asked Trinity later that day, hoping she wouldn't have to pull a full shift.

"I'm not sure. If nothing else has come into the emergency room, I expect the charge nurse will let me go soon." She gave him a suspicious look. "Why? Do you need me to help you with something? Another procedure?"

"I do need your help with something. Have dinner with me."

Her brow lifted. "You need help with dinner?"

"I'll be lonely if you don't join me."

"I seriously doubt you're ever lonely."

He thought about her comment. He couldn't really say that he recalled ever being lonely. He had a full life that he enjoyed a great deal, but the thought of not spending the evening with Trinity, as crazy as it was, did leave him feeling oddly bereft. "You might be surprised."

"I don't think going to dinner together is a good idea."

Why had he known she'd refuse? "Because of last night?"

Her cheeks blushed a rosy pink and she shook her head.

"No?" One eyebrow rose. "Because you don't want to encourage an incorrigible bloke like me?"

Looking torn, she took a step back. "That's not it."

He waggled his brows. "Then you *do* want to encourage an incorrigible bloke like me?"

If her cheeks had been pink before, now they were blood red. "You are incorrigible, but…"

He took her hands in his. "Then you'll help me?"

"You don't understand."

"You have other plans?"

"No, but—"

"No worries, I'll let you choose where we go. I'll even splurge for dessert."

"I don't want dessert."

He shrugged. "Okay, I'm easy. No dessert for you. If you're nice I'll share mine, though."

She let out a long breath. "You really are incorrigible."

He wouldn't deny it.

"What time should I pick you up? You need a ride to your car and it's my responsibility to get you there."

"I'm not your responsibility."

He studied her a moment then rubbed his knuckles across her cheeks. "We're talking dinner and a ride to your car, Trinity, not for ever. Smile and say, 'Thank you, I'd love to go to dinner with you, Riley.'"

Her face screwed up with doubts, she bared her teeth. "Thank you. I'd love to go to dinner with you, Riley."

He laughed and tweaked her nose. "Atta girl."

How had Riley finagled Trinity into doing this?

Going to the hospital Christmas party one night and going on a dinner date the next was just too much for her bah-humbug to digest.

Oh, yeah, she didn't have her car, she justified to herself.

"Jingle-bells, jingle bells," he sang, looking way too

amazing in his jeans and lightweight sweater as he maneuvered through traffic.

Urgh. The only thing worse would be if he was wearing an ugly Christmas sweater.

He glanced her way and grinned. "Penny for your thoughts."

"You don't want them."

"Sure I do."

"I was imagining you in an ugly Christmas sweater. I bet you have a closet full."

Laughing, he arched one brow. "Ugly Christmas sweater?"

"You know, the ones that sport more decorations than a department store."

"Oh, those ugly Christmas sweaters." He grinned. "I might have a few prime specimens tucked away from years past. You wanna borrow one, or are you just making your Christmas gift request?"

"Hardly." But she ruined the effect by laughing at the thought that he might really have a few. Surely not. Covering his shoulders and chest with a knit sweater with sparkly dangly things all over it would be awful.

"Speaking of department stores, do you mind if we swing by and pick up a few strands of lights for my tree before we go eat? I should have grabbed some last week but didn't realize mine were shot at the time."

She bit the inside of her lip. He'd been so kind to her that could she say no?

"I guess that would be okay."

Not really, but maybe she could sit in the car to avoid the hustle and bustle. If he insisted on her going inside the store, she could surely find a happy place in her mind somewhere for however long it took him to get his lights.

"Don't sound so enthusiastic," he teased.

She didn't want to seem ungrateful. He'd transformed the night before into a fun memory…at least the parts she remembered had been fun. He'd not taken advantage when she'd been at his mercy. He'd been gracious and kind, offering to take her to dinner and to get her car. He made her smile. Whether she wanted to or not, she liked the man.

"Sorry, I guess I get a little cranky when I get hungry."

Pulling into a parking spot, he turned off the ignition and reached across the car to take her hand. "If it's okay, I'll do a quick run for the lights while you grab us some sandwiches from the place there." He handed her a couple of twenties and pointed to a sandwich shop. "I'll make it up to you by taking you to my place so you can help decorate my tree. Deal?"

Before she could tell him that decorating his tree would be more like punishment, he got out of the car. "I'll take a club loaded with everything…hold the onions."

A sinking feeling in her gut, Trinity watched him rush toward a seasonal store in the strip mall.

Dinner and decorating a tree? Not what she'd signed up for, but apparently what she'd be doing, all the same, with a forced smile for Riley's sake.

Trinity had to admit the sandwiches were delicious or she really had been hungrier than she'd thought. The tree decorating, well, she was still holding back her opinion on that.

Not that she enjoyed the decorating but she'd have to be blind not to appreciate the view. Standing on a stepladder, Riley leaned and made another snip from the live blue spruce tree that towered several feet over her head. After clipping a few more twigs, he inspected the tree to see if it met with his approval.

From where she stood at the bottom of the ladder, she had to admit he definitely met her visual approval. The man was hot.

"What do you think? Look good?"

Did he have a crystal ball to see into her mind or what? "Oh, yeah."

"Now, that's the enthusiasm I've wanted to see all evening. To think, if you'd had your car you'd have found some excuse to say no."

Trinity closed her eyes and winced. He'd meant the tree, not his rear end. Duh. Of course he hadn't meant his rear end.

"I did say no," she reminded him. The man was persuasive. She'd better be careful or he'd have her agreeing to dress up in a red suit and climb down a chimney proclaiming, ho, ho, ho and a merry Christmas to all.

"You have to admit this is more fun than going home alone." His forehead wrinkled as he inspected the tree and stretched to straighten a branch, giving her another great view of his rear end. "You think I need to take a little more off the top? I want this tree to look amazing when we're done."

What she thought was that no amount of trimming was going to make the tree come anywhere near to how amazing his bottom was. Someone should stick him at the top of the tree and her views on Christmas might brighten more than a little. Definitely, she could get into unwrapping his package.

Urgh. What was wrong with her? Perhaps Riley had placed a spell on her beneath the mistletoe because she'd really like him to climb down that stepladder, take her in his arms and kiss her until her lungs were so deprived of oxygen she had to pull away just to keep from losing consciousness.

Then she wanted him to kiss her some more. More. More. More.

Crazy. She wanted to be kissed right now. And not because of some silly song coming over his surround-sound system about a kid seeing momma kissing Santa either. Riley's belly could never be compared to a bowl full of jelly and the dusky five o'clock shadow gracing the strong lines of his jaw were sexy, not fluffy white tufts that would tickle her face.

"Are you hanging mistletoe?" Oops. Had she really just asked that out loud? Who needed the cozy fire that he must have also turned on to keep the room temperature comfortable? Her face had to have just sped up global warming with a single embarrassing moment.

He glanced down at her, his grin positively lethal. "Would you like me to hang mistletoe, princess?"

How did any good girl in her right mind answer that?

"Um, no, I was just wondering if you were going to, not suggesting you do so, *snowflake*. I mean, if you were going to that would be okay, but if not…" Okay, time to zip her lips because she was rambling and just fanning the flames.

The dimple in his left cheek dug deeper. "You know, I'm a traditional kind of guy so I do have mistletoe. It's in that box over by the sofa if you want to dig it out."

Just to have an excuse to move away from his gaze, she went to the plastic storage container and searched through the labeled boxes inside. When she lifted the lid off the properly labeled one she wrinkled her nose. "You insist on a live tree but have plastic mistletoe?"

"I know. A travesty." He gave a faux devastated shrug. "We should go shopping tomorrow evening to buy me the real deal."

"I wasn't hinting for an invitation."

"I didn't think you were."

"I have better things to do."

"Than to enjoy the spirit of Christmas?" He gave her a horrified look. "What could be better than that?"

"Just about anything and everything."

"Don't you like Christmas?" Obviously he found the possibility that someone might not like Christmas so absurd he didn't wait for an answer, just climbed down the ladder to survey his handiwork.

"It's not my favorite holiday," she muttered under her breath, glad that at least for the moment she didn't have to stare up at his amazing butt.

Her answer caught his attention and he glanced at her. "Which holiday is your favorite, then?"

Not that she'd ever discussed her aversion to Christmas with anyone, but no one had ever asked her which holiday was her favorite. She thought for a moment.

"New Year's Day." She blinked at the man standing right in front of her.

"Why's that? You like making resolutions no one ever keeps?"

"And people think I'm cynical?" Smiling, she shook her head. "No."

Besides, she tended to keep the few New Year's resolutions she made each year. Somehow she'd bet Riley did his best to keep any resolutions he made too. He just seemed like that kind of guy.

"After New Year is when everyone takes all their Christmas decorations down and gets on with their real life, instead of wasting a month dreaming dreams about a man in a red suit bringing them their heart's desire."

"Ouch." He placed his hand over his heart and took a step back as if she'd struck him a vital blow. "You're a mean one, Miss Gr—"

She held up her hand and squinted at him. "Don't you call me names, snowflake." She tossed a loose piece of mistletoe at him, smiling when he easily caught it and blew her a kiss.

She puckered up and kissed the air. Electricity sizzled between them and she clung to their conversation to keep her mind away from just how much she wanted to feel his lips against hers for real. "Not liking this superficial holiday that's a bunch of marketing hype to get people to spend money that they don't have does not make me a bad person…or a green one."

His lips twitched, as if he knew what she was doing, as if his lips had a few wants of their own. "Agreed, but I'd really like to know why someone who's as sweet as you wouldn't like the most wonderful time of year."

"First off, whether or not Christmas is the most wonderful time of the year is a matter of opinion." Was he moving closer or was she imagining that the distance between them was shrinking? Oh, please, let the distance be shrinking because if he didn't kiss her soon, she might just bury herself in mistletoe and present herself to him. "Obviously," she continued, as if her heart wasn't pounding in her chest, as if every cell within her didn't leap toward him, "I am not of that opinion."

"Second?" He'd definitely moved closer. A lot closer. She could feel his body heat, could feel his breath brush across her lips, could smell his musky male scent that sent her senses into hyperdrive.

"Second..." she stared into his eyes, her lips parted, her pulse throbbing "...you don't know me well enough to know how sweet I may or may not be."

"I disagree." He covered her mouth with his, moved his lips in a caress that was teasing, tasting, erotic and sensual. Hot and demanding. Everything she'd just been longing for. Him. His kiss made her feel as if someone had strung lights on her and she twinkled from the inside out.

"Oh, yeah, you're sweet," he whispered against her lips when he pulled back. "Sweet as candy canes and gumdrops."

"Right," was all she could manage, because what she really wanted was to pull his mouth back to hers. Desperately she wanted another kiss, wanted him. That terrified her. "Let's get this tree decorated so I can go home."

After a brief pause, in which he studied her, Riley threw his head back in laughter. "You know, princess, if I didn't know any better, I'd think you like me even less than you profess to like Christmas."

"Good thing you know better, then, eh?" she retorted, handing him one of the new strings of lights. "Get to hanging or I'm out of here."

Because at the moment she was having a difficult time recalling all the reasons she shouldn't want him and needed not to trust in him.

"Yes, ma'am." With a wicked gleam in his eyes he reached for the mistletoe and went to hold it above her head. "I'll start with your favorite decoration."

"No!" But she ruined her denial by having to suppress a laugh. She pointed to the tree. "Decorate."

He gave an exaggerated sigh. "I didn't know you were such a slavedriver."

She gave him the sternest look she could muster when he looked so darned cute and remorseful with his mistletoe. "Like I said, there are a lot of things about me you don't know."

"Yet," he clarified, with what she was quickly realizing was his usual optimism. Or was stubbornness a better label? "Don't worry," he continued. "I plan to know everything there is to know about you, princess."

Lord, she hoped not. She'd come to Pensacola to escape people who knew everything there was to know about her.

"You'll be coming to me to find yourself," he added, his expression way too confident.

She hoped not on that too because she never wanted to let anyone that close ever again.

"Here, you save this for later." He tucked the loose piece of mistletoe she'd tossed at him into her scrub top pocket. "Any time you get the urge, you just wave that and I'll pucker up."

She rolled her eyes but couldn't keep her fingers away from the cheap plastic greenery in her pocket. "Like a red flag in front of a bull?"

He chuckled. "I hope I have a little more finesse than that." His brow furrowed in mock concern. "I do have more finesse than a stampeding cow, right?"

She gave a little shrug. "Maybe."

His brow rose.

"Okay," she confessed. "A little."

"I'll settle for that for now, but later we'll renegoti-ate your thoughts about my finesse."

If that meant he planned to kiss her again, she should find a reason to leave, but instead she just smiled and secretly hoped that was precisely what he meant.

Prior to placing the lights on the tree, they plugged the strands in to make sure each bulb lit up. Each one shone a brilliant color, sparkling against the tiled floor-ing. Then she held the lights while he went back up the stepladder. They worked together to string them around the tree, starting at top and working their way down.

Every time she started to enjoy herself a little too much, she reined herself in because he made her feel a little too happy, a little too comfy, and that could only lead to heartache, right? She couldn't deal with more heartache so it was much better to keep her defenses high.

Telling herself she really did not like the woodsy scent filling her nostrils and that she'd probably have a rash on her hands from handling the branches, Trinity frowned. "Why do you have such a big tree?"

He waggled his brows, covering the last of the branches with lights. "You know what they say about men with big Christmas trees."

The man was a certifiable nut. She must be too be-cause she almost giggled. So much for her defenses. "They have big trees to compensate for their wee lit-tle...minds?"

He gave her a scolding look. "I could show you my wee little mind and put that theory to rest."

"You wish," she teased, before thinking better of it.

He reached for the snap at his waist.

"Fine." She didn't bother suppressing her eye-roll but tried really hard to keep her blush in check. "Please, tell me, oh great ginormous tree owner, why is your tree so big?"

His eyes sparkled and his grin almost knocked her off her feet. "The bigger the tree, the better to light up her world."

"Her?" He hadn't brought anyone with him to the hospital Christmas party, had spent the evening with her, had spent the night afterwards in her bed and flirted outrageously with her. He'd better not have a "her".

"Your world?" he corrected, looking sheepish.

"I don't need your compensatory huge tree lighting up my world. My world is just fine the way it is."

Even as she made the bold claim, she wondered if perhaps she did because when he clicked a button and his tree sparkled to life, she had to admit, something inside her felt better. Warmer.

Lighter.

As if the button had turned on something inside her too that had been stuck in hibernation.

"Wow," she gasped, unable to quash her surprise. "I have to admit, that's beautiful."

Exactly, Riley thought, but he wasn't looking at the tree. He couldn't drag his eyes away from Trinity.

She was beautiful.

He wanted to light up her world, to see a permanent sparkle in her eyes and a smile on her lips.

Too bad he didn't have a remote control that he could click and turn her on.

To turn her on in more ways than one.

Because he was turned on.

Had been from the moment he'd first noticed her at the Christmas party. Something about her got under his skin and made his body go haywire. Big time. Was it just that instead of chasing him, like most women did, she seemed intent on keeping him at arm's length?

"Just wait until you see it after we've finished decorating," he promised. "My tree, which I refuse to label as compensatory and would still be more than happy to set the record straight once and for all, will steal your breath, guaranteed."

"I..." She glanced away then her lips tightened. "I seriously doubt that, but I do like the lights." She wasn't going to touch his offer apparently. Not that he'd really expected her to. "Let's hurry and finish."

"So you can leave?"

She met his gaze, her lips twitching lightly, letting him know she was fighting back a smile. "So I can have some of that dessert you promised but have totally failed to deliver."

"Touché." He laughed.

Yes, he really liked this woman, even if she professed not to like his favorite holiday. There had to be more to her claim than just a dislike of Christmas.

A more that he wanted to know every detail of so he could prove her wrong and show her the magic of the holidays.

CHAPTER FIVE

TRINITY DIDN'T LIKE Christmas at all and doubted she ever would. But when they'd finished decorating, she did think that Riley's Christmas tree was beautiful. Magical even.

Plus, she had concluded that she did like the woodsy pine smell filling his living room. Why had she practically gagged on the scent for the past couple of years, comparing the outdoorsy aroma to spruce-scented household cleaner?

Because she didn't like this holiday, she reminded herself.

From childhood this holiday had only ever held bad memories. Nothing good had ever come out of Christmas. Not for her.

She'd do well to remember that.

Riley's constant smiles and holiday good cheer made her forget that she didn't like a single thing about the season. Still, she was doing something to help someone who had helped her. Someone she genuinely liked and who hadn't taken advantage of her.

"Thank you."

"For?" he asked, studying her way too intently for her comfort.

She wanted to squirm, like a kid sitting on Santa's lap. "Last night."

"Nothing happened last night for you to owe me any thanks for."

Was that how he saw the night?

"Had something happened," she admitted, "I wouldn't have been thanking you."

"You might have," he teased, but when she didn't smile, he relented. "For the record, I prefer my bed partners to be sober and just as into me as I am into them. Whether or not we were going to have sex last night was never an issue."

"I wasn't into you?" That she had a hard time imagining because the man made her burn from head to toe. Even now she wanted to rip his clothes off him and lick him all over. She squeezed her eyes shut, trying to clear the image of her doing just that.

He shrugged. "We've already established that you drank a little too much."

"Did I want you?" she said, more insistently. What was she saying? Of course she'd wanted him. She still wanted him.

"You said you did."

"Oh." A vague memory of her telling him he could do whatever he wanted so long as he didn't leave her ran through her mind. Fire spread across her cheeks. She had made a complete and utter fool of herself. "I'm sorry." She turned to go, wishing her car was in his drive so she really could escape.

"I'm not." He turned her to face him. "I wanted you, Trinity. I'm not ashamed to say so."

She blushed and he grinned.

"I wasn't inebriated, except by your smile."

"I've said it before but it bears repeating, you're smooth with the lines, Riley."

"No lines," he said. "Just the truth."

"Right."

"Seriously."

"Seriously, I want that dessert now." Anything to get away from this conversation.

"Chicken," he accused, apparently reading her well enough to know exactly what she was doing.

"Bok bok, Mr. Big Tree," she replied, wondering at her sparring back and forth with him verbally when really she should be embarrassed at her out-of-character behavior.

His laugh made her feel warm inside.

"Like I said, fun girl."

"Like I said, give me dessert."

Trinity had expected Riley to insist on coming into her apartment when he'd followed her home, but he didn't. He walked her to her door, kissed her forehead, saw her inside, then left without setting foot into her place.

Go figure.

Staring at the closed door, she wanted to open it, to yell to him that he could have at least kissed her good-night properly.

'Meow.' Casper brushed up against her leg, reminding Trinity that she'd like to be fed.

"I know. I know. I rushed off this morning without paying you much attention." She glanced down at the solid white cat that she'd rescued from an animal shelter when she had been nothing more than a tiny pitiful-looking kitten.

Casper mewed again, staying practically beneath her

feet as she walked towards her small pantry to get a can of cat food. She opened the can, put the contents into Casper's dish and watched the cat dive in with gusto.

"You'd think you were starved," she teased. "But I am fully aware that Riley fed you this morning while I threw on my scrubs."

That he'd been thoughtful enough to do so had impressed her, even if she hadn't made a big deal of him having done so. The man was thoughtful all the way round. He was just a little too good to be true.

Well, all except for the not having kissed her goodnight part. That he could use some work on. ·

Or maybe it was her sanity that could use some work, because she shouldn't want him to kiss her. She didn't want a relationship, didn't want to set herself up for another fall, like the one Chase had delivered.

"I know you aren't starved," she informed the cat.

Casper's blue eyes cut to her for a brief second as if to say, So what?

Trinity laughed then jumped when her phone rang. She glanced at the number. It wasn't one she was familiar with, but she knew who the caller was as sure as she lived and breathed. Should she answer?

Could she not?

"Did you forget something?" she said by way of greeting, because "Hello" seemed all wrong when he had just left.

"Apparently." He sounded confused, frustrated. "I'm standing outside your front door."

Trinity's stomach flip-flopped. Had he ever left? Or had he just come back? Did it matter?

"The usual protocol when standing outside someone's door is to knock, not phone." Her heart pounding in anticipation of whatever was to come, she headed towards the front door.

"I didn't knock because I don't want to come in."

Her hand paused in the process of reaching for the doorknob. "You don't?"

Her stomach knotted. Was he playing some sick game with her? Teasing her? Toying with her emotions?

"I do, but…Trinity, tell me to go home."

If this was his idea of a game, it was cruel and twisted. She wasn't amused.

"Go home," she ordered, and meant it. She'd been hurt enough in the past. She wouldn't let someone sour her future. Not even someone who seemed as wonderful as Riley.

Then again, most of the time when something seemed too good to be true, it really was. So why was she still on the line, waiting for him to say something? Hoping he'd say something. Something brilliant and wonderful that would make her smile instead of feeling as if her eyes were about to spring a leak.

A low laugh sounded in her ears. "That was way too easy for you, princess."

"You have no idea," she muttered, wondering at the silence that followed. She wanted to tear the door off its hinges and drag him inside her apartment and demand he explain himself.

Instead, she leaned her forehead against the cold metal doorframe, wishing she could see through it to the other side, wishing she knew what he was thinking, why he was standing outside her door when she was inside, why he'd called her instead of knocking.

Why was he there at all?

Why wasn't she hanging up?

Urgh. Her head hurt with all the questions plaguing her mind.

"If I knocked, would you let me in, princess?" His voice was barely above a whisper but she heard just fine.

Her hands shook. "I guess you'll have to knock to know the answer to that question, won't you, snowflake?"

Taking a deep breath, he laughed again. "If you had any idea how much I want to rip through this door because I know you're standing just the other side…" He paused, and she'd swear she felt his forehead bump against the door. Was he trying to knock some sense into his head? How was it he kept putting her thoughts into words that came from his mouth?

"As much as I want you," he admitted, "what I want more than anything is to not mess this up."

"Knocking on my door would mess this up?" What was "this", she wanted to ask, but held her tongue. She doubted he knew any more than she did. That he admitted there was a "this" was monumental, had her brain undoing every wall she'd just attempted to erect between them. Didn't he know he should leave those walls alone? She needed them.

"It might. What if you didn't open the door?"

He had a point.

"True, but what if I did?"

Or would that be messing things up even worse?

Riley ground his forehead against the cold, hard metal of Trinity's apartment door and prayed for the knowledge to know the right thing to do.

He wanted to knock.

Whether she would admit to it or not, she wanted him to knock. He could hear it in her voice.

Every instinct warned he shouldn't, that, despite their mutual desire for one another, she wasn't ready to consummate that desire. Not really.

As much as he hated listening to that voice of reason, he trusted his instincts more than the body part that had him wanting to he-man his way into her apartment.

To do that would only satisfy him in the short term and although he had no clue exactly what he wanted with Trinity, he knew that one night would not be enough. If he rushed, she might shut him out for ever. Despite the tough front she attempted to put on, she was vulnerable in ways that made him want to fight every dragon that had ever taken a swipe at her. Although he didn't understand or like how protective he felt about her, he refused to be yet another dragon for her to fend off, even if a well-intentioned one.

"We both know you shouldn't open your door to me. Not tonight." He straightened from the door before he gave in to temptation.

"Then why did you call?" She sounded irked, which pleased him because it meant she wasn't immune to the chemistry between them. That he wasn't wrong.

"Why call?" He loved her logic and her sass. Despite the rebellious throb in his body, he couldn't help but smile. "To hear your voice. For you to tell me I'm crazy."

"You're crazy," she replied, without hesitation.

"About you," he admitted, knowing it was true, that she was different from any woman he'd ever known, and not just because she didn't fall at his feet.

Which was why he'd leave, and smile while doing so. Yeah, he'd like to be on the other side of her door but there was no rush. He'd take his time, woo her, have her begging for more, and then give her more for however long the sparks between them flew.

"You don't even know me," she insisted, much as she'd done previously.

"A problem I intend to remedy."

But not tonight.

Forehead against the door, Trinity held her breath. Surely, any second now he'd knock. He had to knock, right?

He was there.

Just on the other side of her door, teasing her. No, not teasing really. More of a temptation to reach out and take what she reluctantly admitted she wanted.

He did tempt her. Like fresh-baked cookies tempted a starving dieter.

She wanted a bite.

A big bite.

Before she could have biter's remorse, she undid the chain, undid the deadbolt and flung the door open.

"Riley?"

"Hmm?" His response buzzed in her ear.

"Where are you?" Stunned, she glanced down the hallway.

The empty hallway.

"My car."

His car?

He'd left?

Her heart sank.

"You were never really on the other side of my door?"

She might kill him. He'd gotten her all worked up for nothing, had...

"I was there."

Frowning, fighting disappointment she didn't quite understand and definitely didn't want, she went back into her apartment. She should hang up now, before she incriminated herself.

Why was she surprised? Disappointed? She should be glad he'd left, that he'd had reason when she'd temporarily lost her mind. Her stomach knotted and her eyes watered. Great.

Why was she not telling him where to go and turning off her phone?

"Trinity?"

"Yes?" She slumped back against the door, fighting a sniffle. Was he seriously whistling? She might just throw her phone at him for real.

"I like you."

Were they in grammar school or what?

Eyes squeezed closed, she sighed. "So you keep saying, but at the moment, Riley Williams, I don't like you one bit."

He surprised her by bursting into laughter. "There's my funny girl."

"Are you dating Dr. Williams?"

Putting her stethoscope into her scrub pocket, Trinity spun around to look at her coworker. Karen Mathis, Trinity's favorite coworker by far—usually—grinned at her and waited with an expectant look that said she wasn't going to be easily distracted.

"Why would you ask me that?"

"I saw you at the Christmas party," Karen pointed out. "I'd been looking for you because I knew you didn't know many people yet and I was going to have you join the group I was with. I didn't spot you until you were all cozied up with the only cardiologist on staff who makes women's hearts beat faster with just a flash of his smile."

Trinity's heart was beating pretty fast without the benefit of one of his smiles. "We just danced. It wasn't a big deal."

"And sang together," Karen reminded her. "Plus, I hear you arrived at work with him yesterday morning when you both got called in. You rode home with him yesterday at the end of your shift. Despite many females' valiant efforts, I don't know of him ever dating anyone who works here. This all sounds like a big deal to me. So, are you two an item or what?"

Inwardly, Trinity cringed. The hospital gossip mill had sure been busy. How did she answer a question she didn't know the answer to? Because saying he liked her just sounded a bit second grade to her. She didn't really know what they were other than that she liked him too.

"Did you also hear that she's going to eat with me after work tonight?"

Both women turned at the newcomer to their conversation.

"Dr. Williams." Karen's cheeks flushed almost as bright as Trinity imagined hers were.

"Riley," she gasped, her eyes devouring the man before her, searching his eyes for some trace of the man who'd spent hours on the phone with her the night before. Hours and hours. He'd blown her away. They'd talked long into the night without awkwardness or long bouts of weird silence. The man was way too easy to talk to. "Anyone ever tell you it isn't polite to eavesdrop?"

She almost called him "snowflake" but caught

herself just in time. Yeah, that would have had some tongues wagging all over the cardiac unit.

"Never. Most people like having conversations with me." He waggled his brows, his eyes not leaving Trinity's. The twinkle there said everything. That he knew what she was thinking, was thinking the same thing himself. "Good morning, ladies."

Trinity mumbled a good morning, glancing away because all she could think was that this was the man with whom she'd fallen asleep while on the phone with him the night before.

He'd stayed on the phone with her because he'd said he really did want to get to know her without the physical getting in the way. Honestly, she just didn't know what to think about him. He was unlike any many she'd ever met.

Chase sure hadn't worried about the physical getting in the way.

Sex had gotten in the way of their relationship.

Big time.

Not because they'd rushed into a physical relationship. They hadn't, despite Chase's constant pressure to do so. Perhaps she should have held out longer. When she'd finally given in, it had been the beginning of the end. She'd flopped in bed.

Chase had had no qualms announcing that juicy little tidbit to the world.

So a man who put emphasis on getting to know her rather than on her bedroom performance was good. Raised her odds of success, right? Or just set up her expectations to where her failure would sting all the more?

"Trinity?" Riley interrupted her thoughts. "We *are* going to eat after work today?"

She blinked, thinking him too good looking for his own good. He was so used to getting his own way that she almost said no just to be difficult. But that wasn't any way to start a relationship. Or to maintain one.

A relationship. Was that what they were doing? What she wanted?

"Yes," she agreed, knowing she wasn't going to deprive herself of spending the evening with him, even if she still didn't trust him. "Just as long as we don't do anything Christmassy."

For answer, he just grinned. "Would I ever ask you to do that?"

"Never." Trinity couldn't keep a smile from curving her lips. She tried. Really, she did. After all, she had sworn off men, but there was something about Riley that couldn't be ignored. Okay, so everything about him refused to be ignored.

Karen stared back and forth between them. "So the gossip is true?"

Trinity blushed.

Riley grinned. "If they're saying that I'm pursuing the hottest nurse at Pensacola Memorial then, yeah, it's true."

Had he really just said that? Trinity's face caught fire and her mouth dropped. Chase had always been so private, not wanting anyone to know how much he cared about her, saying that with them both working for the hospital they should keep their relationship on the quiet. Ha, he'd sure blown that at the end.

Then again, had he really cared about her at all? She'd certainly thought so. They'd dated for nine months. She'd thought she was going to get an engagement ring for Christmas. Instead, she'd gotten a horrendous public humiliation and a reminder about why she disliked the holiday so much. Or perhaps it was Christmas that disliked her. Maybe she should ask Riley for a rain check until New Year.

Karen smiled. "I'll be sure to let everyone know you're off the market, Dr. Williams."

"I didn't know I was ever on the market. But you do that. My free time is definitely going to be occupied by this little lady so long as she'll let me hang around." Riley winked and nodded towards the cardiac care patient rooms. "How's Mr. Ryker this morning? Holding his own?"

Still not quite believing how he'd just essentially given Karen permission to tell everyone that he belonged to her, Trinity shook her head in wonder.

Take that, Christmas party trio who'd called her "tonight's lucky pick".

She was this week's lucky pick.

Or something like that.

Then again, she had to wonder just what he had to gain by hanging out with her. Why he'd want to. Ultimately, how much did they have in common? Was he so used to women chasing him that he had to dazzle her so she'd follow suit?

Sure, she'd enjoyed talking to him into the wee hours, but everything was different when you were bone tired, right?

Still, she'd be lying if she said she hadn't enjoyed spending time with him the evening before, despite what he'd had her doing. She'd definitely be fibbing if she said she hadn't derived deep pleasure from falling asleep to the sound of his voice, to his breathing on the other end of the phone, to him asking her thoughts and dreams.

No one had ever asked her those things.

"Oxygen sats are staying at 97-98%, but he's still on two liters per minute," she told him, referring to the patient she'd just finished checking prior to Karen's inquisition. "Cardiac monitoring is normal. His vitals are stable. Ins and outs are normal. A physical therapist had him up walking not long ago."

"That's what I like to hear."

It's what she liked to report. No nurse wanted to deliver bad news regarding a patient.

"Come round with me?"

He was her superior so of course she'd go round with him if that's what he wanted. Based on the past couple days, she'd do a lot of things with him if that's what he wanted. If he could get her to decorate a Christmas tree, she was pretty much at his will to command.

Lord, she hoped that wasn't really so.

"Y'all have fun and don't do anything that will get Mr. Ryker's heart racing," Karen teased, looking quite pleased at Riley's admission.

He laughed and Trinity didn't say a word. Honestly, as impressed as she was at Riley not caring who knew he was interested in her, she hated the thought that she was the focus of hospital gossip. Even if it was positive gossip regarding her and Riley, because all good things came to an end and then what? She'd once again be poor pitiful Trinity who'd been dumped, because realistically she acknowledged that he'd be the one to end their relationship.

Would he humiliate her publicly, the way Chase had?

Of course, to give him credit, Chase had been drinking too much. Would he have otherwise announced her shortcomings so cruelly at their hospital Christmas party? Probably not, but once done he'd been unable to take back his words, couldn't stop the teasing that had ensued at Trinity's expense. Why had she stayed in Memphis so long after that horrible Christmas? Had she purposely been punishing herself for being so stupid as to put her hopes in a man? At least she hadn't started drinking, the way her mother had after being deserted by Trinity's father.

She should have removed herself from the situation much sooner. She hadn't wanted to run but, really, after her mother's death she'd had no ties. She should have left. Next time she'd know.

Next time?

Was she already planning for the demise of any relationship between her and Riley? Whatever that relationship might be. She really didn't have a clue what he wanted from her.

If he'd just wanted sex, wouldn't he have knocked the night before instead of talking to her into the wee morning hours?

Riley tapped on the patient's door then entered the private cardiac room. "Good morning, Mr. Ryker."

The man stretched out in his bed smiled at Riley and then at Trinity. A clear tube ran around his face with a nasal cannula delivering oxygen. Multiple wires and leads were attached at various points to his body.

"Your nurse tells me that you're ready to dance a jig and you want to blow this joint as soon as possible. That so?"

Not her exact words.

"If it would get me home earlier, I'd dance a jig or

two," the heavy set man admitted, raising the head of his bed and scooting up, wincing a little as he did so. "Other than the pain in my chest and leg from being cut open, I feel great."

"If all goes well today, I'll release you to go home tomorrow morning and see you back in the office in a week or so."

The man's wife, who'd been sitting quietly in a chair next to his hospital bed, got wide-eyed. "You're going to let him go home that soon? Is that safe?"

"If everything goes as expected today, yes, I am. It's safe for him to go home. Actually, the sooner I can get him home, the less risk there is of secondary infections such as a resistant strain of staph or C. diff."

"Oh," the woman blanched and she pushed a heavy-framed pair of glasses up the bridge of her nose. "What if something else happens? I won't know how to take care of him."

"If it's a problem, we can have a home health agency come out and dress his chest wounds and the surgical site on his leg. But, honestly, he should be fine as long as he doesn't overdo it."

The woman's relief was evident.

"But the first thing we have to do is get you through today." Riley placed his stethoscope on the man's chest, moving the diaphragm from spot to spot to listen to the man's heart sounds.

"Can you tell if the bypass is taking, based on what you hear?" the man asked, looking concerned. "I keep wondering what I'd do if my heart rejected the graft."

"That's unlikely to happen as it's your own tissue. But no worries, we'll take another look at the blood flow via an echocardiogram to make sure everything is working properly. You're in good hands."

Trinity wouldn't argue with Riley's claim. He did have good hands. Expert hands that worked magic with hearts.

Which, of course, made her wonder about what those hands were going to do to her heart.

Or should she even worry about that since Chase had tattered it to shreds and despite her move she knew there were only broken pieces where once a strong heart used to beat?

Maybe she was immune to Riley hurting her because she didn't have a heart left to be broken.

Somehow she doubted that because already she knew she'd miss him terribly if he left her life.

That scared her more than she cared to admit. Maybe she should run while she still could.

Only could she, even if she wanted to?

CHAPTER SIX

"THIS ISN'T DINNER," Trinity pointed out when Riley pulled into the crowded mall parking lot that evening. Although he looked handsome in khakis and a polo and was in way too good a mood to have worked all day, she was still in her scrubs, hungry, tired and really didn't want to fight the crowds. She'd told him she'd have dinner with him, so dinner they would have.

Somehow she hadn't envisioned him taking her to a shopping center for a slice of pizza or Chinese. Then again, she knew next to nothing about his eating habits and they had eaten sandwiches the night before.

"True," Riley admitted, not looking one bit guilty as he parked the car in a just-vacated parking spot.

One more thing to not like about Christmas. Everywhere was packed. Parking lots, shops, streets. It was as if every person came out of hibernation and crowded every public place, searching for that great deal on the perfect gift that they'd spend money they didn't really have to spend. Trinity would much rather be at home with a good book and Casper curled up in her lap than dealing with all the holiday hoopla.

Her car door opened and she glanced up at the man

waiting for her to get out of the car. Really? She'd rather be with her cat than with this gorgeous man?

Okay, so not really. But hanging with Casper would be a lot easier on her emotions in the long run.

Please, don't hurt me, she silently pleaded. All day she'd questioned why he'd taken an interest in her when there were so many women out there who would gladly kiss his rear end and had to be more suitable than her. She was just Trinity Warren from the wrong side of the tracks, so to speak. He was a cardiac surgeon who'd obviously led a privileged life. They couldn't be more different.

"Come on, princess." A big smile on his face, he motioned for her to get out of the car. "We're just going to do a little shopping before we eat."

What? He wanted her to go in there and face the shopping frenzy? Had he lost his mind?

"I don't think so. You didn't mention anything about shopping."

"Didn't I?" He pretended to look repentant. "Must have slipped my mind." He took her hand and laced their fingers together. "No worries, princess. I promise to feed you, too."

As if skipping a meal or two would hurt her.

Still, the last thing she wanted was to go into a mall all decked out with Christmas decorations and sales. Maybe she really was a Scrooge.

"I don't like shopping." Had she sounded petulant? It hadn't been her intent, but she felt like digging her heels in and refusing to budge. Seriously, the man did not have to have his way on everything.

"Every woman likes to shop."

She snorted. How stereotypically male!

"Shows how much you know about women," she countered, chin high at his arrogant comment.

He stopped walking and gawked at her. "How can you not like shopping? Especially at this time of year? Every store is a smorgasbord of treats just waiting to make someone happy."

Her stomach roiled. "It's especially at this time of year I don't like shopping and my guess is that that smorgasbord of treats causes more problems than happiness. Someone has to pay for all that stuff bought that no one really needed to begin with."

Wow. She sounded a lot like her mother.

Which she really didn't want because, God rest her soul, Trinity didn't want any similarity between herself and the woman who'd given birth to her. Still, facts were facts. People went crazy at Christmas.

"Bah, humbug."

"Make fun of me all you like, but I prefer if we eat and then you take me home before you do your shopping." If his lower lip stuck out any further she'd swear he was pouting. "Or you can just take me home now and you can come back and do your shopping. We can do dinner some other time."

"We're not doing my shopping and no way am I taking you home without feeding you first."

This time she was the one who stopped walking. She stared at him as if he was making no sense. Actually, he wasn't making any sense.

"Whose shopping are we doing?"

"Yours."

Her face squished and her nose curled in disgust. "Mine?"

He nodded, tweaking her nose to unfurrow the wrinkles.

"I don't need to do any shopping." Her needs were simple and she wasn't running low on anything. Who would she buy something for? She barely knew anyone in Pensacola and as much as she liked Karen, she wasn't sure they were at a buy-each-other-Christmas-gifts point in their friendship. Although she did like the woman and Karen had seemed happy for her regarding Riley's interest, so maybe… Trinity usually just ordered a few gift cards online to have on hand in case she needed a quick gift. Last year she'd used most of them herself come January because she just hadn't had anyone to give them to.

"Sure you do," Riley countered with so much confidence that her insides heated a little.

She blew out a frustrated sigh. "Riley, I don't like it when you assume things about me."

A serious expression slid over his face. "Noted. I don't mean to railroad you into doing something you don't want to do, princess. But I also feel it my personal responsibility to get you into the Christmas spirit."

His personal responsibility? Poor guy. He had no clue what he was in for.

"Good luck with that."

"Thanks."

She shook her head, not surprised her sarcasm had fallen short. Riley only seemed to see the positive, regardless of what she did or said.

Still, Christmas was pushing it. Why couldn't they have met at a Halloween party? Or, better yet, a New Year party? Anything but Christmas because taking away the fact that he was a gorgeous doctor and she was just her, the fact they'd met at a Christmas party spelled doom from the start.

So far as she was concerned, nothing good had ever come out of Christmas.

But the sooner they got this shopping ordeal over with the sooner they could eat and the sooner she could go home and over-analyze the past few days yet again. "What am I shopping for?"

"It's less than two weeks until Christmas Day and you don't have a single decoration up or a single wrapped present in your apartment."

That was a problem why? Her apartment was the one place she could escape from all the holiday craziness.

"I hate to burst your bubble, Riley, but most single people without kids don't go all out with decorations and presents. They have better things to do with their time than decorating for themselves."

Like take out the trash and give the cat a bath. Important things like those.

He shook his head in mock disappointment, his eyes twinkling. "I bet you were one of those kids who never believed in Santa and took joy in telling other kids that he wasn't real."

Although she doubted he'd meant his comment to hurt, she felt a sharp sting in her chest and a defensive shield popped up. "I never told other kids Santa wasn't real."

He stared at her incredulously. "But you never believed in Santa? In the magic of Christmas? Not even as a kid?"

Swallowing the lump in her throat at memories she didn't want rising to the surface, she shook her head.

"Then who did you think climbed down your chimney and left all the Christmas morning goodies? The tooth fairy?"

She didn't think anything. Not about the tooth fairy or Santa. Or the Easter bunny or any other mythical creature who was supposed to do something good for her. Why would she?

"Apparently your Christmas mornings were very different from mine." At her house Christmas had just been another day. No big deal. Actually, if she'd made the mistake of mentioning the holidays, Christmas morning had been worse than other days because her mother would go into a bigger than normal rant. New Year had never been able to get there soon enough.

"Were you so naughty that Santa didn't visit?" His tone was teasing, but Trinity had to look away because she'd swear something had blown into her eyes. Probably a bit of fake snow off the ginormous tree gracing the entryway of the shopping mall.

Stupid tree. Stupid fake snow. Stupid shopping trip. Stupid her for coming here and dredging up all these memories.

She was not going to let him see her cry, had learned long ago to hide her pain. Most of the time, at any rate. So she slid her game face on, the same one she'd worn year after year.

"Apparently so, because he never did."

Riley stared at Trinity, trying to decide if she was joking. The pale undertones to her skin and tight set to her mouth before she'd turned away from him said she wasn't but that she would just as soon he thought she was.

He'd really stuck his foot in his mouth on this one. He'd been teasing her, wanting to make her smile, wanting to make her reveal more about herself, and she had. But he felt awful. Surely, she was over-exaggerating?

"Not even once?"

Her eyes downcast and expression somber, she shrugged. "It's not a big deal, Riley. We've been through this already. Christmas is just a commercial gimmick to make people spend money. I didn't need Santa bringing me presents. Not then or now."

The lift of her chin declared she didn't need anything and dared anyone to claim she did. Was that what she really believed? If so, shame on her parents.

"Didn't your parents believe in Christmas? In the joy of giving?" He couldn't imagine his own parents not making a big deal out of the holidays. It was the one and only time of the year his father took time away from work. His mother had barely been able to wait to get her house decorated. Pretty much the minute she had removed the remains of the turkey from the table at Thanksgiving, she'd have him and his brothers start carrying down precisely labeled totes of decorations. Despite whining, those times were some of his best memories.

Although he hadn't given it much conscious thought, he was carrying on in her footsteps right down to how he stored his Christmas goodies.

"Oh, my mother believed in the joy of giving all year long." But the way Trinity said the words conveyed a very different message from the one Riley had meant.

Poor Trinity, not having similar holiday traditions. As crazy as his family was, his Christmas memories were all good ones, except for those first few following his father's death when his mother had seemed lost and forlorn. Riley had vowed to give her back her Christmas mojo and he had. Their shopping and decorating spree the previous week was proof enough of that.

Trinity rubbed her hand across her forehead, sucked in a breath and stared into an electronics store window as if their display was the most fascinating thing she'd ever seen. For a brief moment he thought her eyes watered, but not a single tear fell so he might have been wrong.

But he doubted it.

"What about your father?"

She gave a low laugh. "I have no clue about my father's thoughts on Christmas, or anything else for that matter. He left before I was born."

That he could relate to on some levels, because although his father had lived in the same house he'd rarely been home. Except at Christmas.

He'd wanted to know more about Trinity and her comments had revealed more than any other statement that she'd ever made. Yet all it had really done was to pose more questions. Questions that he didn't think walking in a shopping mall was the right time to ask. But someday he wanted to tear down the walls she hid behind.

"Well, Trinity Warren, this is your lucky year, because this Christmas is going to be your best ever." He squeezed her hand, knowing if he'd brought joy back to his mother's holidays he could do so to Trinity's too. "I promise."

"It's really not a big deal." But the no big deal had her voice choking a little beyond what she was able to hide. Maybe her eyes really had watered.

"Christmas is just another day," she continued, protesting a little too much perhaps. "I usually volunteer to work. I really don't mind and really don't need a 'best ever' Christmas."

In years past, he'd volunteered to work as well so that others with children could be at home with their loved ones. He imagined he'd do the same this Christmas Day, too. His family all understood that he could be called away from celebrations at any time, but fortunately he'd always been at the family get-together for at least most of the day.

He loved the craziness of his family under one roof, of kids running around everywhere, shaking packages, wanting to know what Uncle Riley had bought them this year, and his mother warning that he'd better not have bought them anything that was going to cause a ruckus in her house. And, of course, he always did.

"My mom cooks a big Christmas lunch. My whole family goes. And I do mean the whole family. There's a bunch of us—aunts, uncles, my mother, two brothers and two sisters, and more nieces and nephews than I can count these days." He smiled at the thought of his family. "It's a bit of mayhem, but in a good way. Maybe you'd like to go with me?"

Her gaze cut to his and a panicky look shone in her eyes. "Why?"

Why? Good question because Trinity going with him would raise all kinds of questions and expectations in his family's minds. He'd never brought a woman home for the holidays.

"Because I'd like to take you with me." Despite whatever teasing and questions her presence triggered, he knew he'd never spoken truer words. "I want you to spend Christmas Day with me, to be there with me and my family, to see what Christmas is really like."

Because no way could she go with him and not be enchanted with the holidays.

Her eyes definitely a little misty, she sucked in a deep breath. "Like I said, I'll probably be working, so I shouldn't make any plans. Thanks, though."

That was a cop-out if he'd ever heard one. Why was she being so stubborn when he was offering to include her in his life? Something past girlfriends had begged for. He was offering to take Trinity to his most important family get-together, one he cherished and had never risked an outsider disrupting, and she was tossing it back in his face?

"But if you're not working, you'll go?" He resented having to push when she should be happy to be invited, but he wasn't going to let her be vague with her answer. She'd wiggle out of going if he let her.

"I'll be working."

He arched his brow. If having to work was all that stood in the way of her going with him, he'd find a way to get someone else to work in her stead. Even if it meant slipping someone a nice fat Christmas bonus out of his own pocket. He wanted Trinity with him and, as crazy as it was, he'd do almost anything to ensure she was. She needed to experience the magic of Christmas and what better way than with his family?

"Fine." She relented at his look.

He could tell she was only agreeing because she didn't think that whether or not she'd be working was an issue. She planned to work, would probably beg to work. A spark of annoyance flashed through him. Surely she didn't think he'd let her get away with that?

"If I'm not working, I'll go with you to Christmas dinner with your family." She gave him a stern look.

"But the next time you ask me out to dinner, there had better actually be food involved rather than shopping because, in case you couldn't tell by looking at me, I'm not one of those girls who skips meals."

He threw his head back in laughter. "Funny girl. You're perfect just as you are, princess, and should never skip meals. No worries. I will feed you. Right after we buy your decorations."

CHAPTER SEVEN

THE LAST THING Trinity wanted in her apartment was Christmas decorations. She certainly didn't want to waste her hard-earned money on glittery, glowing fake trees and wreaths and garlands. Just having to walk through the aisles of ornaments and bows made her skin crawl.

She fought the urge to throw her hands into the air and run out of the store. This was pure torture.

Telling Riley the truth about her childhood had been torture. Why had she done so?

She'd never told anyone. Not even Chase. She'd not wanted to see the look of pity in his eyes, hadn't wanted anyone's pity. She was doing just fine, had a good life overall. She didn't need some man coming along and stirring up all kinds of childhood hang-ups to go along with the new ones Chase had hand-delivered two years ago.

She hadn't liked the sympathy in Riley's eyes. She didn't need his sympathy. She hadn't needed him to invite her to spend Christmas with his family out of pity.

"What about this?" Riley asked, pointing out a box of red glass balls. He'd already pointed out more than two dozen decorations, all of which she'd turned down.

She could tell he was losing patience with her. Good. Hopefully, he'd soon take the hint that she really didn't want to be doing this. Maybe she could fake a stomach growl to speed things along. She willed her stomach to let loose with a loud rumble, but didn't even manage a tiny one.

Great, the one time she wanted loud body noises around a hot guy and she couldn't even force one out. It figured.

Barely glancing at what he held, she shook her head. "No, thank you. Not interested. Besides, I really don't need any decorations. Just dinner."

"I've never met anyone who needs decorations more than you." His frustration was obvious and rubbed her wrong.

"I think I'm offended by that comment." She hadn't asked him to take her shopping, had only agreed to dinner, not a stroll down holiday horror lane.

He raked his fingers through his hair, glanced around the aisle then faced her. "I didn't mean it in a bad way."

"Because there's a good way to say someone needs plastic garland, fake glass balls and gaudy red velvet bows?"

"Precisely." Obviously having whipped his frustration into control, he grinned and held up a box of horrid cheap plastic candy canes for her inspection. "What about these? Awesome, right?"

Hoping he'd take the hint, Trinity didn't hide her boredom, just yawned. "If I pretended that my blood sugar was bottoming out, could we go and eat? Please?"

His gaze narrowed suspiciously. "Is your sugar dropping?"

She grimaced then shook her head. "No, but I could fake it."

He touched her chin, tilted her face towards him. "As long as I have breath in my body, I don't ever want you faking anything. I don't want you to even have need of faking anything." His lips twitched. "And I do mean *anything*."

His fingers burned her skin, singeing her flesh with the feel of him. She stepped back before she did something stupid. Like say she wanted to buy mistletoe. Bunches and bunches of mistletoe. Barrels of it.

"Okay, deal," she agreed, hoping he didn't see how his touch had made her pulse race and her breath catch. "Feed me, so I don't have to fake interest in shopping."

He shook his head in obvious displeasure. "If you really want to go, we'll go, but I'm disappointed that we didn't find a single thing you wanted."

She wanted him to touch her again, and in more places than just her chin. Did that count? It should because it was a really big want.

Then she saw it.

At the end of the aisle on a platform. A ten-and-a-half-foot blue spruce fake tree decorated with snowflakes and angels and silver ribbon that twined back and forth between the branches. A toy train set was wound around the base and a few packages assured hidden delights but were probably nothing more than empty promises. No matter. It was what was at the very top of the tree that had caught her eye.

A big shiny star that looked absolutely magical and just like the one she'd seen at her elementary school when she'd been five.

That Christmas she remembered well.

That Christmas she'd gotten caught up in the excitement of her classmates, in the whole spirit of Christmas. Prior to then she hadn't even been sure if she'd known what Christmas or Santa had even been about. She'd written a rudimentary letter to Santa and even crawled up in his lap when he'd come to her classroom. Packed back in her things she had a Polaroid photo of that moment that she'd kept hidden away over the years for some crazy reason. Probably a reminder of what lay ahead when one got one's hopes up and believed in things that weren't real.

With excitement she'd told Santa of what she'd wanted more than anything and he'd told her to be a good girl and come Christmas morning she'd find her surprise under the tree.

She'd been as good as gold. Better than any five-year-old had ever been, surely. She'd gone to bed on Christmas Eve full of hope and had barely been able to sleep because she'd been sure she'd wake up to a pile of goodies but mainly to the pair of new sneakers she'd desperately wanted. Her others had been hand-me-downs and had grown too small. A new pair of stylish pink hightops for school was going to be a breeze with how good she'd been.

Only there had been no surprise. Or even a tree. Her mother had claimed the entire holiday was nothing more than a scam and she wasn't spending hard-earned money on something as ridiculous as putting a tree inside their tiny apartment.

When her mother had found her crying, she'd complained that Christmas was a rich man's holiday invented to make poor parents like her look bad and that

Trinity should feel ashamed for making her feel bad. Then she'd gone off and drunk until she'd passed out.

The same as she did the other three hundred and sixty-four days of the year. Only without Trinity having set herself up with false hopes that the day might bring something different.

She had stopped believing. Right then and there at five years old she'd quit believing in Christmas and Santa. Sure, she'd still gone through the motions at school and, after she'd graduated from college, at work. But she'd never believed the holiday to be anything more than commercialized hype meant to build false hopes and to disappoint. How absolutely fitting had it been that Chase had broken her heart at a Christmas party?

"Stars are magic," Riley said from beside her, pulling her back from the past to the present, obviously clueless about where her thoughts had gone. How could he know? Although she'd revealed more to him than to any other person ever, she'd rather die than have anyone know the true depth of her shame.

"Just like the star that led the wise men and the ones that guide sailors through the sea," he continued, his voice low, mesmerizing. "They lead us where we need to go if only we'll follow. Anywhere in particular you'd like to go, princess?"

Trying to keep her cynicism to a minimum and any dream of going somewhere magical well tamped down, Trinity looked at him. "It's just a cheap piece of glass and tiny light bulbs."

"Use your imagination."

"I don't have one."

"Sure you do." He laced their fingers. "Close your

eyes and picture that star, Trinity. Picture it leading you where you want to go."

"That's the most ridiculous thing I've ever heard." So why were her eyelids so darned heavy all of a sudden?

"Do it," he ordered in his Dr. Williams voice.

"You're crazy."

"About you."

That was twice he'd implied he had feelings for her. Trinity glared. "You're not going to run off when I close my eyes, are you?"

"You couldn't run me off. I'm right where I want to be."

"At the mall, shopping?" She gave him a doubtful once-over. "You sure you're straight?"

"With you," he clarified, shaking his head at her. "And if you'd like me to give a demonstration of my straightness, I'll gladly do so."

She gulped back the image of Riley proving to her that he preferred the opposite sex. Even when she was tired and irritated at him, the man could send her libido through the roof. Wow.

"Fine." She closed her eyes and did as he said. Or tried to. The image of his straightness refused to budge from her mind.

"Do you see where you want to go?"

"Oh, yeah, I see where I want to go and you offered to take me there, but for some reason I'm still quite hungry and there's no food in sight."

He laughed then surprised her by leaning forward to drop a kiss on her lips. Just a quick peck, but a kiss all the same. Had he read her thoughts?

"Come on, Scrooge," he relented, not sounding angry

but definitely not his usual happy-go-lucky self. "I'll feed you."

Guilt hit her. He was trying to be nice. It wasn't his fault she was being so otherwise.

"Hey." She feigned surprise, wanting his sparkle back. "I take back everything. That star thing worked!"

After staring at her a brief second, he grinned. "I never thought it wouldn't. Glad to know you were imagining me kissing you."

Wondering if he'd just played her with his probably feigned disappointment, she shook her head. "Keep telling yourself that, lover boy, but it's the promise that you're finally going to feed me that I referred to."

His grin way too endearing, he lifted her hand to his lips and kissed her fingertips. "You keep telling yourself that you weren't imagining my arms as where you want to be but I'm going to prove otherwise to you."

Unfortunately, Trinity couldn't argue with him because she feared he was right.

Trinity managed to make it through the next week without Riley dragging her shopping again. Thank goodness.

However, that didn't keep him from dragging her to the local soup kitchen where everyone greeted him by name. They helped serve over a hundred meals and whether it was in the name of the Christmas spirit or whatever, Trinity felt good about doing so and promised herself that she'd sign on to help on a regular basis. Not only that, she'd look for other charitable places where she could volunteer.

Of course, with Christmas being only a week away she couldn't escape the festivities. Who would have guessed that people who lived at the beach would be so into the ho, ho, ho swing of things?

At work, everyone was wearing Christmas print scrub tops and a few of the docs had Christmas ties, Riley included.

Having just returned to the nurses' station and spotting him, she rolled her eyes at the tie currently around his neck. "Seriously? You have a reindeer with a light-up nose on your tie? That's what you wore while you saw patients at your office all day?"

Waggling his brows, he grinned. "Yep, I'm quite disappointed that no one asked me to guide their sleigh tonight." He shifted to where he could look behind her at her bottom. "How about you, princess? You want me to light up your world and guide your sleigh tonight?"

That he could light up her world she had no doubt. In the past week she'd smiled and laughed more than she had…well, maybe ever. The man was a nut. And brilliant. And kind. And generous. And…

She was getting way too dependent on him. It was barely a week since he'd kissed her under the mistletoe at the hospital Christmas party and every free waking hour had been spent with him. When she wasn't with him, she was thinking of him, dreaming of him.

"Sorry, I'm fresh out of sleighs and there's not a bit of fog in sight."

If spending a week with him could have her feeling so clingy, she really needed to get a hold of herself before she did something silly. Like fall in love with him. That would be nothing short of a tragedy.

And something she needed to guard against.

"This Santa is flexible. How about we grab a bite to eat then catch that new Christmas movie?"

"Not tonight."

His smile morphed into a frown. "You have other plans?"

Trying to keep a straight face because he read her way too easily, she nodded.

"Am I invited?"

Was he invited? What kind of response was that to a woman saying she had other plans? Really, the man was too much.

"Do you want to be invited?"

"If you're going to be there? Yes, I want an invitation. A VIP pass even."

Although she was pretty sure she'd just scolded herself for being so dependent on him, she found she couldn't say no, didn't really want to because to say no would mean depriving herself of the twinkle in his eye, the mischief in his grin, the wit in his words.

"Fine. You can go with me."

He grinned and she wondered if that meant he'd known he'd get his way all along. "Where are we going, princess?"

She had no clue because she'd just made up that she had other plans in a panicky moment. She should have known better.

"It's a surprise." To her too since she probably would have just gone to her place for grilled cheese sandwiches and a rerun of some TV series. She still might.

"Aw, are you taking me caroling?" he teased.

She squinted at him in a forced glare. "That would be a surprise, now, wouldn't it? But, no, I'm not a caroler. That would contradict that whole don't-like-Christmas thing I have going."

"But you do sing," he pointed out, leaning against the counter.

"In my shower doesn't count."

"I'd like to be the judge of that for myself. You could give me a private viewing tonight. Now, that would be a surprise."

She rolled her eyes again and ignored him and the images of them in the shower flashing through her mind.

"You also sing karaoke," he reminded her.

"Only under the influence of alcohol, which I'd never knowingly do." She made a pretense of being busy.

"It's okay to let loose every once in a while and just enjoy yourself."

"I don't need alcohol to enjoy myself." She winced at how harsh her voice had been. She hadn't meant to bite his head off, yet she definitely had. Unable to just stand still, she headed to a patient room. Anything to escape him.

Unfortunately he followed her, catching her just outside the door. "I didn't say you did. I was just saying it was okay for you to relax and enjoy life. Talk to me."

She didn't want to talk. They were at work. Only Karen was near, but anyone could see them, could hear them if they wanted to eavesdrop. Even if they'd been in private she wouldn't have wanted to have this discussion, but she sure didn't here. She closed her eyes, took a deep breath. "Sorry."

"Okay." He sounded confused. "You want to explain why you jumped down my throat on that one?"

She shook her head. No, she didn't want to go there. Not at any point in the next century or so.

He appeared to weigh his options. "Okay, I'll let it slide."

They both heard his unspoken "for now".

Trinity pulled the covers off Jewel Hendrix's legs to asses them for edema.

"They're only swollen a little compared to what they were when I checked into this joint," the seventy-two-year-old woman with end-stage congestive heart failure said a bit breathily. "I can actually move my toes again."

She wiggled them back and forth.

On arrival in the emergency department, she'd been retaining so much fluid that her skin had been too tight for her to flex her toes. She'd had weeping from her skin on her shins and calves and had had crackles in her lungs. Had she not been brought to the hospital, she would have drowned in her own body fluids.

"There's still enough fluid that I can't make out your pedal pulses, though." Hopefully after another round of diuretics the swelling would go down even more.

The woman glanced at her feet. "Honey, this is a good ankle day in my book." She paused to catch her breath. "I'm pretty sure if y'all would let me up out of this bed, I could even get these boogers into a pair of shoes. Most days I feel like one of Cinderella's ugly stepsisters trying to shove my monstrosity into a glass slipper."

Trinity smiled at her patient. She really liked Jewel. The older woman had spunk.

"What about you? Some lucky fellow slip a glass slipper onto your foot and make you feel just like a princess?"

Why was it that the elderly felt they had a right to

ask questions about one's private life? Why was it that Trinity felt obligated to answer the feisty older woman?

Hoping her face was unreadable, she raised her foot up from the floor to display her solid white nursing shoes. "No glass slipper for me."

"A pity."

"Not really." Trinity slipped the skin protectors back around Jewel's feet to prevent skin breakdown and positioned her feet on the pillows to keep them elevated. "I don't need a man to slip my foot into a glass slipper. I'm way too practical for that. Besides, with my luck a glass slipper would only shatter and cut my foot up anyway."

Trinity smiled at the woman, but Jewel's face was pinched into a frown.

"Maybe the wrong quality of men have been attempting to slip glass slippers onto your feet. You need to upgrade."

Ha. No man had been attempting to slip a glass slipper onto her foot, but she wouldn't admit that to Jewel. Besides, she had no right to complain. Riley treated her as if she really were the princess he often called her. She had to admit that most of the time she liked the attention he showered on her. Who needed glass slippers and a Prince Charming when you had a handsome cardiologist trying to woo you into Christmas cheer?

Trinity tucked the bed sheet and white blanket around her patient's elevated legs. "I'll keep that in mind the next time a Prince Charming asks to see my feet."

The woman chuckled. "I like you."

Trinity shot the woman another smile. "You can sweet-talk me all you want, but I'm still going to give you your medication."

"I never thought you wouldn't." The woman practically cackled. "When's that handsome doctor of mine going to be here?"

"Dr. Williams should be by any time. He was here earlier, but got called to the cardiac lab for a procedure." She'd only caught a glimpse of him, but a glimpse had been all it had taken to get her heart racing. Especially with how he'd winked at her when their eyes had met. Karen had teased her on that one, but Trinity hadn't really cared. Most of the time he made her feel good. And confused.

Although everyone at the hospital had accepted that they were a couple, Trinity just wasn't sure exactly what they were. Other than a few brief kisses and holding her hand, he barely touched her. What was his game? "I expect he'll be finishing up some time soon."

Did she mean with the patient or with her?

Jewel sighed. "I'd like to be home for Christmas. Maybe he'll let me leave this evening."

"Maybe," Trinity said, adjusting the setting on Jewel's intravenous pump. The woman wasn't receiving any fluids currently as her problem was fluid overload. However, her diuretics were being given intravenously and Trinity had just hung a new bag of the medication. "But I doubt it. You were a really sick lady when you got here yesterday morning. We really need to get more fluid off before you can go home."

Jewel eyed the bag of medication. "But I'm a lot better than I was and that stuff there is going to help even more."

"True, but you're also heavily medicated and Dr. Williams will want to keep a close check on your electrolytes for at least another day, probably longer. Your medication can deplete your potassium and if that happens, a whole new set of problems could occur."

"We can't have that."

"Which is why I don't think he'll discharge you any time soon. Or at least not until after you've had your echocardiogram."

Jewel sighed. "That's the ultrasound thing with the sticky stuff on my chest?"

"Yes, ma'am. No pain involved." Trinity entered the data from her assessment of Jewel into the in-room computer and that she'd begun administration of the medication ordered.

"How's my most beautiful patient doing this evening?"

The old woman's brow rose. "I'm your only patient? A brilliant doctor like you? That's surprising and a bit worrisome."

Riley laughed and winked at the older woman. "You're a quick one, Jewel."

"That I am." The woman beamed.

Trinity smothered a smile and clicked to save and sign the data she'd entered.

"You going to let me go home today?"

Riley shook his head. "Now, why would I do that when your nurse just told you the reasons why you should stay?"

Jewel shrugged her heavy shoulders. "I was just checking."

"Anyone ever tell you what a testy thing you are?" Riley teased the older woman, pulling his stethoscope from his pocket and cleaning the diaphragm with an alcohol swab.

"Only my husband." The woman's face took on a happy glow. "God bless him."

Riley laughed and placed his stethoscope on Jewel's chest.

The breathy woman watched his every move. Glancing up, she noticed that Trinity also watched his every move.

Jewel motioned towards Riley then waggled her drawn-on eyebrows.

Noticing the movement, Riley glanced up, caught just enough that he glanced back and forth between them. "Okay, you two, what are you cooking up?"

Trinity shook her head. No way was she going there. Jewel would have to do her matchmaking elsewhere because as sweet as Riley was to her and as fine as he seemed to be with everyone thinking they were a couple, she didn't fool herself that he was a Prince Charming who was going to slip a pair of glass slippers onto her feet.

Or even a pair of pink hightop sneakers.

She'd do well to remember that.

CHAPTER EIGHT

LETTING HIS GAZE soak up the sight of Trinity in her dark navy scrubs, Riley stepped up beside where she worked at the nurses' station. "Dr. Stanley is having a small impromptu get-together tomorrow night, just dinner and drinks, to celebrate the holidays."

Trinity looked briefly at Riley then went back to studying the computer monitor.

"Would you like to go?"

"No, thank you," she immediately replied, without another glance his way.

Tempted to scream with frustration, Riley sighed. "Do you know any words other than those?"

"Yes."

"Great." He rubbed his hands together in glee. "You really do. We should get you in the habit of using them more often. Let's practice. Trinity, will you go to a Christmas dinner party with me tomorrow night?"

She arched a brow at him. "You want me to be a yes-girl?"

Did he?

"I want you to be an open-minded girl who answers questions based on more than her preconceived notion that she doesn't like Christmas and wants no part of any celebration of it."

"You're missing the point completely."

He leaned against the desktop and stared down at her. "Which is?"

"That I really don't like Christmas so why would I purposely choose to celebrate it?"

Had a more stubborn woman ever walked the face of the earth?

"Okay, fine." He sighed. "We won't go to my boss's Christmas party that he invited me to and mentioned bringing you with me." Was it wrong that he was laying on the guilt as thick as could be? "What would you prefer to do tomorrow night?"

"Just because I don't want to go, it doesn't mean you can't go, Riley. You go ahead and have enough fun for both of us."

Ouch. "You want me to go to a party without you?"

"If it's a Christmas party? Yes." She put a lot of emphasis on the word. "I do."

What woman wanted her man to go to a party without her? Or maybe she didn't think of him as her man? He'd purposely fought to keep the physical side of their relationship at bay because she was so obstinate she'd be likely to use them having sex against him. If he went to a party without her, she'd likely do the same.

He shook his head. "What if I'd rather be with you?"

"Then maybe we could go for a walk on the beach," she surprised him by suggesting. He'd expected her to insist on him going, on her insisting she had other plans. She rarely said yes without him having to sweet-talk her. He didn't like it and kept waiting for her to quit playing such games. Maybe she finally had.

"To be so close to the Gulf," she continued. "I've barely been there."

"My place okay?"

Without looking at him, she nodded. "Yes." She put great emphasis on the word. "That would be fine."

Wow. Maybe they really had reached a turning point. Good, because keeping his hands to himself was growing more and more difficult. He wanted her.

"You want me to grill some salmon fillets? We could walk on the beach afterwards then sit on my deck and enjoy a glass of wine?"

Make love under the stars, in his bed, his shower especially, because ever since he'd mentioned her giving him a private viewing he hadn't been able to get the image from his mind. Or maybe they'd just sit on his deck and talk. Just so long as she let her guard down long enough for them to enjoy the night, he'd be a happy camper, sex or not.

"I don't drink," she said, but at least she hadn't said no.

"Cool. We'll sip juice on my deck." Other than the occasional glass of wine, he generally didn't drink either, so wine or juice wasn't a big deal to him. Plus, he wanted a completely clear mind if and when they touched. "I'll pick up some fillets on my way home and let them marinate tonight. You want a spinach salad? Maybe some sautéed asparagus in butter sauce?"

Trinity blinked up at him. "Are you for real? I just made you grilled cheese for your surprise dinner the other night."

"Pinch me and see." He waggled his brows, feeling lighter than he had in days. He hadn't realized just how frustrated he'd grown. "I'll pick the spot."

Her lips twitched with a smile she couldn't hold back and his entire insides warmed. Finally they were making real progress.

"I should do just that. Only I'd have to pick the spot."

"I'm game. Anywhere in particular you'd prefer to start? I could offer a few suggestions. Maybe give you a few pointers on my preferences?"

She looked up as if she was going to roll her eyes, but her smile was now full blown. "You really are crazy, you know?"

He thought about reminding her of exactly what he was crazy about, but just grinned, happier than he should be that she'd agreed without him having to talk her into doing so.

"I don't want to keep you from your boss's party, Riley," she relented, but he could tell she wasn't enthused at the prospect. "Not if it's something you want to go to."

"Not a problem." His insides felt light. "I like our plans better anyway."

Her smile made her eyes sparkle with the brilliance of twinkling green Christmas lights. "You're sure?"

"Positive."

"I feel guilty that you're going to cook for me. Is there something I can do?"

He nodded.

She arched a brow.

"Come with hunger in your belly and a smile in your heart."

She hesitated a moment then met his gaze head on, making his heart stutter a time or two.

"That's all you want me to bring?"

A dozen different responses ran through his mind.

An open mind. A spirit full of Christmas. Open arms to embrace him. A willing heart. He settled for something simple.

"For now."

Okay, the man was really too good to be true. Because Riley had not only cooked for her, he'd lit candles.

Candles.

At no point in her life had a man given her a candlelit dinner. Actually, never had a man cooked for her either.

Riley had done both and was merrily singing while he did so.

What was this? A romantic seduction? Didn't he know he could have had her at any point over the past week?

She'd like to think not, but truly, had Riley pushed, she'd have invited him into her bed any of the nights that he'd seen her into her apartment then left with little more than a kiss.

Not only were there candles on the dining table, but they were scattered around the room as well. Plus, his tree sparkled with the thousands of lights they'd strung around the branches. Garlands hung over the doorways. Gorgeous burgundy and gold ribbon bows accented the centers and twined outwards. A nativity scene was spread out over a coffee table. His sofa cushions had been replaced with ones with a smiling Santa on them.

He even wore a "Kiss Santa" apron tied around his waist.

Leaning against the deck railing, she shook her head. "I do have to wonder how old you are sometimes."

A breeze ruffling his hair, he glanced up from where

he stood at the grill. "A person is only as old as they feel so I'm about…thirteen."

Smiling, she glanced through the glass windows making up the back of his house and door leading into his open living and dining area again. Her eyes caught on the toy train set on the floor beneath the Christmas tree. Her lips twitched. "Gee, I was thinking more along the lines of six. Maybe seven."

"Nah." He shook his head, moved away from the grill long enough to plop a kiss on her lips. "Six- and seven-year-old boys couldn't care less about girls and I definitely am into girls. Specifically, I'm into you."

Trinity's belly did a few somersaults. "Point taken, and I'm glad."

Because as scared as she was of getting hurt, she was honest enough to admit that she wouldn't have wanted to miss out on being the center of his attention. For however long it lasted, Riley was into her and that was a glorious thing. Her defenses might warn she should run while she still could but another part of her admitted that it was already too late.

Perhaps it had been too late from the moment at the Christmas party when she'd looked into those devilish blue eyes and he'd assured her he was a man who aimed to please. No one had ever made her feel the way he did. Worthwhile. Wanted.

"You look beautiful, by the way."

Point in case. Trinity's cheeks burned. He was always complimenting her, making her look in the mirror and wonder what he saw that she didn't. That no one other than him had ever seen. Because despite their nine-month relationship, Chase had never called her beautiful. Neither had he ever made her feel as if she was.

Why had she fancied herself in love with him?

Because she hadn't known any better? Hadn't known what a good man was really like and she'd been settling for what had been right in front of her rather than looking for something more? Something real?

Something like Riley.

No, she wasn't in love with him, although it would be so easy to fall in love with him. The man was a phenom. She didn't know how any woman could spend any amount of time with him and not fancy herself in love with him. He was that kind, that considerate, that witty, that sexy, that everything.

"I hope you're hungry, princess." He lifted a tin-foil-wrapped salmon fillet off the grill.

"Starved."

Starved for food, but maybe for much more than she'd bargained for. Nothing in her life had prepared her for Riley. She was supposed to be taking charge of her life, learning to deal with her Christmas aversion. She was not supposed to be becoming so entangled with a man she'd have a difficult time ever letting go of, and yet she didn't regret being here with him. She cherished every precious second of his company, of his attention.

She'd given up pretending otherwise.

"Starved?" He grinned. "That's my girl."

His girl. He didn't care who knew, who saw them together, or who saw him brushing his knuckles across her cheek or just giving her hand a quick squeeze. If anything, he acted possessive, as if he wanted everyone who saw them to know they were together. As if he was proud she was with him.

It had been months before Chase had wanted anyone

at the hospital to be aware that they were dating and then he'd acted more embarrassed than proud.

"Why are you so nice to me?" she mused out loud.

"Huh?" Obviously, he had no clue what she meant. Which made her happy inside. He wasn't putting on airs or trying to impress her, just being himself.

"I'm just curious why you're so nice to me."

"I already told you the answer to that, princess. More than once."

"What's that?"

"I like you." He smiled and she deep-down knew he believed what he said. He liked her. "A lot."

"This is good," Trinity praised twenty minutes later, the lemony grilled salmon practically melting in her mouth. "Much better than my grilled cheese the other night. I think you missed your calling."

"I happened to like your grilled cheese the other night, although perhaps not the butt-kicking at chess that followed." He grinned. "You really think I should give up cardiology and cook for a living?"

She snorted. "When you word it that way, probably not, but you are a very talented man and I am well aware that I barely won that chess game."

"Glad you noticed and appreciate my efforts."

"Oh, I notice." Every detail about him. She took another bite. "You have a beautiful place, Riley."

"I like it. When I was looking to buy, I knew I'd make an offer on this one the moment I stepped inside, even though it's a little further from the hospital than I'd intended. It felt like I was coming home."

She glanced out the windows towards the sea. "Great view."

"It's better tonight than usual."

But when she turned to him, he wasn't looking at the gulf. He was looking at her.

Heat infused her entire body. "You don't have to say things like that, you know."

"I know. I want to."

"Why?"

"Why?" He sounded confused. "Why wouldn't I?"

"I don't know. You're just always complimenting me and I don't want you to feel it's necessary."

"But complimenting you is necessary. Very necessary."

She wanted to ask why again, but didn't want to sound like a broken record. So she smiled. With Riley, when in doubt about what to do, smiling seemed to work best. "This house suits you. Functional, beautiful—"

"Christmasy?" he interjected, grinning.

"Christmasy," she agreed, unable to deny his claim. He was everything Christmas should be. Everything that Christmas had never been. Not for her. But everything he did made a long-suppressed part of her memory pull forward.

Enough so that she experienced a twinge of panic, but the evening was too nice to let doubt ruin it.

They finished eating and together cleared away the dishes, stacking them in the sink. Trinity tried to load them into the dishwasher, but he shook his head.

"Not now. Let's go for that walk on the beach. I've been looking forward to it since you first mentioned doing so earlier."

"Okay." She set her plate down on the marble countertop and picked up the jacket he'd set out earlier for their walk as the wind was brisk. "You talked me into it."

Putting on his own lightweight jacket, he laughed. "That's my girl."

As much as she kept telling herself that she wasn't in love with this man, that she wouldn't fall in love with him, she couldn't argue with his statement.

She was his girl.

Indisputably.

Hand in hand, Riley and Trinity walked along the beach. Ignoring how much he wanted Trinity was getting more and more difficult. He didn't want to rush her, didn't want to make wild assumptions, but from the moment she'd arrived all he'd wanted to do was pull her into his arms.

Her mind stimulated him.

Her quick wit stimulated him.

Her curvy little body stimulated him.

It was the latter that was currently tearing his resolve into bits. He felt as if he was in a constant state of stimulation.

He couldn't recall ever feeling this way. Not even when he'd been a randy teenager.

Letting go of his hand, she'd ran ahead of him, laughing as the waves lapped at her bare feet. She turned to beckon him to join her. Wind whipped at her hair.

Temptation whipped at his soul.

What he wanted was to push her down in the surf, rip her clothes off and make love to her right then and there, with the waves crashing around their naked bodies.

He swallowed, watched her dance around in the white foam.

"Riley, hurry," she called. The water crashed around

her ankles and she laughed, looking and sounding freer than he recalled ever seeing her.

Like a child set loose to play.

Like the most tantalizing woman to ever tempt man.

"I ate too much to hurry," he called, enjoying watching her play too much to rush.

"Right." She laughed then plopped down just beyond the water's reach, her toes stretched out towards the sea, tempting the water to move closer and closer.

"You know you're going to get wet, right? Then you'll be cold."

She shrugged. "At the moment I don't care. This is wonderful."

He glanced out to sea then back at the smiling woman leaning back as if offering herself to the moon shining above them.

If so, he was jealous of the moon.

Because he wanted her to offer herself to him that way.

Every way.

He wanted her to come to him, for her to initiate their lovemaking, for her to have no regrets and for him to have no worries that he'd talked her into something she hadn't really wanted.

He'd thought himself a patient man, but looking at her body stretched out under the bright moonlight, the surf nipping at her toes, he had none.

"Besides, if I get cold, you'll warm me up, right?"

He hadn't realized she was watching him. He gulped back the knot her words caused to form in his throat and willed the one forming in his pants to go away.

"Riley?"

"Hmm?"

"Are you afraid to join me?"

Terrified. Because getting close to her might mean losing control and seducing her right out of her panties. What would his neighbors think? Although, honestly, he wasn't sure how many were even home at this time of year. A lot of the houses along this stretch were owned by wealthy snowbirds looking for an escape.

"Scared you'll get wet?" she teased, digging her fingers into the sand beside her.

"Nope." To prove his point, he sat down next to her on the sand. "But I should warn you that I'm very turned on and perhaps you should get up and run while you can because what I really want to do would get me arrested."

Arrested? Trinity blinked, wondering if she'd misheard him over the waves. "Do what?"

"You heard me. Just what I said. You're beautiful and totally do it for me. I look at you and I want you. I have wanted you from the first moment I set eyes on you propped up against that hotel ballroom wall. Tonight, here on the beach, I want you so badly I may explode from it. I feel weak. If I did with you what I want to do with you, I'd be arrested."

He wanted her. Really wanted her. A heady sensation, but the other thing he'd said played in her mind.

"I make you weak?" She didn't want to make him or any man weak. Especially not when he made her feel strong, stronger than she recalled ever feeling.

He picked up her hand, pressed it to where his heart beat. "Does that feel as if you make me weak?"

His heart pounded beneath her fingertips. She shook her head.

"My resolve is what's weak. You make me feel alive,"

he clarified. "As if everything I do is bigger, brighter, more than anything I've ever done."

That she understood because it's how he made her feel. It amazed her that he could possibly feel the same. How could he when that seemed so unlikely? "I do?"

He nodded.

"I want you, Trinity, but I didn't mean to tell you like this."

She glanced around at the beach. Although there were other houses along the stretch of beach, they were essentially alone. The moon shone bright above them. The sea crashed foamy white waves that played a perfect love song. He'd just cooked her a delicious dinner and he'd lit candles. She couldn't imagine anything more romantic, more seductive.

"What's wrong with this? With this very moment?"

"Earlier I thought..." he shook his head. "It's too soon."

He was probably right. Less than two weeks was too soon. Still, they'd been together every night and if you put that on regular dating terms of weekend dates, they'd been seeing each other for months. Or was she just reaching?

Probably.

Because her hand had moved from his chest to his face. The grit of sand still lingered on her fingers but his skin was smooth, perfect.

"It's not too soon," she whispered, knowing it was true, especially when she heard his intake of breath above the crash of the waves. "But I should warn you that if we did, you'd be disappointed."

"Never."

She laughed ironically at his faith. If only. "I wish that was true, but I'm not very good at…well, you know."

"Sex?"

Staring at where her hand caressed his jaw, she nodded. "I can pretty much guarantee that you won't want me any more once we do."

This time it was he who laughed. "You'd be wrong."

"Again, I wish that was true."

"Why?"

Could she write him a thesis on all the reasons why? Things like that he made her feel good about herself? That he made her believe in things that she shouldn't believe in? That he'd taken away the loneliness that had iced her insides for so long that she'd believed the cold-ness was a permanent part of who she was?

"Because I like you," she said instead, using his usual response to sum up all the emotions bubbling inside her. "A lot."

In the moonlight, she saw his mouth curve upwards.

"Good to know," he admitted, taking her hand. "I was beginning to wonder if this relationship was one-sided."

"Is that what we're doing? Having a relationship?" Not that it didn't feel like a relationship. It did. Plus he carried on at the hospital as if they were. But, still, there was no one around but the two of them and she wanted a straight answer from him.

"If you have to ask me that, I'm doing something very wrong," he teased, scratching his head as if trying to figure out what that something might be.

"I…I just wasn't sure." Which sounded quite lame at the moment, with how his eyes searched hers. Even in the moonlight she could see desire flickering in the blue depths.

"After the past two weeks you aren't sure that I'm totally fascinated by you and want to spend every second of my time with you?"

Wow. That's all that her brain could register. Just wow. Wow. Wow. Riley's words seemed so foreign, so far-fetched, yet she heard his sincerity, saw the truth in the way he looked at her. He looked at her as she'd never been looked at, as if she was the most precious being on earth.

"I'm scared," she heard herself say, knowing her words were as true as his, shocked, though, that she was admitting her fear to him. Wasn't that exposing just how vulnerable she really was?

"Don't be scared of me, Trinity. I'd never intentionally hurt you."

Intentionally. Which meant she likely would be hurt at some point down the line. Her life had taught her to expect no less. But she wasn't going to hold back, wasn't going to let the past or fear dictate who she was. Not when it came to Riley. Was she?

At this moment she was a woman sitting on a romantic beach, touching a fantasy man who was quickly encompassing her whole world.

He wanted to be here, with her. He thought she was beautiful, he wanted her, and he didn't mind telling her, showing her.

When he was with her she didn't get the impression that he wanted to be anywhere except right with her. When he looked at her she didn't get the impression that he wished she were someone else.

He wanted *her*.

He lifted her hand to his lips, kissed her fingertips.

"I have sand on my fingers." And tears in her eyes. Why was she crying?

"Doesn't matter." He kissed the top of her hand, gently turned her arm to press his lips to her wrist, then he kissed her there. Gentle kisses where his lips lightly brushed across the tender skin, heating her blood. Brilliant kisses that made her mind go in thousands of directions, all of which involved him.

She shivered and scooted closer to him, grazed her knuckles across his clean-shaven jaw. "Smooth."

He chuckled. "The better to kiss you without worrying about scratching you."

"I'm not a dainty flower that easily wilts."

"You want scratched?"

"I want kissed."

"I'm a man who aims to please."

When his lips covered hers, he didn't kiss her with the gentle pressure he'd kissed her goodnight with each night. No, he kissed her with the mouth of a man who was hungry. Hungry and wanting to devour her.

As if he wanted her so much he couldn't not kiss her that way.

The sensation was heady.

Trinity's head spun she felt so light, so good, so unreal.

Riley was unreal.

Because no way was such a beautiful man kissing her as if he couldn't get enough, as if he wanted, no, needed, everything she could give him.

She wanted to give him everything.

But if she did, would it be the beginning of the end, the way it had been with Chase?

Would Riley find her so lacking between the sheets that he wouldn't want her any more and would wonder why he'd ever thought he had thought her something special?

Or did sex even matter that much to him?

His mouth moved lower, to her neck, trailing hot kisses, making love to her skin.

Um, yeah, this was a man who cared about sex. No doubt about it.

Which meant she was in big trouble.

CHAPTER NINE

RILEY FELT THE difference in Trinity's response and pulled back. "You okay? Am I coming on too strong? I didn't mean to move too fast."

He'd known better than to rush things, but he'd thought… No matter what he'd thought. The reality was they'd only known each other for two weeks and he had moved too fast. She was scooting away from him, standing, brushing the sand off her clothes, and was a million miles away from him.

"You're fine."

Fine? Not the adjective he wanted to be called when he was on fire for her and had just been kissing her with a great amount of gusto.

Mindless kisses that had been all about feeling and emotion and had had little to do with thought or intentions.

"The wind just felt a little chilly. That's all. I want to finish our walk now."

Just what every man wanted to hear when he was on the verge of making love to a woman he was crazy about. When he'd been overcome with passion and she'd…she'd decided she wanted to finish their walk. Oh, yeah, he'd pushed too soon. Only had he really?

She'd wanted him, too. Had he done something wrong? Or was she playing games with him?

"Okay, we'll walk." He stood, brushed his clothes off, and took her hand.

He wasn't sure she wanted him holding her hand either, but he wasn't going to let her shut him out after the kiss they'd just shared.

She'd told him she was scared. Was that why she'd pulled away?

She'd also told him that she wasn't very good at sex.

Based on how she kissed him, he'd say she couldn't be more wrong.

But maybe she really believed otherwise. He was reaching, but there had to be some reason why she was now lost in thought instead of in his arms, and he sure didn't want to believe it was that she was a tease. The vulnerability he sensed within her assured him that wasn't the case.

"You're a very good kisser."

Her head jerked toward him.

"An amazing kisser," he added, seeing the doubt in her eyes. Hell, someone had really done a number on her.

"You're the one who's a great kisser." She shrugged as if it was no big deal, but he could see that his praise pleased her. "I just follow your lead."

"Thanks for saying so, but you don't give yourself enough credit. You drive me wild, Trinity."

She gave him a weak smile and squeezed his hand. "Thank you."

"You're welcome." As much as his body urged him to pick up where they'd left off, to take her in his arms and kiss her until she was breathless and begging for

the release he craved, he just clasped her hand in his
and walked.

Patience might not be his virtue, but some things
were worth the wait. He had no doubt that when he and
Trinity made love, and they *would* make love, the wait
would be worth having the patience of Job.

How could her schedule have been changed? No one
ever wanted to work on Christmas, so surely she
wouldn't have been randomly taken off the schedule?

She stared at the holiday work schedule. Her name
was not on the twenty-fifth anywhere. Christmas Eve,
yes, but not the big awful day itself.

She had been on that list. How had her name been
taken off?

"What are you looking at?" Karen asked, stepping
up behind Trinity and looking over her shoulder to see
what had her so captivated.

"There was a message in my inbox about last-minute
holiday schedule changes and for everyone to recheck
the hours they'd be working."

"Yeah, I saw that."

"I'm no longer scheduled for Christmas Day."

"Lucky girl."

"Not lucky girl." Because if she wasn't working, she
had to go with Riley to his family dinner. Not that there
wasn't a teeny tiny part of her that wanted to go, to meet
the people he spoke of with such love, but the thought of
a Christmas Day dinner was too much. Plus she'd have
to buy them presents. Not that she was such a tightwad
that she minded spending the money, but what the heck
would she buy people she'd never met and who were
from such a different social background from her own?

"You sound as if having Christmas Day off is a bad thing." Karen grinned at her. "Enjoy yourself, spend some time with family."

Time with family? Ha. Her only family had been her mother and she'd died several years ago from liver problems.

But Riley's family?

"Or that good-looking man you're dating. Now, there's a way to spend Christmas Day. Unwrapping really great packages." Karen waggled her brows.

Panic tightened Trinity's throat. She glanced at the schedule again. "You're supposed to work. Let me take your place."

Karen looked at her as if she was crazy. "Why would you do that?"

"Because I moved here from out of state, remember? I don't have any family. I'll be by myself if I'm not working. I should work and you go enjoy your day with your family."

Karen shook her head. "No way. Pay for Christmas Day is always double time and I need the extra money. I'd put in to work and was glad for the schedule change as I'm helping put my kid sister through school. Besides, I seriously doubt Dr. Williams is going to let you spend Christmas Day alone."

Okay, so convincing Karen to swap with her wasn't going to work. Maybe one of the other cardiac nurses would swap with her.

No such luck.

Trinity couldn't work out why not a single one of the nurses scheduled to work on Christmas Day preferred to have the holiday itself off. Not a single one of them was willing to let her work instead of them. Unbelievable.

What was up with this hospital anyway? Didn't they have any Christmas spirit? They were supposed to want to be at home, to be with their families, to…not be like her.

Annoyed at herself, she went into a patient room and forced a smile onto her face for Jewel's benefit.

"Not working."

"Huh?" she asked, confused by her patient's immediate comment. "What's not working?"

"That fake smile." Jewel pursed her lips. "I take it you still haven't found that pair of glass slippers?"

"If you recall our conversation, you'll remember that I don't want glass slippers. Way too impractical for a practical girl like me."

Jewel snorted. "You can talk big all you want, but when I look at you I see the truth."

Scary thought, but somehow she believed Jewel really did see more when she looked than most people did. As if age had given her insight beyond the surface.

"What truth would that be?"

"That you're a romantic through and through."

Trinity made a face then put her hand across Jewel's wrinkled forehead as if taking her skin temperature. "Uh-oh. I think we'd better call your doctor because you're delirious."

"And you, my dearie, aren't fooling this old gal. You crave romance."

Wondering at why she sounded as out of breath as her patient, Trinity shook her head. "Wrong. Pink hightops were my dream shoes, not glass slippers. I run from romance."

Riley paused outside Jewel's door, fascinated by the conversation he was overhearing. Perhaps he should feel guilty for eavesdropping, but he didn't. He needed an edge with Trinity, something to push him in the right direction where she was concerned, because she confused him.

And frustrated him.

Since the night on the beach she'd gone right back behind her wall, and had also erected a barrier between them. A new barrier because he wasn't convinced there had ever been a point where she hadn't had a protective wall between them.

Except perhaps for a few moments there on the beach when she'd been touching his face. When she'd looked at him, touched him, she'd been unguarded.

He'd liked what he'd seen, what he'd felt. A lot.

He wanted that woman, that unguarded Trinity, all the time.

The one he knew was buried within her who claimed to not like Christmas, to not believe in the magic of the season. He wanted to see her laugh as she had in the surf, to let herself loose with him and just embrace life.

Not for her to beg every nurse on the schedule to let her work for them on Christmas Day so she could get out of spending the day with him.

That had almost had him losing his temper. Even now the idea that she'd do that got his hackles up. Then again, perhaps he couldn't say a thing because he'd already ensured none of them would swap with her, and without bribery.

Just because Trinity claimed not to be a romantic, it didn't mean the other nurses on the cardiac floor were immune to romance. When he'd told them he'd planned a Christmas surprise for Trinity, they'd all oohed and ahhed. Yeah, the other cardiac nurses were as much suckers for romance as…as he was.

Because he wanted to give Trinity romance and lots of it. He wanted to show her what Christmas was all about.

"Why on earth would you run from romance? Especially in a pair of pink hightops?" Jewel sounded as confused by Trinity's claim as Riley himself was.

"Because romance is all about building up expectations and making promises that won't come true, not in the real world, so of course I run."

That's exactly how she described Christmas.

"Honey, like I said before—" Riley could just see Jewel's head bobbing back and forth "—you've been hanging out with the wrong Prince Charming."

Riley frowned.

She'd been hanging out with him.

Was he the wrong Prince Charming for Trinity?

For that matter, did he even want to be a Prince Charming? It wasn't a role he'd ever envisioned for himself. He worked long hours, was dedicated to his career and would never want to do to a wife and family what his father had.

He wasn't looking for happily-ever-after, but there was something about filling Trinity's world with goodness and dreams come true that made him long for the ability to wave a magic wand and give her the world, to slip that glass slipper on her foot and be her Prince Charming.

"I like the man I've been hanging with. He's a great guy."

Riley's chest puffed out a bit at her admission. Oh,

yeah. That was him she was talking about. She liked him and thought he was a great guy.

"If he's such a great guy, where's the glass slippers on your feet and the dreamy look in your eyes?"

Leave it to Jewel to point out the harsh reality.

Trinity laughed, the sound sparkly and warming something inside Riley.

He wanted to make her laugh that way.

"He tries, Jewel, he really, really tries, but I'm damaged goods."

"Damaged goods?"

"Lots of baggage. Plus, Christmas isn't my favorite time of year."

"Not a crime, but why not?"

"Long, long story, but the most recent installment would be that my boyfriend dumped me quite publicly a couple of years ago at our hospital Christmas party. I wasn't much on the holiday prior to that, but gave up completely at that point. Nothing merry about a day that only reminds you of bad memories."

"Sounds to me like I was right. You have been dating the wrong Prince Charming." Jewel made a sound that could have been her clearing her throat or could have been her faking a gag. "Let's hope this current guy you say you like has more sense."

"Let's hope."

Trinity's voice held a dreamy quality that could only be defined as real hope. She hoped he had enough sense to be her Prince Charming? Was that it? Was he not giving her enough romance? He hadn't really tried to be romantic, just himself. Although most men would say that cooking a candlelit dinner for her should have won him more than a few romance brownie points. He'd done more for her than he'd ever done for any woman. Was it not enough?

Still, she'd given him food for thought.

He'd planned to go in, check Jewel and see if sending her home for the holidays was a remote possibility.

Instead, he walked away from the room wondering what one had to do to be Trinity's Prince Charming? Her *right* Prince Charming?

And wondering why making sure he did just that was so important when he wasn't a happily-ever-after kind of guy.

Christmas Eve. Only a few more days of this nonsense and then the world would be focused on out with the old and in with the new and how many resolutions could everyone make that they didn't really intend to keep.

Trinity could barely wait.

Sure, so far she'd made it through the holiday season with a lot fewer tears than last year.

Actually, she hadn't cried much at all, and she knew why.

Riley.

Since the Christmas party they'd been together pretty much non-stop and she hadn't had time to dwell on Christmases past.

Just Christmas present.

No way would she even consider Christmas future. She had to make it through the rest of the current holiday season first.

As in, what the heck was she going to buy his family? She'd forced herself into a few shops and hadn't found one thing that said, *Buy me because Riley's family will love me.*

How the devil was she supposed to know what to purchase for people she'd never met? She'd considered buying everything from gourmet cheese and fruit to the latest bestseller. She'd even done several late night frantic internet searches on gifts for people one didn't know.

Nothing had seemed just right.

She'd yet to see Riley today as the cardiology group he was a part of had closed up shop for the next two days, but she knew he'd be by at some point to check on his hospital patients. He was the kind of doctor who would do a round on his own patients rather than have the on-call doc do so.

"Hey, before you leave today, make sure you find me," Karen said as she came around the nurses' station. "I have a little something for you."

"You do?" Trinity asked, thankful for the little something she'd picked up for her coworker while searching for Riley's family something. The small gift was stuck inside a Christmas bag with Karen's name on it inside her purse.

"Well, yeah." Karen gave her a "duh" look. "We are friends, aren't we?"

"Well, yeah." She mimicked Karen's tone, mostly to cover the odd emotion moving through her chest. Karen had gotten her a Christmas gift. And just called them friends. "But we never discussed gifts, so I didn't expect you'd get me anything."

"What? You didn't get me anything? Guess that rules out that new Corvette I've been wanting." Karen feigned a sigh. "There's always next year."

"I didn't say I didn't get you anything," Trinity pointed out, "but you're right, there's not a Corvette sitting out in the employee parking lot with a big red bow and your name on it. At least, if there is, I'm not the one who got it for you."

Karen grinned. "Maybe we should check the parking lot out to see."

They both laughed.

"So what are your Christmas Day plans?" Karen asked, but sounded as if perhaps she already knew the answer.

"Well, unless I can convince you to let me work in your place, I'll be going with Riley to his family Christmas lunch."

"Wow. I figured you'd be spending the day with him but a family get-together? Are you two that serious?"

Heat infused Trinity's face. That serious. How did she answer that when she didn't know the answer herself? "It's just a meal."

"When a man takes a woman with him to a family holiday meal, it's never just anything. It's a big deal."

"Maybe he just felt sorry for me because I'm new in town." Yet another reason why she didn't want to go. She didn't want his pity.

"Are you kidding me? I have seen the way that man looks at you. He is smitten."

Which sounded good but also a little too good to be true. She kept expecting him to snap out of whatever spell he'd fallen under. Then where would she be? Lost.

"What are you wearing?"

Trinity shrugged. She hadn't even thought about what she'd wear. What was wrong with her? She should have thought about it. Only she was so used to just wearing hospital scrubs that she didn't give much thought to anything else.

Laughing, Karen shook her head. "Okay, so you've

no clue what you're wearing. How about gifts for Riley's family?"

If her face had been hot moments before it was deathly cold now.

"I wish I knew. I've been searching for something from the moment I realized I was going to have to go to this dinner, but what do you buy for people you've never met?"

Karen paused a moment then shrugged. "Nothing big or fancy, just some token of appreciation that says thank you for including me and, no, I'm not a total loser that your son's dragged home to meet you."

"Maybe I am a total loser when it comes to Christmas, because I don't have gifts for them and don't know what to buy."

Karen looked thoughtful then waggled her brows. "Anything at home you can re-gift?"

Re-gift? As in give away something that someone had given her once upon a time? That would be assuming that she'd received gifts over the years. She rarely had.

She winced and met her friend's gaze. "What am I going to do? I'm running out of time. Tonight, after work, is the last chance I have."

Shaking her head in mock sympathy, Karen laughed. "I guess you are going to join the throng of last-minute shoppers who are hitting the stores the minute they get off work tonight and pick something from whatever is left on the sales rack."

Trinity closed her eyes.

Go shopping for Christmas gifts on Christmas Eve.

Oh, joy to the world.

CHAPTER TEN

RILEY HAD PLANNED to spend Christmas Eve with Trinity, but obviously she'd had other ideas because when he'd asked her to come over for dinner, she'd refused.

Something she hadn't done for a while so she'd caught him off guard. He'd just assumed they'd spend Christmas Eve evening together and hadn't even considered any other possibility.

He paced across his deck, staring out at the sea. The wind was up a bit and held a chill. The waves crashed noisily against the beach, the pounding sound matching his mood.

What if Trinity refused to go with him tomorrow? What if she refused to see him on Christmas Day, period?

What kind of glass-slipper-wielding Prince Charming could he be if she wouldn't even let him have a go at her feet?

Besides which, he wasn't quite sure how he was going to pull off everything he had planned. His sports utility vehicle was packed to the brim with what he'd planned to give her, but the reality was that he might have put a whole lot of effort into something he wouldn't even be able to pull off. It wasn't as if she even had a chimney for him to shoot down. Besides, breaking and entering with her asleep in her bedroom seemed a little too stalker-ish.

He closed his eyes, breathed in the salty scent of the sea.

Where was she? What was she doing?

Surely not mourning over the idiot who'd dumped her? Ever since he'd overheard her conversation he'd wanted to strangle the guy.

And to hold her tight and never let go.

At least he understood the walls she hid behind a bit better.

Raking his fingers through his hair, Riley sighed. He didn't like feeling at a loose end. They'd only started spending time together two weeks ago. A single night away from her had him antsy?

Maybe Trinity was missing him as much as he was missing her. Only one way to find out.

He slid his hand into his pants pocket to call her. His phone started ringing before he could even press a single key.

The number on the screen had him letting out another sigh, this one full of relief and something akin to pleasure that she'd taken the initiative.

"Trinity." No hello, just her name. "I need your help."

His help? Panic hit him. Was she in trouble?

"Anything." There were few things he wouldn't do for this woman.

She told him what she needed and he burst into laughter.

"Okay, princess, I have everything you need. I'll save your royal hind end."

* * *

From the corner of her eye Trinity watched Riley trail a long curly ribbon across the floor, enticing Casper to pounce, which the cat quickly did, only to have Riley tug the string a little further away.

"She'll never tire of that, you know," she warned, liking it that he was a cat kind of man. That he hadn't minded that she'd brought Casper with her. Chase had been more into dogs. She liked both. "She likes to play."

"Smart cat." He dangled the ribbon out in front of the cat, causing Casper to swat at a curl.

"Because she likes to play?"

"Every good girl should take time to play."

"That a dig at me?"

"No, ma'am, but if the shoe fits."

If the shoe fit? Ha, if he only knew that Jewel was hoping he'd shove her feet into a pair of glass slippers he wouldn't be making jokes about shoes fitting.

He nodded then glanced at where she was attempting to fold wrapping paper around a box. "Are you sure you don't want me to do that for you?"

"I can wrap a present."

His gaze dropped to the box and he scratched his head. "I'm sure you can, but maybe I could help you. It's not a crime to accept help from time to time."

She glanced down at the bunched-up paper and then at the previous package she'd wrapped. "They certainly don't look like the ones in the store," she mused, casting a longing eye at his perfectly wrapped present then onward to his Christmas tree. "Or the ones under your tree."

"They don't have to look any certain way," he assured her, helping her straighten the wrapping. He gently pushed Casper out of the way when the cat attempted to pounce on the paper, obviously not finished with having Riley's attention. Her cat really was smart. Brilliant, even.

"It's not the packaging that matters, Trinity," he continued, smoothing the paper Casper had managed to crinkle. "Like a lot of things in life, it's what's inside that counts."

"Yeah, well, I'm not sure about what's inside either." She gave the packages a skeptical look, handed him the string so he could occupy her cat while she attempted to wrap presentable gifts. "It wasn't easy buying something for someone I've never met."

"You did fine. My mom will love her gift and that you brought her something. She loves presents." He tugged on the string again, sending Casper into another pouncing fit. "For that matter, she's going to love you."

"Let's hope so."

She was nervous about meeting his family, wanted them to like her, had gone out on the worst evening to Christmas shop and fought the crowds to buy them gifts. She'd even picked up little gifts for his nieces and nephews. Her, Christmas shopping. Whatever had come over her?

And then there was Riley's gift. Something silly and ridiculous and so emotionally expensive she hadn't been sure she could pay the price. Yet the moment the idea had struck her, she'd known that's what she wanted to give him.

Something she hoped would have meaning to him and make him smile.

She pulled off a piece of tape and stuck it to the box she was working on. She managed to get all the box covered with paper, but she used a lot of tape in the process. At the rate she was going, they'd have to make a tape run soon.

Much to Casper's delight, Riley tossed the curled string of ribbon onto the floor. Grinning, he scooted over beside her and cut a new sheet of the wrapping paper the stores she'd been at had sold out of. Thank goodness, he'd been more than willing to not only share, but to help out with all the other things she hadn't even thought of asking him if he'd had, such as tape, name tags, and ribbons.

"Here." He set another box in the center of the cut paper. He placed his hands on her face and forced her to look at him. "Let me show you how I do this then you can develop your own technique."

Trying to ignore the bolts of electricity zooming through her at his touch, she grimaced at the roughly wrapped package sitting beside her. "I certainly need to lose my current technique. I'm horrible at wrapping."

At lots of things. Things she wanted to be good at. To be mind-blowing at.

"You just need a little guidance and then some practice." He stroked his thumb across her cheek. "I'm more than happy to oblige."

"Is sex that way, too?"

That had his eyes bulging and her grimacing.

"What do you mean?"

Her and her big mouth. Why had she had to say anything? Then again, she really did want to know. Because she thought about sex with this man a lot. Sometimes in a good fantasy way and others as in a scary way that would have him changing his phone number and running when he spotted her in the hospital hallways.

"I told you I'm horrible at that, too," she admitted, wondering if she was like the worst woman ever in making her admission. Then again, if she'd thought she could fake it successfully, they'd have gotten naked on the beach the night he'd cooked for her. She'd wanted to but had been scared of losing him, something she hadn't been ready to admit, much less risk. "Is sex something you'd instruct me in and then help me practice?"

"Princess, happy doesn't begin to convey how I feel about helping you with sex, but I've kissed you and know how wonderfully sensual you are. My guess is that you're better than you think."

If only. She knew she wasn't. She'd been there. And if she hadn't been, well, Chase had told her and the entire Christmas party how awful she'd been in the sack.

"No, I'm not."

Twisting a piece of ribbon around the package, he frowned. "Not that I believe for one minute that it's true, but what makes you say that you're not any good at sex? Are you a virgin?"

"No," she said quickly. Did he think she'd just made up that she lacked bedroom skills? That wasn't exactly the kind of thing a woman went around tooting her horn about. At least, none she'd ever known. "My ex told me how terrible I am."

"Your ex was an idiot." His words were immediate and matter-of-fact.

"Well, yes, he was." Chase had been. She could see that now. "But, unfortunately, on that matter, he was right. I didn't enjoy sex and won't be winning any Oscars for my bedroom performance."

"If you didn't enjoy sex, then he was the one who was lacking, not you." Riley's gaze bored into her, making her want to squirm. "It's his job to see to it you're enjoying sex, Trinity. If you weren't and he blamed you, he was an even bigger idiot than I thought."

Than he thought? She'd barely mentioned Chase to him, because mentioning her ex just brought her down, made her worry that Riley would move on as well. Riley was so much more than Chase had ever been. Why wouldn't he move on?

"What do you know about Chase?"

For once, it was he who averted his gaze and started wrapping the present, but as if he realized what he'd done and didn't like the action, he met her gaze head on. "Just what little you've told me...and what I overheard you tell Jewel Hendrix."

"You were listening to my conversation?" Her cheeks heated. That would teach her to have inappropriate conversations with older women who went on and on about glass slippers and Prince Charming.

"Perhaps I shouldn't have, but I did."

She digested that, trying to recall just what all she and Jewel had said about Chase...and Riley himself. "What else did you overhear?"

"That he dumped you at a hospital Christmas party. Sounds like a jerk."

"He did and he was."

"He didn't deserve you," Riley said immediately, with such conviction that she had to stare at him in wonder. He believed that. He believed in her. The question was, could she believe in him?

"No, he didn't." Warmth lit inside her and spread through her chest. "Funny that it's taken me two years to realize that."

Riley paused from wrapping the present to take her

hand and kiss her fingers. "Is he why you don't like Christmas?"

"Partly."

"And the other part is the lack of Christmas while growing up?"

She wasn't sure she liked him knowing so much about her, the real her beneath the surface. Riley and Jewel had a lot in common.

"Not in the way you probably mean," she admitted softly, wishing they could just not have this conversation.

"Which is?"

"It's not that I expected grand presents or anything, it just would have been nice to have had a little bit of normalcy during my childhood."

Wow. She couldn't believe she was saying the words out loud, that she was admitting that her life wasn't perfect, because to make that admission just begged for someone to want to dig deeper.

For Riley to dig deeper.

She knew he would. So why hadn't she shut this conversation down? Instead, if anything, she'd encouraged it.

His hold on her hand tightened then he let go, started working on the present again. "By normalcy, you mean like a Norman Rockwell painting?"

"Not really." Normalcy, as in a Norman Rockwell painting? As in a mother and a father making a big deal over her, over having a brother or a sister to squabble with over who got to open the first gift. She hadn't ever really thought of normalcy that way, but perhaps, if she had, that's exactly how she would have envisioned an ideal childhood Christmas. "Maybe."

"I should warn you, my family is very non-normal. Christmas with us is more along the lines of a mad-house. The whole bunch are touched in the head."

She could hear the love in his voice and was honestly more than a little jealous. "Must run in the family."

"Must do," he agreed, holding up the wrapped gift for her inspection. *"Voilà!"*

"Nice." Every angle was perfectly aligned and taped down. "Do I have to be a heart surgeon to achieve some-thing similar?"

"Nope, just need a little patience and a whole lot of practice. Here." He cut off a piece of paper and flattened it out on the floor, then placed the box in the middle. "Your turn."

Trinity wrapped the remainder of her presents with Riley's help. The packages weren't as neat as the one he'd done alone, but by the last one she was impressed with the progress she'd made.

"Look!" she exclaimed as she ran the edge of the scissors over the length of ribbon, causing a perfect curl to form. "I did it!"

His eyes were warm, full of praise. "I knew you could."

His faith in her was so evident, so real as to almost be palpable. "You did, didn't you?"

"It was a no-brainer."

When no one her entire life had believed in her, why did he? What did he see that no one else did? "Why's that?"

"You're a smart woman who can do anything you set your mind to."

"Thank you, but you're giving me more credit than I deserve."

"I don't think so. I just think you don't give yourself enough credit. Not where a lot of things are concerned. You really are the most amazing woman, Trinity."

Not knowing what to say to his comment, she made a show of surveying the assembly of presents. "I hope they like them."

His gaze stayed on her rather than the presents. "They will. They aren't picky. They're used to dealing with me, remember?"

He was so close to perfect it wasn't real. His family would see right away that they were from two different ends of the spectrum. A bubble of panic rose in her throat.

"What if they don't like me?"

"They will like you. Weren't you paying attention? They aren't picky." He grinned while he said the last and she knew he was attempting to ease her concerns. His easy smile and confidence did go a long way to dismantling her anxiety. The man's constant good humor was contagious.

She slapped his arm playfully. He had such a way of making her feel better. "Shame on you, Riley."

His eyes twinkled with merriment. "For?"

"Teasing me when I'm nervous about meeting your family."

"No worries, princess. I know they are going to love you. Besides, turnabout is fair play and you can tease me when I meet your family."

Which was yet another reason why she should have shut this conversation down a long time ago. She bit the inside of her bottom lip. "Won't happen."

His brow rose. "You don't plan to keep me around

long enough to have need to introduce me to your family?"

His tone was teasing, but a real question shone in his eyes.

"It's not that. We both know you'll be the one to get bored with me and walk away. Not vice versa." She hated the thought of him doing so. If she'd felt a panic bubble before, she felt a panic volcano now. "If you think back, I told you that I don't know my father, and my mother died a few years ago." Right before she'd started dating Chase, actually. "There's no family for me to introduce you to."

"No uncles or aunts or cousins?"

If there were she'd never met or heard of any of them. She shook her head.

"Oh, princess, that's terrible. Come here." He wrapped his arms around her and hugged her close, much as a parent would a child.

Trinity couldn't say her lack of family was terrible, just her reality, but Riley's arms around her felt good so she wasn't going to argue with him. Instead, she snuggled against him and rested her cheek against the hard plane of his chest, soaking in his strength.

"I'm sorry, honey. I didn't know."

"It's okay." How could he have known? How could anyone have known when she kept all her emotions bottled up inside her? Even now she wondered if she'd made a mistake, letting him know so much. "Does it matter?"

He pulled back to stare down at her. "Of course it matters. Family is one's support system and you've had to face life without that."

Her mother had been her only family and, honestly,

she hadn't been supportive, at least, not that Trinity could recall. More that Trinity had been an unexpected nuisance that had come along and interrupted her buzz.

"Not all families are supportive."

"True, and there are times mine drive me crazy, but I wouldn't trade them for the world." He kissed the top of her head. "Well, you'll see what I mean after you meet them tomorrow."

With that, a renewed dread of meeting his family, of having to endure a Christmas dinner and be smacked in the face with what all she didn't have in her life hit her. A renewed fear of what this Christmas Day would bring because, seriously, Christmas was never good for her. "You're really going to make me go?"

"You know I am. You gave me your word."

She nodded. She'd expected no less. "What should I wear?"

"Clothes. If you don't, my mother will be highly upset with me," he said with a deadpan expression that was unlike him.

"Okay, smartypants, what kind of clothes? A dress or just something casual?"

He grinned and she realized he'd once again purposely tried to distract her. "Casual. There's a lot of us, and I do mean a lot, and we're very informal. Just dress in whatever you're going to be most comfortable in."

"Okay." She leaned her head against him, drawing on his strength yet again and hoping she didn't disappoint him. "Thank you, Riley."

"For teaching you to wrap presents?"

"That, too, but I meant for just being here with me, period."

"With you is where I want to be. I was a bit lost without you tonight. I've gotten quite accustomed to eating dinner with you and hanging out afterwards. Being without you left me at a loose end and I didn't like it."

"I feel the same."

He tilted her chin to where she had to face him. "You do?"

With everything else she'd already told him, what was one more admission? "I think about you from the time I wake up until the time I go to sleep and all the time in between."

Okay, so maybe that had been a big admission.

"And your dreams? Am I there, too?" He spoke so close to her mouth that she could feel the warm moisture in his breath.

Her own breath caught, held, and blew out in an excited little burst of anticipation of his lips touching hers. He was going to kiss her. She knew he was. She wanted him to. Needed him to.

"Oh, yes, Riley, you are in my dreams." She lowered her lids then met his gaze head on, not trying to hide what she knew was in her eyes. "You and mountains of mistletoe."

CHAPTER ELEVEN

THINKING HIMSELF THE luckiest man alive, Riley accepted the invitation she'd just tossed out. He wanted to kiss her more than he wanted his next breath.

Her lips were hot and met his with a hunger that surprised him.

A hunger that matched his own.

His hands were in her hair.

Her hands were in his hair.

Threading through the locks, pulling him to her, grasping tightly as if she never wanted to let go.

His mouth left the lushness of her lips to travel down her throat, to sup at the graceful arch of her neck. She smelled of heaven, she tasted even sweeter.

Her hands had gone to his waist, were running over his lower back, pulling him towards her with an urgency that had his head spinning.

He groaned. He wanted her more than he'd thought it possible to want someone. He wanted her to the point his body ached with need, but more than that his mind craved her. Craved knowing what she looked like with pleasure on her face, craved knowing how she sounded when she experienced full and total release, craved the knowledge that he'd put that look on her face, made that sound escape her perfect plump lips.

He kissed and supped and touched.

She rubbed and massaged and arched against him, exposing the beauty of her neck more fully. He took full advantage, moving lower and lower.

He didn't consciously consider cupping her breasts, but his hands did so as if they had a mind of their own and had taken charge. No wonder. Her breasts were amazing and made him want her all the more, which he'd have thought impossible as he already wanted so much.

"That feels good."

Had she said the words or him?

His mouth must have developed an agenda of its own, too, because when his hands pushed away her top and bra, his lips covered the perfection of her creamy breast. His gut clenched.

He'd changed into jeans when he'd arrived home. Now he longed for the comfort of his loose slacks because his jeans had grown way too snug.

As if she'd read his mind, Trinity's fingers undid his jeans and slid beneath the material of his shirt. She ran her fingers along his abs, tracing lightly but with the effect of lightning bolts, before moaning and pulling him close enough that their bodies molded together.

"More," she demanded, her fingers going into his hair and pulling his mouth to hers. The moment his mouth covered hers, they both began to make haste with his shirt buttons, with her pushed-aside shirt, until they both stood bare chested against each other.

More sounded just about right. He wanted more. Lots more.

* * *

Somewhere in the recesses of her mind a small voice warned Trinity that she needed to stop. Sure, everything was going just fine at the moment but she really wasn't any good at this. If she didn't stop, Riley was soon going to discover that fact for himself, and then what?

But her body wasn't listening to her brain. Her body was way too busy discovering new and wonderful sensations that his mouth and hands were distributing all the way through her.

In a minute she'd stop, but for now she just wanted to feel everything he so generously gave. Surely that wasn't so wrong? After all, it was Christmas Eve.

So rather than cover her breasts when her shirt fell to the floor, she dropped her head back and basked in the absolute glory of his eyes feasting on her. They did. As if her body was the most beautiful thing he'd ever seen. Wow. How did he do that? Make her feel so good without saying a word?

So when his hands and mouth returned to work, she wasn't surprised that the rest of her body wanted to get closer, to get in on the action. Her hips ground against him, marveling at the hardness pressing against her, marveling at how he breathed raggedly, at how absolutely turned on he was. By her.

His hands sliding her pants down her hips felt natural, like the most perfect thing ever. Standing before him, his eyes eating up the image of her in only her peach-colored panties could never be wrong as long as he looked at her with that light in his eyes. He wanted her. More than she'd ever been wanted, Riley wanted her. Being the object of his desire was a heady high.

One that left her wanting more. And more. And more.

Unable to stand still another moment, she moved to him, kissed him, ran her fingers over the beauty of his shoulders, his chest.

Strong, chiseled, the way a man's body should look. He was so beautiful. So much so she should probably feel intimidated, but how could she when he was so obviously affected by her, when his eyes had been soaking up the sight of her body like a starved man? When he now touched her with that same urgency?

The open snap of his jeans dug into her belly, reminding her they were in her way. She slid her hands down over the hard planes of his abdominal muscles and into the edges of his waistband. She gave a hard tug. His hands immediately joined hers in removing his clothes.

Then they stood in front of each other, he in navy boxer briefs, she in panties that were growing more and more damp.

"You're beautiful."

She shook her head. "You are."

He smiled.

She smiled back and nodded. She knew better than to do this. Especially at Christmas, but she wasn't stopping.

Trinity sighed with contentment in her sleep, rousing herself. Without opening her eyes, she smiled.

Really, really smiled.

Because Riley had been right. Chase had been wrong. She hadn't been horrible at sex. She'd just been having sex with the wrong man.

And Riley was the right man.

A bubble of panic flitted through her, but her body glowed with contentment and her joy was too great to let doubt take hold. Not now. Now she wanted what she hadn't had the first time she'd woken up with Riley. She wanted to wake him up with kisses, make him smile.

Then, she hadn't believed herself capable. Now, she knew better. He'd woken a siren within her. And not one who was horrible either.

Smiling, she rolled over, only to come shockingly fully awake.

She was alone.

Alone.

She reached out and touched where Riley had been in the bed beside her, her hand running over the cool sheet. Apparently he'd been gone for some time. Was he in the other room? Or perhaps out on the deck? Regardless, he wasn't in this bed next to her.

Where she wanted him to be. Where he should be.

Her heart twisted in grief. Had she been wrong? No, he had enjoyed the sex as much as she had. She knew he had. She might not be the best he'd ever had, but she had given him pleasure. A lot of pleasure.

But maybe sex was all he'd wanted from her and now that he'd gotten it, he was done. Perhaps having left her in his bed was his way of telling her not to get too attached, that they wouldn't be waking up in each other's arms.

Really, she'd known better. Had known that when she'd had sex everything would come to a screeching halt. She hadn't needed it to be Christmas to achieve that feat, but she doubted the day of the year had helped any.

Would she never learn?

Recalling all the touches she and Riley had shared, the way their bodies had melted as if made to fit together, the way she'd seen stars flash in front of her eyes and cried out his name, the way he'd growled hers in a torrent of release, she couldn't regret the night before. Whatever Riley's reasons for not being in this bed, it wasn't that she had been horrible in bed and for him giving her that knowledge, freeing her from that burden Chase had saddled her with, for that she was grateful. Not only had he shown her otherwise, he'd given her the greatest experience she'd ever known.

Not just the sex, though. Every moment in his company was precious. He was precious.

She loved him.

Despite all the reasons she knew better, she loved Riley Williams.

She should leave. She should go let her cat out of his guest bathroom and she should leave.

Instead, she closed her eyes and pulled the pillow that his head had once rested on over her head, cursing her stupidity for falling in love with a man who was so far out of her league and who could never really be her Prince Charming, even if he did call her princess.

Had the past taught her nothing?

The tears that burned her eyes were nowhere near as hot as the ones that seared her heart.

His mind racing, Riley carried the last box of his supplies into Trinity's apartment. He hit the front door with his hip, wincing when it closed a little more loudly than he'd intended.

No one might be home but he didn't want any of her neighbors calling the law on him either. Then again, maybe they'd just think it was Santa making all the noise. He felt like Santa.

He'd worried how he would be able to pull off her Christmas gift without her knowing what he was up to. Leaving her warm, sexy body naked in his bed hadn't been easy, but her surprise would be worth it.

He couldn't suppress the grin on his face.

He'd promised Trinity the best Christmas ever and he was going to deliver.

She'd already given him the best Christmas ever.

The best night ever.

The best everything ever.

She'd rocked his world. In so many ways. Trinity had certainly knocked him for a loop. A good one. Like a carnival ride that thrilled and made you want to just keep coming back for more.

He glanced around her living room, smiling at his efforts. What would she think?

She professed to not like Christmas, but he'd never seen anyone more starved for the magic of the holidays. He wanted to give her that magic. He wanted to make all her dreams come true.

To make her day feel as if she lived a fairy-tale. He wanted to make every day of her life feel like a fairy-tale.

Which struck him as odd. His thoughts were those of happy-ever-after, not those of a man who knew he couldn't do to a woman what his father had done to his mother. Yet he couldn't bring himself to think of a future without Trinity.

Because he loved her.

Oh, hell.

He couldn't love her.

But he did.

Yet what kind of Prince Charming could he be when he'd forever be called away from her for his career?

With shaky hands and a heavy heart he finished what he'd snuck her keys out of her purse and driven to her apartment to do.

No Prince Charming had ever done better.

Too bad he was a Prince Charming who couldn't give a happy-ever-after.

Maybe if she didn't open her eyes, she could just pretend she wasn't awake and could sleep straight through Christmas. Darn whoever had changed the schedule at work and left her home alone today.

Only she wasn't at home.

She was at Riley's. In his bed. Alone.

She tugged on the covers, trying to pull them over her head, but they wouldn't budge. Which had her eyes popping open to see why.

"Good morning, princess."

"But..." She stared in shock at the man sitting at the foot of the bed, looking sexy as all get-out with only his jeans on. Wow. Maybe she *was* dreaming.

She stared at him, trying to reconcile the fact that he was here, that he was smiling and teasing her. Had she dreamed waking up in his bed alone? Dozens of conflicting emotions swirled inside her.

Last night had hurt. A lot. But he hadn't left because he was right here in front of her.

Of course he hadn't left. She'd been in his bed, in his house.

"Why?"

He looked confused. "Why what?"

"Why are you here?"

His brow arched. "Is that a trick question? I live here." His expression darkened. "Don't you want me here?"

How did she answer that? Did you tell a man that you'd woken up and found the bed empty and had assumed the worst? That you'd cried yourself to sleep and erected a hundred new walls to replace the ones he'd torn down because she'd realized she was in love with him?

"I woke up and you weren't here." Did she sound whiny?

She'd thought he would take a hint and tell her why he'd left his bed, but he just shrugged, as if his absence was no big deal. Only he didn't meet her eyes and he wasn't smiling.

"Sometimes a man has to do what a man has to do. Now, out of bed. Time's awasting."

He might convince her to get out of bed except there was an itsy bitsy tiny problem. "I'm naked."

"Good point." His smile was lethal and he suddenly seemed intent on lightening the mood between them. "Forget getting out of bed. I'll get back in with you. Much better idea." With that he dove towards her, tugging on the covers she had tucked beneath her chin.

"No." She wiggled and squirmed, trying to prevent him from uncovering her body. "No, I don't want you to see me like this."

He stilled. "Like this? I saw everything there was to see about your body last night. Up close and personal from all angles. Have your forgotten?"

"No, but..." How did she explain that when she'd woken and he hadn't been there she'd felt such devastation and had grieved and erected those walls to where she just didn't trust letting them back down. She didn't want to let them back down. Right or wrong since he obviously hadn't really left, she still felt defensive.

Or perhaps it was her other realization during the night that had her so defensive. She didn't want to be in love with him.

"Riley, I don't want to do this today."

"This?"

"You know."

He blinked and tugged at the covers again.

Holding them tight, she shook her head. "No."

He let go of the comforter. "What are you saying?"

Her grip on the comforter tightened. "Last night shouldn't have happened."

"Because?"

What could she say? That she was so damaged by her past that she couldn't bear any more pain? That she'd fallen in love with him and although she'd thought she was strong enough to be with him and survive when he got bored with her crazy hang-ups, last night had shown her otherwise?

"Fine," he agreed between gritted teeth. "Last night was a mistake."

She couldn't tell if he was being sarcastic or angry.

"At least get out of bed and come and see what Santa left you."

Her heart dropped somewhere to the pit of her stomach. "Please, don't."

Because she just couldn't take such comments this morning. She just couldn't pretend she was the same as him, that she could spend the night in his bed and go and be all jolly with his family. She couldn't pretend that she didn't love him and that she was terrified of that realization.

"Don't?" He raked his fingers through his hair then scooted up beside her, gently forced her to look at him. "Talk to me, Trinity. I thought you'd wake up smiling this morning, not looking at me as if I'm the Grinch who stole Christmas."

"No, that would be me. I'm the one who dislikes Christmas, remember?"

"That's just because you're so stubborn and refuse to give Christmas a chance. Quit being otherwise, get out of bed, and let's enjoy our Christmas morning together before it's time to leave for my mom's. We'll discuss last night some other time, but for now I promised you the best Christmas ever. Accomplishing that does require some effort on your part."

A sick feeling settled in her stomach. "What have you done?"

Because she didn't want him going and setting a precedent that every other year would have to live up to and never would. She didn't want him being nice to her because he felt sorry for her that her mother just hadn't been into Christmas. That Chase had messed with her head and heart. She didn't want to be another of Riley's charity cases.

"I didn't say I did anything. But maybe you were a very good girl this year, and Santa came to see you last night."

She didn't want him making her depend on him even more than she already did. That was becoming more and more difficult each day and after last night... She shook her head. He probably thought her a charity case all the way round. Maybe that's what the past few weeks had been about. She was this year's Christmas project. "No, whatever it is you've done, just undo it."

His jaw tightened. "You want me to undo your Christmas morning?"

She nodded. "I don't want you being nice to me."

"Now I'm really confused."

"Don't you see?" She fought sniffling. "You've got to stop doing this."

His eyes filled with concern. "I don't see at all. You've stumped me. What exactly do I have to stop doing?"

"Making me want to believe."

He reached over, ran his finger across her face and tucked a hair behind her ear. "Now, why would I want you to stop believing when the whole idea is to make you believe in Christmas?"

Only she hadn't been talking about Christmas.

She'd been referring to him.

CHAPTER TWELVE

RILEY SCRATCHED HIS head in total confusion while Trinity got out of the bed without his assistance and with the comforter wrapped around her delectable body. He'd have liked to have woken her up with kisses, but he hadn't wanted her to get the wrong idea.

Which meant there was a right idea.

He wasn't exactly sure what that was, but he figured he had some time to figure it out. To figure them out because he wasn't a forever kind of man and she deserved her own happy-ever-after.

At least he'd thought he had time and had told himself he just wouldn't think about the future today, that he'd focus on the holiday and giving Trinity a day to remember always.

He just didn't understand why she'd be back to bah-humbugging after the night they'd shared. He'd thought the night amazing, had expected all smiles and happiness on his favorite day of the year. Instead, she'd seemed determined to be contrary. Did she want to ruin their day? To fight?

Frowning, he slipped his shirt from the night before back on and went into his living room, surveying the room and trying to see it as she would.

He hadn't gone overboard at his house, just hung on his fireplace mantel a stocking with her name in glitter on it. Plus a few presents. He'd wanted her main gift to be a complete surprise. Had he not done a little something for her, she'd definitely have suspected.

He wanted to catch her off guard and blow her mind. "Riley?"

He hadn't heard her step up behind him.

"What is all this?"

She'd put on one of his T-shirts and a drawstring pair of shorts that came down past her knees. She'd combed her hair and tied it back with a rubber band. Her face was freshly washed and ethereally beautiful. She looked like an angel.

One he was now afraid to touch for fear of upsetting her further. For fear that his feelings might show and set up expectations he couldn't follow through on.

"Christmas morning."

She glanced around the room, taking in where he had their breakfast cooked and waiting on the table, taking in the small package sitting beside her plate, taking in all the details of the room but not smiling. Instead, she looked distraught. "Why?"

He could list any number of reasons and all of them rang with truth. The panicky paleness to her face warned he might have miscalculated who she really was. "Because I want to make you happy."

But had obviously failed miserably.

Her face pinched with obvious disappointment. "You think you have to give me things to do that?"

"No." He frowned. She was taking all his efforts the wrong way. Not at all how he'd envisioned. "Haven't you ever heard it's more blessed to give than to receive?"

Without saying anything, she walked over to the fireplace mantel, ran her finger over the red velvet stocking with her name on it.

"There are presents inside."

She glanced down at the bulges in the stocking. Her face was still pinched. "I see that."

"They're yours." He'd wanted to watch her tear into the presents with excited gusto, wanted joy to sparkle on her face and laughter to curve her lips. He'd wanted her to throw her arms around him and wish him a merry Christmas. Instead, she appeared to be somewhere between starting to cry and darting out of the room.

"I...I'm not sure."

She didn't intend to open his gifts? What the...? He sucked in a deep breath. "Fine. If you don't want to open your presents, we can eat breakfast first."

"I'm not really hungry."

Determined that he was somehow going to lighten her mood without letting her ruin his, he waggled his brows. "If you don't want to open presents and you aren't hungry, then whatever do we do to pass the time until we go to my mom's house?"

Her gaze narrowed. "Not what you're thinking."

Yeah, her "Last night was a mistake" had clued him in that she wouldn't be dangling any mistletoe over her head any time soon. He crossed his arms. "You don't know what I'm thinking."

"Sure, I do."

"Then you should be ashamed of yourself."

She didn't crack a smile.

"Come on, Trinity. Lighten up. It's Christmas and

we're young and healthy and have a lot of things to be thankful for. I've done my best to give you a special Christmas morning. Why are you acting this way?"

Trinity felt like a grade-A heel. She was being an ungrateful pain when he was doing his best to make the most of the morning. She realized that.

Just as she realized that she wanted to give in to his cajoling. But what would be the point?

Last night had blown her away then blown her to bits.

She was in love with him. Just look at how she'd fallen apart when she and Chase had ended. Chase had been nothing compared to Riley.

Nothing.

She'd given her word she'd go with him today, but beyond that she couldn't do more. Couldn't risk more.

He was a good man. He deserved more. Deserved better than she could ever be.

He deserved someone who could look around at the effort he'd made to make her Christmas morning special and express her appreciation, not clam up with fear and panic. Someone who could give him good things in return.

Casper mewed at her feet and she bent over to pick up the cat, stroking the silky fur.

"I fed her some tuna. Hope that's okay and that I didn't do something else wrong."

Ouch. Usually he was so patient, but he must have reached his limit. She couldn't fault him for that.

Walking over to the table where he'd prepared a small feast, she sat in a chair, putting Casper in her lap. The cat nuzzled her a brief moment then jumped down to rub against Riley's leg. She didn't blame her cat. She'd choose rubbing against Riley's leg over her lap, too.

She and her cat could mope over him together when he was gone.

Her gaze fell on the brightly wrapped present next to her plate. "I don't have your present with me."

"You got me a present?"

Embarrassed, she nodded. "It's not anything big. Just a little something that you will probably think silly."

"Not a problem. We'll go by your place on the way to my mother's. I figure you will need to shower and change anyway."

"Actually, I have a bag in my car and could grab a quick shower here if that's okay." Because if she went home, he might not prise her back outside the door to go to his mother's. She might be a coward, but she wasn't a liar. She'd told him she'd go, so she would go. If he still wanted her to. "I keep a change of clothes in my car because of never knowing when I'm going to get off work."

"Whatever is fine. Can I get it for you?"

She shook her head. "Sit down. You've obviously worked hard this morning getting all this together. The least I can do is co-operate."

She could tell he was disappointed. By her words and her actions.

She just wanted this day over.

"Will you please open your presents?"

Glancing at the package, she nodded. Really, how could she say no?

With shaky hands she unwrapped the present, her breath catching at what was inside. An angel tree-topper.

"Thank you." She didn't point out that she didn't have a tree.

"You're welcome." He sounded as awkward as she did.

That the packages inside her stocking contained various Christmas ornaments didn't surprise her. Not really. What an optimist he was.

Part of her knew she'd treasure the gifts always. Another part wondered if she'd ever be able to look at them without remembering that the day he'd given them to her had been the beginning of the end.

Apparently, he was going to fail at giving Trinity a magical day. Not that he wasn't trying, but he could only do so much when she wouldn't look him in the eye and even her smile was fake.

Maybe he should have just taken her home instead of torturing himself with failure for the remainder of the day.

He didn't deal well with failure.

Especially when he didn't know why he was failing. He loved this woman and wanted to make her day special. Why was everything coming out wrong?

Because he was the wrong Prince Charming?

"You can take me home if you've changed your mind about wanting me with you today."

"Hell, no," he snapped, knowing he sounded harsh, but seriously, if that was her game and she'd purposely been aloof all morning to get out of spending Christmas with him, she could think again.

"Fine, but just remember that I did offer."

He tried to hold her hand as they walked around the car, but she pulled away under the pretense of helping him carry packages. He frowned but figured that her refusing to hold his hand was par for the course today.

Fine. She could act all weird if that's what she wanted, but today was Christmas and he was going to enjoy the day if it killed him.

His mother's house was in chaos as usual, being Christmas Day. There were easily more than thirty people present. They all looked to be having a great time and happy to be there. Except Trinity didn't want to be there and was doing a poor job of hiding that fact. Several times on the trip from the car to the house he'd thought she might make a run for it.

"Please, don't make me do this."

Frustrated beyond belief, he stopped walking to glare at her. "You act as if being here is making you a martyr."

She winced. "I'm sorry. It's just that I—"

"Uncle Riley is here!" Timmy, his sister's oldest, screamed, and came racing toward him. The seven-year-old launched himself at Riley, cutting off whatever Trinity had been going to say. "Did you bring presents?"

"Have I ever come to Christmas without presents?" he snapped, and regretted it even before Timmy's face fell. "Sorry, bud," he apologized to his favorite nephew, who stared at him as if aliens must have invaded his body. Riley sighed, gave the kid a hug, then sat him down on the pavement. "There are more in the car if you want to round up a posse to help unload."

Still looking at him as if trying to figure out what was up, Timmy and several of his other nephews, who seemed to appear out of thin air, ran towards his car.

Setting down the presents that he held, he turned

to face Trinity. "I know you don't want to be here, but Christmas is special to my family and I don't want the day ruined for my mother. She's been through a lot. Try to at least pretend you want to be here with me, okay?"

Looking pale, Trinity just nodded and was then overwhelmed by his mother and sisters. Being cornered by the Williams women could be compared to nothing less than an all-out assault.

"Oh, look at you, honey. What a pretty little thing you are!" his mother said, her hands on Trinity's shoulders as she studied her.

"Mom, you're embarrassing her," said Riley's younger sister, who then proceeded to do the same but pulled Trinity into a hug that she remained stiff through.

"Nah," said his sister, who was currently eight months pregnant and looked as if she was about to pop. "All women like to be called pretty and little."

"Hey, pretty little sister," Riley greeted her, stressing *pretty* and *little*. He kissed her cheek. "Mom, Becky, this is Trinity. We work together at the hospital."

Because what more could he say?

"You more than work together or she wouldn't be here with you." That had come from his brother, who'd joined them and slapped Riley across the shoulder.

Riley wanted to laugh, to shake his brother's hand and make a joke of his comment, but instead he just shrugged. "It's no big deal, really."

"Right," his older sister said, wrapping her arms around him and kissing his cheek. "Great to see you, little brother. And Trinity." She turned to a pale Trinity and did the same. "We're so glad that Riley has finally brought a woman home with him. We've all been placing bets as to what you looked like."

"Bets?" Trinity's eyes resembled those of a doe in headlights. Her skin was pasty white and her posture stiff as a board.

Riley winced. "Sis, you're scaring her."

"Nah, if she's with you, she isn't easily scared."

His siblings all burst into laughter but Trinity remained quiet, and regret filled Riley. He'd made a mistake, bringing her here.

After the disaster of a morning they'd had, maybe he should just admit that everything about them was a mistake. He couldn't give her what she deserved and she didn't want anything he tried to give.

Maybe she really didn't like Christmas.

Or him.

Ending things as soon as possible was inevitable.

Trinity had made a mistake in coming here with Riley. Seriously, she should just hibernate through Christmas each year. She'd be a happier person if she did.

Those around her would be happier because she knew she was ruining Riley's day and that was a shame, but she felt unable to snap out of her melancholy.

She'd had sex with him the night before. Amazing, beautiful sex where they'd not held anything back from each other. Today she could barely look at him for the panic filling her mind.

Would he dump her on Christmas, as Chase had? Perhaps publicly do so in front of his family? His affluent family? She might not know the actual values of cars but the cars in Riley's mother's drive weren't at the low end of the market.

They couldn't be more different.

They'd probably all lost their bets because she

doubted any of them had bet on Riley bringing a charity case.

"Jake here thought you'd be tall and a buxomy redhead." A woman who looked a lot like Riley clarified her earlier comment, oblivious to Trinity's inner torment. "I thought you'd be tall, thin and blonde. Becky thought you'd be brunette."

"And I thought you'd be the luckiest girl in the world to be here with my wonderful son," Riley's mom butted in, shooing them all further into the house. "Come on in so we can say a blessing for our meal." The kids came running through with more packages. "Boys, y'all put those under the tree for now. We'll open presents after we all have full bellies."

"But, Nana!"

"Don't Nana me. You heard me." But her voice was full of love, rather than threat.

They were all being friendly, trying to include her, had smothered her with hugs and attention.

But Trinity felt the difference in Riley and knew she had no one to blame but herself. She'd known better than to come here, to become involved with him from the very beginning, and yet she had.

Because she had felt something when she'd looked at him that she hadn't been able to resist and she'd made the mistake of falling in love with a man she could never have.

"Don't pay them any mind." A very tanned, very blonde woman who looked like she'd stepped off a vacation ad for Florida advised her. "The whole Williams clan are nothing but troublemakers."

Trinity just blinked at the gorgeous woman.

"Hi, I'm Casey, Jake's wife. You must be Trinity.

Come and sit by me. I'll protect you from the Williamses."

"Hello," Riley interrupted with a scowl, stopping Casey from taking Trinity's arm. "In case you've forgotten, you are one of us Williamses now, too."

The woman flashed pearly-white teeth that contrasted brightly with her tanned skin. "Happiest day of my life."

Jake wrapped his arm around her waist and planted a kiss on the woman's mouth right there and didn't stop with just a quick peck either.

Blushing, Trinity glanced around, but no one was paying the couple any heed. Apparently showing affection was the norm at the Williamses' house. No mistletoe required.

"Uncle Riley, will you sit with us?" the little boy Riley had called Timmy asked, jumping up and down near Riley as if he had ants in his pants.

"At the kids' table?" Riley scratched his jaw. "Not this year, Timmy. I've brought a guest with me. She needs me at the adult table with her. I have to protect her from the big people."

Not hiding his disappointment, the boy gave Trinity a disgusted look. "She's just a girl, Uncle Riley."

"Just a girl, he says." Riley ruffled the boy's hair. "I'll have to remind you of that in a few years."

Trinity found herself watching Riley's family interact, watched the open affection, the laughter, the genuine gladness to be together, and she tried not to feel envious. She also tried not to feel guilty that Riley frowned more than smiled. She wasn't the only one who noticed and, unfortunately, various family members would shoot them curious looks from time to time, but no one asked what the problem was.

They had to be wondering, though. Why would he bring someone who so obviously didn't fit in with their wonderful lives? Why did it even matter? After all, she wouldn't be seeing these people ever again. Riley wouldn't want her to.

He'd given in to his nephew's repeated requests to come and check out the new video game Santa had brought him or he'd just given up completely on her. Either way, he'd disappeared some time ago, which was probably for the best because something his brother had said to him had made him almost growl earlier.

In a room full of people, yet oddly alone at an open archway leading into the foyer, she took a sip of hot cinnamon apple cider, liking the mix of sweet and tangy flavors and wishing it would settle her nerves.

Wishing her insides didn't twist, her mind didn't doubt, her stomach didn't roil. That she really was a part of this family and could go and play video games with Riley and the kids. Or even lounge comfortably with the crew that was settling in to watch a football game and talking back and forth about which team was going to win.

She wished she could be a glass-half-full kind of girl, rather than what stared back at her in the mirror. How did one go about changing one's reflection?

She rested her head on the archway and wished she could blend into this love-filled family.

"She doesn't seem to be having a very good time. Neither do you, for that matter."

Ouch. Was she supposed to have been able to over-hear Riley's youngest sister? The pregnant one. She couldn't remember her name. She'd met so many different people today. Easily more than forty, although it might as well have been hundreds for how they'd made her head spin.

"We are a bit much to take in," Riley said defensively. Trinity's heart lurched at his defense but then crumbled at his next statement. "But you're right. I shouldn't have brought her here today, but she doesn't have any family and I didn't want her to be alone. Not on Christmas Day." He paused and she couldn't hear what his sister said. "Maybe, but, regardless, I made a grave miscalculation where she was concerned. One I dearly regret."

He wished he hadn't brought her? Well, duh, of course he wished he hadn't brought her. She was ruining his day with his family. What a Christmas-killer she was.

Determined not to dampen his day or this lovely family's day any more than she already had, she forced a smile onto her face and joined the closest group of adults to her.

Somehow she'd fake her way through the rest of the day.

Christmas couldn't end soon enough. Was she doomed to feel this way for ever?

Taking a quick glance toward Trinity as he pulled the car out onto the highway, Riley sighed. "You're quiet."

She'd been quiet most of the day. With him, at any rate. When he'd come out from trying to make up to Timmy for snapping at the boy, Trinity had joined a group playing cards. She'd laughed and had seemed to enjoy herself. Except when he'd come near. Then the silent treatment had rolled in.

"Sometimes it's better to say nothing at all."

"Than to say something bad?" On the day after they'd first made love. Christmas morning. The entire day should have been filled with smiles and happiness. She'd clammed up and shut him out rather than embrace the goodness of what they could have shared on what was probably the only Christmas they'd spend together.

"You think I would say something bad?"

Why was it he stuck his foot in his mouth so easily where she was concerned? He loved her. He didn't want to pick a fight with her. Not really. Or maybe he did because he felt so frustrated by the whole situation. At this point he wasn't sure what he wanted.

"No, I don't think you would say anything bad. What I think is that you'd sit quietly and answer a thousand questions as politely and concisely as you possibly could then go right back to being quiet, as if you'd taken a vow of silence rather than make any effort to make conversation."

Her face flushed pink. "I made an effort to talk to your family."

Keeping his eyes on the road and one hand on the steering-wheel, he raked his other hand through his hair. "I wanted you to like my family. To not have to make an effort to talk to them, but for it to flow naturally. I wanted them to like you."

"I did like them."

He heard her swallow and figured he'd said too much. That he should have held in what he wanted, because what he wanted didn't seem to matter.

"Did they not like me?"

A damn of emotion broke loose within him and he failed to hold his irritation in.

"They knew something wasn't right between us. I finally brought a woman home and they all kept asking me if we were arguing. I was embarrassed." He knew he should stop, that he should just zip his lips and not say a word more, but his insides felt raw from walking on eggshells for most of the day. "And I guess we are, because from the moment I woke you up this morning you've been determined to fight with me. Thank God you only ruined my day and not my family's."

"I ruined your day?" Her hands were folded neatly in her lap and she stared straight ahead through the windshield, not even bothering to look his way.

This was the woman he'd made love to, the woman he had wanted to give a special Christmas to. Instead, everything had gone horribly wrong.

"I can honestly say this wasn't how I envisioned us spending Christmas Day together."

"I imagine not." Now she glanced toward him, her eyes full of emotion that he wished was focused on the positive instead of whatever had occupied her mind all day.

"Which means what? That you've deliberately needled me because you didn't want to go with me to my mother's? That you've deliberately undermined our day together?"

Because he'd had that impression all day, but why she'd do that made absolutely no sense to him. No sense whatsoever.

"From the moment of the hospital Christmas party you've refused to listen when I tell you something about myself and you claim it means something else, something that's what you want to hear. Then, when, like today, I'm not what you envisioned, you don't understand why I'm not. Well, hello, Riley, but I am a woman with real needs and real wants and real desires. If I say I like something or don't like something, guess what? That means I like something or don't like something. And you want to know something else?"

"You're obviously going to tell me whether I want to know or not." He pulled his car into his driveway and parked beneath the covered awning.

"I don't like you after all." Trinity jumped out and headed to her car.

He felt a first-class jerk. How had the day gone so wrong? Why was he going after her when it would be better to just let her leave? They had no future. Yet he couldn't let her go.

"Where do you think you're going?" he asked, putting his hand over the car door to prevent her from being able to open it.

"Anywhere you aren't," she spat at him.

"Trinity, why are you doing this?"

Her? Trinity fumed. He was trying to blame this on her? Him and his goody-two-shoes, perfect, rich, Christmas-loving family could just get over themselves. Okay, so she'd liked his family, had enjoyed playing cards with his sisters, mother and aunt, had found herself thinking that this was how families should be. How Christmas should be.

She'd longed to be a real part of his family, had been saddened that she would always be on the outside of such family moments, of real Christmas joy.

But that didn't give Riley reason to blame her for the day going wrong. She'd told him she hadn't wanted to go and he'd finagled her into doing so and then blamed her when things hadn't gone as he'd hoped. Why was that her fault?

She'd taken blame for enough things during her life. For her mother's problems. For her father leaving. For Chase finding her lacking. For Chase leaving her. She refused to take blame any more for not being what someone thought she should be.

"Because I don't want to be here. I don't want to be with you. I didn't from the beginning but I got caught up in this fairy-tale you tried to create. Well, guess what, Riley? Fairy-tales don't exist. They don't come true. Not everyone gets a Prince Charming or a happily-ever-after or even a pair of pink hightops. The whole concept of happily-ever-after is as fake as…as Santa Claus himself."

"You really believe that?"

She nodded, saw the look of disgust in his eyes, the disappointment. No doubt she'd been one big disappointment for him. From last night through today.

"I also believe that I don't want to see you any more. Just leave me alone, please. We're finished." She shoved past him and got into her car.

This time he didn't try to stop her.

CHAPTER THIRTEEN

THROUGH HER TEAR-CRAZED haze, Trinity realized she'd left her cat at Riley's. How could she have forgotten Casper?

Then again, she couldn't exactly be faulted for not thinking rationally. She'd just had a crazy few hours.

She'd had sex, amazing sex that had proved at least on one count Chase had been wrong. She wasn't frigid. She might not be a dynamo in bed, but she at least now knew what all the fuss was about.

She'd met Riley's family. She'd liked them, regretted that she'd probably never see again the wonderful women she'd come to know.

She'd realized she was in love with Riley and then proceeded to fight with him all day.

Christmas. What a blasted day! A day when everything seemed to always go wrong. Only could she really blame everything that had gone wrong today on the holiday?

She'd expected everything to go wrong and had pretty much rejected his sweet, thoughtful gifts. He was right.

She'd been the problem.

How could she have been so blind?

How could she have dirtied something so good? Because Riley was good to her. Good for her. He'd genuinely liked her. Genuinely wanted her. Thinking back to how he'd looked at her, how he'd held her and touched her, she had to wonder if maybe he genuinely loved her.

She'd acted immature, scared, prickly. All because she'd fallen in love and didn't want to be hurt again. In the process she'd been the catalyst that had set the disastrous domino effect into play.

Today she'd been a one-woman demolition crew.

She would see him again. He had her cat. They worked together.

But before she saw him again, she needed to get her head straight. Needed to figure out who she was and what she wanted.

She went up to her apartment, still lost in thought about what she needed to do next. Was she woman enough to trust Riley? To trust in him? Because if she wasn't, then she just needed to let him go, let this be the end rather than continually looking for problems and dragging him down in the process.

If she was woman enough to trust him, if he'd forgive her for today, which was questionable, then what? Where did they go from there?

Distracted, she unlocked her apartment door and stepped inside, only to rub her eyes in disbelief at what she saw.

A nine-foot tree dominated her living room.

A gorgeous tree decorated with twinkling white lights and silver and glass ornaments.

Perhaps he'd meant the angel ornament he'd given her at breakfast to go at the top, but she didn't see how as the tree was amazingly decorated. At the top, brushing against her ceiling, was the silver star they'd seen at the shopping mall. The one that was so reminiscent of the one from her childhood classroom when Christmas had been magical to her.

Riley paid attention to details.

She walked over, touched a clear plastic ornament. A princess ornament. The entire tree was decorated with various princess paraphernalia. Cartoon princesses. A pumpkin coach. Tiny glass slippers. A magic wand. A crown.

A single medium-sized package was under the tree.

How had he done this?

When had he done this?

Last night. When she'd woken up and he hadn't been there. He'd been here. At her house. Decorating. Trying to bring the magic of Christmas into her life.

He'd played Santa.

A tear slid down her cheek.

She plopped down on the floor, picked up the package. A tag read, "Don't open until December 25th".

Being careful not to tear the paper, she undid piece of tape after piece of tape. A shiny silver box was inside. She lifted the lid, moved away white tissue paper.

Her eyes widened at what she saw. "Wow."

She kicked off her shoes. Holding her breath in anticipation, she slipped her foot into one pink hightop and admired the perfect fit. Oh, yeah, the man paid attention.

"I had to guess your size."

"Riley." She spun towards the door. Her open door. She'd been so distracted when she'd stepped inside that she hadn't closed it. He stood there, filling up the doorway with her cat in his arms.

"Sorry, I didn't mean to interrupt, but the door was open."

Her cheeks flushed. With joy that he was there. She didn't need the magic of Christmas in her life.

She needed Riley, because he made every day magic.

He *was* magic.

"You're not interrupting. Not really." Not at all. Never had she been happier to see anyone. Would he think her crazy if she ran and threw herself at him? Wrapped her arms around his neck? Her legs around his waist?

"I brought Casper." He glanced around, looked awkward then set the squirming cat down. Casper took off towards the tree, intent to check out the new items invading her space.

They both watched the cat sniff and check out the tree, the open package, and then settle into the box lid as if it was the most comfortable of beds.

Riley put his hands in his pants pockets. "I won't keep you."

He turned to go. Every fiber of her being screamed to stop him. To risk everything and fight for this man. Whatever came, pain, loss, suffering, a single moment in his arms was worth taking that risk.

"Please do," she called out to his retreating back.

He turned, his forehead wrinkled. "What?"

She stood, took a deep breath. "Please do keep me, Riley."

She wanted him to keep her for ever.

"I don't understand."

She took a step towards him then another, until she stood right in front of him, one shoe on, one shoe off. She stared up into his beautiful blue eyes.

"I want you to keep me, Riley. For ever."

He regarded her for a moment. "What are you saying, Trinity?"

"That I'm an idiot who is so scared that you won't love me, that you will leave me, that I've made it impossible for you to love me and all too probable that you'd leave."

"You pushed me away."

She nodded.

"Why?"

"Because I was scared of how I feel about you."

"Which is?"

"I feel as if I can't breathe when you aren't around."

Some of the tension around his eyes started to ease. "And?"

"And as if I can't breathe when you're around because you take my breath away."

"Keep going," he insisted, crossing his arms over his chest. But his eyes had lost the cloudiness that had hidden away the sparkle she loved. Now that sparkle had come back and gave her strength. If she wanted this, wanted him, she was going to have to confront her fears, not let them overpower her the way they had for the entire day, for years. "You aren't going to make this easy, are you?"

"Lady, when I finally have you admitting that you care about me and want me in your life, you'd better believe that I'm going to keep pushing."

"I…" She shrugged. "I didn't know why you were so nice to me, why you wanted me, why you chose me. I thought maybe I was just another charity case."

"Why wouldn't I choose you? You're everything to me. All day I've kidded myself that we were a mistake, that we should just call it quits, that I could let you go because I'm not a forever kind of man. But from the time you drove away, I knew I couldn't ever call it quits with you." He ran his fingers through his hair. "I don't know what to do, Trinity. I never saw myself as marrying or having kids. Not with my career. I didn't want to be one of those dads." He paused. "I didn't want to be my dad."

"Your dad?" she asked, reeling at all he'd admitted, reeling that he'd said he loved her.

"He worked all the time, was always gone. That's why Christmas is so special to my family. It was the one and only time of the year that my dad didn't work. We had a day of him being with us, playing with us, with us being the center of his attention for an entire day. When the holiday was over, he was back at work and we rarely saw him until the following Christmas. I don't mean to whine. I know I was blessed. He was a good man, provided a good living for his family." Riley shrugged. "It's just that it seemed he was only there as part of our family at Christmas."

"Him working so hard allowed your mother to always be there for you kids, though."

"You're right," Riley agreed. "I know that in my head."

"But in your heart?"

"In my heart, I don't want to be like him."

"Which is?"

"A husband whose wife was lonely. A father whose children longed for his presence. A man I only have good memories of from Christmas."

"I'm sorry," she said, and meant it. "But at least you do have those memories. And now I understand why Christmas is so important to you, to your family."

Riley nodded. "The first few Christmases after he'd

died, my mother was devastated. My brother and sisters and I decided we were going to make sure to always be there for Christmas, to spend a good portion of the day with her, to bring her as much joy as possible."

"I'd say you were a success. She couldn't stop smiling and laughing today."

"But the other woman I wanted to bring as much joy as possible to wasn't smiling and laughing today. Not with me."

She wrapped her arms around his neck, hugged him tightly to her. "I'm sorry, Riley. I was confused, and last night…last night blew me away."

"Last night blew both of us away." He touched her cheek. "I've been doing all the chasing, Trinity, and you've been doing a lot of running." He gestured to her gift. "You said you weren't a glass slipper kind of girl, that you wanted pink hightops so you could run. When you need to run, run to me, Trinity."

Her eyes misted and she put her palms against his face. "It may take me a while to get my head on straight at times, but I will always run to you. You're my star."

He stared down at her in question.

"The star that leads me where I need to be."

He smiled. "I hope so."

She took a deep breath, rested her forehead against his chin. "For however long you want me, I'm yours, Riley."

"Then you're going to be mine for ever." He took her in his arms, kissed her. "Please, don't ever shut me out again the way you did today. My youngest sister could tell I was in love with you. She commented on how much when we were talking today."

That was what his sister had said?

"You told her that you'd made a mistake, that you regretted bringing me."

"You heard that?" He hugged her. "Our timing was off. We needed today, just you and me figuring out what happened last night and making sure we didn't do anything to mess up it happening again and again. But I couldn't cancel Christmas with my family. I just shouldn't have coerced you into going with me."

"I understand. I wouldn't have wanted you to have canceled. As a matter of fact, what I kept thinking was that I wanted what you had. That I wanted to be a part of that family, to experience the warmth and love of what Christmas should be." She stood on tiptoe and pressed a kiss to his lips. "You are what Christmas and love should be."

Riley kissed her long and hard. "My heart is yours, princess. I don't have all the answers to our future, but I'm yours every day for the rest of my life."

Her breath caught. "Really?"

"Really." His eyes catching on something behind her, he swept her up off her feet, carried her over to the tree then sat her down. "There's something I want to do."

Seeing what his gaze had caught on, she knew what he was going to do. Her heart swelled.

He pulled a chair over and she automatically sat down. He dropped to one knee and picked up the other hightop.

"Thank you for this." She spread out her arms towards the tree. "You make a great Santa."

He shook his head. "Wrong guy."

She arched a brow, not quite sure what he meant.

"I'm not going for Santa in your life."

"What are you going for in my life?"

He grinned and slipped the other shoe onto her foot. "I'm your Prince Charming, of course. Your right Prince Charming."

"My one and only Prince Charming," she assured him, touching his arm.

"I like the sound of that."

"But, Riley, I should tell you."

"Yes?"

"You're my Santa, too."

"Oh?"

She nodded. "Every day I'm with you is like Christmas."

"You're the one who is a gift, princess. You've made my life better."

"Hey, I have a gift for you, too," she recalled, jumping up and rushing to the drawer where she'd stashed his gift.

Smiling, she handed him the bag.

He eyed it suspiciously. "You used a bag rather than wrapping paper?"

She grinned. "I bought this before my wrapping lesson."

He pulled out the paper and lifted out a box about the size of his hand. What was inside made him burst out laughing.

And had his eyes shining brightly.

"It's perfect."

"I thought you'd think so, snowflake."

Holding the ornament as if it was the most precious treasure, he smiled at her, love in his eyes. "I love you, Trinity."

Her heart swelled with Christmas joy, with love. She leaned forward and planted a kiss on his lips. "I love you, too. Thank you for my best Christmas ever."

He grinned. "Until next year's."

EPILOGUE

CHRISTMAS DAY A year later, Trinity wasn't so sure Riley had topped the previous year's Christmas. As a matter of fact, at the moment she wasn't even sure she liked him. Or that she'd ever allow him to touch her again.

She moaned with pain.

There was just something about this day.

"Come on, sweetheart, you're almost there."

Okay, so she probably would let him. After all, she did love him with all her heart and was loved by all of his heart.

"Breathe, honey."

She was breathing. Trinity grimaced at her husband, who dabbed at her sweaty face with a washcloth. Her calm, patient, always-positive husband who had brought so much joy into her life. So much happiness. So much security and magic.

He'd given her Christmas.

And so much more.

"When the next contraction hits," the obstetrician said, "and when I tell you, I want you to push as hard as you can."

She felt as if she'd been pushing for hours, but in reality not that much time had gone by. She'd woken up during the middle of Christmas Eve night, had found Riley missing from bed and had gone to look for him. Not surprisingly, she'd found him beneath their Christmas tree, playing Santa.

What had been surprising was that before she'd been able to say anything she'd felt a gush of liquid between her legs. A gush of amniotic fluid as her waters had broken.

According to the clock on the wall, it was barely nine on Christmas morning. She was in the hospital. With her husband, The pink hightops she'd insisted on wearing digging into the stirrups. With their soon-to-be-born baby on its way. And their family anxious in the waiting area. The entire Williams clan.

"Push, Trinity," Riley encouraged, clasping her hand and focusing on her. "Look at me and push."

She tried to look at him but kept squeezing her eyes closed in pain as she attempted to turn her insides out.

"Breathe, baby. Breathe."

Breathe. Push. Pant.

Trinity felt a gut-wrenching pain then horrendous pressure.

"The baby's head is out," the doctor praised. "There's lots of hair."

Another contraction, a few more pushes and Trinity cried.

"You have a baby girl," the obstetrician informed them. "Congratulations."

"A girl." Riley said the words with absolute wonder. "We have a daughter."

Exhausted, but amazed at the man smiling at her with all the love a man had ever felt for any woman shining in his eyes, Trinity nodded. "A girl, born on Christmas Day."

"The most precious gift anyone has ever given me."

Trinity tried to point out that Riley was the one who'd given her the precious gift of their daughter.

"Joy Noelle Williams."

Trinity glanced down at the baby in her arms. "I have this feeling that my role as princess is going to be booted by this little sweetheart." She smiled at the man who'd brought so much joy into her life. Who'd made her part of his family, given her a family of her own. "I think you may have a hard time topping this year."

"Perhaps in your delicate condition you've forgotten, but I'm a man who aims to please, so just you wait and see."

Her eyes widened because she recognized that determined look on his face.

He just grinned. "Merry Christmas, darling."

* * * * *

HER MISTLETOE WISH

BY
LUCY CLARK

MILLS & BOON

First published in Great Britain 2013
by Mills & Boon, an imprint of Harlequin (UK) Limited.
Harlequin (UK) Limited, Eton House, 18-24 Paradise Road,
Richmond, Surrey TW9 1SR

© Anne Clark & Peter Clark 2013

ISBN: 978 0 263 89927 6

Harlequin (UK) policy is to use papers that are natural, renewable and recyclable products and made from wood grown in sustainable forests. The logging and manufacturing process conform to the legal environmental regulations of the country of origin.

Printed and bound in Spain
by Blackprint CPI, Barcelona

Dear Reader

Funny and vivacious Reggie has been waiting patiently for me to tell her story, and here it is—the last in the *Sunshine General* series. She's woven her way in and out of stories about her close friends, Mackenzie, Bergan and Sunainah, and now her three friends are right there with her as they watch her fall in love with the fabulous Flynn, clapping and cheering all the way.

These four friends have overcome so much adversity, and I like the way that although they're all very different they have such a tight bond, accepting each other for who they are and simply showing each other love. Friendships are vitally important, it's true, but the other thing I love about these four women are the four men who enter their lives and turn their worlds upside down. Flynn is no different, with the way he bursts back into Reggie's life, clearly still attracted to her and wanting to show her just how much he's changed for the better.

Flynn, John, Elliot and Richard I know will also become the best of friends, throwing another shrimp on the barbecue during their cul-de-sac crew gatherings whilst their wives, Reggie, Mackenzie, Sunainah and Bergan, sit back with a relaxing glass of wine and toast their friendship.

I do hope you've enjoyed the *Sunshine General* series—spreading a little sunshine!

Warmest regards

Lucy

For Melva. You're never too old to make a new friend,
and I'm glad I'm one of yours.
You are a very special person to my mother,
my daughter and to me.
Thank you for sharing your 'wisdom'.
Let's put the kettle on…
Pr 1:7

Recent titles by Lucy Clark:

THE SECRET BETWEEN THEM
RESISTING THE NEW DOC IN TOWN
ONE LIFE CHANGING MOMENT
DARE SHE DREAM OF FOREVER?
FALLING FOR DR FEARLESS
DIAMOND RING FOR THE ICE QUEEN
TAMING THE LONE DOC'S HEART
THE BOSS SHE CAN'T RESIST
WEDDING ON THE BABY WARD
SPECIAL CARE BABY MIRACLE
DOCTOR: DIAMOND IN THE ROUGH

**These books are also available in eBook format
from www.millsandboon.co.uk**

**Praise for
Lucy Clark:**

'A sweet and fun romance about second chances
and second love.'
—*HarlequinJunkie.com* on
DARE SHE DREAM OF FOREVER?

CHAPTER ONE

REGGIE SMITH RACED into the outpatient clinic, smiling and waving to the patients who were awaiting her attention. The clinic was decorated with tinsel and baubles and a sad-looking branch from a gum tree had been potted in the corner, dressed with twinkle lights in an effort to add a bit of festive cheer to the people waiting to see the doctor.

Christmas was Reggie's favourite time of year because it always brought hope and she was a big believer in hope. Plus, in the weeks leading up to Christmas, everyone seemed to be in a happier mood, calling a quick 'Have a great Christmas' or 'Merry Christmas' or 'Happy holidays'. Of course, Sunshine General Hospital was also abuzz with the annual hospital auction to be held ten days before Christmas and as Reggie was part of the organising committee, there was still much to do.

'Four weeks until Christmas and I haven't even started my shopping,' one of her closest friends, Mackenzie, had said to her only yesterday as they'd finalised the venue for the hospital auction.

'I'm almost done.' Reggie had grinned widely.

'Show-off,' Mackenzie had returned.

Even thinking about it made Reggie smile as she

screeched to a halt at the outpatient clinic desk. 'Sorry, sorry,' she called brightly. 'I was held up in A and E. Sorry, sorry.' Her words were genuine as she honestly didn't like to keep people waiting but sometimes, especially where she was concerned, time seemed to have a habit of disappearing.

'It's just like you, Reggie.' Clara, the clerk, smiled as she pointed to a bundle of case notes, indicating they were Reggie's patients for the morning. 'Luckily, the new general surgeon covering Geetha's maternity leave has already started the clinic so you shouldn't be too far behind.'

'I didn't think Geetha was leaving for another week,' Reggie said as she hefted the notes into her arms.

'Handover period,' Clara offered. 'Don't you ever read your emails?'

Reggie's answer was to grin and shrug. 'You know me!' She looked at the top name on the case notes in her arms. 'Er...Mr Searle. Would you like to come on through?'

She waited while Mr Searle, an elderly man in his sixties, stood and started walking towards her, barely leaning on the walking stick in his right hand.

'You're walking really well,' she said, clearly impressed as the two of them walked slowly down the corridor towards her consulting room. 'I spoke to Mackenzie, your orthopaedic surgeon, the other day and she told me how pleased she was with your progress. After today's check-up, you might be able to get a break from this place for a while.'

'I'm looking forward to it,' Mr Searle replied as he headed through into her consulting room. 'No offence intended,' he added.

'None taken,' she remarked, waving her hand in the air with a dramatic flourish. 'I love it when my patients are well enough to get back to living their normal lives.' Her eyes were alive with delight, her voice filled with happiness, but as she turned to close her consulting-room door, the door directly opposite hers opened.

The smile slowly slid from Reggie's face, her eyes widened in shock, and her jaw dropped open in disbelief as Flynn Jamieson—*the Flynn Jamieson*—stood opposite her. He was dressed in a pair of navy trousers, a crisp white shirt and striped university tie. His hands were on his hips as he stared at her with his piercing blue eyes.

'Do you have to be so noisy, Reg?'

At the use of the familiar name, especially as he was the only person she'd ever allowed to call her that, Reggie's eyes flashed with fire as annoyance replaced surprise. 'Please don't call me that. Excuse me.' With that, she closed her consulting-room door, effectively shutting out the sight of him.

She leaned against the door and closed her eyes for a moment, unable to ignore the repressed pulsing desire, the one only Flynn could evoke, and the way her entire body seemed to be trembling just from the sight of him. What on earth was Flynn Jamieson doing here? In Australia? In Queensland? In Maroochydore? In Sunshine General Hospital—*her* hospital?

No sooner had the questions started running around in her head than the answer materialised like magic. 'Surgeon covering Geetha's maternity leave,' she whispered. Why, oh, why hadn't she read her emails? The head of the surgery department was a great communicator, always keeping the surgical staff informed with the latest happenings, but it was Reggie who was the bad receiver of these communications, which meant she really had no one else to blame but herself for being shocked at Flynn's appearance.

'Reggie?' Mr Searle's voice brought her attention back to the present and she quickly opened her eyes and pasted on a smile, forcing herself to push all thoughts of the disturbing Flynn Jamieson to the back of her mind. So what if he was here? So what if she would be required to work with him? She'd worked with him before and they'd made a good professional team. The fact that he'd broken her heart six years ago meant nothing to her now. *He* meant nothing to her now. Nothing at all.

'Sorry, Mr Searle.' Reggie dragged in a breath and placed the pile of case notes on the desk, taking Mr Searle's from the top and opening them up as she sat down in the chair. 'Let's get your examination underway.'

For the rest of the Monday morning outpatient clinic Reggie did her utmost to avoid any and all contact with Flynn, forcing herself to focus on being her usual bright and cheerful self for the sake of her patients. They deserved nothing less but once her last patient for the morning had exited her consulting room, Reggie immediately picked up the receiver of the internal hospital phone and called Mackenzie.

'It's Reggie,' she stated before Mackenzie could even squeeze out a 'hello'. 'We have to meet. Are you free? Coffee shop across the road from the hospital in ten minutes?'

'I think I can do that. What's wrong, Reggie?'

'The worst thing possible.'

'What?'

Reggie could hear the worry in Mackenzie's voice but it was nothing compared to the utter panic and devastation in her own. 'It's Flynn. He's *here*!'

'This is an emergency,' Reggie told her friends fifteen minutes later as they all sat round a table, sipping coffee.

'I cannot believe Flynn is back,' Sunainah said, her sparkling new wedding rings gleaming brightly on her left hand. Reggie tried not to look at them, or Bergan's, or Mackenzie's. During the past eighteen months, all three of her closest friends had found their true loves and were now happily married. She had tried not to let it bother her, had tried to remain as happy and as optimistic as she'd always been, but deep down inside, late at night when she was all alone in her apartment, she had curled into a tight little ball and cried, feeling incredibly lonely.

And now, to top everything off, Flynn Jamieson was back in her life. He was the only man she had ever truly given her heart to, the only man she had ever truly loved, and yet he was the only man who had ever truly crushed her beyond despair.

'What are you going to do?' Bergan asked.

'What do you mean, what am I going to do? I'm going to yell and scream and bellyache and do my best not to fall apart in front of him. I mean…' She spread her arms wide as she slumped back in her chair. 'It's *Flynn*.' Reggie closed her eyes. '*My* Flynn,' she whispered, as Mackenzie put her arms around Reggie and hugged her close.

'How did he look?' Bergan asked.

Reggie sighed and shook her head as though she were a completely lost cause. 'Good. *Really* good.'

'But he is not married anymore, is that correct?' Sunainah asked.

Reggie sighed and looked at her friends. 'Not as far as I know, but then, I stopped reading the latest society gossip of the rich and famous after I saw the picture of him and his blonde, buxom bride splashed across the front pages. A man does not break off an engagement with one woman and then marry another in under a fortnight.' She glared at her untouched coffee, her voice as dark as the beverage.

Less than twenty-four hours after Flynn had taken her out to a romantic restaurant, given her red roses, plied her with the finest champagne and then strolled with her along the beach at sunset, stopping momentarily to go down on bended knee to not only confess his love for her but profess that it was *she* he wanted to spend the rest of his life with—he'd come round to her apartment and called the whole thing off, telling her it had been a mistake.

'Stupid romance. Stupid rich people. Stupid Flynn,' she grumbled, her frown deepening. 'And I thought I was going to have a good Christmas this year. Fat chance of that happening now.' She sighed, trying to figure out how she was supposed to deal with working alongside him every day until Geetha returned from maternity leave, which could be anywhere from six to twelve months from now.

Lifting her gaze from scowling at her coffee, it was then Reggie noticed that her three friends were giving each other very worried looks. They'd all known each other so well, for so many years, having been through so much together, that sometimes there was no need for words to communicate exactly what they were thinking.

They'd met at medical school, all of them having come from very different backgrounds, but their past adversities had been the one thing that had ended up binding them together. None of them had had an easy ride throughout their life but in looking out for each other and offering constant support, they'd formed their own family unit. So Reggie could easily read their expressions and she shook her head.

'I'm not going to fall for him again. I can tell that's what you're all thinking, aren't you,' she stated rhetorically.

'Well…' Sunainah shrugged.

'You've always said he was your one true love,' Mackenzie added.

'I'm more worried about you turning into a crazy nutter again,' Bergan added, her words matter-of-fact but filled with love. 'I mean, after you broke up you not only removed every single trace of Flynn from your life, destroying and disposing of all the very expensive gifts he'd given you, but you cut your hair super-short, coloured it purple and threw yourself into matchmaking your friends.'

'Well, I can't do the last bit anymore,' Reggie pointed out, indicating the wedding rings her friends were wearing, then added thoughtfully, 'I could possibly colour my hair again. I've always wanted to go green. What do you think? Green streaks?'

Before her friends could answer, Bergan's and Mackenzie's phones rang. They quickly answered them and while they spoke, Sunainah reached across the table and took Reggie's hand in hers.

'Just…pause, Reggie. Stop and take a breath.' Sunainah's phone started buzzing with a reminder and she shook her head. 'I am sorry, Reggie. My clinic will be starting in five minutes. I need to—'

'Go.' Reggie waved her hands towards her friends, shooing them away. 'Thanks for giving me probably the only fifteen minutes you had spare. I do appreciate it.'

'Sorry,' Mackenzie said, as she and Bergan stood.

'Emergency,' Bergan added.

'My afternoon theatre list will be starting late so call me if I'm needed to help out,' Reggie told Bergan.

'Will do,' her friend replied.

Reggie picked up her coffee, sipping it as she watched her friends finish their drinks quickly and head back to the hospital. She prided herself on always being happy, always having a bright smile on her face, a genuine smile, one that would bring happiness to others. Forever optimistic—that's what her friends had called her, yet now she wanted to wallow in her despondency, blaming Flynn Jamieson for making her feel this way.

'Definitely green hair,' she mumbled to herself a few minutes later, unable to lift herself out of her grumpy mood.

'I think it would look great,' a deep male voice said from behind her, a voice she instantly recognised and one that set her entire body alight with sparks of joy and excitement. Reggie turned round to look over her shoulder but didn't see him. Had she imagined it? Was she going insane, thinking every deep male voice belonged to Flynn?

She turned her attention back to her drink and almost jumped with fright when she saw Flynn lowering his six-foot-four-inch frame into the chair opposite her. She quickly put her coffee back onto the table before she spilled it. 'Don't do that, Flynn. You know I don't like being scared.'

He nodded. 'I do. Sorry. Couldn't resist.'

'Try.' She glared at him suspiciously. 'How long have you been lurking around here?' She indicated the immediate vicinity around her table. Had he overheard them all talking?

'I came in as your friends were leaving. I received a very cool look from…Bergan, is it?'

'Yes.' She frowned. 'How did you know that?'

'You showed me quite a few pictures of all your friends during our time together in the Caribbean. Don't you remember?'

Reggie sat up straighter in her chair, squaring her shoulders. 'I can't remember a lot of things about the Caribbean. It was so long ago.' She tried to inflect a touch of nonchalance into her tone but could tell from the disbelieving look on his face that he wasn't really buying it.

Flynn nodded slowly then just sat there, staring at her as though he was drinking in the sight of her. 'How have you been, Reg?'

She gritted her teeth at his familiarity, not wanting to give him the satisfaction again of seeing how the intimate name flustered her. 'I'm…fine.'

'Freaked out? Insecure? Neurotic and emotional?' he checked, and she shook her head in annoyance.

'Don't be cute, Flynn.'

He spread his arms wide and leaned back in his chair. 'I don't know how to be any other way.' His smile was big, his eyebrows were raised and his twinkling eyes were clearly teasing her.

'I see your arrogance is still in check.'

He surprised her by chuckling and she instantly wished he hadn't, the warm, inviting sound washing over her like a comfortable blanket. She'd always loved his laugh, always loved making him laugh, but not like this, not through silly barbs and jibes.

Reggie bit her tongue, needing to get her ridiculous hormones under control, to remain cool, calm and collected. 'What are you doing here?

'In the coffee shop?'

She levelled him with a glare. 'Flynn.' There was warning in her tone.

'Oh. At Sunshine General? I'm covering Geetha's maternity leave.'

'So I gathered but…er…' How did she ask this without sounding self-important? 'Did you know I was working at Sunshine General?'

Flynn didn't answer her but instead checked his watch. 'We're going to be late for afternoon theatre if we don't get a move on.'

'I don't care,' she continued to grump as Flynn stood. He obviously hadn't been told the morning elective theatre lists had run overtime. She watched as he shoved his hands into the pockets of his trousers and stared down at her with that crazy little smile touching the corners of his lips. It was a smile that had never failed to set her heart racing and now was no exception.

'You're sounding like Scrooge, Reggie.'

'Bah, humbug,' she muttered as she finished her now-cold coffee and stood. She didn't really want to walk back to the hospital with Flynn because even being this close to him was already causing her body to react with all the hallmarks of years gone past. Her heart was beating wildly, her mouth was dry, her knees were shaking and she momentarily leaned on the table for support.

'How can *you* not be in the Christmas spirit? You, who always wanted it to be Christmas all year round? The woman who loved wishing everyone happy holidays as she walked around the hospital or went to the shops or the gym or, in fact, anywhere.' Flynn pressed a finger to his lips in thought.

'In fact, I remember you animatedly and jovially wishing the Prince of the Netherlands the happiest Christmas one year. Then the next day you gave a homeless man the same greeting in exactly the same way.' He shook his head in bemusement. 'That's one thing I always liked about you, Reggie. You treated everyone, prince or pauper, the same. You afford everyone the same courtesy.'

Reggie glared at Flynn, her anger beginning to rise. 'Don't compliment me.'

'Why not?'

Her mind tried to think of a reason because she could hardly tell him that his words had warmed her heart. She didn't want her heart to be warmed by Flynn. Not now. Not ever. But he was still standing there, waiting for her reply. 'Just…because.' She shook her head and walked out of the café, waving her thanks to the owner and managing to muster a half-hearted smile. She hated herself for feeling this way, for not spreading joy and happiness, as was her wont, but seeing Flynn again, even walking alongside him as he fell into step beside her was throwing her completely off balance.

'Just because? What kind of answer is that?'

'The only one you're going to get.' She pressed the button at the pedestrian crossing with great impatience, wanting the light to turn green instantly so she could walk away from the man who had hurt her so bitterly. Still, she wasn't the same woman she'd been six years ago. Once more in her life she'd been forced to pick herself up and keep moving forward. His rejection of her had only served to make her stronger and because of that she could and would stand up to him.

Drawing in a deep breath, she turned to face him, to give him a piece of her mind, to tell him to leave her alone, but it was only then she became aware of other people coming to join them at the traffic lights, waiting to cross the road. She was forced to step closer to him, to rise on her toes so she could direct her words closer to his ear.

'Whatever happened between us happened a long time ago, Flynn.'

'It wasn't that long ago,' Flynn pointed out, stepping closer to her, dipping his head and heightening the repressed awareness she was experiencing. She closed her eyes, desperate to remain in control of the situation and not be swayed by the cologne he was wearing, the same scent she'd introduced him to all those years ago, assuring him the subtle spicy scent suited him much better than the woodsy one he'd been wearing. She couldn't believe he was still wearing the hypnotic, alluring scent.

The lights turned green, the beeping sound from the pedestrian crossing startling her slightly. She opened her eyes and belatedly realised that while everyone else had moved off, she and Flynn were just standing there, close—too close—looking at each other. She swallowed over her dry throat, desperate to ignore the tingles and sparkles and butterflies and all the other sensations this man had the habit of creating deep within her.

'It was another lifetime ago,' she eventually retorted, before turning and walking across the road, having to run the last little way as the flashing pedestrian sign had already turned red.

'It was a good lifetime, though.' His voice came from behind her and she glanced over her shoulder, not realising he'd crossed the road behind her. 'We had a good time together.'

'I don't want to talk about it.' She stopped walking for a moment and turned to glare at him. 'Why are you here? Why now? Why—?' She broke off, her voice cracking on the words. She looked away from him and shook her head, unable to believe her body and mind were betraying her by reacting to his enigmatic presence and becoming so emotional.

Swallowing, she shook her head and turned away from him, knowing it was better to beat a hasty retreat than say something she would regret. While Flynn may have broken her heart, it wasn't in her nature to be mean or malicious.

She didn't want to look behind her, didn't want to know whether or not Flynn was following her. She didn't want to know his whereabouts, she didn't want to work alongside him in the clinic and she didn't want to deal with him during operating lists. She wanted him to go, to leave the hospital and Maroochydore—in fact, leave Australia…and leave her alone.

So why, after the way he'd been smiling at her in the coffee shop, did she get the feeling that wasn't about to happen?

CHAPTER TWO

REGGIE WAS GLAD she had a busy theatre list to focus her thoughts. It was easier to push the reappearance of Flynn Jamieson in her life to the back of her mind and instead be calm and controlled as she removed Mr Philmott's gallbladder, relieved young Cynthia Schroder of her inflamed appendix and performed a hernia repair on Mrs Grant.

Between cases, she did her best not to run into Flynn, knowing he was operating in the next theatre. At one point, she was in the doctor's tearoom, just finishing a much-needed cup of coffee, when she thought she heard his voice out in the corridor. Panic filled her insides and as she glanced wildly around the room she realised there really was no place for her to hide.

Quickly washing her cup, she headed to the door, intent on slipping out of the room as he came in. Never had she been more grateful to Ingrid Brown, one of the general surgical registrars who had been assigned to assist Flynn in Theatre, because as they came into the tearoom Ingrid was intent on keeping Flynn's attention firmly on her.

'Reg?' Flynn interrupted Ingrid the instant he saw

Reggie standing by the door. 'How's everything going in Theatre?'

'Great,' she offered, and quickly left the room, trying to ignore the spate of tingles that seemed to flood right through her body from the quick glance she'd received from Flynn. Why was it that even after six years, after breaking her heart and making her feel as though she was worthless, he could still create such havoc with her senses?

And that was the way things went for the next week, with Reggie doing her best to quickly slip out of a room the instant he walked in. Keeping a nice, uncomplicated distance between them was helping her to focus on her patients, on the planning for the hospital Christmas auction and on keeping her paperwork up to date. The fact that she was as jumpy as a long-tailed cat in a roomful of rocking chairs every time a nearby door opened or she heard male voices in the corridor meant nothing.

Self-preservation was of paramount importance in situations such as this, but even through all her efforts of avoidance she was having difficulty sleeping because the instant she lay in her bed and closed her eyes, memories of her past encounters with Flynn flooded her mind.

So many memories yet such a short time together. For the first two weeks in the Caribbean, she'd kept her distance from him, trying to figure out whether he was like all the other wealthy people she knew or whether he was, in fact, a normal person. Reggie had had very good reasons for distrusting the wealthy, but thankfully he'd turned out to be the latter...or so she'd thought.

Having been raised in an exclusive and snobbish Melbourne suburb, born to incredibly wealthy parents, Reggie had instantly recognised the name of Flynn Jamieson when he'd arrived at the understaffed Caribbean hospital for his six-week contract. Their fathers had been involved in some sort of business venture together and their elite community had been small, to say the least.

Of course, Flynn hadn't had a clue of her own true identity and after she'd realised he really was interested in providing medical treatment to people in need, not just working there because it had been a good opportunity to advance his career, she'd started to thaw towards him.

She'd allowed herself to be affected by his gorgeous, sexy smile, his bright, twinkling eyes, his smooth, hypnotic voice. And once she'd fallen for him, hook, line and sinker, he'd revealed his true colours, discarding her feelings and dismissing her out of hand.

And yet somehow, all these years later, he still managed to make her knees go weak with one of those smiles, make her heart pound wildly against her chest with a simple wink and make her melt in a boneless mass at the sound of his voice. It was wrong. Wrong that he still had such a hold over her emotions, and she resented him for it.

The following Monday, after she'd managed to avoid him once more during the general surgical elective theatres list, Reggie had stopped by her small office in the surgical block to finish writing up some notes and collect her computer and cellphone. It was late in the day and she was thankful the rest of the administrative staff had already left for the day because the last thing she felt like was talking to people.

'So unlike you,' she murmured, as she hunted around

for her house keys, having already forgotten them twice in the past few days. She blamed Flynn's presence for her lack of joviality and general absent-mindedness and once more wished he hadn't chosen to come to Sunshine General and inadvertently torture her just by being around.

She heard a sound outside in the corridor and instantly she was alert, listening for evidence of Flynn. Deciding to forget the search for her keys, knowing her neighbour, Melva, had the spare set, Reggie quietly locked her office door and all but sprinted out of the department.

Whether or not it had been Flynn she'd heard or one of the cleaners, she didn't care. Bumping into Flynn was too exhausting as it not only set her body into a trembling mass of uncontrollable tingles but also taxed her mind as she tried to fight the urge to throw herself into his arms and press her lips to his. She knew it was wrong to want to do that but sometimes it was difficult to deny the urge.

Reggie headed to the front of the hospital, looking forward to getting home, having a quick bite of dinner and then running a long, luxurious bath where she would soak until her skin was all wrinkled and pruney, washing away the cares of her day…and the acceptance that she was just as much attracted to Flynn as she'd ever been.

She stood at the taxi rank and looked up and down the road, unable to believe that at just after seven o'clock in the evening, on a Monday night, there were no taxis parked and waiting outside the hospital.

'There are always taxis here,' she murmured, spreading her arms wide.

'Not tonight, from the look of things,' Flynn's deep voice said from beside her, the sound causing her heart to flip-flop with delight before a ripple of awareness washed over her. Reggie closed her eyes, trying to pull some sort of shield around herself, but she'd had a busy and emotionally exhausting day and wasn't sure she had the energy for yet another run-in with Flynn.

Dragging in a deep breath, she opened her eyes and turned to look at him, deciding it was easier to face the situation than to make it worse by pretending to ignore him. 'Do you think you might not continue to creep up on me?' she asked, trying to keep her tone polite and impersonal but failing miserably.

'Only if you stop dashing from a room every time I walk in,' he countered, his clever eyes telling her he'd been aware of her avoidance tactics.

She looked down at her feet then cleared her throat. 'Er…how was Theatre this afternoon?'

Flynn stared at her for a split second before nodding. 'Good.' He paused and she noted a small smile twitching at the corners of his lips. 'No patients died.'

'Always a good thing,' she replied instantly, before she could stop herself. It was a private joke between the two of them, extending back to his first operating session in the Caribbean. The equipment at the hospital hadn't been as up to date as that in the hospitals in Australia and afterwards she'd asked him that same question.

'How did things go in Theatre, Flynn?'

'Good,' he'd replied, pulling off his cap and gown. 'No patients died.'

Reggie's laughter had filled the air at his words and it had been at that exact moment that she'd realised

Flynn Jamieson was indeed a good man and she would be wrong not to give him a chance. She, herself, was proof that people shouldn't be judged by who their parents were so she shouldn't do the same to Flynn. 'Always a good thing,' she'd replied as he'd joined in with her laughter. From that day onwards, the two of them had been almost inseparable.

Reggie pushed the memory aside and glanced up and down the street as though willing a taxi to miraculously appear. She shifted her laptop bag to her other shoulder, wishing she hadn't added a few hefty manila folders filled with paperwork to it.

'You remembered,' he said softly, reaching out to take her bag from her.

'It's OK. I've got it,' she told him, grasping the strap and doing her best to ignore his comment. She didn't want to stand here and reminisce about the past.

'Of course.' He dropped his hand back to his side. 'Habit. I always used to carry your bag for you when we were together.'

'But we're not together anymore, Flynn, and I'm a big girl now and can do it all by myself.' Her polite smile was starting to slip and not only was her exhaustion shining through, so was her lack of patience. 'Look, Flynn, do you mind if we don't do the trip down memory lane? I've had a hectic day and I just want to get back to my apartment, eat and have a—'

'Relaxing soak in the tub,' he finished for her, his words indicating just how well he did know her. 'Of course you do.' He took a step away. 'I'll leave you alone.' With that, he turned and walked away without another word, leaving Reggie standing at the front of the hospital, beneath the bright lights, with other people milling around, both patients and staff.

She frowned at his quick retreat. It wasn't that Flynn was leaving her all alone, deserted in the wilderness. He was merely doing as she'd asked. She should be grateful for that, so why was it she felt guilty for sending him away?

'No taxis?' an elderly man asked as he came to stand beside her, looking up and down the street.

'There's an international sporting match being played at the stadium,' another person offered as she came to stand on the other side of Reggie.

'Ah, all the taxis have taken their chances there.' Reggie smiled and nodded, pulling her cellphone from her pocket. 'I'd best ring for one. Would you like me to book one for both of you as well?' she offered, feeling her natural joviality return. The others agreed and within minutes Reggie had ordered taxis for them. 'They said it would be about another ten minutes.'

'Thank you, dear,' the man said. 'I might go and sit down to wait.'

'I'll join you.' But no sooner were the words out of her mouth than a white car pulled up into the taxi rank. Reggie did a double take as Flynn exited the car and came round to her side, taking her bag from her shoulder and holding open the passenger door.

'Your taxi awaits, Dr Smith.'

The others who were waiting with her all laughed and clapped, drawing more attention.

'I've called for a taxi,' she spluttered as Flynn put a gentle hand beneath her elbow and guided her towards his car.

'It won't go to waste,' the elderly man said, indicat-

ing a few other people who had come to the front of the
hospital, hoping to find a swag of taxis.

'So that's settled,' Flynn remarked, as a stunned Reggie sat in the passenger seat. He closed the door then
turned to the other people standing there. 'I apologise
for not being able to be your personal taxi but I do wish
you all the merriest of Christmases and a prosperous
New Year.' Then, with a small bow, he came round to
the driver's side, slipped behind the wheel, buckled his
seat belt and the car merged seamlessly with the flowing evening traffic.

'What…what are you doing?' she asked, the shock
slowly starting to wear off.

'I'm giving you a lift home. I thought that was obvious.' Flynn snapped his fingers at her. 'Keep up, Reg.'

'Don't call me that.'

'Why not? I've always called you Reg. In fact, if
memory serves me correctly, I was the only one you
allowed to call you that.' Flynn's smile was wide and
bright. 'It made me feel special.'

'That's why I want you to stop.'

'I'm not special to you anymore?'

'Flynn, can we just stop this charade?' she said
abruptly, her exhausted temper getting the better of her.

'Which way do I go?'

'You go back to wherever it was you came from, get
out of my life and leave me alone.'

'No. I meant to your house. I don't know where you
live.'

Sighing with exasperation and deciding it was far
better to work with him rather than against him as that
would facilitate her arriving home sooner and thus escaping his presence, she said, 'Turn right at the next

set of traffic lights. Down two blocks then right, left, right, right.'

'Right,' he said, with a small chuckle.

Reggie rolled her eyes and stared out the window, determined not to say anything else. She'd been kidnapped and she was grumpy. Why was it Flynn seemed to bring out the worst in her?

'You always used to say I brought out the best in you,' he offered, and it was only then that Reggie realised she'd spoken out loud.

'That was before.' She shifted in her seat and stared at him. 'I know I shouldn't aggravate the designated driver but as you've basically kidnapped me, I just might.' She dragged in a breath. 'What we had all those years ago, Flynn, is over. I can learn to accept the fact that you'll be here while Geetha's on maternity leave—'

'The next six months,' he offered.

'And I can even learn to work alongside you as a professional colleague, but at no point in the scenario of the two of us working at the same hospital does it mean we're going to rekindle the relationship we had before.' She shook her finger at him to emphasise her words. 'You didn't choose me, Flynn. You broke off our engagement and within less than a fortnight were married to another woman.' Reggie crossed her arms over her chest and refused to say another word.

'Reg.' He turned right and started to slow the car.

'I told you not to call me that. I can't believe you thought you could just waltz back into my life and be so…so…familiar. We are not friends, Flynn. Far from it.'

'Reg.'

'All we are is colleagues. Nothing more. There will

be no cute looks from you, no flirting, no "Do you re-member when?", no—'

'Reg.' He slowed the car to a crawl, peering through the windscreen.

'No "no patients died" type of thing. OK? We are not a couple and we never will be,' she huffed.

'Regina! Shut. Up.' He brought the car to a stop and pointed to the front windscreen. It was then she did as he'd suggested and what she saw made her eyes go wide with horror.

'That's my apartment building. My building…it's on *fire*!'

Reggie opened the door and was out of the car like a shot. 'Reg! Wait!' She heard Flynn's voice in the dis-tance but couldn't wait. Her building was on fire. Her apartment. Her neighbours' apartments. Her neigh-bours.

'Melva! Melva!' she called, as she ran down the street. There were police, flashing lights and people ev-erywhere. The firefighters were doing their job, work-ing hard to take control of the angry orange flames that were engulfing the home where she'd managed to carve out a new life for herself.

In a state of shock she continued to call out Melva's name. Her elderly neighbour would have been getting ready for bed. What if she hadn't been able to escape? What if she was still in there!

'Whoa! Reg!' Flynn was right beside her, grabbing her arms as she barrelled headlong towards the area the police had cordoned off. 'You can't go in there.'

'But she needs me.' Reggie tried to shake loose from Flynn's grasp but he was hanging onto her with a firm grip. 'Melva!' she called again.

'Stop.' A policewoman came across and stood in Reggie's path, effectively blocking her. 'That is a burning building.'

'That's *my* building,' Reggie begged. 'Please? Melva. My neighbour—' Reggie broke off as she saw a fireman coming out of the building with a woman over his shoulder. 'Melva!' She choked on the word and it was only then she felt the soothing and strong presence of Flynn right next to her, his arm around her shoulders, not only holding her back from rushing headlong into a burning building but also providing her with strength and comfort.

'We're both qualified surgeons at Sunshine General.' His words carried authority as he spoke to the policewoman. 'As the ambulances are…' he paused for a second and listened, the sirens easily heard in the distance '…still on their way, and you have a woman there who needs medical assistance, why don't you let us help out?' As he spoke, he pulled out his hospital identification, proving he wasn't lying. The policewoman checked it thoroughly and nodded.

'What about her?' She gestured towards Reggie, who was watching the fireman gently place Melva on the ground a safe distance from the burning building. His fellow firemen were already calling for his return to the building.

'Let her treat her neighbour and she'll be fine,' Flynn said.

The policewoman seemed to dither for a second but when Flynn smiled reassuringly at her she nodded. 'All right. We're already short-staffed. Medical kits are over there next to the police cars,' she said, pointing. The policewoman's partner was already kneeling by Melva's side, pressing his fingers to her carotid pulse then shaking his head.

At her words, Flynn removed his arm from Reggie's shoulders and like a racing horse bursting from the barriers Reggie was at Melva's side like a shot.

'Melva. Melva, it's Reggie. Can you hear me?'

'You know her?' the policeman asked, moving back before Reggie could shove him out of the way. Her hands were busy, checking Melva's pulse, leaning down to see if she was still breathing.

'She's my neighbour.' Now that Reggie was actually able to be doing something, she was much calmer, just as Flynn had predicted. She glanced up to find Flynn returning with the medical kit and oxygen mask, as she continued her attempts to get a response from Melva.

'You live here?'

'Lived. Past tense.' Reggie couldn't even think about everything in her apartment that was in the process of burning. All she cared about was Melva. She kept calling to her, willing her to open her eyes. Her breathing was definitely restricted. Reggie didn't like it.

'Quick. The oxygen,' she said, holding out her hands towards Flynn.

'What about your other neighbours?' the officer asked. Reggie just wanted him to keep quiet but she also knew that he had a job to do.

'The family in number two, upstairs, are interstate. The young couple in the other upstairs apartment should still be at work.' She reached into her pocket and pulled out her cellphone, tossing it at the officer and telling him the names of her neighbours. 'Search through my directory and find their information.' Reggie turned her attention to Flynn. 'Melva's pulse is faint. Her breathing is definitely restricted. We may need to intubate. No patient response.'

No sooner had the words left her lips than Melva stopped breathing.

'She's stopped,' Flynn reported. He opened the medical kit and reached for a face shield and gloves. In another instant he had checked Melva's mouth was clear and had her head tipped back, ready to perform expired air resuscitation.

'Come on, Melva. Breathe.' Reggie's words came through gritted teeth as she counted out the breaths, readying herself in position for cardiopulmonary resuscitation. She kept counting, Flynn kept checking for a pulse.

'Come on, Melva. This is getting beyond a joke, and I'll tell you right now,' she said in time with her movements, 'you are not dying tonight. Not if I have anything to do with it.' Her words were clear and determined and filled with promise.

Flynn did another two breaths then checked for a pulse. 'It's there.' He looked over at Reggie, noting the look of relief cross her face.

'Atta girl, Melva.' She rested back on her heels for a second before helping Flynn to secure the oxygen mask over Melva's mouth and nose. The ambulance sirens had drawn closer and in another moment they were silenced, but the blue and red flashing lights filled the darkness of the night as whoever was driving came up the kerb and onto the grass, getting as close as possible to where they were treating Melva.

'I'll speak to them,' Flynn said, standing up and striding purposefully towards the paramedics.

'She has a few burns to her arms and legs,' Reggie

pointed out, and reached for the medical kit. 'Melva,' she called again, still watching the rise and fall of the other woman's chest. 'We're going to take good care of you,' she said, as the paramedics came over to give them a hand. They wrapped wet towels around the burns on Melva's arms and legs, Reggie very happy when Flynn reported that her breathing was improving.

'Do you know if she has any allergies?' Flynn asked.

'Not that I know of.'

'OK.' He spoke to one of the paramedics. 'Can you get me some midazolam so we can get Melva here ready for transfer?' He returned his attention to Melva as she started to cough a little more.

Reggie quickly hooked a stethoscope into her ears and listened to Melva's breathing. 'Still rasping. Let's give her some salbutamol via nebuliser just to open those lungs.'

'Yes, Doctor,' the paramedic replied.

'Reggie?' As Melva said her name she coughed and Reggie immediately took the other woman's hand in hers.

'Yes, it's me. I'm here. You're going to be fine.'

'So much smoke. Couldn't see.' Melva's words came out broken but there was also a hint of panic in her voice and the last thing they needed right now was for Melva's anxiety to rise.

'It's OK now. Shh. I'm here. I'll take care of you.'

'But the apartments…'

'I'll take care of it. You just relax and leave everything to me.

Flynn looked across at her. 'Reggie, if you need any help—'

'I said I'd take care of it,' Reggie returned, her words a little crisp.

'Of course.'

She frowned for a moment. Flynn? Backing down? Not insisting on being the big, strong hero, coming to the rescue of the damsel in distress? She met his gaze for a split second and saw nothing there but reassurance. Perhaps he had changed. Perhaps he was different from the way he'd been six years ago. There was truth in his eyes, as though he was desperate to let her know that he meant what he said.

Could she really trust him again? Reggie couldn't deny she was relieved he was with her, somehow empowering her with the strength and professionalism she needed to help her elderly neighbour.

Reggie pressed her fingers to Melva's pulse and was pleased to find it a little stronger than before. 'You're doing just fine, Melva.' Reggie held the other woman's hand and kissed it. 'You have an oxygen mask on so just lie still. I'm looking after you.'

'Good. Means I'll be OK.' Melva managed a weak smile beneath the mask, her eyes opening only for a second before she closed them again then started coughing.

'Relax. Breathe easy,' Reggie encouraged, and looked up to see just where Flynn was with getting that salbutamol organised. 'Flynn?' she called.

'Right here, Reg.' He was walking towards her, carrying the portable nebuliser. Soon they had Melva settled, with the salbutamol easing the pressure in her lungs as the paramedics transferred her to the stretcher.

'You'll come with me?' Melva asked, her voice still a little raspy.

'Try to keep me away,' Reggie said with a smile

as Melva was settled into the ambulance. She stopped for a moment then turned and looked at their building. Smoke was billowing out but thankfully the firefighters had managed to contain the raging flames, protecting the properties on either side. People were everywhere, being kept at a distance, more police had arrived to assist with crowd control and another fire engine was just pulling up so the men and women who had already been battling the blaze for quite some time could rest and recuperate.

She knew the drill. She'd been involved in many a rescue situation over the years but now, as she continued to watch the place she'd called home become nothing more than a wreck, she couldn't help an overwhelming sense of helplessness engulf her.

Her eyes filled with tears and although she tried to blink them away, knowing she needed to remain strong, to be there for Melva, she couldn't shift them. Sniffing, she raised a shaking hand to her lips as the scene before her blurred into a watery mess. As a tear dropped from her lashes and rolled down her cheek, she almost jumped when Flynn's warm and comforting arms drew her close.

She knew she should resist. She knew she should push him away, keep her distance from the man who had broken her heart beyond repair, but she couldn't. She wanted his comfort, needed his strength, and for the first time in years Reggie gave in to the vulnerabilities she'd successfully kept at bay for far too long.

'Oh, Flynn,' she murmured against his chest, hating herself for loving the comfort he offered. 'What am I going to do now?'

'Shh,' he crooned, resting his chin on her head and tightening his hold on her. 'We'll figure it out.'

'We?' The word was barely a whisper as she snuggled in a little closer to him, her ear pressed to his chest, and there she could hear that his heart was beating a lot faster than it should. 'We?' she asked again, a little louder, and as she edged back just a touch, lifting her head so she could look at his face, she saw in his eyes determination mixed with a healthy dose of repressed desire.

'We,' he confirmed with a definitive nod.

CHAPTER THREE

'REGGIE?'

She felt a hand on her shoulder rousing her from her light doze. Someone was gently shaking her awake, their deep voice tender and soothing.

'Reg?'

She breathed in deeply, recognising the sound of Flynn's voice. Oh, Flynn. How she'd missed him. The way he'd always held her close, supporting her, listening to her, comforting her. She'd loved the way he'd called her 'Reg', the one syllable sounding so special and unique and perfect from his lips. She sighed with happiness, letting the dream of his presence wash over her.

She remembered the first time he'd kissed her, *really* kissed her, not just a quick peck on the cheek. She'd all but melted into his arms and kissed him back with equal abandonment. Until that moment she'd never known kissing someone could feel so real, so right, so romantic.

They'd known each other for only two weeks and she'd been astounded at how his thoughts had been so aligned with hers. 'I just knew it would be perfect between us,' he'd whispered against her mouth when they'd finally come up for air. As though by unspoken mutual consent, from that moment onwards they'd been a couple. They'd strolled hand in hand along the beach at sunset, worked side by side at the hospital, gazed longingly into each other's eyes. She had accepted his words, his touch, his love, and she'd thought it would last forever.

Sadness crept into her soul and she started to rouse from the dream, wishing she had the chance to go back and rewrite her past. Oh, Flynn. Why? Why? She shifted, trying to shake off the tender hand on her shoulder...the one that was trying to wake her.

'Reg?' She heard his voice, more clearly now. She felt his breath fan her face and slowly her mind lifted itself from the fuzziness of that state between dreams and reality. Reggie opened her eyes and looked around, taking a moment to remember exactly where she was.

She was in the female ward, sitting in a chair by Melva's bedside. She'd obviously fallen asleep, the exhaustion of the day having finally caught up with her. A busy day at the hospital and then...and then the fire. The fire that had burned her apartment and all her belongings to the ground and had almost taken Melva's life. She looked at Flynn, realising he was crouched down beside her chair, his lips curved in a small smile.

'Hi, there.'

'Was I snoring?' she asked, and was delighted when his smile increased.

'Not that I can report. I'll have to check with Ayana, though,' he said, indicating where the night sister was seated at the nurses' station, writing up some paperwork.

Reggie looked back at Melva, pleased to see her friend sleeping soundly. The echo-cardiograph was still monitoring Melva's heart rate and from what Reggie could see, everything looked to be within normal parameters.

'She's doing well,' Flynn confirmed, and stood when Reggie eased herself out of the chair, wanting to read Melva's latest set of observations. Feeling stiff from sitting too long, Reggie stretched her arms up over her head, shifting slightly from side to side as she worked out the kinks in her back. As she lowered her arms she glanced at Flynn, surprised to find him watching her every move. She blushed and straightened the hem of her knit top, which had ridden up a little.

'Er…' She cleared her throat as she tried to focus on the information on the monitor. Come on, Reggie. Pull yourself together. It's not as though Flynn hasn't admired your body before. Good heavens, she used to go swimming with him in the sea wearing a bikini. But that had been then, when they'd been together as a couple. This was now, when he was nothing more than a colleague…and possibly a friend?

He had stated he was going to help her out and he'd held her so tenderly, so carefully, so…lovingly? She pushed the thought away and gave her thoughts a mental shake.

'All her vitals are steady,' Flynn continued. 'Her heart is strong, the burns on her arms and legs are bandaged and will eventually heal,' he continued.

'And on top of all this she now has the emotional trauma of dealing with losing her life-long possessions, reminders of her husband and family and all those trinkets she's collected over the years. She shouldn't be forced to start again, not at her age.' Reggie reached for Melva's hand and held it in hers. 'She has been such a good friend to me since I moved into the apartment block. I need to do whatever I can for her…and for the other tenants.'

'The fire wasn't your fault, Reggie,' he pointed out. 'Preliminary findings show there was a fault with the wiring.'

'Then I should have been more diligent, forcing the landlord to check these things out more thoroughly.' She pressed a kiss to Melva's hand before she turned and walked to the end of the bed. 'I feel as though I've failed her. What sort of Christmas is she supposed to have now?'

Flynn put both hands on her shoulders then turned her to face him. When she didn't immediately look at him he placed his fingers gently beneath her chin and lifted it so their gazes could meet. 'It's not your fault.' His words were earnest and intent.

'But—'

'It's not your fault.' He spoke with carefulness, as though he was desperate to get the words to sink in.

'Still, there has to have been something I could have done to prev—'

He silenced her by pressing his index finger tenderly to her lips, knowing the touch would effectively silence her. He leaned in closer, bringing his mouth closer to her ear so she could hear him when he whispered clearly, *'It's not your fault.'* Then he gathered her into his arms and held her tightly. 'You're not going to do yourself any favours by playing the what-if game, Reg.'

She closed her eyes as his message finally began to penetrate through her thick skull. 'I know you want to rewind time, to do anything you can to spare Melva the emotional upheaval she's going to go through, but you can't.' His words were barely above a whisper as she once more allowed herself to rest within his arms.

How she'd missed this. Having someone with big strong arms hold her, comfort her, support her in times of need. How she'd missed Flynn. She felt so comfortable and secure in his arms that a moment later, she yawned, a big, long yawn.

'You're exhausted,' she heard him murmur, but now that she'd mentally accepted there was nothing she could have done to alter tonight's outcome of the fire, it was as though her entire body was starting to shut down.

Plus, Flynn was making it very comfortable for her to stand there, leaning into him, knowing his big, strong arms would support her and keep her safe. At this particular moment it didn't matter one jot what had happened between them all those years ago. What mattered was that Flynn was offering comfort and she was going to be selfish and accept it.

The memories from her past, the memories she'd tried so hard to push away, to ignore, to never think about again, were returning with a vengeance as she continued to lean against him. She knew he wouldn't let her fall, that he would support her, and for a wild moment she desperately wanted to go back in time. Back to when Flynn had professed his love for her. Back to a moment when her life, for the very first time, had felt…complete.

'Go back,' she mumbled into his chest, her words incoherent.

'Reggie?' Flynn eased away just slightly to look down at her, but she only seemed to snuggle in closer. Who was he to argue? He closed his eyes, allowing himself to absorb the sensation of once again having his Reg in his arms. It was clear the attraction they'd felt for each other all those years ago was still alive and well...at least, it was on his side. Could she feel it, too?

'Reggie?' He tried again and when the only answer he received was her steady and even breathing, he realised that the day had definitely taken its toll on her. Not only had she been watching over Melva for the past few hours but she'd also answered a barrage of questions from the police, providing them with whatever information she could. Thankfully, both her other neighbours had been contacted and although they were devastated at the loss of their belongings, at least none of them had lost their lives. Therefore, he wasn't the least bit surprised at Reggie being so completely wiped out that she was literally asleep on her feet.

'Come on, Reg,' he murmured, shifting her slightly in his arms so he could guide her as they walked quietly out of the ward.

'Where are we going?' she asked, half roused. He couldn't help but smile down at the gorgeous sight of her, her short, black hair sticking out a little at the sides and her eyelids half-closed.

'You need sleep,' he replied.

'Good idea. Residential wing will have a bed free.'

'Goodnight, Ayana,' Flynn called quietly as he waved to the night nurse. 'If there's any change in Melva's condition—'

'I'll call you and Reggie immediately,' Ayana promised. 'Get her to a bed, and soon, Flynn. She really is asleep on her feet, isn't she?' Ayana smiled as Reggie continued to lean against Flynn. It would be far easier for him to scoop her into his arms and carry her through the hospital but he was already mindful of the looks they were receiving with her snuggled so closely against him. The last thing he wanted was for Reggie to have to deal with a barrage of gossip on top of everything else that had happened to her.

They headed out of the ward towards the lift, Reggie more than content to let him guide her. That way she didn't have to think about anything. She couldn't remember being this exhausted since she'd been an intern, trying to cope with the all-nighters followed by a full day shift. Perhaps the trauma of losing all her possessions, of the impending frustration and stress of dealing with the insurance company, of having to go out in the morning and buy new clothes and shoes and… She didn't even own a toothbrush. Not anymore.

'And all the Christmas presents,' she groaned, her words muffled as she spoke into Flynn's chest, another layer of stress falling on her shoulders.

'What?' Flynn bent his head so he could hear her more clearly.

'I'd finished my Christmas shopping. Now it's all gone.' She wanted to cry, she wanted to scream and bellyache and wail, but she was just too exhausted.

'We'll sort it out,' Flynn promised her as they headed out into the humid December night.

'Thank you, Flynn. You always were so reliable… except, you know, when you broke my heart.'

'You're mumbling, Reg. Can't understand a word,' he told her. 'And you're starting to trip over your own feet,' she heard him say, and the next instant she felt as light as a feather, floating along in the breeze. She looped her arms around Flynn's neck and rested her head against his shoulder, only belatedly realising he'd scooped her off her feet and was carrying her, striding purposefully towards the residential wing like the gallant hero she'd always thought him to be.

'*Flynn,*' she sighed as her head was finally placed onto a soft pillow. She had no idea just how much time had passed and could have sworn she'd been strapped into a car at one point. Perhaps Flynn had decided to drive around to the residential wing rather than carry her the entire way.

At any rate, she was simply glad to finally be in a bed, a sheet being pulled over her, the ceiling fan whirring gently above to keep her cool throughout the night. Someone was removing her shoes and once that was done she drew her knees up and snuggled into the inviting world of dreams.

'Sleep sweet, Reg.'

Flynn's glorious deep words washed over her and then she dreamed he'd placed a kiss on her forehead. 'Mmm, Flynn. I've missed you,' she whispered.

He straightened up and stared down at the woman sleeping in his spare room. She'd missed him? Really? Was that just the exhaustion talking? Did she mean 'miss' as in she'd wanted to see him again? Because from the moment he'd seen her at the hospital the impression he'd gained had definitely been the opposite, especially as she'd spent the better part of the last week avoiding him.

With her breathing settling into an even rhythm, letting him know she was definitely sound asleep, Flynn knew he should leave yet he couldn't seem to move. Watching Reggie sleep made his heart contract with pain and pleasure as his mind was flooded with a round of what-if's.

She was the woman he'd once loved with all his heart, the woman he'd planned to marry and spend the rest of his life with, the woman who had managed to show him he was a person of worth, to accept him for exactly who he was…and then everything had exploded. He'd been weak, had allowed himself to be manipulated, and it had brought him nothing but pain and mortification.

'Not anymore.' He shook his head and exhaled heavily. When he'd accepted the job at Sunshine General, he hadn't known Reggie was working there, not until a few days before his starting date, when he'd had a meeting with Geetha to fill in the remaining paperwork.

'The staff here are very friendly, especially Reggie,' Geetha had told him after they'd finished dealing with the red tape. Flynn had literally frozen at the name.

'Reggie?' It might not be the same person, he'd rationalised, astonished to find his heartbeat had increased. The name 'Reggie' might actually be referring to a man named Reginald, not a dynamic woman called Regina who had the biggest blue eyes, fringed with dark lashes and the most encompassing laugh he'd ever heard.

'Reggie Smith, she's one of our general surgeons.' Geetha had shaken her head. 'Incredibly talented, should have been head of department years ago but instead she prefers to work as a functioning member of the team, at least that's what she tells me.'

'Reggie Smith.' Flynn had settled back in his chair, his heart racing at the thought that soon he'd see Reggie again. Was that a good thing? He'd thought about her constantly over the past six years, especially when his marriage had broken up. He'd been tempted time and time again to find her, to track her down, but what would he say to her when they met again? *I'm sorry I broke your heart. Can we try again, please, because I can't seem to get you out of my mind?*

He'd also presumed she would be happily married with a couple of children, that she'd moved on with her life…her life without him. Thoughts like that had stopped him from trying to find her. Reggie deserved the world of happiness, especially after the abominable way he'd treated her, and if she'd found that happiness with some other man, he did not want to know about it.

Now, though, not only had he been granted the opportunity to see her but to also work alongside her. She wasn't married, didn't have children, and if the way she'd just whispered his name into the pillow was any indication, perhaps there was a small spark of hope. It was clear, on his part, that the attraction he'd felt all those years ago certainly hadn't diminished. The question was, could Reggie forgive him for his past behaviour? If she couldn't, there was no hope of them moving forward together.

His phone started to ring and he quickly left the room, wondering who would be calling him at this hour of the night. Another emergency? He hoped not. He didn't want to leave Reggie alone in his town house, concerned she'd wake up and not know where she was.

He checked the caller ID and saw it was Violet. He quickly answered the call. 'Hey, Vi. Everything OK?'

'It's Ian,' she told him. 'He has a temperature. I don't know what to do. You know I fall to pieces when he gets sick.'

'What are his symptoms?' Flynn walked through to the lounge and slumped down into a comfortable chair as he listened to Violet describe five-year-old Ian's symptoms. 'It does sound like it's just a tummy bug, especially as you haven't been feeling well. You've given him paracetamol?'

'No. No. Good idea. I'll do that. Hold on. Don't hang up.'

Flynn closed his eyes, feeling strange receiving a phone call from Violet while Reggie was asleep in the next room. It was as though the two different parts of his life, family and the separate life he was trying to build, were once more colliding. He'd been given a second chance with Reggie and he wasn't going to blow this one. If she knew he was still in contact with Violet, that might jeopardise everything, and the fact that she'd just been murmuring his name in her sleep was a good sign that things *were* progressing the way he was hoping.

However, he also knew he'd have to tell her about Violet…at some point. Right now, though, he was going to do his best to keep his two very different worlds as far apart as possible. He didn't want anything jeopardising the chance that he and Reggie might be able to pick up where they'd left off six years ago. Now, that certainly would be something to dream about.

Reggie opened her eyes, stretching her arms above her head. She'd had a wonderful sleep but a moment later, as her mind began to wake up, she remembered the events of yesterday evening. Her apartment had burned down.

'Melva!' She sat bolt upright in the bed, thinking fast. She'd get out of bed and go check on Melva, then start figuring out what to do next. No doubt she'd have to go shopping as the clothes on her back were literally the only clothes she had. She could borrow some from Mackenzie and…

She frowned, looking around the room, taking in her surroundings. This wasn't a tiny room in the residential wing. 'Where am I?' As she continued to inspect the room, she realised she was in Sunainah's spare room… or what had previously been Sunainah's spare room. Her friend had moved out of this town house when she'd married Elliot. The town house had been vacant since then and listed on the hospital's bulletin board. Her eyes widened as realisation dawned. 'Oh, no!'

Reggie flicked back the covers and checked the floor for her shoes, quickly slipping her feet into them as she tried to piece together what she could remember of last night's events *after* the fire.

She'd been at Melva's bedside. Sunainah, Mackenzie and Bergan had all come to find her once they'd heard the news—her friends were always there when she needed their support. Then, being the stubborn woman she was, she'd refused to leave Melva's side until her neighbour had been settled in the ward. She could remember sitting by Melva's bed…then…she'd fallen asleep. Someone had woken her up and—

'*Flynn!*'

Reggie shot to her feet and opened the spare-room door, pushing her hands through her hair as she walked through the lower part of the town house towards the kitchen—Flynn's kitchen. She was in Flynn Jamieson's town house and by the scents of coffee and pancakes wafting from the kitchen it appeared he was making breakfast.

Sure enough, she found him standing at the stove,

expertly flipping pancakes in the air and catching them in the frying pan. 'Flynn?'

'Ah.' He turned and looked at her over his shoulder, his smile bright and welcoming. 'Good morning, Reggie.' He indicated the table, which was set with plates, knives and forks, a glass of juice and a bottle of maple syrup in the middle. 'Take a seat and I'll bring you your breakfast.'

'You know how to cook now?' Still trying to wrap her head around this surreal moment, of having Flynn cook breakfast for her, she moved towards the table and dropped down into the chair, glad of its support. 'Back in the Caribbean you weren't sure how to boil water.'

He grinned at her. 'I wasn't *that* bad but, yes, during my time there I realised a lot of things about myself and how I needed to become more self-sufficient.' He checked the pancake again. 'Almost done.'

'You always were full of surprises,' Reggie murmured, her tone indicating that some of those 'surprises' hadn't always been good ones.

Flynn's answer was to wink at her, and her insides instantly flooded with a tingling warmth. Why, oh, why couldn't she be immune to his charm? She immediately looked away from him and stared at the empty plate in front of her, trying to get her thought processes jump-started.

'I've called the hospital,' Flynn said a moment later, 'and been informed that Melva has slept peacefully throughout the night and was sitting up, drinking a cup of tea.'

Reggie lifted her head and sighed with relief. 'That's great news. Thanks for the update.'

'You're welcome. Coffee?'

'Uh…most definitely, please.' She frowned as she watched him pour her a cup of coffee, not adding any milk or sugar before placing it on the table before her.

'You still take it black, right? No sugar?'

'Correct.'

'That's because you're sweet enough.' He smiled brightly. 'Isn't that what you always used to say?'

'Flynn, stop it.'

'Stop what?'

'Trying to take us down memory lane.' She spread her arms wide. 'What are you doing here?'

He stared at her as though she'd gone completely loopy. 'Did you hit your head last night? Are you feeling all right?'

'Flynn,' she growled, her teeth gritted, her tone filled with warning. He had the audacity to laugh.

'Reg, I'm not exactly sure what you mean.'

'Here. In *this* particular town house.'

'It was listed on the bulletin—'

'I know. I know it was listed but why did *you*, of all people, have to move in?'

'I don't follow.'

'Sunainah used to live here and Richard lived here before her and before that Richard's parents and before that…I don't have a clue, but the point is, you're living slap bang in the middle of my three closest friends.'

'And the problem with that is…?' he asked, carrying the frying pan towards her and placing a perfectly round, perfectly cooked pancake onto her plate.

'Thank you,' she said politely. 'It's just odd that *you*, the man I was once going to marry, is living *here*. Among my friends. In the town house they wanted me to move into. Joining the cul-de-sac crew.'

'There's a crew?' His eyes were alive with delight at this news. 'Do they get together for movie nights and dinners?'

'Flynn, be serious.'

'I am. Do you know how much I've always wanted to be accepted as just part of a crew, part of a team?'

That stopped her. 'You have?' She was surprised at his words and stared at him for a moment, realising there was still so much she didn't know about him.

'Anyway, you were saying your friends wanted you to move in here?'

'Yes, but I was more than happy where I…was.' Reggie sighed as the weight of the previous evening's events fell on her shoulders like a tonne of bricks. She slumped forward and buried her head in her hands, not even the delicious scent of the pancakes able to help in this situation.

Flynn put the frying pan back on the stove top, adding more mixture before coming over, placing his hands on her shoulders and gently starting to massage them. 'I'm sorry your place burnt down, Reg.' His words were simple, effective, perfect.

'So am I,' she said, leaning back a little to grant him more access to her neck, her eyes closing at the touch of his hands. How did he still manage to know exactly what she needed? Straightforward words and a bit of support. No flowery sentiments, no immediate solutions to problems. Just support. That was all she needed at this moment and he was offering it in a caring and gentle manner.

'You still have magic hands,' she sighed after a few minutes. 'And thank you for the pancakes. They're my favourite.'

'I remember.'

'They do make me happy, Flynn, I just can't…'

'You can't show it the way you usually do. The ever optimistic, happy and bubbly Reggie. I get it.'

'Get what?'

'With me, everything's different. You think there's too much water under the bridge between us. That it would be impossible for things to move forward between us.' He nodded. 'I understand.'

'Do you?' Did he really understand just how much he'd hurt her all those years ago?

'I might even be so bold as to declare that I understand *you*, Reggie.'

She laughed without humour. 'I've changed.' She shifted a little in her chair, acutely aware of the way he was making her feel with his hands on her shoulders, massaging gently. The air between them seemed to be charged with unspoken conversations, things they should have said but hadn't…things they shouldn't have said but had.

'Everyone changes, Reg, but hopefully not in essentials,' he offered, releasing her shoulders. 'I think you're still the same Reggie, wanting to help others, smiling, laughing, spreading sunshine wherever possible. I watched you do that when we were together in Sint Maarten, amazed and in awe of your ability and—' He dropped his hands and quickly pulled out the chair next to her and sat down, facing her, his expression determined. 'I'd like to help, Reggie. I'd like to take a leaf out of your book and spread a little sunshine.'

'Wha—? Flynn?' She closed her eyes and shook her head for a moment. 'I don't understand.'

'I want to help you and your friends. I can help by

relocating Melva and your other neighbours.' His words were intense and earnest. 'And…' he held up a hand '…before you say I'm doing what all wealthy people do and throwing money at the problem, I want you to know that's not entirely true. My intentions are pure and honourable. Even if these people weren't your friends, even if they were complete strangers, if I'd heard about their hardship, I would still have wanted to help.'

Reggie thought on his words for a moment, seeing the truth in his eyes. He seemed so completely animated at the idea, his eyes twinkling with anticipatory delight. She wished he wouldn't look at her that way because right now he was far too handsome for his own good and that simply made it all the more difficult for her to keep her distance. Besides, who was she to stop him from helping others? 'I think that would be a nice thing to do, Flynn. Thank you.'

'So you'll accept my help?'

'Yes. I think my neighbours and I would be very grateful for your help, especially if you can help with relocation. Trying to find a new place to live this close to Christmas? It really *would* take a Christmas miracle to pull it off.'

'Then be prepared for a miracle.' He stood and returned to the stove, expertly flipping the pancake. 'Because I already have a plan with regard to temporary accommodation for you and your neighbours.'

'You do?'

'Yes. I've had a look online and there's a small apartment complex, near shops and public transport, with three partially furnished vacant apartments.'

'Three?'

'Yes. One for Melva, once she's ready to leave hospital, and the other two for your other neighbours.'

'What about me?' she asked, her tone a little indignant.

'Ah. Now, for you I have the perfect place. It's not going to be too far from Melva and the others, it's close to the hospital, it's furnished and the landlord has said you can move in today.'

'Today? It sounds like a miracle. Where is this place?'

Flynn winked at her and spread his arms wide. 'It's here. You're going to live with me!'

CHAPTER FOUR

'What?'

Reggie stared at him as though he'd grown another head but Flynn either didn't notice or didn't care. '*Live...* with you?' Her heart was pounding wildly in her chest at the mere thought of living with Flynn, of sharing the same intimate space as him, of seeing him last thing at night and first thing in the morning. She was glad she was sitting down as her entire body had turned into a trembling mass of jelly.

'Why not? It makes perfect sense. I have a spare room and you'll have sole use of the bathroom. I can use the *en suite* and we work at the same hospital.' He shrugged one shoulder. 'It makes perfect sense.'

'And you're sure this other place you've found only has three free apartments?'

He smiled and nodded as though humouring an indulgent child. 'Yes, Reg.'

Could he hear the hysteria in her voice, see the panic in her eyes? She was positive he could from the way he was still trying to sell her on the idea. 'So what do you say, new roomie? Let's start the day with a healthy...' he stopped and looked down at the pancakes '...or sort of healthy breakfast.'

Reggie continued to gape at him, her mouth hanging open as he plated up his pancake and carried it to the table. Before he sat down, he removed bowls of fresh strawberries and whipped cream from the fridge, placing them on the table next to the maple syrup. As far as he was concerned, this was a done deal. She had no say in it and anger started to replace her earlier incredulity.

'I am not moving in here.' She enunciated each word crisply.

He considered her words for a moment then asked logically, 'So where will you go?' He added strawberries, cream and syrup to his pancake, behaving as though this was just another ordinary breakfast conversation.

'I'll go to a hotel for a while.'

'And waste your money when there's a perfectly good room—free of charge—here for you? Until the insurance money comes in, you're better off using your funds to buy clothes and shampoo and other essentials you'll need, rather than having to pay for accommodation.' His words were matter-of-fact and logical and she hated him for them.

She sighed again, her frustration clear. Didn't he realise that with what had happened between them, with the way he'd taken her to the highest of highs when he'd confessed his love and proposed to her then plummeted her to the lowest of lows less than twenty-four hours later when he'd broken her heart by cancelling their engagement, that there was no way she could move in with him?

'Mmm, smells good.' He pointed to her plate. 'Come on, Reg. Eat up. We're due at the hospital in an hour's time.'

'What?' She blinked at him in astonishment. 'You're not even going to suggest I take the day off? That given the circumstances of my recent emotional trauma, of losing practically everything I own, except for my laptop, my phone and the clothes on my back, I shouldn't stay in bed and rest?'

'I know you, remember.' He leaned over and spooned some strawberries onto her pancake. 'Regardless of what may or may not be happening in your life, the last thing you would ever do is let your patients down. You're not about to cancel a fully booked outpatient clinic because of personal reasons. You and I both know that being with your patients, helping them out and making their lives just that little bit easier, is going to be the best medicine to take your mind off things…at least, for a little while.'

She frowned at him. He did know her, at least on some levels. On other levels…she'd kept a lot hidden from him, previously rationalising that they had a lifetime together to discover all there was to know about each other.

'True. Working will help me to process everything that's happened,' she rationalised, including Flynn's offer for her to stay with him. 'Working will keep my mind focused.' She would go to work, see her patients, help people out, spread a little sunshine, as Flynn had termed it, and then, she was sure, life would seem a little clearer. At least, so she hoped. She looked down at her pancakes and breathed in appreciatively. 'These do smell good.'

'They taste good, too.' He ate another mouthful and winked at her, the action causing Reggie's insides to start fluttering. Why was it that one simple look from him, whether it was a wink or a smile or one of his long stares across a crowded room, made her feel so... special, so unique, so feminine? Flynn had always had been able to turn her insides to mush, to make her want to fan her face because her cheeks were tinged with heat from excited embarrassment. Now was no exception and it was far easier to concentrate on eating than trying to avoid his hypnotic gaze.

She really had no intention of permanently staying here with him because even the thought of living under the same roof as Flynn set her entire body on fire. The man was too dangerous at the best of times but to be around him both at work and at home, no doubt dreaming about him whilst she slept, would make it nigh on impossible for her to keep her emotions in check.

Still, his offer did solve her immediate problem so for the moment she would just let everything roll. She would have breakfast and a shower, mentally and figuratively washing the grime of yesterday away before popping over to Mackenzie's to borrow some clean clothes. She was glad he'd mentioned that he'd use the en suite because even thinking about standing naked beneath Flynn's shower, with him in the same house, made her feel all flushed with self-consciousness. Perhaps it would be better to just go to Mackenzie's and shower there.

After eating half of her pancake and enjoying her coffee, she was about to tell him of her plans when he beat her to it.

'I need to dash to the shops before we head to the hospital so why don't you make free use of the place? Wash away all the bad things that happened yesterday and reconnect with your usual optimistic self?' He smiled encouragingly as he said the words. 'Oh, and I contacted Mackenzie last night and she's brought over some clothes for you. They're in the drawers and the cupboard in the spare room—or *your* room as it now is.'

'You…contacted Macken—' She stopped and shook her head, unable to believe how thoughtful he'd been. 'It would have been very late.'

'Your friends love you, Reg.' He spoke softly and with sincerity. 'They don't care what time of day or night it is, they're there for you. That type of friendship is rare and incredibly special.' He looked down at his plate for a moment before meeting her gaze once more. 'Only a fool would throw away such a thing.'

His words were slightly pointed and she wondered whether he was calling himself a fool. Was he admitting that he'd made a mistake all those years ago? Was he saying he wanted to reinstate himself into her friendship circle? Was he a friend who…loved her?

Reggie found it difficult to look away. There, seated opposite her, was the man who had always been in perfect control. He'd been immaculately groomed and dressed from the first day they'd met in Sint Maarten. Being raised in a wealthy, controlled environment where most decisions had been pre-set for him had been something he hadn't even thought of rebelling against until he'd met her. He'd told her she'd liberated him, shown him a different side to life, and that his love was hers forever. And she'd stupidly believed him. She should be wary not to make the same mistakes twice.

She tried to swallow but found her throat exceedingly dry. Reaching for her orange juice, she was surprised to find her hand trembling a little. Still, drinking the cool, refreshing liquid helped to break the intense moment.

'Had enough?' he asked, pointing to her plate and breaking the moment. She nodded quickly, not trusting her voice to work. Flynn stood and quickly cleared the table. She watched him for a few minutes as he moved comfortably around the kitchen. He had such swift and defined movements, those broad shoulders of his looking firm and in control, the material from his crisp, white shirt pulling tautly across his triceps.

Reggie breathed out slowly, her gaze hungrily taking in every nuance of the man. She swallowed and cleared her throat, and when he looked her way, she realised she quickly looked away. 'Er…' She racked her sluggish mind for something to say. 'Breakfast was delicious. Whoever taught you to cook did a good job.'

'That would have been my cooking teacher at the community centre.' His tone dipped a little as he spoke, his eyebrows raised in silent question, his eyes letting her know he'd been well aware of her visual caresses.

Reggie frowned and looked away. 'Not your wife?'

'My ex-wife,' he replied pointedly, then shook his head. 'She had no idea how to cook either. One of my patients put me onto the class and the next thing I knew I was learning how to make a beef Wellington.'

'You can do a beef Wellington? I can't even do that.'

He grinned. 'Then I shall have to make you one.' He gave the countertops a final wipe. 'Perhaps there are quite a few things you don't realise about me.' Like how he was determined to show her he'd changed, that he was willing to make amends for the way he'd treated her all those years ago, like how he was almost desperate for her forgiveness.

'Perhaps,' she said, surprised at the huskiness in her voice. What was it about this man that set her alight so instantly? They'd met, they'd worked together, they'd tried to fight the natural attraction that had sprung up between them but had failed. Flynn had confessed that perhaps it was a good thing, perhaps the mutual chemistry they felt for each other was one of those rare gifts that shouldn't be ignored, so they hadn't bothered to try ignoring it at all and thus had begun the happiest, most wonderful weeks of Reggie's life. Flynn holding her. Flynn laughing with her. Flynn kissing her.

Six weeks. They'd known each other for just six weeks. Friendly colleagues for two weeks, dating for two more and then falling in love for two blissful weeks. So fast, so quick, so incredibly perfect.

As he stared back at her from the other side of the kitchen, she really felt powerless to look away, as though the past and the present were colliding and both of them could sense it. When her cellphone rang, she almost jumped out of her skin. Flynn chuckled before reaching across to the bench where he'd obviously put it last night. He'd even plugged it in to recharge the battery. How thoughtful. She frowned for a moment. Had he been this thoughtful six years ago?

'Mackenzie,' he remarked, looking at the picture of her friend that had come up on the display.

'Oh...uh...thanks.' Reggie rose from her chair and accepted the phone, taking it into the spare room so she could have some privacy. 'Mackenzie?'

'How are you doing this morning?'

'I'm at Flynn's place!' She leaned back against the door, ensuring it was closed. 'I must have been so tired he brought me home with him and put me to bed!' Her words were half whispered, half squeaked as she spoke at the speed of light.

'I know.' Mackenzie chuckled.

'Oh, of course you do. You came over and helped him by delivering some clothes! Why didn't you wake me up?'

'Not on your life, Reggie. You needed sleep.' Mackenzie said in her best motherly voice. 'Flynn sent me, Bergan and Sunainah a text message telling us you were staying with him. I think it's a great idea.'

'But he doesn't just want me to stay for last night, he wants me to *move in with him*.'

'I know.'

'Do you know everything? Does everyone else know what's going on in my life except me?'

'It's not like that, Reggie.'

'And I'll bet you all think this is a good idea? Are you insane? This is *Flynn* we're talking about. The man who broke my heart into tiny little pieces and scattered them to the wind.'

'I remember.'

'I cried on your shoulder, I ate too much ice cream, I went over and over everything he'd ever said to me, trying to figure out what I'd done wrong to chase him away.'

'I remember.'

'I talked about him ad nauseam, I drove you insane. I told you time and time again that I was over him but I was just kidding myself and then, when I finally *did* get over him and moved on with my life, he swaggers back in and *takes over*.'

'He's not taking over. He's only trying to be nice and helpful, especially as since it's Christmas the majority of hotels are already booked up. Add to that the fact that Bergan doesn't have room because Richard's parents are coming home for Christmas, Sunainah's place is full because she married into a ready-made family and I have one of John's sisters and her family arriving the day after tomorrow.'

Reggie slid down the door, crumpling into a heap on the carpet, realising the truth of what Mackenzie was saying. 'I'd forgotten all that.'

'Not surprising. Look, honey, I'm not trying to make light of you losing everything in the fire, it's completely devastating and it will take a while for you to process things, both with the mounds of insurance paperwork and on an emotional level, but staying at Flynn's keeps you close to us, to *your* family, and right now you need to be surrounded by family. We're all here for you and we'll do whatever we can to help—and so will Flynn,' she added. 'He's a good guy, Reggie, and no matter what happened between the two of you all those years ago, you know, deep down inside, that it's true.'

'It's not a question of whether he's good or not, Mackenzie, it's a question of whether or not I can resist him,' Reggie blurted.

'Oh.' Mackenzie said the word slowly as though realisation was just dawning. 'Ah. Yes. I hadn't thought of things from that angle, just the logistics of your present predicament.'

'Well, start thinking that way. I can't stay here with Flynn. I can't stop staring at him, remembering how it felt to be held by him, to be kissed by him, to be in love with him.' She closed her eyes, the pain from her past beginning to return. 'He hurt me, Mackenzie, and, yes, it's all in the past, but what if I allow myself to get close to him and he hurts me *again*?'

'What if he doesn't? Reggie, the one thing I remember you telling me a few years after you'd broken up was that you thought Flynn had never really opened up to you, that the attraction between you two had happened so fast—'

'And the break-up even faster,' Reggie put in.

'That at times you wondered if you ever really knew him. Plus,' Mackenzie continued before Reggie could say another word, 'there was also a lot about your past that you never told him.'

Reggie opened her eyes and looked at the blank mushroom-coloured wall opposite her. 'True.'

'Maybe this is the chance to rectify that.'

'What point is there in opening up to him now? Rehashing the wounds of my past?'

'Call it finishing unfinished business. You always wondered how Flynn would react once he learned who you really were. Now is your chance. Who knows? It might be cathartic. Once he knows the truth of your past, if he reacts the way you always thought he would—'

'By rejecting me, like everyone else from that world,' she interrupted again.

'Then it might help you get him out of your system once and for all. Then you can really move forward with your life.'

'I have moved forward,' Reggie declared, not wanting to open the box she'd hidden in the back of her mind, the one she'd marked 'Do Not Open'. 'I've changed a lot. I'm happier than I used to be. I've put myself out there. I've dated other men and—'

'And secretly used Flynn as your yardstick the entire time. No man was ever good enough. Or, on the flip side, you'd end up solving your date's problems and helping them get back together with their old girlfriends.' It was Mackenzie's turn to interrupt. 'Think about it, Reggie. You and Flynn have unfinished business. Talk to him. You might be surprised at what you discover.'

Reggie pondered Mackenzie's words for a moment, realising there was a hint of common sense in them. 'I didn't know he could cook and those pancakes were delicious.'

'There you go, then. Plus, if you think about it, with the way Christmas tends to get hectic in surgical theatres, you'll probably be spending most of your time at the hospital, rather than catching up on sleep at Flynn's place.'

'It does get busy.'

'Then after Christmas you'll have plenty of time to look around and find somewhere to live that suits your needs, and once the insurance money comes in, I'll gladly volunteer to go furniture shopping with you.'

'Yeah.' Reggie sat up a little straighter, her confidence beginning to return. 'I don't need to stay here forever, just the next few weeks.' She thought it through rationally. 'And I do spend a lot of time at the hospital over Christmas. I really wouldn't be here all that much.'

'See?'

'And it was very nice of him to offer.'

'He's a nice man and, if you let yourself admit it, I think you'll see he's also a good friend.'

'Friend?' She tilted her head to the side and considered the word. 'I guess I've never really thought about Flynn that way, as a friend. It was so powerful and intense between us we didn't really have the opportunity to truly become friends.'

'So you'll stay?'

'You know…' Reggie levered herself up off the floor '…I think I will.'

'Yay! A temporary member of the cul-de-sac crew.'

Reggie laughed at Mackenzie's words, feeling a return of her usual optimistic self. 'I can already hear your thoughts, Kenz. Dinner parties, games nights and Christmas parties.'

'You know me too well, Reggie.' Mackenzie laughed along with her friend. 'Feel better?'

'I do. I really do, which, given I've lost practically everything, is not a bad feeling to be having.'

'Good. Oh. I've gotta go. Ruthie's just woken up.'

'Right-oh. I'll talk to you later.'

'You know it, cul-de-sac crew member!'

Reggie was still smiling as she entered the bathroom, finding a set of towels waiting there for her along with a fresh bar of soap. 'How thoughtful.' And he really was, she realised. Taking care of her last night, making her breakfast this morning and offering to help relocate her neighbours. 'Friends,' she repeated to herself as she stepped beneath the soothing spray of the shower. 'I can be friends with Flynn.' She was proud of the conviction in her words.

By the time he returned from wherever he'd had to go, Reggie was showered and dressed in the borrowed clothes.

'Wow.' Flynn's eyebrows shot up as he saw her standing there dressed in a navy skirt, white shirt and navy jacket. Her short feathered black hair was still drying and her face was clear and fresh and devoid of make-up…and she looked incredibly beautiful. 'You look—'

'Like Mackenzie?' Reggie shook her head and looked

down at the demure clothes in disgust. 'No colour. No vibrance. No pizazz.' She snapped her fingers as she spoke, which only made Flynn laugh as he carried the shopping bags through to the kitchen. He dumped them on the table before turning to look at her once more.

'I mean, I love her and everything and I really do appreciate the loan of the clothes but we have absolutely nothing in common as far as how we dress,' she continued as she followed him.

'It's true that you prefer to wear bright colours, sometimes even mixing and matching different print materials that ordinarily should *never* go together but somehow look completely perfect on you.'

Perfect? She brushed the thought aside. 'You're a textile expert, eh? Now, *that* I definitely didn't know. Please, continue, oh, wise fashionista.'

Flynn's eyes flashed with repressed humour and, while keeping a straight face, he slowly walked around her, murmuring and nodding as though deep in thought. 'Yes. Yes. I can see what you mean. It *is* rather conservative for the likes of Ms Regina Smith, General Surgeon Extraordinaire, but I think I can solve the dilemma quite easily.'

'You can?' She couldn't help the way she felt so incredibly self-conscious with him walking around her, looking her up and down, and although she knew they were only pretending, somehow his visual inspection had become more of an intimate caress. She fought against the sensation, determined not to spoil this lighthearted moment. They'd always been able to joke together, to tease each other in a good-natured way, and now that it was happening again she started to realise just how much she'd missed him.

'Oh, yes, indeedy I can.' He crossed to the bags he'd placed on the table and reached inside, pulling out a small white box. He held it out to her.

'What's this?' she asked.

'Open it.'

Dropping all pretence, Reggie accepted the gift box with surprise. It wasn't tied or secured in any way and after she gently eased the lid off she saw white tissue paper. She glanced at Flynn, who only nodded with encouragement. She moved the folded tissue paper aside to reveal a bright and beautiful Christmas-patterned silk scarf.

'Oh!' She stared at it in astonishment for a moment before carefully pulling it from the box. Flynn instantly took the box from her hands as she ran the silken threads through her fingers. 'Flynn. It's...' she met his gaze '...lovely.' To her astonishment, she felt tears begin to gather behind her eyes and she quickly looked away, desperate to pull herself together and gain some sort of control over her emotions. Always difficult when Flynn was so close.

'I thought you might need a bit of colour in your life, particularly this morning, and I couldn't go past the bright Christmas theme.'

'It's perfect. Thank you.' Reggie continued to sift the scarf through her fingers as she tried to ignore the lump in her throat. Then, out of nowhere, logical thought seemed to click in and she looked at him, angling her head to the side, a slight frown marring her brow. 'Wait a moment. It's not even eight o'clock in the morning. How did you manage to buy this when the shops aren't even open?'

Flynn shrugged. 'I know a guy.'

'Of course you do.' Reggie shook her head, remembering how easily things came to wealthy people. It annoyed her that the knowledge put a dampener on what was yet another thoughtful gesture from Flynn. He'd gone out of his way to do something nice for her and she shouldn't care about the logistics. Deciding to ignore it, she tied the scarf around her neck, the bright reds and greens instantly bringing more colour to her outfit.

'Definitely perfect.' Flynn stepped forward and fixed the back of her collar before bringing his fingers to his lips and blowing a kiss into the air. 'Very festive. The fashionista has done it again.' He raised one arm in the air with a flourish.

Reggie's previous annoyance instantly fled in light of his antics and she laughed. She'd always believed that if a person didn't want to be in a bad mood, they could simply decide not to be, that they had the power over their own emotions to change the way they were feeling, and that was exactly what she was going to do right now. She wasn't going to dwell on the fact that Flynn came from money, that he'd lived a pampered life, that his family's wealth had been one of the reasons for him breaking their engagement.

No. She was going to step forth into her new life. The life where she was Flynn's housemate for the next few weeks. The life where she had the opportunity to buy new things, to start afresh. The life where that fresh new start might even include Flynn.

CHAPTER FIVE

REGGIE TOLD HERSELF she didn't feel self-conscious driving to work with her new housemate, that she didn't care if people saw them pull into the doctors' car park together or that they walked side by side into the hospital and onto the ward for the early morning round. She and Flynn were friends and colleagues and it wasn't uncommon for friends and colleagues to carpool. So many people working here did it. Being with Flynn, constantly, was nothing to be remarked on.

'Whoa, Reggie,' Ingrid, the general surgical registrar, commented quietly as they waited in the nurses' station for the rest of the ward-round participants to arrive. 'Did I just see you arriving at work with Dr Gorgeous Legs?'

Reggie couldn't help but grin widely at the nickname. 'Dr Gorgeous Legs?' she asked with a hint of incredulity.

'Sure. Nice long legs that lead up to a firm torso and a perfectly handsome face.' Ingrid eyed Flynn as she spoke.

'You're almost licking your lips.'

'Who could blame me?' Ingrid sighed then looked

pointedly at Reggie. 'So give. How did you score a lift with him?'

'My car's still being fixed at the garage, you know, after those joyriders smashed into it the other week.' She shook her head innocently, hoping to change the subject. 'There it was. Legally parked on the side of the road while I did my grocery shopping and, wham—the next minute it was destroyed as they smashed fair into it. Still, at least it can be repaired. After the fire and all last night, the last thing I would have wanted was to have to buy a new c—'

'Yes, yes. I'm sorry about your car and your apartment.' Ingrid impatiently waved her words away. 'That doesn't explain how Gorgeous Legs gave you a lift.'

'Oh. That's easy. Flynn and I are old friends.' Reggie said the words as matter-of-factly as possible, picking up a pen and pretending to study that day's ward-round sheet with great interest. Ingrid wasn't being sidetracked or fooled by Reggie's faked nonchalance.

Ingrid's eye brows almost hit her hairline. 'Really?' There was an insinuation in Ingrid's very interested tone and Reggie was sorely tempted to spin her a yarn, to say that they were actually a long-lost brother and sister, separated at birth. Or that Flynn had saved her life by donating a kidney. Flippant and funny. Anything to hide her true self behind a mask of bright happiness, but as she looked over to where Flynn was chatting with a heavily pregnant Geetha, who was doing her final ward round before handing over her patients to Flynn, Reggie realised that he deserved better.

'We worked together during our final year of general surgical training.'

'Oh.' Ingrid was clearly disappointed with her answer and as Geetha was calling the ward round to order, there was no time for the registrar to say anything else. Throughout the round Reggie frequently found herself standing beside Flynn, remembering past ward rounds they'd conducted together in that small Caribbean hospital.

'Do you remember the first time we did a ward round together?' he asked her as they walked towards the cafeteria to grab a quick coffee before their clinic started.

Reggie smiled. 'You were dressed in a three-piece suit.'

'You wore a bright yellow sundress.'

'We were working in the Caribbean, Flynn. It's hot there.'

'It was practically see-through, Reg. Gave my heart a mighty big flutter.'

She grinned at his words, hearing the teasing note. 'Really?'

'I'd been working in the UK, where it had been freezing cold and raining, before catching my flight. I literally got off the plane in the Caribbean, raced to the hospital and arrived three minutes before the ward round started. You were the first person I saw and you were…a vision of loveliness.'

'Oh.' She could feel her cheeks beginning to suffuse with colour at his sweet words.

'For a moment I thought I was hallucinating.'

'Really? You looked very uncomfortable.' She laughed nervously, trying to disguise the fact that his words had affected her. He'd really been that instantly attracted to her? She couldn't remember him telling her that. She gazed up at him, their eyes locking, silently communicating. The moment between them was start-

ing to stretch, starting to change, starting to become
more intense than she was ready for. She needed to
lighten the mood somehow.

'I was.'

'But you were determined not to show it.'

'I was exceedingly stubborn back then.'

'Yes. Yes, you were.' As they stood in the cafeteria
line, she smiled up at him. 'And very stiff and rigid.'
She picked up his arm and gave it a shake. 'You're much
more loosey-goosey now.'

'Loosey-goosey?' Flynn chuckled as he reached out
with his free hand and straightened the bright Christmas
scarf around her neck. He exhaled slowly as Reggie released his arm, their fingers brushing lightly, almost ca-
ressing. The smile started to disappear from his mouth
as he continued to gently tug and pull the scarf, smoothing it with his fingers.

'All fixed, Mr Fashionista?'

It was the sound of her voice, a little softer, a little
huskier than normal, that made him shift his gaze to en-
compass her. 'Yes,' he replied softly. 'Perfect. As usual.'

'Perfect?' There was that word again and Reggie
cleared her throat, desperate to try and keep their previous light-hearted banter in her words.

'As usual,' he repeated, his intense gaze penetrating
deeply into her soul.

'You thought I was perfect?' The words were barely
a whisper and for a moment she wasn't even sure she'd
spoken until he nodded, the movement small but definite.

'Always.'

'Oh.'

'Are you two moving forward in the line or do you

mind if I cut in front of you?' the impatient male nurse said from behind them.

'Er…' Reggie blinked, looking away from Flynn, unable to believe she'd been standing in the busy hospital cafeteria line just staring at him. Her only saving grace was that he'd been staring back at her. Flynn stepped aside and gestured for the nurse to precede them.

'We're not in as much of a rush as you. Please,' he offered politely. The nurse rolled his eyes before walking between them and advancing before them in the line.

'You really are more…I don't know.' Reggie shrugged her shoulders and gave him a quirky smile. 'Relaxed, I guess, is the best word to describe you.'

'Plus, I'm not wearing a three-piece suit.'

'True,' she said, indicating his navy trousers, white shirt and tie, which had a parachuting Santa Claus on it. 'Very loosey-goosey.'

'And…' he remarked, picking up the end of his tie and pressing it.

A moment later Reggie heard 'Jingle Bells' playing in an electronic, tinny way. It lasted for a whole ten seconds and she couldn't help but giggle.

'Your tie plays "Jingle Bells"?' She was amused but also pleasantly surprised. When they'd first met all those years ago he would never have worn anything like this.

'Yes.'

'Your tie plays "Jingle Bells" and you're only showing me this *now*.'

Flynn grinned widely as they edged forward in the line. 'I knew if I'd shown you before ward round you would have wanted to play it for every patient and ward round would have taken way too long.'

'That's exactly what I would have wanted to do.' She pushed a hand through her hair and shook her head in stunned amazement.

'I know you, Reggie.'

'So you keep reminding me.'

As she said the words she felt the smile begin to slip because there was still so much he *didn't* know. How would Flynn react when he found out about her past, about what had happened to her, what she'd lived through? She'd managed to hide it from him before but would it make any difference now to their burgeoning relationship?

After the way they'd just openly stared at each other, it was clear the attraction was alive and well and yet she had no real idea what she felt for him, apart from enjoying his company, and right at this moment she wasn't sure she was ready for that to end. Flynn made her feel special and pretty and feminine and no other man had ever been able to achieve all three...and most certainly not with a simple lift of an eyebrow.

They ordered their coffees, Flynn paying for them before she could pull her money from her pocket, and after thanking him, something she seemed to be doing a lot of lately, they headed to Outpatients.

'Now you're both late?' Clara said as they walked in together. She pointed to the different piles of case notes waiting for them both. They grinned at the outpatient clerk. 'One day I'd love it if clinic could actually start on time,' Clara said pointedly.

'We'll try and make it a Christmas miracle,' Reggie promised as she scooped up the notes, ensuring she didn't spill her coffee in the process.

'I'll believe it when I see it,' Clara joked, smiling and shaking her head in bemusement.

Today Reggie was in no hurry to avoid Flynn. Instead, she was delighted every time they met in the corridor or headed out to call in a patient at the same time. It was as they were almost finished with clinic that she received a call from Bergan in Accident and Emergency.

'Reggie? I need you.'

'OK. Can you give me fifteen minutes or—?'

'Now,' Bergan interrupted, and before she rang off she added as an afterthought, 'And bring Flynn. I need him, too.'

'OK.' Reggie hung up and headed out into the corridor. Instead of calling in her last patient, she knocked on Flynn's consulting-room door. They'd have to leave it to Ingrid to finish up with the clinic list but, thankfully, there were only two or three patients left to go.

'Yes?' he called, and when she entered it was to find him and one of the clinic nurses helping their elderly female patient to her feet, the nurse ensuring the woman's walking frame was stable. 'Ah, Dr Smith. Good timing. Could you hold the door for Mrs Baladucci, please?'

'Certainly.' Reggie held the door as the nurse and Mrs Baladucci exited the consulting room, then she turned to face Flynn, who was quickly writing up the case notes before closing them and adding them to the 'completed' pile.

'Let me guess. Emergency?' Flynn asked.

'How did you know?' She stared at him for a moment before shaking her head in astonishment.

'You have a…certain look in your eyes and around the corners of your mouth whenever there's an unknown medical problem.'

'I do?' Reggie touched her fingers to the corners of her mouth, feeling a little self-conscious.

'I know you.'

'Oh, will you stop saying that? Please?' She spread her arms wide. 'There's actually quite a lot you don't know about me, Flynn. Yes, you knew me six years ago and, yes, we were very close and, no, I may not have changed in essentials, but will you stop constantly pointing out that you know me because, in reality, you don't.' The words tumbled out of her mouth before she could stop them.

Flynn stared at her in surprise. 'I didn't realise it upset you so much.'

'Well, it does.' Reggie gritted her teeth for a moment. 'I don't know what you want from me, Flynn. I don't know if the offer to help relocate my neighbours or having me stay at your place comes with any sort of strings attached but I just can't deal with too much more right now.'

'There are no strings attached,' he said quickly. 'And what I want from you, Reg, is quite simple.' He stood and looked her directly in the eyes. 'I want your forgiveness.'

'Forgi—' She stopped, too stunned to speak. She couldn't remember anyone ever asking her for her forgiveness before, especially someone who had hurt her so badly.

'So…we're needed in A and E?' he asked, breaking the moment and tidying the desk.

'Y-yes.' Reggie blinked, working hard to compartmentalise her thoughts. Flynn wanted her forgiveness. Bergan needed her in A and E. Patients. Trauma. Expertise. That's what she needed to focus on right now and, dragging in a breath, she pushed her personal thoughts aside. 'Retrieval team.'

'I'm part of the retrieval team? I don't remember—'

'Bergan said she needed you.' Reggie threw her arms in the air in complete exasperation. 'That's all I know.' Then she turned and headed out, wanting to get down to A and E as soon as possible so she could concentrate on something other than the way Flynn was constantly spinning her first one way then the other. She wished he'd stop because the motion was starting to make her feel ill.

In A and E, several of the retrieval team had already changed into the blue and yellow jumpsuits that stated they were part of the medical team at Sunshine General. Reggie headed over to where Bergan was gathering everyone together in the nurses' station, feeling rather than knowing that Flynn was directly behind her.

She tried hard to switch off her awareness of him and focus on whatever Bergan had called them down to assist with. Professional. She needed to be professional. After all, she'd worked alongside Flynn before; in fact, they'd worked exceptionally well together in the Caribbean…and that had been part of the problem. Too good, too close, too quickly.

Bergan cleared her throat and everyone around fell silent, waiting for her to speak. 'The key players are here. We're just waiting for Mackenzie but she's just getting out of Theatre so we'll begin without her.' Bergan pointed to the computer monitor, which was revealing a picture of the main beach in Maroochydore. 'We've had a report from the surf lifeguards that a shark has been sighted on the beach. They've closed the area but have just spotted a person, out to sea, floating. One male, approximately in late fifties to sixties. They're sending out a boat now and request immediate assistance.'

She turned to Flynn and Reggie. 'You two, go in the chopper. You both have the relevant experience when it comes to shark attacks, having treated and operated on victims before. I want you at the scene, stat. The instant they have that body out of the water, you need to be standing by.'

'Is there just the one victim?' Reggie asked, her mind going through the different injury scenarios they might be facing.

'That's the report at this time. Go and change. Get to that chopper.' With that, Bergan turned her gaze to the rest of the team. 'Everyone else, listen for your posts.'

'Change rooms are this way,' Reggie said, before Flynn could ask. They walked quickly along the corridor, down the side of A and E towards the changing rooms. 'Retrieval suits will be just inside the door. Once you're changed, we'll meet back in the corridor, grab the retrieval gear and head up to the chopper.'

'I guess all that experience in the Caribbean has come in handy. I hope I can remember what we need to do,' Flynn remarked as they hurried along. 'I've been working very much inland for the past few years.'

Reggie smiled at him reassuringly as they reached the changing room doors. 'You'll be fine and if you forget, just ask me.'

'I'll do that,' he promised, as he punched in the code for the male changing rooms at the same time she tapped in the code for the female changing rooms. 'See you in five minutes.'

'Or less,' she remarked, pushing open the door.

Ten minutes later, they were both changed, seated in the chopper with their medical retrieval backpacks and ready for take-off.

'Any word from the surf lifeguards?' Reggie asked their pilot through the headset.

'I'll patch you through to Bergan,' he replied.

'What's the latest?' Reggie asked a moment later as they headed out towards the sea.

'They've got the man in the boat. Left arm is partially detached, incision bites to left side of abdomen,' came Bergan's clear words. 'There is also a report of a second victim. Young girl, twelve years of age. Lacerations to right side, unconscious, right foot missing.'

Reggie closed her eyes as Bergan spoke, knowing full well that Flynn could hear every word through his own headset. She tried to picture the victims' wounds, tried to keep her mind focused, imagining herself moving through the motions of treatment. At times like these they couldn't afford to think about the personal, about those poor people who had suffered such horror. In order to remain professional, they needed to remain detached.

'The boat should be on the beach in two minutes.'

'What's our ETA?' Flynn asked the pilot, watching Reggie closely, whose eyes were tightly shut. He knew she was trying to think things through, to imagine the wounds and the treatment they'd require. He could also remember the first time she'd been like this. Their very first retrieval together.

They'd been sitting in an ambulance, being driven from the hospital on Sint Maarten, towards a luxury hotel where several guests had been crippled with a gastro bug. As they'd been the only surgical residents at the hospital, it had fallen to them to treat the patients. Flynn had met Reggie only the day before and while he'd been instantly attracted to her, he hadn't been at all sure how she performed under pressure.

'She's far too happy for her own good and although she did well in ward round, I have to wonder if she's got what it takes to cope in emergency situations,' he'd told Violet when he'd spoken to her on the phone after his first day.

'I'm sure she'll be fine, Flynn,' Violet had responded. The two had known each other since they'd been toddlers, their mothers the best of friends, and Violet had been the closest thing he'd had to a sister. Their mothers had always said that one day the two of them were destined to marry, but both he and Violet had laughed it off, preferring to remain just good friends. 'If she's a qualified doctor and doing the same surgical training you are, then she must have some smarts,' Violet had wisely pointed out.

Flynn had frowned, unable to believe the instant attraction he'd felt towards his new colleague. Perhaps doubting her abilities was his way of dealing with that unwanted attraction? At any rate, he'd hoped she was good because he hadn't really fancied having to carry the weight of running the surgical team on Sint Maarten on his own for the next six weeks. 'I'm still not convinced.'

'Anyway,' Violet had continued, 'Tell me about the more relaxed pace of life. Nice and slow? Sunshine all the time? I hope so because seriously I thought your parents were going to pressure you into a coronary if you hadn't left.'

'You're exaggerating, Violet,' he'd returned.

'Six weeks of sun, surf and drinks with little umbrellas in them. Utter bliss.'

'Sunburn, sand stuck everywhere and incompetent colleagues.'

Violet laughed at him, not taking his words seriously. 'She must be pretty if you're already labelling her as incompetent. You always do that, Flynn. It's a protective measure. Any time you feel out of your depth, you look for the negative.'

'I do?'

'Look, Flynn, just promise me you'll stop burning the candle at both ends and try to enjoy yourself. Get to know this colleague of yours. What did you say her name was?'

'Regina Smith. Although she's already informed me that she hates being called Regina, that she much prefers Reggie—like she's some sort of trucker. Then she throws her arms around me in one of those uncomfortable friendship-hug things, telling me what a wonderful time we'll have working together. Far too happy for her own good.'

Violet wasn't able to stop laughter from flowing down the telephone line. 'She sounds fantastic, Flynn, and perhaps just what you need for the next few weeks. A little holiday romance, eh?'

'Bite your tongue. You know I'm not interested in any sort of relationship. Not with the pressure our parents are putting on us.'

'It'll never happen, Flynn. You and I are destined to be best friends. Nothing more. Now go. I have a feeling that this Reggie Smith may just surprise you.'

And she did. As they travelled in the ambulance,

heading towards that luxury hotel, Reggie's eyes were closed as though she was trying to catch up on her sleep.

'Conserving your energy?' he asked.

'No.' She spoke the single word before opening one eye to look at him, the corners of her lips turning upwards. 'Concentrating.' She closed her eye and lapsed back into silence.

'Er…OK. Well, would you like to talk about what sort of scenarios we might encounter and how you envisage us handling the situation to ensure an effective and prompt outcome?'

'That's what I'm doing,' she replied. 'I like to close my eyes and picture the situation, visualise myself treating the patient. That way I know exactly what equipment I need and the best way to handle things.'

'You…*picture* yourself doing this?'

'Yes. Try it.' She opened one eye again and looked directly at him. 'Close your eyes.'

'I don't think—'

'We have another five minutes before arrival. Just try it at least.' She closed her eyes again and, feeling utterly stupid and knowing he probably looked ridiculous, Flynn eventually closed his eyes.

'Let's say the patient complains of right-sided abdominal pain with localised tenderness in the middle. I see myself palpating their abdomen, ensuring it isn't appendicitis or hernia. Although there's an outbreak of a gastro bug, it doesn't mean that one of our patients isn't suffering from that but is rather suffering from something far more serious. Not that I'm trying to imply that gastroenteritis isn't a serious condition but simply pointing out that we need to be on top of things.' She paused to take a breath but before she could start again he jumped in.

'You're a talker,' he stated, opening his eyes, feeling mildly silly for agreeing to do things her way but impressed she'd actually managed to get him to comply.

Reggie's grin was bright and wide, like her gorgeous blue eyes as she opened them to look at him. She leaned forward in her seat, as far as the seat belt would allow and looked directly into his eyes. 'I've been told the only way to shut me up is to kiss me.' She waggled her eyebrows up and down suggestively and then sat back in her seat and openly laughed at the stunned look on his face. 'Relax, Flynn. I don't bite.' She winked at him. 'Not unless you want me to.'

The old cliché somehow sounded fresh coming from Reggie's lips and it was only then he realised he'd been staring at her mouth, as though his thoughts were more than willing to follow her lead.

And indeed, the first time he had kissed her had been to shut her up. He couldn't remember what she'd been talking about but he did remember not hearing a word of what she'd been saying, more fascinated by the way her lips moved, wanting desperately to kiss them, to show her just how desirable she was.

Now, many years later, with so much water having flowed rapidly under the bridge between them, Flynn wanted nothing more than to lean forward and kiss those incredibly perfect lips of hers…lips that fitted so snugly against his own. How he'd yearned for them over the years. How he wanted to pick up where they'd left off. How he wished he'd been stronger back then and had stood up for what he'd really wanted out of life.

'Preparing for descent,' the chopper pilot said.

'Copy that,' Reggie returned, and opened her eyes. She looked directly at Flynn. 'Ready?'

'Yeah.' He nodded his head for emphasis and cleared his throat, unsure whether she'd heard him properly through her headphones. He needed to pull it together. To be professional. He knew Reggie—and their patients—were counting on him but sometimes it was difficult to be around her, especially when there were so many memories of their time together intruding into his thoughts.

As the chopper landed and they disembarked, Flynn tried not to notice the way even the blue and yellow overalls made Reggie look sexy. Carrying their gear, they headed over to where the surf lifeguards' boat was being pulled up onto the sand. Reggie was taking the lead on this one and he'd learned, that first day, as they'd treated over thirty patients at the hotel for various complaints, that she was indeed an exceptional doctor.

Bright, talented and absolutely gorgeous. A lethal combination and one he was far from being immune to.

CHAPTER SIX

ON THE BEACH, the surf lifeguards had set up a shield to give them some privacy while the man, whose name was only given as Kev, was carried from the lifeboat to where Flynn and Reggie were opening their emergency backpacks, ready to get to work.

'Establish IV line, get that plasma up and going, stat,' she stated, and Flynn nodded.

'Agreed.' Although they both knew what they were doing, it was important to communicate effectively and clearly exactly what procedures they were undertaking.

As soon as Kev was placed in front of them, they both had their gloves on. As Kev was wearing a wetsuit, Flynn took out the heavy-duty scissors and immediately began cutting away the neoprene fabric so they could better see what they were dealing with. After peeling away the section from his chest, most of which was covered in blood, Reggie hooked her stethoscope into her ears to check Kev's heart rate while Flynn grabbed a large bandage and applied pressure to Kev's left arm, ensuring it was as secure as possible to assist with stemming the bleeding.

'Hi, Kev,' she said to the man, who was semiconscious. 'I'm Dr Reggie Smith with Sunshine Gen-

eral. This is Dr Flynn Jamieson. We're here to help you.'
She smiled at him as she unhooked the stethoscope.
With the paramedics on the scene, one of them came
over and was able to hold Kev's head stable until they
could get a neck brace onto him.

'The girl.' Kev spoke the words through gritted teeth
as Flynn picked up a penlight torch from his medical
kit and performed Kev's neurological observations. As
they worked, both Flynn and Reggie called their findings to each other.

'Heart rate is elevated.'

'Pupils equal and reacting to light. Best to put the
line in his foot,' Flynn remarked, before looking down
at Kev. 'The girl's been found. The surf lifeguards are
bringing her in now.'

'She was…being taken farther…out to sea. Had…
to save her.' His words were disjointed but understand-
able, which showed his cognitive function was clearly
working.

'You did great, Kev. Now I need you to try and relax.
We're here to help you.' Reggie was taking the tubing
she required from the sterile packaging. She checked
both feet for pulses and reported they were both there.
She also asked Kev to wiggle all his toes for her and
although it hurt, he was able to do as she asked. 'You'll
feel just a little scratch,' she told him as she prepared
to insert the cannula into his foot.

'I've felt more…than that today,' he retorted. 'What…
what are you doing?'

'You've lost a lot of blood, Kev,' Flynn told him. 'We
need to replace those fluids as soon as possible. Once
we have some fluids into you, we can give you some-

thing for the pain. Can you wiggle the fingers on your right hand for me?'

'I'm not important,' Kev told them.

'I beg to differ,' Reggie replied, as one of the other paramedics came over to help. She left him to finish off inserting the drip and turned her attention to Kev's abdomen. 'I just need to have a little look around, see what the damage is, and then we can give you something for the pain,' she told him.

'The girl. The girl…is all that's important,' he said, his teeth gritted in pain. 'Need to save the girl.'

'You did save her,' Flynn reassured him.

'I did?' At this news, Kev seemed to relax a bit. He closed his eyes. 'Couldn't save my own girl but…this is good.'

Reggie and Flynn briefly looked at each other, wondering what on earth Kev could be talking about. The bite marks on Kev's abdomen were clear but deep. Flynn had already packed one of the puncture wounds with gauze and Reggie grabbed another bandage from her kit and applied pressure to one area on Kev's lower left abdomen.

'Hold this,' she instructed the paramedic, who had now finished setting up the drip. 'I think it's time we gave you something for the pain,' she told Kev. 'Are you allergic to anything?'

'No. No, but had a heart attack…six years ago now… but good since,' Kev replied, unable to shake his head as the paramedic was now attaching a neck brace to keep Kev's head as still as possible.

'And you're not taking anything? No fish oil?'

'Vegan now,' he told her. 'Flaxseed oil.'

'Good. That's all fine.' Reggie reached into her medi-

cal kit for the syringe that had already been drawn up
with the medication and clearly labelled. 'Check ten
milligrams of morphine,' she said.

Flynn glanced over, checked and confirmed the
medication she was about to give Kev, before reply-
ing, 'Check.'

'There you go, Kev,' she told him as she administered the medication via the butterfly cannula. A few
moments later Kev's features began to relax.

Now that Kev was out of pain, Flynn was able to
increase his investigation of the abdomen. 'Not sure if
the patient has voided, given the wetsuit, but possible
bladder and kidney rupture, large and small intestinal
damage but both lungs appear fine. Suspected fracture
to left neck of femur and probable pelvic bone damage.'

'And the arm?' Reggie asked, after she'd rechecked
Kev's heart rate. She took the stethoscope out of her ears
and met Flynn's gaze. He didn't need to say anything—
the look in his eyes told her that the arm didn't look at
all good and the chances of Kev keeping it were mini-
mal.

'Took the brunt of the attack.' Kev's words were
barely audible. She nodded, indicating she understood
exactly what he was not saying. The salty sea wind
was whipping around them and she was glad of the
screens the paramedics had erected. The lifeguards on
the beach were keeping the onlookers at bay as best they
could. When a shark alarm was raised, it tended to send
a thread of panic through everyone who was around,
whether they'd been in the water nor not.

'The boat? The boat?' Kev asked, still concerned,
even though the morphine was definitely working. 'Is
it in? Where's the girl?'

'The sea's a bit choppy,' one of the paramedics reported. 'They've got her in the boat. They're on their way,' he reassured their patient. Still, Kev seemed slightly agitated again. Something was clearly bothering him.

'Wasn't supposed to…turn out like this,' he mumbled, and Flynn frowned.

'Let's get him back to the hospital so he can be prepared for surgery. With the sounds of sirens in the distance, it appears the cavalry is on the way so we can leave the girl to Bergan and her team.'

'Good thinking.' Reggie pulled her walkie-talkie from the medical kit and contacted the helicopter pilot. 'You ready to head back?'

'Got a patient for me?' he asked.

'Copy that. Name is Kev—that's all I have at the moment. We'll stretcher him now. ETA six minutes.'

Now that the transfer was organised, Reggie did a final check of Kev's vitals, pleased to see he was responding well to the fluids and pain medication, and yet he still seemed uneasy. Then again, he'd just been bitten by a shark but her intuition told her it was more than that.

'Good news, Kev,' she said brightly. 'We're getting you off the beach.' She checked the bandages they'd applied, pleased with his situation. They'd managed to get to Kev as quickly as possible and even though he was in his late fifties, it was clear that he was the type of man who looked after his health.

'Wait. Wait.' Kev's eyes snapped open, the look in them as wild as the sea. 'The girl. Is she OK? I need to know. Please? Please?'

'They're still coming in, Kev, but the other staff from

Sunshine General have arrived. They're brilliant and know what they're doing. They'll take good care of her.'

'We need to get you back, Kev. Your abdominal injuries need further treatment and surgical interven—' Flynn started.

'I need to give you…a message,' Kev interrupted, his tone forceful.

'For whom?' Reggie asked, trying to use her calming voice to placate him a little. They needed him transferred as soon as possible but she didn't want to risk agitating him further by not giving him the respect he deserved.

'Write it down.'

'It's all right. We can do this back at the hospital. You're nice and stable now and we'd like to keep it that way,' she told him.

'Please? I need to give you a message…for my wife.'

'You're going to be fine, Kev. You can tell her yourself when you see her.'

'No. No. She hates me.' He closed his eyes at the words. 'Write it down.'

Reggie looked across at Flynn, who shrugged one shoulder. 'He's the patient. It's his call.' She nodded and pulled off her bloodied gloves before reaching into the medical kit, finding a pen but no paper.

'Wait a moment,' one of the paramedics said, unzipping his overalls and digging into his trouser pocket before pulling out a clean napkin. 'Use this.'

'Thanks.' Reggie accepted it from him then looked at Kev. 'What do you want me write?'

'I hope saving this girl…makes up for not saving ours.' Kev closed his eyes as he spoke and for a moment Reggie's throat closed over, an immediate lump forming there, which was difficult to swallow over. Kev had lost his daughter? 'Did you get that?'

'Uh…' She quickly scribbled down his words. 'Yes.'

'Also, tell her to remember…remember Coffs Harbour at New Year's…and the dingo dance.'

'Dingo dance?' Reggie raised her eyebrows as she looked at Kev. 'Sounds interesting.'

'You got that?' he asked again, and she nodded.

'All written down,' Reggie reassured him, before tucking the pen and paper into a pocket in her retrieval suit. 'What's your wife's name?' she asked.

'Michaela.'

'OK. That's all done. Now, I really think it's time we get you onto that chopper and back to the hospital.' Reggie smiled down at him.

Once again Kev seemed to relax a bit more but he looked determinedly at her and asked, 'You'll let me know about the girl?'

'As soon as we know anything, we'll let you know,' she told him. With the assistance of the paramedics they transferred Kev to a stretcher. 'Take him over to the chopper. I'll just quickly debrief Bergan and Mackenzie,' she told Flynn, who nodded. She watched for a moment as the screens were lowered and the lifeguards did their best to stop onlookers from taking photographs on their cellphones. The police were there as well, a few of them clearing the way for Kev to be carried to the helicopter.

As she started to walk away, a police officer came running up to her.

'Is it all right to talk to the patient now? We need to try and piece together what happened.'

'He's been given morphine and Penthrane so he

might be a little vague on details but give it a go,' she encouraged. 'We need to have wheels up in five minutes.'

'Understood,' the police officer said, and headed off after Flynn and the paramedics who were carrying Kev's stretcher towards the chopper.

Reggie quickly trudged her way through the sand towards Bergan, the wind still whipping at her hair. It was at times like these she was glad she'd cut her hair short. Reggie looked around at all the beachgoers, some packing their things up and leaving, others standing behind the area the police had cordoned off, teenagers taking photographs with their cameras and cellphones.

Emergency personnel were doing their jobs, working together like a well-oiled machine. Reggie hadn't even been aware of the police arriving but without them who knew how many people would have tried to sneak a look around those screens while she and Flynn had been treating Kev.

'We are a curious species,' she murmured to herself as Bergan walked over to her, the two meeting out of earshot of onlookers. 'Hey, there.'

'Your patient all ready for transfer?' Bergan asked.

'Yes. Left arm almost completely torn off. Amputation is a definite consideration but I'll get John to consult when we get back to the hospital.' Reggie pointed to where the surf lifesaving boat, after battling high waves brought on by an oncoming storm, was finally reaching the beach. 'You and Mackenzie OK to take care of the girl?'

'Yes. You'll probably be in Theatres by the time we return but I'll keep you informed.'

'Kev—my patient—was really concerned about the girl so I'd appreciate that.'

'No problem.'

Reggie turned and jogged towards the chopper, looking back to see them lifting the young girl from the boat and carrying her to a second screened-off area, away from prying eyes. She certainly hoped the girl was strong enough to make it through.

'Excuse me!' a woman called from behind the police tape, and when Reggie looked at her, the woman quickly ducked beneath the tape and ran towards her. 'I'm looking for Kev.'

'I'm sorry,' Reggie said, her tone filled with apology. 'You'll need to wait behind the tape.'

'I'm his…er…wife. Michaela.'

Reggie nodded. 'Yes. He's told me about you. Come with me. You can ride in the chopper with us.'

Michaela face turned pale. 'So he really has been attacked. I thought it was a bad joke.'

'We need to go now,' Reggie urged, breaking into a jog and urging Michaela along. 'Kev needs immediate surgery.'

Michaela shook her head. 'I never come to the beach. I can't stand it but he loves it.'

'Never mind about that now.'

'But you don't understand. I only came down so he could sign the divorce papers. I've been pressuring him to do it for months but he kept refusing.'

They'd reached the chopper and Reggie's heart went out to the woman as she read guilt and remorse in Michaela's eyes. She placed her hand on Michaela's shoulder, her words warm. 'Focus on being brave for Kev.

It doesn't matter what's happened in the past, he needs you now. Can you do that?'

Michaela seemed to consider that for a moment before she nodded. 'Yes.'

'Good. Let's get you into the chopper.'

'Why does everything bad happen at Christmas?' Michaela muttered as she climbed into the chopper, sitting down and allowing herself to be strapped in by the pilot. Reggie introduced her to Flynn, who had just finished doing Kev's observations.

'Can he hear me?' Michaela asked, as the rotors of the helicopter started to whirr above them.

'He's been given pain relief to make transport easier,' Reggie said apologetically as she strapped herself in and donned her headphones.

'Six minutes and we'll be at the hospital,' the pilot announced, then the chopper lifted smoothly upwards.

'Call through to the hospital and have John Watson standing by,' Reggie instructed.

'Copy that,' the pilot returned.

'Is that Mackenzie's husband?' Flynn asked, and Reggie nodded.

'Excellent orthopaedic surgeon,' she told him as both she and Flynn kept a close eye on Kev's condition. Thankfully, the trip was non-eventful and John was there waiting for them when the pilot landed the helicopter safely on the roof above the A and E department. A short lift ride down and they were wheeling Kev's bed through to the treatment room. After transferring him to a hospital bed, Reggie and Flynn performed observations again, Michaela standing in the corner out of the way, watching and listening in disbelief as Reggie spoke clearly, giving details of Kev's condition to the A and E staff, as well as John.

'I can't believe it. I just can't believe it,' Michaela kept repeating. Kev was still drowsy from the analgesics and it was clear he needed to go to Theatre as soon as possible. Reggie took Michaela out of the treatment room, down the corridor to a small waiting room, where she started to explain the operation to her.

'Michaela, we need you to sign the consent forms as you are his next of kin.'

'But we're supposed to be getting divorced. I have the papers here for him to sign and then that's it.'

'However…' Reggie tried to remain calm, to get her point across in the most straightforward way because the longer they had to delay taking Kev to Theatre, the worse the outcome would be for him. 'In the eyes of the law you are still listed as his next of kin.' Reggie looked into Michaela's eyes. 'I know all of this has come as a shock but he really does need surgery and we can't progress until—'

'Dr Reggie Smith. Dr Reggie Smith,' came the call over the A and E intercom. 'Code Blue, TR One.'

'What?' Reggie was on her feet and racing back towards trauma room one, her mind going faster than her body as she thought through a thousand different scenarios in the thirty seconds it took her to return. 'What happened?' she asked as she pulled on a pair of gloves and a protective disposable gown.

One of the A and E nurses was performing cardiac massage on Kev.

'Blood pressure dropped. We lost output. He went into defib,' Flynn announced, as he prepared to push fluids, John readying the crash cart. 'Vitals dropped suddenly.'

Reggie was checking Kev's pupils. 'Come on, Kev. Stay with me. You can do it.' She shook her head. 'Not reacting to light.'

'Give me one of adrenaline,' Flynn ordered, as the nurse continued cardiac massage, another of the nurses bagging Kev to pump air into his lungs.

Reggie checked for a pulse and when she couldn't find one Flynn put his stethoscope into his ears and listened for a heartbeat.

'Nothing.' Flynn shook his head and glanced at Reggie. She nodded encouragingly, her eyes eager. 'Push fluids. Get ready to shock him.' Flynn looked at John, who nodded.

'Come on, Kev. Come on. You've come too far. You're a hero, Kev. An absolute hero,' she told him, as she watched Flynn administer the fluids. She closed her eyes for a second, wishing for a miracle, but even she knew the situation was bad. Kev had lost too much blood and even though they were continuing to do everything they possibly could to revive him, there was no guarantee he'd make it through surgery.

'Charging,' John said.

'Clear!' Flynn called, and everyone stepped back from the patient. 'No output.'

'Shock him again,' Reggie instructed, and again John charged the machine.

'Clear!' Flynn called once more, and after the shock had been administered, Reggie pressed her fingers to Kev's carotid pulse.

'Again,' she instructed.

'Reggie—' Flynn began.

'Again!' There was desperation in her words.

'Charging,' John called.

'Clear!' Flynn said, but after the third time there was still no output. 'I'm calling it.'

Flynn met Reggie's gaze, holding it for what seemed an eternity. She knew it was the right thing to do, that Kev had already been through so much, that he simply hadn't been able to fight any longer. He'd done his bit. He'd saved a twelve-year-old girl's life and he was a hero.

Flynn walked round to where she stood and put both hands on her shoulders, looking intently into her eyes. 'I'm sorry, Reg.'

'We did our job.'

'Do you want me to talk to his wife?'

'No.' She patted the pockets of her retrieval suit, looking for the napkin on which she'd written Kev's last words. 'I'll do it.'

'I'll go with you. Support is always good at a time like this.'

Reggie nodded and walked on wooden legs down towards the small room where she'd left Michaela not that long ago. Flynn's nearness really was comforting and she momentarily wondered whether he hadn't been offering support for *her* rather than for Kev's wife.

With the bright and cheerful Christmas music playing softly through the hospital's system, they entered the waiting room and just the forlorn look on Reggie's face must have adequately conveyed the situation to Michaela as the other woman instantly burst into tears.

'We did everything we could,' Reggie said, the words sounding hollow and inadequate as Michaela crumpled into a chair. Reggie put her hand on the other woman's shoulder, wanting to offer her support. 'His heart couldn't handle the stress of the attack. He passed away a few minutes ago.'

'No. No. This isn't the way it was supposed to happen.'

Reggie swallowed and looked up at Flynn, who nodded encouragingly for her to continue. She held the napkin between her fingers and looked down at the words she'd scribbled there not that long ago. 'He did leave a message he wanted me to pass on to you.' Reggie paused for a moment, not sure she could get the words past her lips but knowing she had to. 'He said he hoped saving the little girl today made up for not saving yours.'

At that, Michaela let loose with a fresh round of tears and Flynn quickly offered her some more tissues. It was incredibly difficult in these circumstances to know what to do or say and although they'd been trained in how to handle these sorts of situations, having the theoretical knowledge and watching someone's heart break into pieces because a loved one had passed away were two very different things.

'He said for you to remember Coffs Harbour at New Year's and the dingo dance.'

Michaela raised her head, hiccupping as she spoke. 'Why on earth would he say that?' she asked, blowing her nose amidst the tears.

Reggie shrugged, unsure what the relevance was. She was about to say she didn't know when Flynn spoke.

'Perhaps he wanted your last memory of him to be a happy one,' Flynn said, his voice deep and soft and filled with compassion.

Surprise lit Michaela's eyes. 'Oh.' Then she nodded.

'The dingo dance.' A small smile touched her quivering lips. 'He was so funny that night.'

'Is there someone we can call to come and be with you?'

Michaela took her phone from her handbag and nodded. 'I can do it.'

'OK. I'll get one of the nurses to come and bring you a drink. We'll be back as soon as possible.'

'Yes. Of course. You must be busy.' Michaela nodded and dabbed at her eyes with a fresh tissue. 'I don't know how you do it, how you cope.'

The lump was back in Reggie's throat and after they exited the room she quickly walked down one of the side corridors of A and E, needing to have a moment or two to herself. Bergan's office was down this secluded corridor and she quickly dug around in her pocket for her hospital pass card, but her fingers seemed to have turned into sausages. She needed the escape, to slip into Bergan's room, to cry and let the pain out, but the tears were already beginning to flow.

'Just let them go,' Flynn's voice said from behind her, and she jumped a little, not having heard him follow her. She turned and in the next instant she was in his arms, their firm warmth providing her with a protective shelter from the stormy emotions pounding at her heart.

'I've got you, Reg. I've got you,' he murmured softly near her ear, but as he spoke, Reggie could hear the thickness in his tone and as she buried her face into his chest, her body racked with sobs, she realised that Flynn was also shedding a few tears.

She was touched at this deeply personal, deeply sensitive side to him that she couldn't remember seeing before. They'd worked together on patients before, they'd lost patients before, but in all the time she'd spent with him he'd always managed to keep a close rein on his most intimate emotions.

Now he was sharing them with her and she couldn't help but feel…quite privileged.

CHAPTER SEVEN

REGGIE WASN'T SURE how long they stood there, their arms wrapped around each other, supporting each other. The job they did wasn't easy. It was bad enough when they were in Theatre and things didn't go their way, the patient dying during surgery, but to have gone out to the beach, to have spent time with Kev, having him confide in her, giving her the message to pass onto Michaela… and then to lose him.

Yes, it hurt, but it also felt incredibly good to have Flynn's strong arms about her. The pain was there but the fact that it was shared really did provide a level of comfort. It had been so long since anyone had just held her, without a hidden agenda, without wanting anything from her. Flynn was offering her comfort and she hoped in some way she was giving him back just the same.

She had no idea how long they stood there and a part of her never wanted it to end but she knew it must. It was their job to pull themselves together, to head back into the fray, as it were, and to help someone else who was still alive and who needed their expertise.

Slowly Reggie's tears started to subside but she was more than happy to stay where she was, at least for the moment. The memory of having Flynn's arms around her...of the way he would sometimes rub his thumbs in small circles in her lower back, giving her a gentle and sensual massage. Would he do that now? Did he want to do that?

Before the emergency, he'd asked for her forgiveness. The fact that he'd done that and also the way he'd been so incredibly thoughtful and helpful and wonderful and supportive was making it far too easy for her to fall in love with him all over again.

She knew he was here at Sunshine General covering Geetha's maternity leave but then what? What were his plans once Geetha returned in six months' time? There were just too many questions. Too many emotions. Too much...Flynn. She knew she needed to pull back, to try and find some sort of perspective where he was concerned, although how she was going to do that she had no clue.

Feeling a little better, Reggie started shifting slowly in his arms. She was becoming far too aware of how perfect his torso was, how he smelled of that deep, earthy spice that had always been intoxicating to her senses, and how she wanted nothing more than to ease back, lift her head and have him press his lips to hers.

He'd done it time and time again in the past and as his arms loosened, allowing her to shift a little more, she couldn't help but look up at him. His gaze automatically dipped to take in the contours of her mouth, the atmosphere between them changing from one of supportive colleagues to one of experienced familiarity.

She looked into his gorgeous eyes, hooded by those gorgeous long lashes, his straight nose, his cleft chin and his slightly parted lips. His arms were no longer protective and supportive but instead were bands of warmth, heating her up all over. Didn't the man have any idea just how powerful his hold was over her? She wanted him to kiss her, to follow through on the urge that seemed to be so tangible between them you could have cut it with a knife.

'Reg.' Even the way he spoke her name was filled with repressed desire. 'I really want to kiss you.'

At his words she gasped, her lips parting and her eyes widening at the bold but honest statement. Her hands were still halfway around his back from holding him close while she'd wept but now she brought them around to the front, to rest against his chest as she continued to look at him.

She really wasn't sure what to say or do because although she was longing to have his mouth pressed to hers once again, knowing she would be able to experience those thrilling sensations only Flynn had ever been able to evoke, she also remembered the pain he'd put her through when he'd broken her heart. She could forgive him. She knew that but could she trust him with her heart again? Was his desire to kiss her simply born from the moment they were sharing or was it something deeper?

He lifted his hand to run his fingers through her short dark hair. 'I like this colour. When we met it was longer and a honey brown and you were the most effervescent and wild and crazy and most wonderful person I'd ever met, and even then I had trouble keeping my lips from yours. It appears, all these years later, that the urge is as strong now as it was then.'

He cupped her chin with his hand and brushed his thumb over her parted lips. If she'd thought she'd been on fire before, his sweet and gentle caress had only enhanced the power surging between them.

'I know I'm being selfish, Reg,' he continued a moment later when she hadn't spoken. 'Especially after the way I treated you all those years ago, and I really need to tell you how sorry I am. I was arrogant and rude and didn't take into consideration that your feelings were much deeper than I'd originally thought.'

'You asked me to marry you, Flynn!' Reggie shook her head and twisted from his embrace. Flynn instantly released her, dropping his arms back to his sides. 'You proposed marriage and I accepted. Then, the next day, you turn up at my room and tell me you need to call it all off. Just like that. No explanation, just that you'd made a mistake and that you were no longer…free to pursue a relationship with me. Less than two weeks later I read—in the society columns—that Flynn Jamieson, of the well-known wealthy Jamieson family and heir to the Jamieson Corporation, had wed his childhood sweetheart, Violet Fleming, a young philanthropic socialite who was on the board of so many charity organisations it was almost impossible for the newspaper to list them.'

'Reg…I—'

'What, Flynn? Please tell me what happened back then because I've spent the past six years trying to figure things out. What did I do wrong? Was I too enthusiastic? Did everything just happen too fast? Sure, I may be spontaneous and, yes, in my life, once I make a decision, things tend to move really fast and I'm off like a rocket, but what a lot of people don't realise is that I think about things far more deeply than anyone would ever guess, and when you proposed to me I didn't take it lightly or as some sort of flippant twenty-four-hour whimsy.' She shook her head and spread her arms wide.

'I'm just not sure how you could have misconstrued my true feelings for you, especially as when you proposed I threw my arms around your neck and smothered your face in kisses while saying "Yes, yes and yes" over and over again! Don't you think that during the time we were together I hadn't dreamed of you asking me that question? That I didn't feel that strong and abiding connection that—stupid me—I thought you'd felt, too…or at least I believed you when you said you did.'

'Reg!'

'What?' Reggie leaned her head against Bergan's office door, wishing she had her pass key on her so they could at least enter and have a bit of privacy. She was tired and edgy after the retrieval, and then having her patient pass away…it was all becoming too much. Now they were just waiting for the young girl to arrive in A and E, in case she required surgery.

It definitely wasn't the time for them to be having *this* discussion, the one she'd wanted to have with him ever since he'd come back into her life—to ask him why he'd really called off their engagement. Apparently time just wasn't on her side at the moment.

'Will you let me get a word in edgeways?'

'Go for it.' She turned and leaned her back against the door, closing her eyes and waiting for him to speak.

He was quiet for a moment before saying softly, 'It was a mistake.'

Reggie was glad she hadn't been looking at him when he'd spoken those words because the pain that instantly pierced her heart, she knew, would have been clearly reflected in her gaze. She tried to focus on the

Christmas music playing through the speaker above, hoping that her days really would be merry and bright, but how could they possibly ever be that way again when Flynn had just confirmed that proposing to her had been a mistake?

'Thanks for confirming that,' she returned, realising she needed to get away from him. In some ways it was the last thing she'd expected him to say, to admit that what they'd had in Sint Maarten had been a mistake, but he'd said it to her back then and he was only confirming it now, all these years later.

The sounds of ambulance sirens nearing the hospital could be heard over the Christmas music and the next instant both her and Flynn's pagers started to beep. She dragged in a deep breath, pushed her personal thoughts aside and stepped away from the door.

Raising her gaze to hover just near the top of retrieval suit, focusing on his Adam's apple, she mumbled, 'Looks like we're needed again.'

With that, she edged past him, ignoring the way her body burst with excitement as her arm brushed against his. Retrieval suit or not, the slightest touch from Flynn would no doubt always set her on fire and it was probably something she should simply learn to accept, rather than fight. She was attracted to Flynn. Fact. He thought the two of them together was a mistake. Fact. All of this made it highly plausible that she would no doubt die from a broken heart.

'Clamp,' she instructed the theatre nurse, Susan, as they entered their fourth hour of surgery. The young girl, Lola, had a perforated bladder and kidney and her bowel was in a bit of a state. 'Nothing we can't fix,' she and Flynn had reassured Lola's poor parents.

Working in conjunction with the urological surgical team, as well as Mackenzie and John for Lola's orthopaedic injuries of an amputated right foot, Flynn and Reggie were determined that this young girl would live. Kev had given his life for her and there was no way any of the team was going to do anything but their best for Lola, no matter how tired they might be.

Lola would need to be on dialysis while her kidney healed and then there was the inevitable right-foot prosthesis she would require, but for the moment both Reggie and Flynn were concentrating on performing an ileostomy, having already successfully completed a resection on the large intestine. They'd had to make a large cut down the centre of Lola's belly in order to gain access to the area. Usually the procedure was performed laparoscopically but in Lola's case that hadn't been an option.

Between the dialysis and the prosthesis, Lola would also have to deal with the temporary stoma they'd been forced to insert—where they attached her small intestine to the outer wall of her body. Her stools would need to go through the stoma into a drainage bag outside her body. All of that was a lot for a twelve-year-old to cope with, especially as it would all be combined with the emotional trauma of being swept out with the ocean current into dangerous waters until Kev had come to her rescue.

As Reggie pulled off her gloves quite some time later, handing Lola's care over to Mackenzie and John, who were the next surgeons to treat Lola's plethora of injuries, she was physically and emotionally drained.

'That poor kid,' Flynn murmured, as he de-gowned in the anteroom next to Reggie.

'Her whole life has just changed,' she replied, removing her mask and cap before running her fingers through her hair, fluffing it up.

'It'll never be the same again.' Flynn continued to watch her, both of them now dressed in their scrubs. Bits of Reggie's dark hair stuck out at all angles, making her look cuter than ever. A lopsided smile slowly tugged at the corners of his mouth and, unable to resist the chance to touch her, he stepped forward and brushed his fingers through the locks so they didn't look so wild and unruly. 'Lovely,' he said.

'Tired,' she returned, unable to put her shields up. After what Flynn had said to her before Lola's surgery Reggie had most definitely wanted to put a bit more distance between them but right now all she really wanted was to find a nice, comfortable bed, curl up and go to sleep.

The feel of his fingers in her hair, his hand cupping her cheek, the way he looked down into her upturned face, the way he looked into her eyes for a brief moment before nodding, as though reading her thoughts, was lovely. To have him here, have him near, have him caring for her. It was something she'd dreamed about for such a very long time that when he put his arms around her shoulders and led her out of the anteroom, she was more than happy to let him.

'Get changed. I'll write up the notes and meet you back here in ten minutes. OK?'

'Sounds good,' she murmured, and headed into the female changing rooms. She was at that stage of exhaustion where she had so many thoughts running through her head that none of them made any sense. One thought blurred into another and they all continued to tumble until she was unable to process anything. So much had happened today and as she slowly changed out of her clothes, almost falling over once or twice, feeling light-headed as though she was drunk, all she could think about was getting to that nice, comfortable bed.

'You're starting to make a habit of this,' Flynn murmured not too much later as they headed to his car. There was a light smattering of rain outside but the air was still rather sticky and humid. She knew he was referring to the exhaustion she'd felt last night…. Had it only been last night? She liked it when her days were full, when time didn't drag, but the past few days had been filled with far too many conflicting emotions, even for her.

'I'm sorry if I'm being a nuisance,' Reggie remarked, the balmy weather having woken her up a little, but Flynn instantly dismissed her words.

'You're not. You've been through a lot, Reggie, and your mind needs time to process everything. At least I don't need to carry you to the car tonight.'

Reggie frowned at him. 'Stop talking about me as though you're the authority on me,' she protested as he unlocked his car and opened the door for her. She stepped forward and only realised a split second later that they were standing facing each other with only the car door between them. She lifted her chin, annoyance making her brave.

'Why not?'

'Because you don't know me, Flynn. Because you've admitted to me that you and I were a mistake, one that should never have happened, that you regret—'

'What?' He frowned as he interrupted her. 'I never said that.'

'Yes, you did. Just before Lola's surgery. We were outside Bergan's office and you admitted it was a mistake to—' She stopped talking again but only because Flynn had put his finger across her lips, startling her and causing her body to be flooded with a mass of tingles at the feather-light touch.

'You once told me the only way to effectively shut you up was to kiss you and I'm very close to doing that, Reg.' He breathed out a calming breath but she could see his eyes flashing with a mixture of desire and frustration. 'What I said to you before Lola's surgery was that it was a mistake to have treated you the way I did. It was a mistake to allow myself to be persuaded by my family. It was a mistake to turn and walk away from you.'

Reggie stared at him then blinked one long blink as though she was desperately trying to process his words. 'A mistake to...'

'Walk away from you. I have many regrets, Reg, and...' He cupped her face, the frustration leaving him as he gazed into her eyes as though she really was the most important and precious person in the world to him. Her legs started to quiver, to turn to jelly, and she quickly put out a hand, clutching the edge of the car door in order to steady herself. 'You are perhaps my biggest regret of all.'

'I am?'

His smile was instant and gorgeous and his eyes were twinkling with mild amusement. 'Yes.' Flynn indicated to the car. 'Get in, Reggie. I think it's time we talked.'

She did as he suggested, trying not to fumble with her seat belt as his words reverberated around her head.

Time they talked? Talked about what? About the past? About how he'd left? About how she'd been utterly devastated and heartbroken? Because if they did that, then that discussion would lead to the present and she wasn't at all sure she was ready to reveal to Flynn just how incredible he made her feel.

She loved being near him, spending time with him, laughing with him, and it was also what she wanted more than anything in the world...but...had too much already passed between them? Was it possible she could forgive him for hurting her all those years ago? For breaking her heart and leaving her feeling as though she'd been living a lie ever since?

'You must talk about this,' she could well remember Sunainah saying a few months after she had returned from the Caribbean. 'Talk about your love for this man, this Flynn. It is important for you to do.'

'No, it isn't.'

'It is not healthy, Reggie. If you keep it all bottled up inside, then a day will come when you are unable to contain it any longer. It will bubble up and burst everywhere, making an awful mess,' Sunainah had persisted.

'I can cope with this, Sunainah. I've coped with worse. You know about my past. You know the betrayals I've coped with. Flynn's betrayal is just another one to add to the pile.' She'd shrugged then shaken her head.

'It's my own fault, really. I, in all my romantic stupidity, thought Flynn was different. That he was a man who truly cared about me, who meant it when he said he loved me. Turns out he didn't. He's no different from any other rich man. Only out for what he can get.' Even as she'd spoken the words her heart had been pierced with pain, her voice breaking on the last words.

Sunainah had hugged her close and a fresh bout of tears had fallen on her friend's shoulder. 'What will you do?'

'What I always do.' Reggie had sniffed and dabbed at her eyes with a tissue before blowing her nose. 'I'll cry and then box everything up in my mind and shove it into a dark corner. Then I'll pick myself up and rely on my awesome friends to be there for me.'

'We are pretty awesome.' Sunainah had chuckled.

'And I will be as bright and cheerful as I know how. If I fold a facade around me, one I can control, letting people believe I am forever the happy-go-lucky girl, I'll be able to cope.'

'I hope you are correct.'

Reggie had hugged Sunainah close before standing up to pace around the room. 'I will be happy. I'll lock my love for Flynn away and never think about it again.'

'That is impossible.'

'Probably.' She'd stared at a photograph of the two of them together, standing on the beach at sunset, holding big, colourful drinks with little umbrellas in them. 'Goodbye, Flynn,' she'd whispered, then kissed the photograph and handed it to Sunainah. 'Hide this somewhere for me.'

'Are you sure?' Sunainah had asked.

Reggie had closed her eyes, a single tear falling from her lashes before she'd taken a deep, cleansing breath and slowly released it. Then she'd opened her eyes, forced a smile onto her lips and laughed. 'Positive.'

'Is that the answer to my question or your projected attitude?'

'Both.'

And Reggie had done her best to be that happy-go-lucky girl for the past six years, doing her best to redirect her thoughts whenever she'd accidentally caught herself thinking about Flynn, wanting to know what he was up to, where he was working, whether or not he had children with his stunningly gorgeous wife. She'd stopped reading the social pages, turning off the television or radio at any mention of the Jamieson Corporation. She hadn't wanted to know.

She'd focused on her work, an ever-present smile on her face, her bright and cheerful attitude becoming less forced and more of who she really was. And whenever she had slipped for a minute and indulged herself by wondering what the heir to the Jamieson Corporation was doing with his life, she would force herself to go out on a date. There was no shortage of handsome men working at the hospital but none of them had ever been able to break through the walls she'd erected so firmly about her heart.

Then Flynn had appeared, standing across the corridor from her clinic room, and everything had started to crumble. Now he wanted to talk? Now he wanted to set the record straight? He *hadn't* thought the two of them together was a mistake? Was this a world she wanted to enter again? Surely a leopard didn't change its spots. Surely, given that Flynn had hurt her once, he would do it again.

He switched the radio on as they drove through the quiet streets of Maroochydore but where Reggie had wanted nothing more than to sleep before, Flynn's words had been like a shot of adrenaline and she was now very much awake.

He wanted to talk. That could mean anything, so what on earth was he going to say…and was she going to like it?

CHAPTER EIGHT

'ANOTHER LONG DAY,' she murmured as they walked into his town house. She didn't know if she could face this 'talk' with Flynn on top of the day they'd had. Maybe she should just go straight to her room and hide there for as long as she could.

'I'll put the kettle on,' he said. 'Why don't you sit in the lounge and I'll join you in a moment?'

'Actually, Flynn, if you don't mind…' Reggie eased her way through the kitchen, aiming towards the downstairs bedroom. 'Can we talk later?'

'No.'

'But I'm exhausted.'

Flynn looked at her for a long moment before shaking his head. 'No.'

'No?' she questioned, feeling her annoyance beginning to rise. 'You can't make me sit down and talk about something I'm not sure I want to talk—'

Without a word, he moved quickly, gently scooping her into his arms and pressing his mouth to hers in one swift motion, effectively shutting her up, just as he'd warned her earlier. Reggie barely had time to register his movements before a flood of delight and excitement zinged around her body like an out-of-control pinball.

He knew how to move his mouth against hers in order to garner a response of pleasure and it appeared he wasn't above using this knowledge and skill right now.

At first, though, he didn't move his mouth, just pressed his lips to hers as though needing to reacquaint himself with her gloriousness, but after breathing her in, after closing his eyes and allowing the drug that was Reggie to once more flow through his system, Flynn eased back ever so marginally and deepened the kiss.

Slowly, slowly, slowly. As though inflicting the most exquisite torture on their senses, he coaxed her lips to part gently, the taste of her fuelling his desire. She was all sweetness and light and sunshine, bringing her unique brand of pleasure back into his life. It was what she'd done all those years ago, breaking down his barriers, wanting him, needing him, teaching him how to lighten up, not to take things so seriously, to be free from repression.

'You're too stuffy,' she'd once told him, and he'd been impressed with the way she'd teased and laughed at him, so unlike any of the other women he'd met throughout his life. Most of them had only wanted one thing—access to his family's fortune.

'Women aren't interested in *you*, son, and they never will be,' his father had told him time and time again. 'All they want are clothes and shoes and jewellery and anything else your money can buy them. Sure, they might show a smidgen of affection for you in the beginning but it'll wane. It always does.'

'So...you and Mum?' Flynn had questioned him. 'What? Mum only married you for your money?'

'Your mother had money of her own, son. That's the point. Marry someone who already has money and you know they don't want you *just* for your money.' His father had dragged heavily on his expensive Cuban cigar, then coughed. 'Even then, they're happy to take whatever you give them. Everyone has their price.'

And yet, when Flynn had met Reggie, he'd had the distinct impression that she really *didn't* have a price at all. All she'd wanted out of life had been to be happy and to spread that happiness to others. She was a clever, caring and charismatic woman who had completely turned his head.

They'd both been staying in the short-term accommodation apartments owned by the hospital to house the doctors who spent time working in Sint Maarten, so they'd bumped into each other quite frequently. Then one night, in the apartment complex's large, almost empty dining room, when Flynn had been sitting alone at a table, Reggie had pulled out the chair opposite him and sat down.

'Well, it seems completely ridiculous for the two of us to be eating by ourselves, especially as you're new here,' she'd offered by way of explanation. Before he'd been able to say a word, the waitress had brought over their meals and he'd found himself eating—and enjoying—dinner with Reggie Smith.

The more time he'd spent with her, the more intrigued he'd become. She was so carefree, crazy and challenging, making him re-evaluate some of his ideals. Soon he'd been unable to stop himself from kissing her and before his time in Sint Maarten had ended, he'd found himself proposing to the most wonderful and exhilarating woman he'd ever known.

Now Flynn gathered her as close as he could, unable to believe he was permitted to hold her once again, to tenderly caress her back, to continue to absorb her delightful response to the kisses he was pressing to her lips. Didn't she have any idea just how perfect she was for him? How he'd wished he hadn't been so spineless all those years ago and had stood up for what *he'd* wanted instead of continuing to allow his overbearing father to dictate his life?

But that was then and this was now. He'd made the break, he'd taken control over his own life and somehow he'd found his way back to the one place he'd always felt like he belonged—with Reggie's arms wrapped around him, her mouth responding enthusiastically to his.

'Flynn.' She whispered his name as she reluctantly broke her mouth from his, her breathing erratic and uneven. She put both hands on his shoulders and eased back. 'We can't do this again.' She tried to shake her head but instead found her lips once more captured by his. She moaned with delight, wanting his glorious torture to continue forever as well as wanting it to finish as soon as possible so she didn't end up revealing just how much she still cared for him.

She knew she should push him away, to break the contact. Self-preservation was usually high on her list of priorities but this was Flynn and where he was concerned she'd never been able to think straight. When they'd first met he'd turned her mind to mush. When they'd argued he'd turned her mind to mush. When he'd smiled at her, hugged her, kissed her, he'd turned her mind to mush.

At first, in Sint Maarten, she'd done her best to keep their relationship strictly professional, wanting to deny the uncharacteristic desire she'd felt towards him. She hadn't dated wealthy men. That had been her one rule and even though Flynn hadn't told her about his excessively rich family, from the moment she'd met him she'd known exactly who he was.

She'd appreciated his skills as a doctor, she'd liked the way they'd seemed to work together so seamlessly, enjoying the inventive ways and solutions he'd devised for dealing with a variety of situations. What she hadn't expected was to find herself wanting to spend more time with him, to talk to him, to tease him, to laugh with him outside working hours.

And then he'd broken her heart, he'd rejected her love and he'd left her. Even though she wanted to see where this frightening natural chemistry that still existed between them might lead, she wasn't sure her heart was strong enough to endure another rejection from him. As the pain from her past, the pain she'd locked away so tightly, started to bubble up and over, she felt a surge of power course through her and pushed her hands against his shoulders.

'No!' She broke from his embrace and took a step away, bumping into the wall and almost tripping over. Flynn instinctively reached out a hand towards her, wanting to help her, but she shifted farther away.

'Reggie?'

As she looked at him, she was pleased to see he was equally as out of breath, as shaken up with repressed desire as she was. It was nice to know she wasn't the only one affected by the raw, animalistic power that still existed between them.

'I can't do this, Flynn.'

'Do…what?'

'This!' She indicated the distance between them,

the thick, heavy attraction that was surrounding them, wanting to draw them closer.

'Why? What is it that's stopping you?'

She stared at him with incredulity. 'Er…how about the fact that you broke my heart?' She turned to walk away, not wanting to relive the pain and mortification he'd inflicted on her. She'd been very disciplined *not* to think about it and she wasn't about to start now, especially *not* in front of him.

Flynn nodded. 'If it's any consolation, I broke mine as well.'

That stopped her. Frowning, she turned to face him. 'What?'

'As I said before at the car, walking away from you that night was not only the hardest thing I've ever done but also the stupidest.'

'Stupidest?'

Flynn raked a hand through his hair, his agitation quite evident. 'I was a fool, Reggie, and for years I've wanted to humbly beg your forgiveness. Now that you're here, in front of me, willing to listen to me, that's exactly what I'm doing.' He looked into her eyes. 'Will you? Can you…forgive me?'

Reggie stared at him in utter astonishment. 'But… wait a second. If breaking up with me broke your heart as well, why did you do it?' She spread her arms wide, her eyes revealing just how perplexed she was with what he was saying.

'My parents.' He shook his head. 'Pressure from my father, emotional blackmail from my mother.' He raked a hand through his hair. 'All my life I'd been told that women would never be interested in *me* for *me*. That when they looked at me all they would see was a walking chequebook. Money would always win out against love, or so I'd been led to believe. But the other fact was that my mother was very ill back then, and there was some controversy as to whether I should even go to the Caribbean in the first place. Although I haven't necessarily seen eye to eye with my parents over the years, they're still my parents and I'm honour bound to them.'

Reggie snorted at his words. '"Honour bound". Ha. What honour? The world of the wealthy. It has its own way to bully and oppress.'

'Er…yes.' He seemed astonished she understood.

'I take it her health improved as you did indeed come to the Caribbean.'

'Yes, and while I was there, while I was with *you*, I started to see the world differently. *You* helped me to see it differently and I started to realise the world I'd been raised in had certain…flaws.'

'One being that it was OK to think for yourself?'

'Yes.' Again he was surprised at her insight.

'And the marriage you entered into the instant you left me?'

'It was my mother's final wish.'

'Let me guess. Your mother was good friends with Violet's mother?'

'The best of friends, yes.'

Reggie shrugged and turned away from him, walking into the lounge room and slumping down into a chair, closing her eyes.

'As ridiculous and as old-fashioned as it might sound, our mothers had always talked of Violet and I marrying, all our lives. We were to have children who would bind our two families together forever.'

'And how did you and Violet feel about this?'

Flynn shrugged. 'Violet was more like a sister to me. Neither of us have siblings. As far as the arranged marriage went, I guess as I'd always been told that was what was expected of me, I didn't think about it much. Until...until I met you.'

'You were OK with having an arranged marriage?'

'Back then, I guess I was...but as I've said, then I met you and everything changed.'

'But the wealthy are supposed to marry the wealthy.' She shook her head, looking at him through her lashes. 'It's snobbish and elitist and not to mention outdated.'

'And yet it's still happening even today.' Flynn sat down on the lounge next to her, facing her, needing her to understand. 'My mother's health deteriorated while I was in Sint Maarten but I didn't know that as I hadn't been answering their calls. I'd wanted to shut out my life, ignore the pressures waiting for me once I returned to Melbourne. I wanted to live in the world you and I had created for ourselves, to stay happy in our bubble.'

'And when you finally reconnected with that world?'

'I was told my mother had been admitted to hospital only a few hours before. Guilt swamped me, especially when my father continued to lecture me about my irresponsible behaviour of not staying in contact. And there I was, calling them to tell them the good news, to let them know that I'd found the woman of my dreams and that I was engaged.

'When I told my father that I'd most certainly come home but that I was bringing my new fiancée with me, he told me I might as well stick a scalpel directly into my mother's heart and kill her instantly. He blustered about how the wedding to Violet was set. That it was my mother's final wish to see Violet and I married and that was what was going to happen.

'He talked to me long and hard about my duty, my honour, my need to step up and do the right thing. He convinced me that there was no way any woman—*you*—could ever feel anything deep and abiding for me, nothing that would stand the test of time.'

Flynn closed his eyes and shook his head. 'He'd sent his private jet to the airport for me and I was to be on it the following afternoon. Alone. I was so eaten up with guilt. My mother had been ill and I'd been selfish enough to shut her out simply because I'd been with you.

'I paced around, thinking things through, trying to rationalise whether or not you truly loved me, and yet somehow…my thinking changed. I did find it difficult to believe that you could really love me for me, that you must know about my family's money and that was the only reason you'd even given me the time of day.'

'You were angry with me.' Reggie's statement was soft but clear. 'I could see it in your eyes.'

He closed his eyes for a moment as though recalling that horrible scene in her room when he'd called off their engagement. 'I was, but only because I'd convinced myself you couldn't possibly love *me*,' he admitted honestly. 'It was easier for me to break it off with you if I believed you'd only been interested in me for my family fortune.'

'The wealthy can behave however they like and nine times out of ten they do. A law unto themselves.'

Flynn looked at her with a hint of surprise. 'I disagree with that statement, at least as far as I'm concerned.'

'Perhaps now, but not back then. Your father dictated

your path and you just let him. You let his voice get into your head and control you, just as it always had.'

'I know, but…' Flynn shifted in his seat, defence at her attack on his father grating on him, even though he knew what she was saying was absolutely true. 'My mother was ill. *Gravely* ill. She passed away five days after the wedding.'

'And was she happy?'

'Seeing me married to Violet? Yes, she was. It was what happened after that which I didn't appreciate.'

'Being stuck in an arranged marriage?' she guessed.

'Well, there was that, but, more importantly, not three days after my mother's funeral my father threw a large wedding reception, inviting everyone who *should* have been invited to what he termed was "the society wedding of the year".' Flynn waved his hand in the air as though he was announcing a headline.

'Did you know about it?'

'Of course.'

'And you couldn't stop it?'

'I wanted to but everyone kept saying it was what Mum had wanted, that she'd helped to plan it and that if it didn't go ahead, we were dishonouring her memory.'

'And there's more guilt piled on.'

'Exactly.' Flynn reached over and took Reggie's hand in his. 'I was also highly conscious of you. I kept wondering what you must be thinking.' He looked down at her fingers, stroking them lightly. 'I knew you probably hated me and I wouldn't have blamed you for the atrocious way I'd behaved. You didn't know that because of my social status, because of my family's wealth, my picture would be splashed around on every glossy magazine in Australia.'

'Actually…' she nodded '…I did know about your wealth.'

He angled his head to the side, frowning a little. 'You mean after I left the Caribbean?'

'No. I knew exactly who you were from the moment we met.'

'What?'

'I knew you were the heir apparent to the Jamieson Corporation.'

'You did?' He looked down at her hand again, before meeting her eyes. 'That wasn't why you…?'

He trailed off, feeling stupid for even voicing the thought, but suddenly he recalled his father's bitter words, the doubts that he had placed in Flynn's head once upon a time. Caught up in the grief of losing his mother, breaking things off with Reggie and being pressured to marry a woman who was more a sister than a wife, Flynn's temper had exploded when his father had refused to back down about the wedding reception.

'If you go ahead with this, I will not attend,' he'd told his father.

'Don't be ridiculous, Flynn. Of course you'll be there.'

'No. I've only just buried my mother and I want time to grieve before we go splashing our fake happiness around the society pages.'

'Fake happiness! Violet is a fine woman and she'll make you a fine wife. She's perfect for you, Flynn. She always has been.'

'I think Violet might have something to say about that.'

'Violet does whatever she's told. She doesn't have an

original thought in her head. She's been told her whole
life that she's going to marry you and she's accepted it.'

'Then she's wrong.' Flynn had shaken his head. 'I
love someone else, Dad.' There. The words had finally
been spoken and where Flynn had somehow thought
they would make a difference, his father had flicked
the statement aside with a wave of his hand as though
he had been shooing away a pesky fly.

'What do you know about love? Some gold-digging
nurse you met in the Caribbean? A holiday romance?
That's not serious, Flynn. All women see when they
look at you is dollar signs. They want your money, not
you. That's where Violet is different. She comes from
money.'

'And the fact that you and her father are merging
your businesses has nothing at all to do with this.'

His father had spread his hands wide as though indicating he had nothing to hide. 'Just seizing an opportunity, son.'

'Sure.' Flynn had stalked to the window and looked
out at the extensive grounds. So green when everywhere
else in the country had been brown due to drought. 'She
wasn't a nurse and she wasn't a gold-digger.' He'd spoken the words more to himself than to his father, needing to reassure himself of the real reasons Reggie had
admitted to loving him.

'You think that, if it helps you sleep at night but, rest
assured, if she knew you had money, that would be the
only reason she latched onto you.' His father had tapped
his own chest. 'I've just saved the company tens of
thousands of dollars in settlement fees, not to mention
protecting us from having our private affairs splashed
all over the papers.'

'Oh, but splashing this wedding reception all over the papers is fine?'

'It's controlled. Now, go and find Violet and thank your lucky stars you had a mother who was looking out for your best interests by finding you the right wife.'

Flynn exhaled slowly as he ran his fingers over Reggie's hand once more, marvelling at her soft, silky skin. These were the hands that had performed intricate surgery on twelve-year-old Lola, the hands that had held his as they'd walked along the beach, the hands that had caressed his face before she'd whispered the words 'I love you' near his lips.

'Are you trying to ask me if I fell in love with you because of your *money*?' She all but spat the word at him.

'Er...um...'

'You don't sound too sure about that, Flynn.' Reggie pulled her hand from his and stood from the lounge, pacing up and down. 'Do you know, it was *because* I knew you came from money that I tried to keep my distance, tried to keep the relationship between us strictly professional.'

'You hugged me on my first day as a way of greeting. That wasn't keeping a distance, Reg,' he stated.

Reggie shrugged. 'That's how I greeted everyone. I didn't want to call attention to the fact that I knew who you were by doing anything different.'

'So you didn't love me?' Flynn felt compelled to asked as he watched her. It was difficult not to stand and drag her back into his arms because when Reggie got fired up like this, she was more dynamic, more beautiful, more alluring than ever.

'Well, of course I loved you...back then. I did agree to marry you and, contrary to how *you* may do things, when I accept a marriage proposal, it's because I'm in love with the man who's asking.' She glared at him, almost daring him to comment.

'I was in love with you back then, too,' he said. 'But I'd been raised to do my duty to my family and... No.' He shook his head again before standing and walking towards her, his hands open, palms up, indicating he had nothing to hide. She stopped pacing for a moment and looked at him. 'No. No more excuses. I hurt you, Reggie and for that I apologise.'

She gave him a brief nod, showing she accepted his words, and while part of her wanted nothing more than to throw herself into his arms and press her mouth to his, the other part was still simmering with repressed anger. Flynn came from money, from a wealthy and prestigious family, and she knew, firsthand, that those types of people couldn't be trusted. Had he changed? Well, he was divorced from his pretty socialite wife, or so the tabloids had reported a while back, but who was to say that was actually true?

She angled her head, needing to check. 'You *are* divorced from Violet, aren't you?'

'Yes.'

Reggie clenched her jaw and crossed her arms over her chest. 'But you still want to be sure that I didn't chase after you for your money, don't you? You'll always be wondering, right?' When he didn't immediately answer she rolled her eyes and started to pace again.

'Well, you'll be pleased to hear, Flynn, that I have *never* been interested in one single penny of your precious Jamieson Corporation millions. Not then and most definitely not now. Even accepting your help with relocating my neighbours, knowing the big corporation was footing the bill and no doubt using it as a tax dodge, was a big hurdle for me to personally overcome.'

'I didn't offer the corporation's money to help those people, Reg,' he quickly interjected. 'I'm offering my own. The wealth, as you term it, that I have now has nothing to do with my father's corporation. The money I have came to me after my mother's death. My inheritance. I was cut out of my father's will and, therefore, any claim to the corporation the moment I signed the divorce papers.'

That stopped her pacing. She stared at him in surprise. 'You…you've walked away from your father?'

'From his blackmail, from his controlling presence, from his world? Yes.'

'Oh.' She dropped her arms back to her sides. 'I didn't realise.'

'It's been three years now.'

'You've been divorced for three years?'

'Officially, yes.'

'Oh,' she said again, the anger starting to dissipate. 'And you didn't…?' She stopped. How could she possibly ask him if he'd thought of her during that time? Whether he'd tried to find her? Had he even really cared about her amidst all his other family politics?

'Didn't what?' he prompted, but she shook her head and thankfully he dropped the subject. Flynn took a tentative step towards her and when she didn't back away he tried another and another until he was standing before her. 'It was a mistake for me to marry Violet.'

'Yes.'

'It was a mistake for me to treat you so badly.'

'Yes.'

Flynn reached out and brushed his fingers through

her gorgeous black locks. 'Do you think we can try again?'

'Try again…as in…what? What does that mean?'

'It means…' he reached down and linked his free hand with hers '…that we see if, after everything we've been through, whether we're still…compatible.' His tone was soft, smooth and inviting. Reggie could feel herself beginning to crumble, could feel the walls she so desperately wanted to keep in place begin to weaken, and when he bent his head and brushed a soft and tantalising kiss across her cheek, her eyelids fluttered closed and she breathed in the scent of him.

Good heavens. The man smelled fantastic. How did he do that after such a busy and stressful day?

'I don't…' She stopped and swallowed over the dryness of her throat. 'I don't know, Flynn.'

'Why? Because I hurt you before?' He brushed a kiss to her other cheek, lingering a little longer.

'Mmm-hmm,' she sighed, parting her lips to allow the pent-up air to escape.

'Do you think you can trust me again?' He whispered the words near her mouth, keeping such a marginal distance that she started to yearn for his lips to be on hers once more. From their very first kiss to their very last, his mouth had always fitted hers perfectly, as though they'd been made for each other. 'Do you?'

'I don't know.' The whispered words were barely audible and Flynn drew back slightly. He cupped her face with one hand and brushed his thumb over her parted lips. She gasped with surprised delight, opening her eyes to stare into his. 'The attraction is clearly alive and well.'

'Yes.'

'And I know you trust me as far as work is concerned.'

'Yes.'

'And you know I'd never force you to do anything you didn't want to so I can safely say that you can trust me with your honour.'

'Yes.'

'So what is it, Reggie? What is it that is holding you back from giving me...giving *us* another chance?'

Reggie bit her lip, the intrusive thoughts from her past bursting forth into her mind at his question. Why couldn't she give him another chance? 'Because you're wealthy and I don't trust wealthy people.'

'What?' He eased back, dropping his hand to her shoulder. 'I don't understand.'

'Wealth corrupts. Even the nicest, strongest people. It corrupts them.'

'And you know this how? Because of me being unable to stand up to my father all those years ago?'

'No. This has nothing to do with you, Flynn. It does, however, have everything to do with me.'

'You? You've been hurt by wealthy people before?'

Reggie couldn't believe the way her repressed memories, ones she'd carefully locked away in a mental box with 'Do Not Touch' written all over it, continued to flood her mind. Her anxiety and agitation started to increase and she turned away from Flynn, needing distance, needing space. She sucked in a breath and then another one, trying not to hyperventilate while she desperately searched for her self-control. She breathed out, unable to believe the fear rising within her, making her throat go dry, almost choking her. Flynn frowned, noting the paleness of her complexion.

'Reg?' She could hear the concern in his voice.

She closed her eyes and shook her head, knowing she needed to say these words to Flynn. It was true that she would love to have another chance with him and where all those years ago she'd been unable to talk about her past, unable to open up to him and tell him the disgusting things that had happened to her, she knew if there was ever any hope of any sort of future for herself and Flynn, she had to tell him the truth.

'I can't say it.' The words were a whisper and when he crossed to her and put his hands on her shoulders, coaxing her to look at him, all she could do was close her eyes and shake her head vehemently.

'It's all right, Reggie. Whatever you have to say, I'm here.' He'd never seen her like this before, so small and childlike. The Reggie he'd always known had been larger than life, vibrant, funny, with the most infectious laugh. 'You're starting to really worry me,' he said, and it was then, when she heard the tremor in his voice, that she knew she had to do this.

She swallowed again and opened her eyes. As she lifted her chin so she could meet Flynn's gaze, her heart was pounding furiously in her chest.

'Easy. Gently. It's all right, Reg. I'm here. Right here. Nothing you can say will change that.'

'You haven't heard what it is I have to say.'

'Trust me, Reg.' He brushed a feather-light kiss across her lips, not to break the mood or for any romantic reason but rather to give her courage. 'Please?'

Reggie breathed out again and nodded, his hands on her shoulders helping to calm her anxious brain. 'OK.' She breathed out, unable to believe she was really going to open that hateful box and expose herself, her inner self, to Flynn.

'All those years ago, when we first met, I knew who you were because I was raised in Melbourne, not far from where you lived.'

'What?' It had clearly been the last thing he'd expected her to say.

'I hate wealthy people because…my parents were wealthy. In fact, my father knew your father.'

'What?' She'd clearly stunned him.

'When I turned eighteen I changed my name by deed poll to Regina Smith.'

'Why?' Flynn was starting to get a bad feeling in his stomach at what she was saying. 'What name were you christened with?'

She forced calmness into her words as she spoke. 'My name was…Regina Anne Catherine Elizabeth Fox-Wallington.'

'Fox-Wallington?' He whispered the surname with incredulity and disbelief.

'I see you remember my family well.'

'You're *that* Regina? The young girl who was abused by her parents?'

She forced herself to keep her chin up, to keep looking into his eyes, seeing his own disbelief at what she was saying. 'Yes,' she confirmed. 'I'm *that* Regina.'

CHAPTER NINE

'OH, REG.' FLYNN shook his head, anguish in his voice. 'I remember. It was in the papers, on the news. They'd been abusing you for years. Physically as well as emotionally.'

Strangely enough, now that she'd come this far, now that she'd confessed the secret of her real identity to Flynn, the pressure of the anxiety started to dissipate. She cleared her throat, amazed at how normal her voice sounded when she spoke. 'For years my parents made sure their private physician looked after me, treating my wounds, isolating me when they took longer to heal than expected.'

'What?'

'Wealth corrupts. That doctor had no problem with being paid off and when the truth finally came out, he had the gall to state that he would often suggest they send me to another boarding school in order to save me from their wrath. I was nothing but a punching bag to my father and my mother would slap me around and then put her cigarettes out on me. The physician was struck off the register and is doing gaol time.'

'Oh, Reg.' Tears came into Flynn's eyes as she recounted the events with little to no emotion. It was a defence mechanism, he knew that, but, still, the traumas she must have endured. 'How did you finally managed to bring it all to light?'

'The last school they sent me to, when I was sixteen, was rife with bullies and, quite frankly, by then I'd had enough of being everyone's punching bag. I'd tried to talk to my teachers at school, to counsellors, but no one would ever believe that the great and powerful Walter Fox-Wallington would ever hit his own child.

'As I was treated by their private doctor, there were no medical records of my injuries, of my broken bones, of my extensive bruising—no *proof*—so why *would* anyone believe me? As far as the teachers and counsellors were concerned, I was a spoiled and wealthy brat who was clearly troubled and who loved to make up stories about her parents.

'Besides, if they actually did find the courage to question my parents, which a few of them did, my father would pull his financial support from the school or slap a law suit on anyone who dared question his word.' Reggie shrugged both her shoulders, Flynn's hands rising and falling with the action. 'You can do anything with money. At least, that was my father's motto and one he used to spit at me every time he "donated" enormous sums of money in order to keep people quiet.'

'But surely someone knew he was corrupt?'

'I'm sure plenty of people did but blackmail, self-preservation and the power of wealth go a long way to buying silence. Besides, he'd simply smile brightly and tell people I was a delusional teenager, a spoiled brat with a grudge against her parents.'

'So…how did you…escape that life?' He was agog at what she was saying.

'I ran away from boarding school. I stowed away on a goods train and ended up in Sydney. There, I found a drop-in centre and a solicitor, Elika, who wasn't afraid to take the case on. Pro bono, of course.'

Flynn was still stunned as he stared down into her face. She'd been through so much and his heart ached for her. No wonder she hated people with money. She had good reason to. 'I remember the story breaking.' His words were soft. 'I remember my father doing everything he could to distance himself from the Fox-Wallington fiasco, as he termed it. He also pulled any and all investments he had in your father's companies.'

'So he wasn't as much concerned with what had happened but rather with protecting himself.'

Flynn shrugged. 'Everything was business to him. Even my mother and myself, although my mother knew what sort of life she was signing up for when she married him.'

'The wealthy have their own set of rules and heaven help anyone who dares to stand up to them or go against them.'

'Ain't that the truth.' His words were filled with heartfelt honesty and as Reggie looked into his eyes she saw that perhaps, just perhaps, there was a possibility that Flynn really understood what it was she was trying to say.

'So where are your parents now? I can't remember what happened.'

'They're dead.' The words were said with no emotion, no relief, no bitterness, no pain. 'When my father realised he couldn't buy off the solicitor, he and my mother left the country for Spain.'

Flynn rolled his eyes. 'No extradition.'

'Exactly. They lived there for almost two years, in perfect luxury, before dying in a boating accident.' She frowned, her voice dropping just a little. 'I wasn't sad when I was told of their deaths. Instead, I demanded to see the bodies—just to make sure.'

'You did? It wasn't…traumatic?'

'I'd just started medical school, so I'd seen my fair share of cadavers. Besides, I'm not meaning to sound callous but I needed to know if it was true. To help me come to terms with the horrific things they did to me, I needed to see their cold, dead bodies on that slab.' She looked away from him. 'I'm sorry if that sounds harsh but—'

'I understand, Reg. Those people weren't your parents, they were the monsters who had made your life a misery.'

Reggie jerked her head up in surprise. 'Yes. Exactly.'

'You had to be sure it was really over.'

'And it was. I identified their bodies and with Elika's help organised for their cremations. There was no funeral, no wake, no chance for people to "honour" those monsters.'

Flynn rubbed his hands along her shoulders, knowing he shouldn't be at all surprised at the inner strength this woman possessed. He gazed down into her eyes. 'You are incredible, Reg. So strong and always so happy and bubbly and yet you've been through so much pain. How did you cope?'

'Well, for a start, I found some wonderful friends at medical school. Sunainah, Bergan and Mackenzie have all been through their own pain and anguish and somehow, although the four of us are incredibly different, we bonded because we all understood what it was like to be a victim.'

'And it's a friendship that's as strong and as true over twenty years later.'

'Yes.' She smiled, thinking of the way she and her friends had stuck together through thick and thin…and how they'd all managed to find the man of their dreams, that one special person they could always rely on, no matter what. The smile started to slide from her lips as she gazed up at Flynn. Was *he* her one special person? The one she could rely on, no matter what?

She'd thought so once before but he'd let her down. Was it possible she could take a chance again? Put her heart out there? Would Flynn hurt her again, especially now that he knew the truth about her past? He was looking at her as though she was the most wonderful, most special and most precious person in the world to him. Was that real?

He'd mentioned the attraction between them being still as strong…possibly stronger than before and he'd been right. When he put his arms around her, she felt as though she'd come home. When he kissed her, she felt as though her entire world was filled with sparkles and rainbows and pure happiness. When he gazed down into her eyes, as he was doing right now, her heart constricted and her breathing became shallow, wanting him to look at her that way always, to support her always, to love her always.

Could they try again?

'Reg, you are special to me. I hope you believe that.'

'I want to,' she whispered.

'Then do it.' He cupped her face and smiled at her before dipping his head to brush his lips lightly across hers. Reggie closed her eyes, wanting to absorb every sensation he was evoking within her, wanting to lose herself in the pleasure and happiness only Flynn could give her. They'd been so good together all those years ago. Perhaps now they could be better. She parted her lips to deepen the kiss but Flynn edged back. 'Reggie?'

'Mmm?' she sighed, her eyes still closed.

'There's just one thing I need to know.' There was a tentativeness in his tone and she immediately looked at him, worry piercing her.

'What?' She searched his beautiful blue eyes and instinctively realised what it was he was still confused about. 'The money?'

'Yes. Your father, from what I can recall, was worth a lot of money.'

'He was. He left it all to my mother, expecting her to outlive him. She, however, hadn't made a will and as their daughter I inherited it all.'

'You did?'

'I did.'

'So…you're wealthy?'

She shook her head. 'No. I didn't want a penny. I signed the entire fortune over to Elika, the solicitor who helped me, the one person who I knew was unlikely to be corrupted. Then I changed my name. My past was gone. Erased. I had a clean slate and I could start again.'

'Wait.' He eased back and held up one hand. 'Let me get this straight. You gave the *entire* Fox-Wallington fortune away?'

'Yes.'

'But that would have been…billions.'

'Wealth corrupts.' She tried to edge away from him

but he immediately put both his hands on her shoulders again.

'But what about medical school?'

'What about it? I did what normal people do. I accepted government funding to pay my university fees, found a cheap place to live and worked all sorts of jobs in order to have enough money to eat.'

'And this solicitor, Elika, what has she done with all that money?'

'Ever heard of the Moffat Drop-in Centres?'

'For teens and abused children?'

'Yes, as well as children and teenagers living on the street, or those who are having a hard time. There's a centre here in Maroochydore that Bergan and Richard do a lot of work with.'

'That's you?'

'No. That's Elika, the solicitor. Well, she's more of a businesswoman nowadays and well into her sixties, but she's still making a difference and the drop-in centres are just the tip of the iceberg. She works with various organisations both in Australia and overseas to help people in need.'

'You just gave all that money away?'

'Why wouldn't I? As far as I was concerned, it was blood money and, besides, it had never brought me happiness. All I've ever wanted was to be normal. A normal girl, doing a normal job, living a normal life.'

'Wow.' He shook his head in wonderment.

'What?'

'You're…so strong.'

'It took me years to piece myself back together, to figure out who I wanted to be as an adult, and with the help of my friends I think I've done a pretty good job.'

'Why didn't you tell me any of this all those years ago?'

'Because it's also taken me years to learn who to trust. It's not an easy thing for me to do and, for the record, I had planned to tell you everything the day after we became engaged, but—'

'But I broke it off.' He closed his eyes, unable to believe how ridiculously stupid he'd been back then. 'And I turned out to be yet another wealthy person you couldn't trust.'

'That's how I saw it.'

'But, for the record, Reggie—and I'm not trying to defend my actions back then or justify my behaviour— I wasn't corrupted by money. I was corrupted by guilt. I didn't marry Violet because my father threatened to cut me off without a cent. I did it because my mother was dying and it was the one thing that would make her happy, to see her son happily settled.'

Reggie looked up into his eyes and for the first time since they'd been talking reached up and brushed her fingers across his cheek. 'You loved your mother.' It was a statement because she could see clearly in his eyes, hear it in his voice.

'I did. Very much.'

'You wanted to make her happy in her last days.'

'Yes, but I let myself get pressured into doing something I should never have done. I resent that now.'

'But you're not that man anymore. I can tell. You're stronger now. You're more...*you*.' She shook her head. 'I'm not explaining that well.'

'No. You're right. I am different.' He gave her a cute, lopsided smile. 'Perhaps these six years apart haven't been a total waste of time.'

'Perhaps we both needed to do some more growing up.'

'Exactly. I've found the courage to change, not because anyone's told me to but because I needed to, for myself. I needed to find out who I was, without my parents, without Violet and without any other pressure.'

'And have you?'

The smile on his lips increased as he shifted towards her, his arms coming about her waist to draw her near. 'Yes. It took me a while to realise it, that I needed to change my life because I wasn't happy.'

'It can be the most difficult thing in the world to do, to take a stand and follow your heart, to do what you know is right.'

'Yes.' He smiled at her. 'And now I need to do what I know is right, to follow my heart and kiss you once more, Reg.'

Reggie loved hearing those words from his mouth and as she sighed against him she couldn't help but raise one teasing eyebrow. 'Only once more?'

His grin widened as he settled her into his arms. 'I like the way you're thinking.' And with that he lowered his head and claimed her mouth in a kiss filled with passion and promise. Exactly what those promises might be she had no idea, but for now she was more than happy just to go with the fact that she'd managed to work up the courage to tell Flynn about her past... and he hadn't rejected her. He'd understood. He'd supported her. He'd accepted.

He was also doing the most wonderful and delectable things to her mouth, tantalising and teasing her senses. The love she knew had never died welled up in her heart, bursting forth with delight throughout her entire body. She loved Flynn. She always had but she knew of old that to love someone didn't necessarily mean there would be a happy ending.

Still, he knew just how to hold her, just how to kiss her, just how to drive her completely crazy with longing. He knew that rubbing small circles at the base of her spine caused tingles to explode within her. He knew that pressing sweet butterfly kisses along her cheek, towards her ear and then down to her neck made goosebumps break out over her entire body.

He knew that whispering words of delight, telling her just how attractive he found her, how he was drawn to her, how he couldn't get enough of her, all drove her almost to distraction.

Soon she was light-headed and swooning, leaning against him for support as her knees started to give way. Within another second Flynn had scooped her up into his arms and carried her to the lounge. He sat down, settling her in his lap, his arms shifting to hold her tightly, his mouth not leaving hers for an instant.

Reggie sighed against him, unable to believe she was finally back here again, back in his arms, back where she'd yearned to be for so very long. Flynn was here. *Her* Flynn, and he was kissing her exactly as he had during all her dreams about him.

'Mmm,' she moaned as he continued to wreak havoc with her senses. She could feel his restraint, feel he was trying to keep things soft and steady, not wanting to scare her away, but didn't he realise that she didn't scare easily? She wanted him. Couldn't he feel that?

The fact that he was taking things slowly was only making her desire for him increase and when he eased his mouth from hers to trace her lips tantalisingly with his tongue, knowing how the action drove her crazy, his breath mingling and blending with hers, Reggie thought her heart would burst.

'Flynn,' she breathed. 'I want you.'

'I know.' He kissed her cheek.

'This can't be wrong. Not a second time.'

'No.' He kissed her other cheek.

'Shouldn't we go…somewhere a little more comfortable?' The words were a husky whisper as he continued to kiss her neck, Reggie tilting her head to the side to grant him all the access he desired.

'No.'

Reggie's eyes flew open, his one-word answer like a stylus scratching its way across a record. 'No?'

'No,' he repeated, his voice thick with repressed desire.

She shifted so she could look at him better and as she did so he seemed to take it as a sign to remove her from his lap and to settle her next to him on the lounge. 'Flynn?' She swallowed over the confusion even she could hear in her voice.

'Reg, I don't want to rush things.' He bent and kissed her lips as though needing her to know he was still very much on board with what was happening between them. 'This time we need to take things slowly.'

'Because we didn't take things slowly last time?'

'Exactly. And…' he brushed the backs of his fingers across her cheek and then pushed some of her dark, spiky locks behind her ear '…you deserve better. With everything you've confessed to me, plus with everything that's happened in the past few days, I think we're definitely starting to move way too fast again. Don't you?'

Reggie stared at him, unable to believe the words

were coming out of his mouth. How was it possible he could be even more wonderful, more considerate, more chivalrous than she remembered? He cared about her. He *really* cared about her and he was willing to prove that by slowing things down. She opened her mouth to agree with him but found the words were stuck behind the bubble of emotion, so she nodded instead.

'I was wondering, just this morning, how you were able to deal with your home burning down so easily, how you could just accept the fact and not wallow and cry and scream, as you most certainly have every right to do, but now...' Flynn brushed his thumb over her lips before bending and mimicking the same action with his lips '...with everything you've been through, you've built up an amazing resilience to things beyond your control. That, my beautiful Reg, is an amazing quality and you have it in spades. You just pick yourself up and keep on moving forward and I want you to know just how much I admire you.'

'Oh, Flynn.' She couldn't believe he was saying such nice things to her and quickly fanned her face with her hand, needing to lighten the atmosphere around them with a touch of humour. It worked because he smiled warmly in response. 'You say the sweetest things.'

'I meant every word.'

She dropped the pretence for a moment and nodded. 'I don't doubt it.'

'Good, because I think the next thing we should discuss is getting some sleep—me upstairs, you downstairs and, no, that isn't a euphemism or meant as a *double entendre.*'

Reggie laughed; the sound lighter and freer than she could ever remember hearing before. Flynn removed his arm from around her shoulders, then stood and pulled her to her feet. He held her hand as he walked her to her room. 'Make free use of the bathroom. I'll use the en suite.'

'OK.' She stood at the door to her room and looked up at him. She smiled then stood on tiptoe and kissed him. 'Who said chivalry was dead?' she asked rhetorically.

'Taking things slower is a good thing.'

'Yes.'

'We deserve the time to really get to know each other again.'

'Yes.'

Flynn smiled and took her hand in his, raising it to his lips. 'Sleep sweet, Reg.' Then he bowed from the waist and headed up the stairs, blowing her one last kiss from the top. Reggie couldn't help but giggle as she entered the room, sighing romantically.

'Oh, Flynn, you really do know how to make a girl feel special,' she whispered, and it was so true. She could trust him. He was showing her that by not rushing into things. He cared about her and it was still a little difficult for her to get her head around that realisation. Was it possible that this time they'd be able to really move forward with their life together? A normal life together? After all, wasn't Flynn the most perfect man for her?

Surely, with everything they'd discussed tonight, there was no way he'd ever hurt her again. Right?

CHAPTER TEN

FROM THE NEXT morning, even though they hadn't specifically discussed it, they appeared to be back together. When Reggie had come into the kitchen for breakfast, Flynn once more having already made the coffee and toast, he'd crossed to her side, given her a hug and brushed a light kiss across her lips.

'Good morning,' he'd said, smiling warmly at her.

'Morning,' she'd returned, before hugging him back, unable to believe how wonderful it felt to be so familiar with him again. He drove them to the hospital but still kept his distance in front of their colleagues, which she was happy about because she wasn't ready for everyone to be staring and gawking at them when she was still trying to figure things out.

He took her shopping for clothes and shoes and all the other little things she needed, not appearing bored by any of the shops they visited or insisting she shop at the most expensive places. She modelled clothes for him, twirling and laughing and smiling and trying to remember when she'd last been this happy. Her car was returned from the garage and he insisted she leave it in his garage, parking his own car in the driveway.

The little girl, Lola, who had been attacked by the

shark, was starting to make progress with her recovery and while it would indeed be a long journey, all the surgeons involved in her care were happy with the way her body was coping with the trauma.

Things were also building up for the hospital's Christmas auction and Reggie and Mackenzie spent quite a bit of time finalising the details.

'One of the outpatient ward clerks signed me up for the bachelor auction that very first morning I was in Outpatients,' Flynn told Reggie when she noticed his name on the sign-up sheet.

'But you're not a bachelor anymore,' she felt compelled to point out.

'Well, technically I am as I'm not married.'

'But we are in a…relationship…' She looked at him with concern. 'Aren't we?'

Or did he just think their time together was a fling? Something to keep him occupied during his six months at the hospital? Had she grasped the wrong end of the stick again? Did she feel more for him than he felt—

'Stop,' he commanded, and when she looked at him, her eyes wide with concern and worry, she noticed he was smiling at her, slowly shaking his head from side to side. 'I can hear your thoughts from here, Reg.' He cupped her face and brought his lips down to warm hers. 'Of course we're in a relationship. Together. Both of us. Mutually exclusive. But apart from our closest friends, no one at the hospital knows that. To pull out of the auction now would raise suspicion.'

'And you don't want to do that?'

Flynn tugged her into his arms, nuzzling her neck once more. 'I like having you all to myself, Reg. I like not having people gossip about us as we walk by. During our lives, and for different reasons, we've both been the topic of discussion and while I know it will happen one day, that the cat will be out of the proverbial bag, I just want a bit longer to have you all to myself.' He pressed his mouth to hers, making her swoon with delight from his glorious kisses.

'I guess it is for a good cause,' she rationalised.

'And I'm absolutely positive that there's a very special woman who's going to ensure she wins the auction.' He glared pointedly at her.

'Really? Which woman is that?' Reggie giggled but pretended to ponder the question. 'Ingrid Brown? She's very interested in you.'

He wrinkled his nose. 'A great surgical registrar but not my type.'

'Clara from Outpatients? Or perhaps—' Her words were cut off as Flynn kissed her into silence.

'You are going to win that auction, Reg,' he whispered in her ear after tantalising her with a thread of butterfly kisses, a spate of delighted goose-bumps flooding her skin. 'Even if I have to give you every last cent.' He lifted his head and looked into her eyes. 'I don't want to be with any other woman—except you.'

Reggie sighed into him as his wonderful words penetrated her heart, accepting the way his mouth continued to create havoc with her equilibrium.

She was still walking on feathers, on pillows, on air when she met Bergan, Mackenzie and Sunainah for coffee. Christmas wasn't that far away and everywhere she went there were people collecting for charity, Santa Clauses in every store, tinsel, carollers and a generally festive atmosphere that was difficult to ignore.

'So…you and Flynn? Still super-happy?' Mackenzie asked.

'Do you even need to ask? Just look at her,' Bergan pointed out. 'It's as plain as the nose on your face,' she remarked, before sipping her coffee.

'You are even happier than usual,' Sunainah added.

'And this time,' Mackenzie remarked as she grinned widely at her friend, 'the happiness you're shining out at the world isn't forced—it's real.'

Reggie giggled, nodding her head at the three of them. 'It's so wonderful and exciting and new and scary and—'

'We've all been there.' Bergan's tone was matter-of-fact. 'A mixture of emotions that keeps your insides churning with angst and delight. You don't need to go on about it.' She wasn't usually one for gushy sentimentality but she reached over and pressed a kiss to her friend's cheek. 'And I couldn't be happier for you,' she said softly, and all of them laughed.

'So are there any plans for a wed—?'

'Stop!' Reggie held up her hand, cutting off Mackenzie's sentence. 'There has been no discussion about anything except that last time we rushed into things far too quickly and this time, well, Flynn wants to take his time.'

'Are you two sharing…a room?' Bergan asked coyly.

'No. Again, he wants to take it slowly.'

'But you have told him about your past? He knows who your parents were?' Sunainah asked quietly.

'Yes.'

'Then it is good he is wanting to take it slowly.' Sunainah nodded in approval. 'I am liking this Flynn Jamieson more and more.'

'But it would be great if we could get to know him better,' Mackenzie pointed out.

'Uh-oh.' Bergan rolled her eyes. 'I'd know that organising look anywhere. Warning. Warning. Cul-de-sac crew gathering imminent.'

Reggie laughed. 'I think it would be great for Flynn to get to know the rest of you much better, too.'

'No doubt Elliot, Richard and John will want to take him under their wing, teach him the dos and don'ts of dealing with the four of us?' Mackenzie clapped her hands. 'Oh, it's just the way I've always wanted it. The four of us, living near each other, helping each other, being a family together.'

Reggie wanted to point out again that nothing was permanently fixed between herself and Flynn but one look at Mackenzie's brightly smiling face and Reggie swallowed the words. For now she could keep her concerns to herself. Like Flynn, she wanted to take things slowly, make sure that they were both on the same page, that they wanted the same things out of life.

For example, she had no idea whether he planned to live in the Sunshine Coast once his contract at the hospital had ended. Did he want to have children in the future? Did he want to travel? How did he see their working relationship? Did he want to work at a different hospital from her? When would he be ready to take their relationship to the next level? Was he still in contact with his father? Did he want her to meet his father? What had really happened between himself and Violet, his ex-wife?

When they'd been together in the Caribbean, he'd occasionally spoken of Violet and his family. 'I'm an only child and so is she,' he'd once told Reggie as they'd walked hand in hand along the beach, admiring the breathtaking sunset.

'Our mothers are the closest of friends and although Violet is a few years younger than me, the two of us have sort of been raised together. We went to the same schools. I was told to look out for her. We played together when we were young. We celebrated birthdays and Christmases with each other's families.'

'So she's just a friend?' Reggie had asked, slightly jealous of the wonderful life he was describing.

'Yes. Nothing more than a friend,' he'd confirmed.

And yet not too long after they'd had that conversation he'd been married to Violet. Now that he'd told her the true circumstances surrounding that union, Reggie still had questions. Was he still friendly with Violet? If so, *how* friendly? Or had their forced marriage been the undoing of a lifetime of friendship? Was that why he didn't talk about her much?

That evening, as they sat watching an old movie together, Reggie really wanted to ask him about Violet, find out some of the answers to the questions that were spinning around in her head, but every time she opened her mouth to speak, she found the words simply wouldn't come out. Surely if he was still in close contact with Violet he would have said something. Wouldn't he? Perhaps the fact that he hadn't spoken much about her indicated their marriage had indeed wrecked the friendship and now the two of them were estranged.

'What am I supposed to do?' she asked Mackenzie as the two of them put the final touches on the ballroom, ready for tomorrow night's Christmas auction. They'd worked closely with the event co-ordinator and she had to admit that the room did indeed look incredibly festive, with green and red tinsel around the place, twinkle lights and a large Christmas tree in the corner. Still, they were responsible for the table decorations and as they'd spent the last few weeks making them, as well as getting people to donate things for the auction. But no matter how many great items were up for bidding, the bachelor auction was most definitely the highlight of the night.

'You're supposed to talk to him,' Mackenzie told her. 'If you want to know about Violet, just ask him. He'll tell you.'

'It's not that I don't trust him,' Reggie began, and Mackenzie raised one eyebrow in question. 'OK.' She spread her arms wide. 'So perhaps I do have a few trust issues. I just want to be sure, this time, that he's not going to up and leave me again. I won't be able to live through the pain a second time. I just won't survive.'

'And you think he's still in touch with Violet?'

'He has to be. Their families are connected and yet he's said nothing about seeing his father at Christmas, or—'

'OK. OK,' Mackenzie interrupted, and put her hands on Reggie's shoulders. 'The only way for you to get rid of this stress and anxiety you're heaping on yourself is to talk to him.' Mackenzie's phone rang and she stared at Reggie for a moment longer before answering it.

'You're right. You're right. I know you're right,' Reggie said, more to herself than to her friend. 'I'll talk to him about it tonight. He'd be open to the discussion...' She bit her lip. 'I hope.'

Mackenzie finished her call. 'That was John.'

'Emergency?'

Mackenzie grinned. 'Yes, but not of the medical

kind. Ruthie's having a sleepover at a friend's house and my husband *needs* me.' She waggled her eyebrows up and down and Reggie couldn't help but laugh.

'Then you'd better get out of here.'

'I can stay and help you finish up here and—'

'Just go. You're lucky enough to have a husband who is crazy about you, so don't go keeping him waiting.'

Mackenzie hugged her friend close. 'Thanks, Reggie.'

Reggie sighed as Mackenzie went, going through the motions of setting up the rest of the table centrepieces before standing back and surveying the room. It looked fantastic. The auction night would be wonderful. They were going to raise a lot of money and she was prepared to pay top dollar for Flynn. No way in the world was she letting Ingrid Brown or any other woman secure the auction prize of a dinner date with the man she loved.

'I'm looking forward to winning you at the auction,' she'd told him the previous night. 'Then I'll have my very own slave.'

'Hey, that's not the terms of the contract. Whoever wins the auction gets to have dinner with me. That's it.' He'd shaken his head and waggled his finger at her. 'No one said anything about slave duties.'

Reggie had playfully slid one hand up his arm and then walked the fingers of her other hand up his chest, and Flynn's grin had widened. 'That depends on what you classify as *slave duties*.'

'Hmm.' He'd accepted the kiss she'd placed on his lips. 'I guess it does.'

After that, they didn't talked much for a while, the two of them completely absorbed in each other, but when things started to get a little heated, Flynn was the one to put on the brakes. 'You make it very difficult to take our time and to go slowly with this relationship,' he murmured against her lips. 'Especially when you are so incredibly delectable and addictive,' he continued, pressing kisses to her neck.

'Likewise,' she returned, plunging her fingers into his hair and bringing his head back so their lips could meet once more. 'It's difficult, Flynn. I want you so much.'

'I know.' He pressed his mouth to hers, slowing things down before lying next to her on the soft rug on the living-room floor. He continued to hold her in his arms, the two of them just lying there. 'I like just... being with you. There's no stress or tension or pressure to be something I'm not. I can be myself with you and you can be yourself with me, and all of that means more to me than anything, Reg.'

He levered himself up onto one elbow and looked down into her beautiful face. 'I don't want you to think I take you for granted. I know what we have between us is rare and unique and incredibly special and I just don't want to mess it up.'

Reggie grinned. 'Slow it is, then.'

'It's the right thing for both of us,' he remarked, before looking past her and frowning.

'What's wrong?' she asked, a frisson of concern churning within her belly.

'Huh?'

'You're frowning. Is there anything I can help you with?'

The frown cleared at her words. 'Nothing's wrong.'

'Really?' Reggie shifted her head so she could see him better. 'Is it your father?'

Flynn shrugged one shoulder. 'I haven't seen or spoken to him in over three years and most of the time I'm fine with that but…'

'Christmas can highlight the fact that families are estranged.'

'Exactly.'

'What did you used to do at Christmas?'

'He'll hire caterers, hold a huge, lavish affair at his house with lots of people he doesn't know, as well as all the people who work in his companies. They'll all get drunk, make mistakes by sleeping with the person they like least and wake up the day after with a multitude of regrets.'

'Sounds like a riot,' she remarked blandly, rubbing her fingertips over the frown lines on his forehead, wanting to do whatever she could to ease them. 'Do you want to see your father?'

'No.' The answer was immediate. 'I've tried in the past to make contact with him and he hasn't appreciated it one little bit. As far as he's concerned, he has no son.'

'Oh, Flynn.'

He swallowed and she knew if she pressed him on the issue he might clam up. She knew what it was like to be disowned by people who were supposed to love you. The wealthy really did have their own set of rules. It was sad that they lived by them. 'So this year,' he said after a moment, 'I am definitely looking forward to starting a new Christmas tradition.'

'Really?'

'With you.'

'Yes.' She kissed him.

'And no doubt the cul-de-sac crew have their big parties and present-giving? Mackenzie and Bergan are already swamped with family. I met Richard's parents yesterday.'

And so they discussed plans for Christmas Day, Reggie more than pleased that it appeared he wanted to spend the day with her. She wanted to ask about Violet. About whether he'd wanted to see her, but she didn't. And now, looking at the festive ballroom, looking perfect for the hospital's Christmas party, she wanted to push aside that one niggling fear of doubt that kept telling her that things seemed too perfect.

'Good things don't happen to me,' she whispered to herself as she headed out into the late-afternoon sunshine. It was such an odd feeling. She had good friends around her. She had a place to stay while all the insurance claims on her apartment were settled. Her neighbours were more than comfortable in the temporary housing Flynn had been generous enough to not only find for them but pay for them. He'd also insisted on remaining anonymous, telling Reggie he didn't need people to be beholden to him.

And above all, she had Flynn back in her life, back wanting to be with her, back wanting a future with her? Hopefully that was the case. Why else would he be insisting they take things slowly? Why else would he be insisting they start their own traditions together?

As she headed down the street towards the hospital, which was only two blocks away, Reggie wondered whether she should tell Flynn that she loved him. Would her declaration change things? Was it what he was waiting to hear before they took their relationship to the next level?

'Oh, why aren't these things as easy as a hernia repair?' she mumbled, as she stopped at the pedestrian lights and pressed the button. She looked down the side street, seeing a family—a mother, a father and little boy—chatting together. A family. A normal family. It was something she'd longed for all her life. The man had his back to her but the woman, with her long blonde hair falling slightly over her face, was folding the stroller and putting it into the boot of her fancy car. The boy was clinging to his father, clearly a little sleepy and more than content to relax in the big, trusty arms that held him.

Reggie sighed, instinctively knowing that Flynn would make a wonderful father. Wouldn't it be nice if that were them? Having spent a lovely day out together, looking forward to heading home and relaxing. Normal people. Normal lives.

The woman closed the boot then held her hands out for the boy. As the man turned to hand the child over, Reggie saw his face. His smiling face—the face smiling at the blonde-haired woman.

'Flynn.' The whispered word left her lips in utter disbelief. The pedestrian lights turned green. Reggie didn't move. Couldn't move as she watched the woman say something to Flynn, both of them laughing brightly. Flynn kissed the little boy and the boy kissed him back, both of them clearly comfortable with each other.

Part of Reggie's mind was racing, panicking, trying to figure out what it was she was seeing, while the other part of her mind was stuck, standing still in stunned shock. Who was the woman? Who was she? Reggie thought back to all those years ago, of the times when she'd read the glossy society mags…and then she remembered where she'd seen that blonde woman. She'd seen her dressed as a bride, she'd seen her looking lovingly up at Flynn as he'd stood beside her—the groom.

The woman was Violet. His ex-wife. After Violet had put the little boy into the car, she'd turned, hugged Flynn close and then pressed a warm kiss to his lips.

Reggie's heart was breaking. It was breaking again. *Flynn* was breaking her heart all over again...and yet it was impossible for her to move. Misery and despair flooded her as the pedestrian lights turned red. Stop. Don't walk. Don't move. Your life is over.

She waited, knowing the inevitable was about to happen, and her heart started pounding out a scared tattooed rhythm against her chest as he began to turn in her direction. In another moment he would see her standing there...watching him.

She shook her head. She didn't want to see him. Didn't want him to see her. Run and hide. *Flee!* Her mind was starting to scream commands at her body but her legs didn't seem able to follow their lead as she remained exactly where she was.

He waved goodbye to the boy in the car, the boy who looked just like him, the boy who was definitely old enough to be his son. If Flynn had a son, why on earth hadn't he told her about him? Was it a condition of his freedom from his father? To hand over access to his son? Was Violet supposed to be in contact with him?

She knew her mind was going into overdrive, clutching at straws to try and make some sort of sense from what she was seeing. The traffic around her was starting to slow again and she became peripherally aware of other people joining her at the pedestrian lights, pressing the button and waiting beside her.

Could they hear the wild pounding of her heart?

Could they feel her pain? Her terror? The one man she'd loved with all her heart had hurt her, not once but twice!

He was turning in her direction, taking a few steps up the street as he continued to wave to the car as Violet indicated and pulled out from the kerb. Reggie couldn't breathe. It was impossible to drag air into her lungs because within a split second he would see her...standing there...watching him betray her.

The moment their gazes met, it was as though the world seemed to stop spinning. Flynn looked confused, then shocked, his eyes widening. His step faltered for a split second, as though he was deciding what it was he should do. He'd just been caught kissing his ex-wife! What would he do?

The next instant he increased his speed, walking with purpose, a determined look in his eyes.

Reggie shook her head and took a step back, even though he was still quite a way away from her. The traffic around her slowed and then the pedestrian lights turned green. The people around her started walking across the street. She looked from the lights back to Flynn and shook her head. Now that she'd actually moved, her body seemed capable of more reaction. Her eyes immediately flooded with tears and her lower lip began to quiver.

'Reggie!'

She shook her head, panic rising within her. She couldn't face him. She didn't want to hear his reasoning, his excuses. All her life people had reasoned with her, provided excuses for the terrible things that had happened to her, and now the one man in the world she'd started to trust, the one man who had captured her heart, was going to break it once again.

'Reg! Wait. I can explain!' His words reached her ears but she brought her hands up, covering them, blocking out his words as she turned and raced across the road just in time. In another instant the traffic started up again, leaving Flynn on one side of the road and Reggie on the other.

Worlds apart, or so it seemed. Flynn had told her she could trust him, that he was different from all the others, but it appeared he'd been lying to her.

Brushing the tears from her eyes so she didn't trip over, Reggie made her way down the street, almost running towards the hospital as though it was her one and only lifeline. The instant she rounded the door, she headed down the stairs, needing to hide herself away, needing to find a place where she could expel the pain from her heart, where she could drag in a cleansing breath, where she could start to make a plan to regroup.

Could she recover from a broken heart yet again? She didn't think so.

CHAPTER ELEVEN

'REGGIE?' BERGAN'S VOICE came over the phone when Reggie had answered the call. 'Where are you?' She'd already rejected several calls from Flynn's cellphone. He was the last person she felt like talking to. How could he? How could he do this to her? She'd opened up her heart, her soul. She'd bared her pain, her horror to him and this was how he thought it was OK to behave? To betray her? No. No. No. The pain in her heart intensified and she choked on another sob.

'Reggie?' Bergan spoke again and it was only the evident concern in her friend's voice that prompted Reggie to answer.

'What?' There was no disguising the tears and pain in her voice as she sniffed and snuffled.

'Where are you? What's happened?' Bergan's tone was insistent and filled with that protective love Reggie had relied on more than once throughout the course of their friendship.

'I… Flynn…' Reggie tried to get the words out but it appeared it was impossible. She'd only just managed to calm herself down, thinking she might be ready to call one of her friends to come and get her, but now that she actually had to put into words what she'd seen,

Reggie found the wave of anguish was washing over her once more.

'He was here in A and E, looking for you, and was quite frankly beside himself with worry. What's happened?'

'Is…is he still th—?' She couldn't finish the sentence, the panic that he might be listening in to this conversation making Reggie skittish again.

'No. I sent him away.'

'Good.' She sighed with relief. 'Good.'

'Where are you?' There was more insistence, more concern in Bergan's words than before.

'When things go belly up, go down, down, down and get as far away as possible.'

'Ah…taking a leaf out of Sunainah's book, eh? Hiding in the basement beneath the stairs. It's a good place, I have to admit. OK. Stay put. I'll be there soon.'

'Don't tell him.' The words were out before she could stop them. 'I don't want to see him. I don't want to speak to him. *Ever.*'

'Relax, Reggie. I've got your back.' With that Bergan disconnected the call and Reggie sat beneath the stairwell in the hospital basement, hugging her knees to her chest.

It was the same place she'd found Sunainah, so long ago now, when Sunainah's life had looked as though there was no possibility for a happy ending. Now her friend was happily married to Elliot, the two of them enjoying being parents to Elliot's wonderful children and even talking about having some of their own. Things had worked out for Sunainah but Reggie couldn't see any possibility of things working out for her and Flynn, not now that he'd betrayed her.

•

Honesty. That was the main thing she needed out of any relationship. Pure and open honesty, and stupidly she'd thought Flynn had thought the same way. Cover-ups, lies and deceit played no part in her life. Hadn't he understood that?

So why on earth had he been warmly kissing his ex-wife?

He'd been holding a little boy who looked just like him and who he appeared to love very much. Reggie had been able to see that clearly in his eyes. Did Flynn have a son? If so, why hadn't he told her about him? Why had he felt the need to keep secrets from her? Not to trust her? To hurt her by betraying her yet again?

She'd been a fool to think that things were looking up for her, that finally she might be able to find the elusive happiness she'd been searching for all her life. Over and over again people came into her life and they let her down. If it weren't for Mackenzie, Sunainah and Bergan showing her it was indeed possible to trust, Reggie would have given up long ago and allowed the spirit of pessimism and depression to invade her heart.

She searched her pockets for a tissue and eventually found one, dabbing her eyes and blowing her nose, knowing she could well play the part of Santa's lead reindeer with her red face.

'Reggie?'

Finally she heard Bergan's voice echo down the stairwell and held her breath, her eyes wide as she listened to the footfalls on the stairs. Were there two people coming down? Had Flynn been lurking in the shadows? Watching Bergan? Following Bergan, knowing she would lead him to where she was hiding?

'Reggie? I'm alone,' Bergan said, as though answering her unspoken question.

'Are you sure?'

'Yes.' There was absolute certainty in Bergan's words and Reggie breathed out a sigh of relief as she wriggled out from her hiding spot and brushed herself off. The instant Bergan stood before her, Reggie threw herself into her friend's arms, fresh tears spilling forth. Bergan placated her, stroking her back as the gut-wrenching sobs started all over again.

'Here's a fresh pack of tissues,' Bergan eventually offered after a minute or two. Reggie eased back, knowing she must look a sight and immediately wiped her eyes and blew her nose. 'Flynn told me what happened.' Bergan spoke softly. 'He says it's not what you think.'

'How would he know what I think?' Reggie asked, a fresh bout of tears stinging in her eyes. 'He lied to me, Bergan. He kept asking me to trust him and I did and I told him all about my past and how people have constantly let me down—all my life—and now he's done it to me. Not once, but *twice*!' Her words were scattered, broken up between sobs and hiccups, her voice high and bordering on hysteria. *'Twice!'* She held up two fingers as though to confirm it. 'Why am I so stupid? Why do I let him do this to me?'

Bergan shrugged. 'I don't know, Reggie, but first things first. We need to get you out of here. I've left Richard in charge of A and E and I'm taking you—'

'Not to the cul-de-sac.' Her words were instant, her eyes flashing with insistent fire. 'You have people staying with you and so does Mackenzie and I don't want to be near Flynn. I just need space. I need to be able to breathe and to think things through and—'

'I understand and I know the perfect place for you to go. Somewhere safe.' Bergan held out her hand to her friend.

'You do?'

'Come on.' Reggie allowed herself to be led away by Bergan, but couldn't help the need to constantly look over her shoulder just in case Flynn was lurking around the corner. 'Relax. Flynn's gone. He left the hospital over half an hour ago. He said he had some things to organise.'

Reggie sighed with relief at knowing Flynn really wasn't on the hospital grounds and when she was safe in Bergan's car she rested her head back against the seat and closed her eyes, her head starting to pound. All she could see, all she could think about was the image of Violet and Flynn, kissing each other. It was as though it was burned into her memory and would remain there forever. At least the last time he'd broken her heart there had only been him telling her it was over—not the vision of him lip-smacked with his ex-wife! How could he have done that to her?

When Bergan stopped the car, Reggie found herself outside the new apartment block where Melva and her other neighbours were staying. The apartments Flynn had organised.

'Melva's place?' There was a hint of hope in Reggie's tone.

'What do you think?'

'This is perfect,' Reggie remarked, nodding. 'I haven't found the time to come and visit my neighbours since the fire and...' She looked at Bergan. 'This *is* just what I need. Some Melva therapy.'

'An escape,' Bergan remarked, smiling at her friend.

'Yes.'

'Go and spend time with Melva. I'm sure the evening nurse who comes to change the dressings on Melva's burns would love the night off, knowing you're going to be staying here for the night.'

'Of course I'll change Melva's dressings. That woman has always been there for me, from the first moment we met.'

'I know.'

'And it's all right with Melva?' Reggie checked as she undid her seat belt and alighted from the car. Her answer was to have her neighbour open the front door and come out to her, walking frame in front in order to steady her.

'Oh, Reggie. What a wonderful surprise. I was delighted when your young man called and said you were coming to stay.'

'My young...man?' Alarm bells instantly began to ring in Reggie's ears as she looked quickly at Bergan, whose answer was to simply shrug one shoulder and sigh.

'I can't take credit for thinking to bring you to Melva's. It was Flynn's idea. He said if you needed space then he would give you space.'

'Flynn organised all of this?' Reggie wasn't sure whether to feel betrayed by Bergan or happy that Flynn had realised she needed space. Darn him for being his usual thoughtful self. It made it even more difficult for her to remember the pain he was causing her. 'That is so like him,' she growled between gritted teeth. 'Why does he have to do something nice when he's hurt me so badly?'

'Perhaps he's trying to show you how much he cares.'

'Then he should care by *not* kissing his ex-wife.'

'Listen,' Bergan said, hugging her friend close and whispering in Reggie's ear. 'I think the man is crazy about you. Even Richard agrees. Flynn is head over heels in love with you.'

'Ha!' Reggie snorted. 'He's got a funny way of showing it. By lying to me. By not telling me about…' She stopped, closing her eyes on the memory that was once more flashing before her eyes. 'You know what? It doesn't matter. *I* want to see Melva. *I* want to spend time with her, so that's what *I'm* going to do.'

'Good for you,' Bergan replied. 'Rest and relax. Get rid of your anxious mind. Enjoy your day off tomorrow. Sleep in. Watch TV. I'll see you at the hospital auction tomorrow night.'

Reggie grimaced at these words. 'I don't know if I want to go. I don't know if I want to see Flynn. It's too soon, especially if he's trying to control my life from afar.'

'Reggie.' Bergan smiled at her friend. 'He's not controlling anything. You are in complete control of all your faculties. Just relax and think about tomorrow when tomorrow comes.'

'Are you coming in for a cuppa, Bergan?' Melva asked from the doorway. 'I've just bought some nice new cups. They're very flash, bone china, and I spent a bit more on them then I should have but then I decided that after everything that's happened, I deserved a treat. Did you know,' Melva continued, 'that apparently we get paid a recovery allowance to help us buy new things while we're waiting for the insurance money to come through? I thought I'd be out of pocket for weeks but at the moment I seem to have more money than I know how to deal with.'

Reggie closed her eyes for a moment, delighted with the beaming smile on her neighbour's face, knowing instinctively that Flynn was the one who had provided that allowance. Insurance companies didn't settle up that quickly. He was using his wealth for the good of others and her heart warmed at the thought.

Perhaps he *was* different from the other people who had allowed money and position to corrupt them. Deep down inside she knew Flynn wasn't like that. He didn't use people and lie to them. So why hadn't he told her about Violet? About the boy? Why hadn't he been able to trust her?

'No, thanks, Melva,' Bergan replied, her words snapping Reggie's attention back to the present. 'Just dropping Reggie off. I need to get back to the hospital.' She hugged her friend again and looked pointedly at her. 'Call me later if you want to talk.'

'No need to worry about that,' Melva said. 'Reggie and I are going to have a great ol' chin-wag, aren't we, love? Now, come on in. Ooh, look. Here's a delivery van pulling up. Good heavens, it's like Grand Central Station out here at the moment.'

Sure enough, the driver of the delivery van was soon walking towards them, a parcel in his hands.

'I'm looking for Reggie Smith?'

Reggie's eyes widened at that, then she frowned in confusion. 'Uh…that's me.'

'OK. If you could sign here.' He waited until she'd done as he'd asked, then handed over the parcel. 'You ladies have a lovely evening,' he said with a polite smile and just as quickly as he'd arrived, he disappeared.

'What is it?' Melva asked, and a stunned Reggie
gave it a quick shake.

'I don't know.'

'Then come inside and we'll open it.' Melva turned
to Bergan. 'Bye-bye, deary. Thanks for dropping her
off. I'll take it from here.' Melva pointedly winked at
Bergan, not being very subtle, but Reggie decided to
let it go for now.

After waving goodbye to Bergan, Melva and Reggie
headed inside to see what exactly was in the package.
'There's no return address, except for a local department store.' Reggie closed the door and walked into the
comfortable lounge room, remembering to admire the
décor of the apartment.

'Ooh. A mystery.' Melva found a pair of scissors and
handed them to Reggie so she could open it.

'Hmm.' Reggie looked slyly at the elderly woman.
'Is it really?'

Melva giggled as Reggie cut open the top of the parcel, then pulled out a toothbrush, a tube of toothpaste,
a pair of soft satin pyjamas and a hairbrush and clean,
new underwear that was scarlet.

'Now, *those* are far more expensive than my tea
cups,' Melva remarked, before whistling, the noise making Reggie blush. 'Is there a note?'

'No, but I think we both know exactly who they're
from.'

'They're from the same person who's found this furnished apartment, who's paying my allowance and who
rang me, not half an hour ago and asked if it was all
right for you to come and visit for the night.'

'What did he say?' Reggie asked softly.

'He said you'd had a shock and he wanted you to

have some space and time to process everything. He thought spending some time with me, the closest person you have to a mother, might be good for you. I told him I was more like your grandmother but I knew what he meant.'

A lump formed in Reggie's throat as Melva recounted what Flynn had said to her. 'You know who he is, don't you,' she stated quietly.

'Of course, dear. I lived in Melbourne for many years. I used to do private hairdressing for the likes of those people.'

Reggie's eyes widened at this news. 'So…do you know who I—?'

'Yes, dear.' Melva eased herself down into a comfortable high-backed armchair. 'I've known from the first moment I clapped eyes on you.'

'And yet you never said anything?' A lump welled in Reggie's throat.

'Why? What was the point in dredging up pain?' She shook her head. 'A person's past is their past. There's nothing they can do to change it. They can only learn from it and move forward into a better version of their future. If you get stuck in quicksand you either stay there, not caring that you can't get out, or you do something about it.' Melva looked at Reggie and nodded, pride in her voice. 'You were one of the strong ones. You were able to leave your past behind you, go to medical school, make something of your life, but sometimes…like with your young man…well, it just takes a little bit longer for people to figure things out. He had to get out of the quicksand and he could only do it for the right reasons.'

'Do you think *I'm* involved with those reasons?'

Melva chuckled. 'What do you think, ya silly goose?'

Reggie frowned, listening carefully to what Melva was saying. She knew the wise woman was right, even though the last thing Reggie wanted was to be rational about all this. Her emotions were mixing again, tumbling over each other in a mass of confusion.

It was true there was no way she could change what had happened in either her past or the one she'd shared with Flynn. The past was the past. She knew deep down inside he was a good man and while they'd both made mistakes—him for leaving her and her for letting him—it didn't change the fact that he'd hurt her.

Logically, she knew time and a bit of distance was necessary for her to sort her thoughts out but emotionally she wanted to be mad at him, she wanted to hold on to her anger. She wanted to continue being annoyed with him, especially as he really did seem to know her very well. He'd realised that her spending time with Melva, away from him, away from Mackenzie, Bergan and Sunainah—being with someone who was completely impartial to all that had gone before—was exactly what Reggie would need.

'Hmm,' she growled softly, the frown still marring her forehead.

'Don't overthink things, Reggie. Sometimes you just need to go with the flow.' Melva waved her hands in the air.

Reggie sighed and turned her attention back to Melva, the frown immediately disappearing. 'How did you get to be so wise?' she asked.

Melva chuckled. 'I'm eighty-two years old, darling, that's how. I've picked up a thing or two about this whole game-of-life thing.' She sighed. 'Now, are you

going to make us a cup of tea in my new fancy cups
and start enjoying yourself or do I have to get cross
with you?'

Reggie instantly smiled as she stood to her feet. 'Tea
it is.'

Even though she'd had a lovely time with Melva, Reggie didn't sleep all that well. Her mind was constantly
churning with everything she knew about Flynn, trying
to piece together exactly what sort of man he was. Before yesterday she would have said he wasn't the type of
man to cheat on a woman but she'd seen the way money
could corrupt even the most saintly of men.

If that little boy was his son, then it was something
she would have to deal with if there was any hope of a
future with Flynn. Did she want a future with Flynn?
Her heart was saying yes, yes, yes, but her mind was
saying no, no, no.

Then what of Bergan? Her strong, determined friend,
who would stand like a guard with swords crossed to
staunchly protect her from any enemy, had crumbled
and gone along with the plan Flynn had put into place.
She knew that happiness came from within and that she
couldn't rely on someone else, couldn't hold them responsible for her own happiness, but she also accepted
that to go through the rest of her life with Flynn by her
side would, indeed, go a long way to making her happy.

She'd tried living without him before and it had been
difficult. If things really weren't as they seemed, if
she'd somehow grabbed the wrong end of the stick then
perhaps…maybe…would she really be foolish enough
to employ some small level of hope?

'Oh, Flynn,' she whispered over her cup of early-morning coffee as she stood looking out of Melva's kitchen window as the sun rose, shining its glorious light all around. The darkest little cracks and crevices changed from a dull grey to vibrant colour. The yellows, pinks, purples and blues. Slowly but surely it was as though the world was waking up, coming to life, wanting to celebrate the new day.

Wasn't that how she'd been since Flynn had returned to her life? Filled with colour? Wanting to celebrate life? She'd forced herself to become a bright and bubbly person, always seeing the glass as half-full rather than half-empty, always wanting to look on the bright side of things, always wanting to surround herself with happiness, but now she knew as an absolute certainty that without Flynn in her life, that's all her life would ever be—forced happiness.

'Good morning, dear,' Melva said as she shuffled into the kitchen, the walking frame supporting her. 'Oh, good. You've already made the coffee.'

'I was going to bring you a cup but I confess to being sidetracked by the glorious sunrise.'

Melva nodded as Reggie quickly fixed her a cup. 'Let's go out onto the balcony and watch it together.' This they did and once they were seated, Melva asked her, 'So what have you decided?'

Reggie's quirky smile was instant. 'You know me too well.'

Melva chuckled but waited patiently for Reggie's answer.

'I think that I at least…I need to hear what he has to say before I can make any other decision.'

Melva snorted at this. 'Really? I think you've decided more than that.'

'What do you mean?'

'This isn't just about listening to the man, Regina.'

'It's not?'

'No.' Melva shook her head. 'What is wrong with you young people these days?' She put her coffee cup down on the table. 'I think it's great you want to listen to him, darling, but this is also crunch time.'

'Crunch time?' It was Reggie's turn to shake her head. 'I don't—'

'Do you love him?'

'Er…I…'

'It's a simple question, Reggie. Yes or no?'

Reggie swallowed. 'Yes.'

'So no matter what he might say to you, you're willing to face the consequences? Fight for him? Move heaven and earth to ensure the two of you stay together this time?'

Reggie's heart fluttered with excited fear. What if Flynn told her that the little boy was his son? Would she be able to accept that? Was she willing to be a part of his son's life? What if Flynn still had a lot of wealthy friends? Would she be able to spend time with them? Melva was right. Was she willing to fight for Flynn? To make sure that his life and her life were intertwined together—forever?

'Yes,' she replied again. 'I am.'

Melva's grin was wide as she nodded her head, as though encouraging Reggie to continue.

'I need Flynn in my life.' Reggie said the words more to herself than to Melva. 'I know I can survive without him, I've done it for the past six years, but I'm not sure if I want to just survive anymore. I've been doing that for most of my life—surviving. I want to be happy,

Melva.' Her chin wobbled as she spoke the words and tears immediately sprang to her eyes. 'I want Flynn.'

Melva chuckled and leaned over to drape her frail arm around Reggie's shoulders. 'That's my girl.'

Feeling happier now that the decision had been made, Reggie had a cleansing shower, realising she would need to head out to the shops at some point to find something to wear to tonight's auction. She surveyed the bright scarlet underwear Flynn had sent as part of her overnight care package. No doubt he'd called one of the department stores where they'd gone shopping last week, asking one of the personal shoppers to gather a few things together and courier them to Melva's apartment.

At least she hoped that's what had happened because even thinking about Flynn, standing in the lingerie section, searching for the perfect matching set of underwear for her…and such a delightfully wicked colour as well…made her cheeks suffuse with colour.

Would he take the time to personally do such a thing for her? Had he left the hospital and gone straight to the department store? He had told Bergan he had things to organise. Had he gone to such great lengths *just* for her?

And that wasn't all. During the course of the morning the doorbell rang twice and each time Reggie's heart pounded with scared excitement at the thought that it might be Flynn. Instead, there were more parcels being delivered, the first a small but perfect Christmas tree, along with a box of decorations. There was a note with it that simply said, 'Enjoy your day.'

A few hours later, once they'd erected the tree and dressed it with baubles and tinsel, the second package arrived.

'This really *is* like Christmas.' Melva giggled as Reg-

gie signed for the parcel. This one, though, wasn't like
the others. It was a long dress bag, with a smaller box
inside. When she opened it, both she and Melva gasped.
There, inside, was the most beautiful scarlet-coloured
dress, perfect to match the underwear she presently had
on beneath her new pyjamas. The bodice was tastefully
embroidered with beads and a few sequins, the skirt
was full and came to just below her knee. The small
box at the bottom of the bag contained a perfect pair
of matching shoes.

'Good heavens. This must have cost hundreds.'

'And then some,' Reggie murmured, instantly falling in love with the dress. It would be wrong of her to
accept it, wouldn't it? Was Flynn trying to lavish gifts
on her in order to buy her forgiveness?

'I should send it all back. The dress, the underwear—'

'But not the decorations. Look how homely they
make this new apartment look,' Melva said instantly.

Reggie surveyed the brightly coloured room and
nodded in agreement.

'And why should you send it all back?' Melva continued. 'The man isn't trying to buy you off, Reggie.
You're far too strong for him to even attempt it. All he's
doing is showing you how much he appreciates you.
He's wooing you. For heaven's sake, girl, let the man
be romantic. Now, off you go to the spare room and try
on that dress. I want my own personal fashion parade
of dress and shoes so we can decide on your hair and
make-up—which I'll do for you. Now go. Shoo.'

She did as Melva had bidden her and they had a
lovely time deciding on make-up and exactly how she
should wear her hair. When the doorbell rang a third

time, Reggie was all in a dither. Dressed in her pyjamas again, she almost raced to the door, filled with excitement to see what Flynn might be sending her *this* time.

When she opened the door, expecting to see a delivery man standing there, waiting for her to sign for the next parcel, she almost tripped over her own feet to see Flynn.

'Flynn!'

She stared at him and he stared at her, both of them drinking in the sight of each other as though they'd been starved for years.

'Hello, Reg.'

'Uh…' She was at a total loss for words, unsure whether to invite him in or just stand there, or whether she should change into her clothes or thank him for all the gifts or… 'What do you want?' she blurted, instantly wishing her words hadn't come out sounding so confronting.

'I…um…' Flynn looked down at his hands, as though completely forgetting why he was here. It was then he seemed to realise he was holding a thick white envelope. 'I wanted to deliver this one. In person.'

'Oh, yes. Sorry.' Manners and a smidgen of coherent thought began to return. 'Er…thank you for all the—'

'It's fine.' He waved away her words with a hint of veiled embarrassment. 'I actually wondered if I could… read this to you.'

'Read it?' He was clearly nervous and it only made him seem more endearing. It was difficult, seeing him standing there—looking incredibly sexy in his blue denim jeans and pale blue shirt, casual but, oh, so delicious—really difficult to remember that just yesterday afternoon she'd seen him kissing another woman.

'Yes.' He dragged in a breath, as though pulling himself together. 'I have a lot of things I'd like to say to you, Reg, and all I ask is that you listen. I'm not looking for an answer or anything. No pressure. Just…please…will you listen?'

Reggie nodded and indicated for him to come inside but he shook his head. 'Here is good.' And without further ado he flicked open the envelope and pulled out a few sheets of paper. 'I wrote everything down, not only so I didn't forget the important things I need to say, because heaven knows that when I'm around you, Reg, my mind tends to turn to mush and all I can think about is holding you close and…' He trailed off and found himself staring at her yet again.

Didn't she have any idea just how adorably perfect she looked in those pyjamas? All soft and cuddly and so *his* Reggie?

'Anyway,' he went on, giving himself another mental shake. 'Here goes.' He cleared his throat. 'Oh, and I'd appreciate it if you didn't interrupt. Just let me get it all out.'

'OK.'

'Good.' He paused, then launched right in. 'Dear Reg.'

'Strong beginning,' she murmured.

'No interruptions.' He glared at her and she nodded again. He tried again. 'I want to apologise for not telling you more about my divorce. I guess as it's a topic I've learned not to discuss in public, I keep forgetting you don't know what really happened all those years ago. Rest assured that Violet and I are just friends.' He stopped and looked directly into her eyes. *'Friends,'* he reiterated, before going back to reading his letter.

'We've always been better friends than anything else. She is also happily married to my cousin, Colin. The child you saw me holding, Ian, is their son.'

'He's not your son?' Reggie whispered, hope filling her voice as he continued to read further.

'Violet and I should never have allowed ourselves to be bullied into the marriage, especially as she'd been in love with my cousin all along. She had broken off her relationship with him, just as I had done with you. Duty and family and all that guff was rammed down our throats and so we did as we were told, desperately trying to make a go of a marriage but instead only succeeding in making each other—and you and Colin—miserable.

'Violet and I secretly separated very soon after the marriage, more than happy to live our own lives, and it was then she began to see Colin again. When she fell pregnant, we all decided it was best to end the farce so that Violet and Colin could stand a chance of being a proper family unit.

'We all knew none of our parents would be pleased with the outcome but we did what we had to and now not only have they had five wonderful years together but Violet just told me that she's pregnant again with their second child. That was why she wanted to see me, to tell me the news in person. Unfortunately, Colin is overseas at the moment and wasn't able to join us.

'Reg, please believe me when I say that there is nothing romantic between Violet and myself. It is *you* I am most desperately in love with and it is *you* I wish to spend the rest of my life with.'

Reggie gasped and covered her mouth with her hand as he looked into her eyes.

'My heart has *always* been yours and I was a fool to

have let you go once. I won't make that same mistake again.' Flynn was no longer reading from the page but instead was staring intently into her eyes. 'I love you, Reg. More so now than I did six years ago.'

She wasn't sure what to do, what to say. What was she supposed to do? She did love him back with all her heart and she wanted desperately to tell him, to let him know that he wasn't standing out on that big scary ledge of emotion all on his own, but somehow, for some strange reason, she couldn't get any of the words past her lips and her feet seemed permanently glued to the spot.

'I know this is a lot to take in,' Flynn continued, clearly not expecting any sort of response from her. 'Hence why I've written everything down. Take this letter, Reg. Read it over and over. Process it. Take your time. Don't rush but, please, believe me when I say that at the moment there's only confusion between us because that's all it is—a silly misunderstanding, and I hope my words have helped clear all that up.

'I'm really looking forward to seeing you tonight at the auction and one simple look from you, a gesture, a word even, will let me know whether or not you accept my apology and my love.'

Then, as she stood there, she watched him fold the papers, putting them back into the envelope with his clever, sure fingers. He held the envelope out to her and with numb fingers she took it…watching in surprise as he bowed his head to her then turned and walked away.

Reggie blinked, several times, wondering if she was still lying in bed, dreaming. Had she fallen and hit her head and was hallucinating? The envelope in her hands was evidence that it was neither and after she'd somehow managed to get her body to function yet again she closed the door, then slumped down into a chair, trying to take in everything that had just happened.

Flynn loved her. Flynn had just stood there, before her, declaring his love for her, letting her know that not only did he love her now but that he'd *always* loved her and always would. He was hers. His love was hers to have…if she wanted it.

'I do. I do want it.'

And yet he hadn't pressured her, hadn't come inside, hadn't talked at her, but instead had read the love letter out loud, sharing with her his thoughts and deepest emotions. He hadn't wanted anything from her, hadn't demanded any sort of response, hadn't forced her into anything.

'But I want him. I love him.' As though it was just too much for her to contain, she raced back to the door and flung it open, staring out into the street to try and see if he'd really left, but there was no sign of him.

'What's going on?' Melva called. 'Is there *another* person at the door?'

Reggie headed back inside and sat down again, surprised to find tears of happiness streaming down her face, a wide grin on her lips. She brushed the tears aside, her heart lifting in complete and utter delight to know that Flynn loved her, that he still loved her, that he'd *always* loved her. She laughed out loud, unable to believe how light and glorious it was to be loved back by the person you loved.

She unfolded the letter and read it again, just to reassure herself that this was really happening, that this was really true. He really *did* know her so well, wanting to ensure she wasn't pressured in any way, and that knowledge made her love him all the more.

'But he doesn't know I love him.' The words tumbled out of her mouth in a rush and she looked around anxiously for her phone. With trembling fingers she dialled his number, heart pounding wildly against her chest as she waited for it to connect. She wasn't quite sure what she was supposed to say; her mind had gone blank. The phone switched through to his voicemail, which meant he was probably driving. She waited for the message to end but when it was time to say something she opened her mouth to tell him that she loved him back, that she loved the dress and the other presents he'd bestowed on her, that she couldn't wait to see him tonight, that she was sorry for being such an insecure ninny and having a big freak-out...but no words came out of her mouth.

She quickly disconnected the call and realised what she must do. She must look her absolute best for tonight. Let Flynn see for himself just how much she loved him. She stood and checked the clock.

'Only three hours to get ready! Come on!'

Flynn stood, dressed in a tuxedo, not caring if he was slightly overdressed for tonight's auction or not. He wanted to look his absolute best when he saw Reggie, hoping amongst hope that his gifts and his letter of explanation, his letter of love, had proved to her that he loved her and that she could trust him. He fiddled with his tie as he stood near the rear of the small stage.

So far, the night had been going for a good twenty minutes and there was still no sign of Reggie. Was she coming? Had something happened? Perhaps he should have organised for a car to pick her up but then he thought she might consider that too controlling and the last thing he wanted was for her to think him controlling. He wanted to cherish her, adore her and love her for the rest of her life, and as he rubbed his sweaty palms down his trousers again, checking the door for the hundredth time, almost wishing her to burst through, he heard his number being called.

'And next up we have bachelor number five. Ladies, he's the latest addition to Sunshine General's surgical department. Please welcome Flynn Jamieson,' Mackenzie, who was the MC for the evening, announced into the microphone. Flynn looked at Mackenzie as if to ask where Reggie was. Mackenzie's answer was to shrug apologetically as Flynn took centre stage, standing beneath the plastic mistletoe hanging from the ceiling.

'Who would like to get the bidding started?' Mackenzie asked, and wasn't surprised when a plethora of hands went up, bids being called out. The previous bachelor had raised well over five hundred dollars and although Flynn wanted to raise money for the hospital, he didn't care if someone only bid five dollars, so long as that someone was Reggie. Where was she?

Mackenzie was taking bids, the price going past one hundred dollars, past two hundred, then three, then four. Up and up the price went, getting to seven hundred dollars. Ingrid Brown, the general surgical registrar, was in a battle with Clara from the outpatient department. Flynn couldn't believe someone would pay that much just to have dinner with him but then again it really was for a good cause.

'Do I have an increase on seven-fifty?' Mackenzie called. 'Seven-fifty going once. Seven-fifty going twice.'

'One thousand dollars!' came a loud female cry from the back of the room and everyone turned to look, turned to see Reggie standing there, dressed in the most glorious scarlet dress and matching shoes, her short dark hair spiked out a little, giving her a radiant appeal. People around her clapped; the hospital's administrator whooped with delight.

'Sold!' Mackenzie called, banging her gavel and ignoring Ingrid's frown. 'Step right on up, Reggie, and claim your Christmas bachelor,' she called. Reggie kept her gaze glued to Flynn's as she made her way through the ballroom, not tripping over a chair or a tablecloth and not overbalancing in the five-inch heels.

Soon enough, she was standing before him. 'Sorry I'm late,' were the first words out of her mouth. 'The taxi broke down and I had difficulty getting another one.'

'You look...' Flynn stared at her, not caring that everyone else was staring at the two of them. As far as he was concerned, there was no one else, no one else except Reggie. 'Stunning.'

Her smile increased as she looked up at him, then motioned to the mistletoe above them. 'Look where you're standing, Dr Jamieson.'

He nodded and moved forward, sliding his arms about her waist and drawing her close. Wolf-whistles came from around them as well as a lot of cheering. Reggie didn't care. She wanted everyone in the world to know exactly how she felt about Flynn.

'Do you think we need it?' he asked, and she slowly shook her head from side to side.

'Thank you for your letter. It was perfect.'

'I hope you don't think I was trying to buy your affection by sending you the things I did.'

'I don't think that. I think you were trying to romance the woman you love.' She slid her hands slowly up his chest to link them behind his neck.

'I do. I do love you, Reggie, so very much. I've never loved anyone like I love you.'

'That's very good news,' she replied, her brand-new heels making her tall enough to lean in closer and line up her lips with his.

'It is?'

'Yes, because I've never loved anyone like I love you either.'

Finally, Flynn smiled at her, a small, secret smile that let her know that, finally, everything really would be all right. 'Marry me?' he asked, their lips only millimetres apart.

'Yes,' she replied instantly, and sealed their new deal with a kiss.

The room erupted into a frenzy of clapping and cheering as the two of them stood beneath the mistletoe, kissing each other with perfect delight.

'I'm sorry this proposal isn't as romantic as the last one,' he eventually said as they made their way out of the ballroom via a side door, not caring about anything at the moment but each other. With the moon above them, the stars twinkling in the night sky and Flynn's arms around her, holding her close, Reggie kissed his gorgeous, loving mouth.

'I like this one best, especially as I now own you.' He raised one eyebrow playfully at her words. 'Don't you realise that spread out over the next fifty years, you would only have cost me twenty dollars a year!'

'A definite bargain,' he returned, kissing her once again.

'Who said money couldn't buy love?' She giggled and allowed Flynn to keep on kissing her…forever.

EPILOGUE

'ARE YOU READY?' Sunainah asked.

Reggie stood dressed in a beautiful white wedding dress that had an asymmetrical split up the side, revealing a generous amount of her shapely legs. Ruffles seemed to be everywhere and as she looked at herself in the mirror, her three friends nodded in approval.

'That dress is *so* you,' Bergan said.

'I love it,' Reggie agreed. 'Almost as much as I love Flynn.' She giggled before turning to face her friends, looking at each of them in turn. She was surrounded by the people she loved and waiting for her in the communal garden area of the cul-de-sac stood the man of her dreams. 'Do you think I'm ready?'

Bergan, Mackenzie and Sunainah looked at each other for a split second before looking back at Reggie. 'Yes,' they said in unison.

'Only you would get married in a car park,' Bergan grumbled good-naturedly.

'It's not a car park. It's a lovely little garden that we all tend and love—'

'Which is right next to where guests usually park their cars when they come to visit,' Bergan added.

'Well, Mackenzie did want me to be part of the cul-de-sac crew and I think this definitely makes it official.'

'Just one more thing,' Sunainah said a moment later, and bent down to pull a rectangular parcel from a bag. It was wrapped in plain brown paper with no other adornments. 'This is for you.'

'Really?' Reggie accepted the parcel and looked at her friend in delight. 'I like presents.'

'I hope you will like this one.' Sunainah, Bergan and Mackenzie all grinned at each other as Reggie ripped the paper off with a touch of impatience and what she saw there made her stare at her friends in wonderment. There, in her hands, was a framed picture of herself and Flynn, standing on the beach in the Caribbean, sipping drinks with little umbrellas, the sun setting behind them.

'You told me to get rid of it but…I could not,' Sunainah confessed.

Reggie shook her head in wonder, then put the picture down and launched herself at her friends, hugging them all. 'Oh, this is perfect. This is the picture from our first real date. Oh, Sunainah, thank you for not listening to me and keeping it safe all these years. You three really are the best friends ever.'

'I am also pleased you decided not to wait and to get married *today*,' Sunainah added, as she set about fixing Reggie's dress once more. 'Christmas Day. Surrounded by everyone that you love most. It is perfect.'

'Yes.' Melva and her other neighbours would be part of the party and after the ceremony they were having a progressive Christmas wedding feast, going from one town house to the next. Reggie had wanted everyone to be included because everyone here was *her* family, the family she'd built around herself and the one in which Flynn now shared.

Since the auction Reggie had met Violet several times, wanting to include her in the planning of the wedding.

'I'm so glad you and Flynn have finally found each other again,' Violet had said when the two of them had been alone. 'He loves you very much. Always has.'

'I know. The past is the past,' Reggie said. 'We can't do anything to change it but what we can do is accept it and plunge right on in to a newer and happier future.'

Violet had laughed. 'Flynn told me I'd like you and he was right. Thank you for making him happy.' The two women had hugged and when Flynn had returned, finding them laughing together, Reggie had seen true happiness reflected in his eyes. They weren't his future wife and his ex-wife, they were the love of his life and his surrogate sister...and they liked each other.

'OK,' Bergan said a moment later, bringing Reggie's thoughts back to the present. 'It's time to go because I have a feeling Flynn isn't going to wait too long for his bride to appear.'

'Right, girls,' Mackenzie said, marshalling her daughter Ruthie and Sunainah's daughter, Daphne, together. 'You come with me.'

'And boys,' Sunainah said, taking her son Joshua's hand and then offering her other hand to Violet's son, Ian, who Reggie had wanted to include in their wedding party. 'You are with me.'

'Out you come,' Bergan said, opening the front door to town house number three and waiting for the bride to precede her. As Reggie was an orphan, she'd decided she didn't need to be walked down the aisle by anyone.

She would stand tall and walk towards Flynn by herself, offering herself to him, her three closest friends and the children behind her.

She accepted her bridal bouquet of bright red poinsettias from Bergan and smiled. 'Yes,' she said to them, before looking towards the garden where Flynn stood waiting impatiently for her. 'I'm ready. Ready for my normal, everyday life to begin. My life with Flynn.'

And with that, beaming brightly she walked towards the man who held her heart, giggling at his expression when he finally saw her, his jaw dropping in gobsmacked delight. Both Colin and Violet were standing in as his 'groomsmen' and with Richard, Elliot and John, as well as the rest of the extended families visiting for Christmas, it was almost difficult to find the wedding celebrant in the mix.

As soon as Reggie stood beside Flynn, she smiled up at him and gave a little shimmy, the ruffles on her dress shaking with the movement. 'Ready to get hitched?' she whispered.

'To you? Absolutely,' he replied, and took her hand in his. 'Now, this is a Christmas tradition I can get behind.'

Reggie laughed, unable to believe she could ever be this happy and it was all thanks to Flynn.

* * * * *

Merry Christmas
& A Happy New Year!

Thank you for a wonderful
2013...

A sneaky peek at next month...

Medical Romance™

CAPTIVATING MEDICAL DRAMA—WITH HEART

My wish list for next month's titles...

In stores from 3rd January 2014:

❏ Her Hard to Resist Husband — Tina Beckett

& The Rebel Doc Who Stole Her Heart — Susan Carlisle

❏ From Duty to Daddy — Sue MacKay

& Changed by His Son's Smile — Robin Gianna

❏ Mr Right All Along — Jennifer Taylor

& Her Miracle Twins — Margaret Barker

Available at WHSmith, Tesco, Asda, Eason, Amazon and Apple

Just can't wait?

Visit us Online

You can buy our books online a month before they hit the shops! **www.millsandboon.co.uk**

Special Offers

very month we put together collections and nger reads written by your favourite authors.

ere are some of next month's highlights— nd don't miss our fabulous discount online!

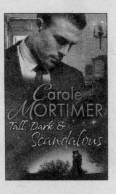

On sale 3rd January

On sale 3rd January

On sale 20th December

Save 20%
on all Special Releases

Come in from the cold this Christmas with two of our favourite authors. Whether you're jetting off to Vermont with Sarah Morgan or settling down for Christmas dinner with Fiona Harper, the smiles won't stop this festive season.

Visit:
www.millsandboon.co.uk

Work hard, play harder...

Welcome to the Gold Coast, where hearts are broken as quickly as they are healed. Featuring some of the rising stars of the medical world, this new four-book series dives headfirst into Surfer's Paradise.

Available as a bundle at
www.millsandboon.co.uk/medical

MILLS & BOON®
Book Club

Join the Mills & Boon Book Club

Want to read more **Medical** books?
We're offering you **2 more** absolutely **FREE!**

We'll also treat you to these fabulous extras:

- Exclusive offers and much more!
- FREE home delivery
- FREE books and gifts with our special rewards scheme

Get your free books now!

visit www.millsandboon.co.uk/bookclub
or call Customer Relations on 020 8288 288

FREE BOOK OFFER TERMS & CONDITIONS
Accepting your free books places you under no obligation to buy anything and you may cancel at any ti
If we do not hear from you we will send you 5 stories a month which you may purchase or return to us—
choice is yours. Offer valid in the UK only and ls not available to current Mills & Boon subscribers to
series. We reserve the right to refuse an application and applicants must be aged 18 years or over. Only
application per household. Terms and prices are subject to change without notice. As a result of this applica
you may receive further offers from other carefully selected companies. If you do not wish to share in
opportunity please write to the Data Manager at PO BOX 676, Richmond, TW9 1WU.